Palais-Royal

PALAIS-ROYAL

Richard Sennett

Alfred A. Knopf · New York
1986

Library of Congress Cataloging-in-Publication Data
Sennett, Richard
Palais-Royal.
I. Title.
PS3569.E62P3   1986   813'.54   86-45356
ISBN 0-394-54538-9

Manufactured in the United States of America
FIRST EDITION

In memoriam
Michel Foucault

Most of the Paris arcades came into being during the decade and a half which followed 1822. . . . They were the forerunners of the department stores . . . the arcades were centres of the luxury-goods trade. The manner in which they were fitted out displayed Art in the service of the salesman. Contemporaries never tired of admiring them. For long afterwards they remained a point of attraction for foreigners.

WALTER BENJAMIN,
Passagen-arbeit

I

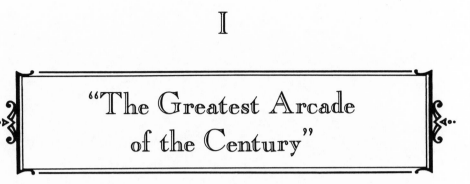

"The Greatest Arcade
of the Century"

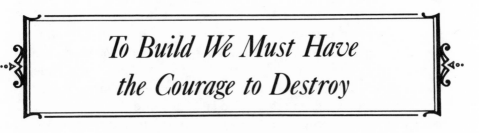

To Build We Must Have the Courage to Destroy

*Letters of Severus Rood, Frederick Courtland,
Charles Courtland and John Courtland
August 1828–August 1830*

Frederick Courtland   *9 August 1828*
in care of M. Fontaine
Ecole des Beaux-Arts
Quai Malaquais
Paris

My dear boy,

I write to you not with a renewed request that you return to your native
land, for when you comprehend the matter I am about to relate, you will
want to fly at the earliest moment; however, I must prepare you for what
awaits you here.

Your father was recently in Swaffham Prior to complete his works for
Sir Geoffrey Hind; it were a mere matter of touches of green in strategic
places, and the ordering of furniture in the new orangery and grotto. To
understand what I must relate, you might be enlightened by a memory
which shall ever be etched on my brain. It is of the time when, your
father newly wed and freshly employed for John Nash, myself also embarked upon a momentous litigation which brought me to the attention of
my most senior colleagues, we two spent a night upon the town to celebrate the Future. Your father was that evening the gayest of dogs, singing
in the tavern where we supped, recounting stories I could fortunately but
half understand. At the conclusion of this revel, perhaps more to tease me
than anything else, your father led me out upon the incomplete works in

the Regent's Park. In the moonlight he sat me down upon a bench; before me lay a short expanse of lawn, then a ditch the depth of a ha-ha, this urban depression housing pipes several feet below the level of the ground; upon the other side of the ditch was the half-finished Cumberland Terrace. Your father disappeared for a few moments; suddenly I heard from the ditch the words of *Macbeth* evoking the moving forest of Birnam Wood, and I saw one young yew tree, then another move before me, as though across a stage. Not content with this harmless conceit, which required the mere parade of some balled and burlapped shrubberies the gardeners had left nearby, your father continued to enact the story of *Macbeth*, like a puppet master; Macduff's words were spoken by an oak sapling, Lady Macbeth's dark plotting issued from, as it seemed, the roots of a rhododendron, the flowers of the plant falling into the ditch as your father shook it in time to her awful poetry. The moonlight fell upon this animated vegetation, making of the bobbing forms almost human shadows upon the road, and he went on and on, drink inflaming him with the necessary strength of an ox to deploy these enormous properties. When a plant had finished its speech, it disappeared into the furrow, and suddenly another popped up to answer, rhododendron speaking to birch, Macbeth the willow—even in excess were your father Knowing—shaking its pliant branches back in horror and then closer, covering the very place where the rhododendron wife had schemed. Finally your father collapsed, the strength which the wine had brought him expended in his veins, and I had to conduct the Pride of Nash's Studio, already hailed in the world as possessing a fastidious eye and a mordant pen, I had to conduct this young genius home as though leading a wretch who had emerged from a bog to shelter, so grimed was he, his hands bleeding from the rough balls of burlap he had heaved up and down, his trousers ripped by lashes of the young, resisting branches.

This taste for freakish sport has never left him, especially at the conclusion of projects like that of Sir Geoffrey Hind's, in which your father has felt ill used or ill at ease—which sentiment is often phantasmagorical, your father knows himself much Acknowledged. But he has deployed his revenging wit once too often, as I told him he would.

Five days ago, he made the final preparations for the unveiling of Sir Geoffrey's grotto. These consisted of secretly, under cover of night, removing the choicest pieces of furniture from Sir Geoffrey's home to the cave: rugs, sofas, candelabra, and tables. His intent was to create a chamber in the most perfect taste of the 15th Louis under ground, and to conduct Sir Geoffrey there the next morning to find this subterranean cavern illuminated as if for a ball. Sir Geoffrey was, evidently, at first no more than surprised and restrainedly annoyed—as any man would be to view precious possessions disposed within damp dripping reaches under the earth. But he reined in his displeasure until he glimpsed a delicate *fauteuil* placed next to a stone water nymph rising from the grotto pool; at this he exclaimed, "That is Helen's chair!," she who was Sir Geoffrey's wife. The bereaved widower rounded upon your father and struck him a savage blow across the face with a riding crop. You must prepare yourself, my dear child, for a revelation which was even more terrible to him who suffered it: the crop slit open John's left eye.

I learnt these horrifying particulars from those who entered into the ensuing pandemonium. Your father fell to the ground in a faint, Sir Geoffrey strode from the grotto shouting he would not pay one farthing for anything; the various rustics who had laboured under John's direction were left to assist the wounded architect.

These labourers appear to have carried your father immediately to one of their rude dwellings, but to have left him there, in hideous pain, for some hours before notifying the rector. This good man, who knew of your father's intercourse with me, and who had even ventured once previously to write to me for a piece of legal advice, now straight away sent a courier to London to fetch me, and dispatched one of the rustics for medical aid in Cambridge. The doctor arrived in all haste; the suppurating wound had already begun to fester, made worse by your father's having fallen from the straw pallet upon which the peasants had laid him to the stone-and-mire floor. After the doctor performed measures which I shall not describe to you as they were described to me, the eye socket was cleaned, your father revived and bled. I arrived, and made arrangements for him to be transported in a landau to my quarters in London.

Whilst waiting for the coach to be prepared I questioned the rustics closely. A confused narrative led up to the slashing and the event itself; they then fell silent. Cunning Savages! They knew what I wanted to know, why no instant succour had been afforded the stricken man; to the obbligato of his moans from within the landau, I, Impotent for the moment to help my errant, dearly loved friend, challenged the rustics to explain themselves before I brought down upon them the full measure of the law. "Squire, he be the law," one yokel proffered. "Your master," I rounded upon him, "is soon to be in gaol himself, along with you." The elder now looked concerned—it dawned upon him that, if not a rational explanation, some excuse was necessary. "Squire taught him his place." At this the others nodded among themselves, as if everything was now satisfactorily resolved, and they turned to me, almost in a friendly fashion, as though I too must be relieved. All I can tell you is that I have been assured the delay of several hours in help in no way provoked the loss of the eye; it simply meant your father suffered longer than necessary.

Your father has now been in my house two days. With the help of laudanum his pain is veiled in sleep. The best medical personages in the town attend John, and, from examining him in his lucid moments, are confident that the damage is contained and that the other eye will continue to function unimpaired. What will it mean for half the window of genius to be forever shut? I cannot bear the thought; your parent, Stoic and Courageous as also I have ever known him, makes every effort to rise above this grief, but the brave, mocking words die on the lips of his consciousness. And can you doubt that in this hour of trial, he calls for you?

Your brother has of course hastened from Gloucestershire. His father shows spark enough to beg "my Jesuitical son" to refrain from "transforming the sick room into a chapel." Poor Charles, he does mean well and is not a little hurt by this parental chaffing. I have soothed him by joining him in prayer. However, none of us has been given the secret of the ways of Providence; 'twere not seemly to ask of the Creator a reckoning for this tragedy. Your presence here will be your sceptical father's greatest solace, and to fit you for his care I have told you all beforehand, that you may comprehend the compass of his need. This unhappily from

your Uncle Severus

Severus Rood, K.C.   *30 September 1828*
6 Inner Temple
London

Snigs,

I turn to you in need as always, my dear and constant friend. I am failing in my Duty. One would think the alarums of parish life would prepare one for the simplest, indeed, the most pleasurable of pastoral cares, that for one's own father, but I simply cannot bear further this light and elegant teasing of my parent, worse because he knows that I harbour Doubt within my breast. It is incessant, his provocation; yesterday I fled the house, fearing I would give way to angry words before him. And yet I know the banter to be bred of pain, and yet again it cuts me. Why, why can I not practise forbearance?

Yesterday a gentleman from the Royal Household came to wait upon him. I received this august servant, who asked me if it be true that my father is at work once more. I replied by leading him into the south room, where fresh evidences of Father's powers were on display, their creator yet absent from the room; the visitor studied the new sketches closely, straightening himself barely in time before Father entered. "Who would have thought it possible?" the emissary had muttered during his inspection; he had searched in his coat pocket for one document, found another about which he muttered again, smiling to himself, "So we shan't deploy that one," and took out the desired paper, holding it in his hand as Father crossed the room. I thereupon quitted the pair, but was told later by my parent that a member of the Royal Family desired that he commence a small commission, "a show of faith," he said, "which confirms that Sovereigns, Charles, like Our Lord in heaven, do in times of need think only to reward the worthy." At this Father smiled slightly; he must have espied the gentleman spying first. It has been thus for a week: *everything,* even his good fortune, he turns to ironical account.

How curious, Snigs, that in moments of family trial we bring to events not the strengths of the man we have become, rather the achings of our boyhood. A few days ago, in washing the socket of my father's eye, I thought of the times when he would shout, in preparation for theatricals, "More colour, Charles! Give your costume more colour, lad!" How could I? I could never see what he saw. For his part, he used to evince dislike for my clerical schoolfellows as "prunes" and "dull magicians," he used to recommend that I leave off all "babble" about that which cannot be seen or touched or tasted.

When I returned to my parish, I sought in prayer God's succour to give me strength as I am weak, and I besought of Him some understanding of the source of my father's provoking, beyond the evident one of pain. Yet to my plea "No man was able to answer him a word," as Matthew says. Perhaps I have not submitted myself in humility to receive God's Grace, perhaps vanity casts me beyond the pale of His charity; throughout the service I thought again and again that were Frederick to nurse Father, they would laugh together. But Frederick has returned to Paris.

Thank you, dearest Snigs, for permitting me to unburden myself in this note.

Charles

John Courtland, Esq.   *4 October 1828*
12 Jermyn Street
London

Dear Father,

It was a smooth crossing. From the moment the diligence left London, though, I thought only of your smile and the sweetness with which you said, "Of course you must return to your work." You know I should have been happy to serve you as draughtsman, as long as you required. Should I have insisted upon return to your atelier now? For hours during my voyage I leant over the rail, pondering the question in some remorse, the placid sea offering me no reply. Perhaps one's taste, as you say, is better formed in Paris than anywhere else. I only know that I should not have left you had I not witnessed the evidences of your mending, and had you not virtually commanded me to return.

I have something of a surprise for you. Do you remember my telling you about the commission M. Fontaine has in hand, the one to build a new arcade entirely of iron and glass, walls as well as roof, in the Palais-Royal? This is the morning the first boards of the wooden galleries in the Palais-Royal were scheduled to be ripped up and carted away; in a month, or at most two, the iron and glass will begin to be placed in their stead. I thought I would not see my esteemed teacher for several days at least, but he presented himself early at my draughting table.

"M. Courtland," he said with a slight smile, "I cannot let the greatest dignitaries in Paris—greatest for our purposes, my boy—see you in a blue smock, you who are usually so elegant. Why have you failed me?"

I hadn't the least idea of the point of his fun.

"Perhaps this is the English way for saying you do not wish to work upon the new Galerie d'Orléans, that you do not like my design, that you would prefer instead the Lyons pumping station for the next six months before asking me for work in Paris?"

I had barely time this morning to rush to my rooms, and change to a costume befitting the occasion. I am sure the honour owes to M. Fontaine's esteem for you, especially as the other two apprentices already have diplomas. The plans are entire, of course, but the use of iron is daring, and I expect that I make some mark when the construction requires experiment.

We made a rather regal progress round the Louvre to the palace, M. Fontaine and his apprentices in a forward carriage, the city surveyor and his assistant in a fiacre behind, followed by a dozen workmen in the enor-

mous carts which are to bear away the wood. It was a fine morning, the
river lively and not yet rank. As always, the journey round the Louvre
struck me by its contrast, on the side of the Seine the windows of the
Louvre clean and the walls sheets of stone gold in the light, on the side
facing the Palais-Royal the Louvre windows coated in dust, the walls
covered with bills and chalk scrawls. As though the contagion had spread
from the smaller palace.

When we arrived at the "Peristyle de Chartres" (formerly known to
you as the west entrance) we were received with some ceremony by a
functionary of the Duke of Orléans, which family, M. Fontaine told me,
has agreed in the end to bear the majority burden in finance of the new
structure. The functionary, resplendent in his peruke, blue breeches and
frock coat, lace at his wrists and throat, stood beside the entrance (the only
one large enough for the workmen's carts) and announced, "Let the Duke's
Architect, the Surveyor of the City of Paris and their suite pass! Open the
gates!" Equally magnificent footmen obeyed him, we passed under the
portico, M. Fontaine and the City Surveyor raising their hats to the functionary, the workmen also raising their caps to him whilst one shouted in
good humour, "Scratch yer arse, Guv'nor!" The high servant glared, and
the gates clanked behind us.

But what a sight! I have told you that the mortar had not set on the last
additions M. Fontaine made to the Palais-Royal exterior when that noble
rectangle began to be disfigured by filth. Some think to blame him, as
always; they say the completed palace is too large, the walls regular and
forbidding like a prison, the streets running round it too narrow; in short,
so inhospitable a building invites defacement. This is why I like to walk the
city at dawn; in those hours the buildings are least troubled by men; I love
particularly the way early light evokes the volume of great buildings without suggesting their density, since you see only the play of planes of surface
against planes of shadow in the uncertainty of new light. However, the
interior court of the Palais-Royal teems with life even at dawn.

M. Fontaine says that in your day the Galeries de Bois were a byword
for the highest fashion, and indeed, the present form retains the old idea:
the two paths cross the gardens of the palace at the original truncation,
and there is still the arcaded barn (for I can call this long, ramshackle
building by no other name) running between the paths, connecting the
opposing stone wings of the rectangle. When the clientele of the Galeries
became more mixed, about four or five years ago, the tradesmen cut
through the north side of the barn, so that shops face outward to the
gardens as well. This was the moment when the Duke decided to act. In
these outer shops are conducted the sale of dubious bills and stocks; there

are many women on offer, even, a thought revolting, young men. In the central shed the trade remains more polite; the wine merchant whom M. Fontaine says you frequented as a boy is still there, although he is enormously ancient.

This morning I did something stupid during our tour of the Galeries de Bois. I presented myself to this wine merchant as your son; he quite honestly replied that he could not recall your name but added, "You are welcome. The English always were, even during the Emperor's time. But follow my advice: keep in future always to the central gallery." Without thinking, I corrected him. "But don't you know? It is all to be torn down; that is why we are here." I regretted these words as soon as I had spoken them; your wine merchant looked searchingly from M. Fontaine to me to another of the apprentices, and then regarded me for a moment longer, before retiring silently into his cubicle.

M. Fontaine glared at me for a moment; my fellow apprentices looked at each other quite pleased. Do you think, Father, that "polish" to one's manners is like the new varnish applied to paintings, the varnish which prevents canvas ever from cracking naturally?

I apologised to M. Fontaine, which he accepted in his own fashion— "Indifference to others is the sublime form of conceit"—and he forgot this little affair in explaining the aim of the House of Orléans. Were the King to live here, he might, I imagine, look from the carved and gilded rooms down upon this perpetual street fair conducted in his gardens and despair of the phrase "Your Majesty." The Orléans family intend to drive the Jews, hawkers and whores in retreat to the boulevard du Temple, drawing an elegant clientele from the rue de Rivoli into our arcade of glass and iron, proof against the elements, filled with plants and discreet shops.

I will confess that, when M. Fontaine conducted us through the present Galeries de Bois, I was surprised at the number of seeming elegant persons who frequent the place. The shops in the Galeries today can be no more than three metres wide (remember: multiply the number of *toises* by 2.03 for the modern measure) and two metres in height; a second row of cubicles in the last decade has been stacked over those resting on the garden earth. To reach the upper shops you climb a ladder, or hoist yourself by a rope, or are simply hauled up by the proprietor who seizes your raised arms and lifts you. I could not believe the sight of a well-known gentleman of fashion in one of these upper cubicles, not crediting that he would have submitted himself to the possibilities of arrival as much as that he should be standing at all, two metres above the surging mass in the aisle, holding some Oriental woven stuff in his lemon-gloved hands, his monocle in place, his silk cravat shevelled, a gentleman perfectly at ease like a noble bird soaring and indifferent in the sanctity of the air to a battle ranging below among diminished human figures. Despite my principles, I found the scene beautiful, as beautiful as the Arabian pandemonium Géricault paints.

My principles. I do have them, you know. Firmly, like my brother. I tried to imagine Charles here, and although this may surprise you, I found it possible to do so. He would look about him in wonder, his eyes rising to the vision of the gentleman in lemon gloves as his eyes sometimes rise in Church; no, he would not find the scene agreeable, but he would be stirred and he would seek to Understand.

I recommence a day later. I can hardly believe my good fortune in being invited to join this work; perhaps you knew beforehand, which caused you to urge me so insistently to return? I wrote yesterday of principles. The plans are based entirely upon them, the roof vaulting in particular bears the marks of genius, yet there is some puzzle in our practise of these principles.

We are building a temple in which the sun rules. The Galerie d'Orléans will consist of two bars of shops, running between the wings of the palace, as did the Galeries de Bois. These buildings will have flat roofs. Between them is a grand central gallery 8.6 metres wide and 65 metres long. It is roofed over by a hip-shaped structure entirely of glass, the panes of glass held in half-round cast-iron bracing. You look up and see, through this half-round roof, the sky everywhere, unobstructed. In scale it is infinitely wider and grander than either the Burlington or the Royal arcades at home. Indeed, what we call arcades are merely buildings close together shielded by a glass roof. Here by contrast, glass is used consistently for almost the entire structure.

On the outside of the two bars of shops will be two further galleries, one giving upon the Duke's gardens, the other upon the courtyard now shared by the Comédie-Française and the City of Paris offices. These outer galleries will have flat solid roofs but walls entirely of glass. Thus our patron, the Duke of Orléans, will be able to walk directly from his blue drawing room out upon the flat-roof parts of the Galerie d'Orléans, invisible to the persons below; the glass skin covering the entire structure will deaden all sound within, and so return to him the privacy of his palace, whilst the rents from the shops below should in fourteen years pay for the structure itself.

The shops are fabricated of iron, glass and mirrors, the outer walls iron frames encasing plate glass so that everything within the shop is visible to those who promenade through the Galerie, the frames cast as graceful Doric columns, the pilasters of the columns mirrored glass, light thus streaming through the roof and bouncing off the columns. The shops are divided into bays by these metal frames, each bay 5.3 metres wide, fourteen shops of one bay width, ten more grand establishments of two bays, and a café which will occupy six bays, and which will form an oasis of peace in contrast to the teeming establishments lining the garden of the Palace outside.

The roof, I say, is the glory of my master's pen. You know how long M. Fontaine's colleague M. Percier resisted the Emperor's desire to erect iron monuments and bridges in the city. My master was also persuaded to avoid metal. Whilst the cost of domestic iron remains as high here as it was during the wars of Napoleon, M. Fontaine says he waited not for reasons of practicality but until he could understand the best use to make of this precious substance. The roof of the wheat market he found beautiful in the way the Baths of Caracalla were beautiful, but the modern version's iron dome he feels exposes too many structural elements. The roof of the Bourse, which I believe you have not seen, was a nearer inspiration; it is an 18-metre span composed as two intersecting ogive vaults. Still, one feels this glass and iron roof weighing down upon the space below. Here, in the Galerie d'Orléans, the roof will seem to float above the space it encloses. For the first time in Europe, man will experience freedom from the force of gravity through an architecture of light.

"I have explained this to the public again and again," he said to us yesterday as we sat on a bench outside his atelier in the Louvre, watching late afternoon on the river. We were all exhausted from the hours spent in the wooden shed, yet M. Fontaine was dustless. We three assistants slumped back on the benches, our feet propped up on the parapet of the Seine wall. The public outcry against his plan upsets our master greatly; even the fashionable papers depict him as bent over the draughting board, a bloody sword in his hand in place of a pen. "I have explained it all but they are incapable of taking in the idea. Thank God those in official positions are more enlightened." The senior apprentices nodded.

I confessed to him that the genius of the plan took me some time to fathom. The senior apprentices looked at one another. I then asked, "These attacks in the press will not harm us?"

He produced for my benefit once more his favorite maxim: "To build we must have the courage to destroy." The senior apprentices had just enough will left to smile knowingly. M. Fontaine met my eyes. I saw it in his; the moment the Galeries de Bois first fell to the wrecking axe spoke also to him.

The lads had set to work upon removing the east end of the north wooden gallery, perhaps the most decrepit part of the present structures. A crowd soon gathered, and I, having witnessed the maelstrom of buying and selling, having seen the smouldering of your wine merchant, I expected some violence to be perpetrated upon ourselves. The passions of the mob are more subtle. Two policemen lounged about, their services unnecessary. The crowd was diverted by the movements of the labourers, as it always is, and indeed made several suggestions about where and how to rip, which annoyed the surveyor and his men. The hammering and sawing began; after the planks had been removed sufficiently to allow the lads to work freely on the ground, the crowd peered into the hole as though observing an incision upon its own exposed body. Each person seemed to recall some adventure; a harlot touched a handkerchief to her eyes, a Jew sighed. And what was the vision laid bare which prompted these regrets? Simply the revelation of a depression in the earth filled with rat's nests, broken bottles, and shreds of fabric. My master was, I am sure, moved as I was by the mob, for the sentiments of the *galériens* were quite genuine as the boards were stripped to reveal these relics. And then they simply walked away; one, two, soon the hundred had disappeared back into the still-standing part of the Galeries de Bois. We were left quite to ourselves. This is the conundrum which was apparent to both of us: what a strange thing it is to destroy life. Though the beauty of what we shall build, Father, is also life.

Knowing your thirst for detail in matters of building, I have sought to slake it with a minute account, and even this omits much. When I have recouped, and if it pleases you, I shall attempt more. In the meanwhile I remain

> yr loving son,
> Frederick

Severus Rood, K.C.   *20 January 1829*
6 Inner Temple
London

Dear Snigs,

Thank you for your words of encouragement. Yes, Hinton does provide a spectacle for the attentive observer and, yes, I am attending to Hinton and to the present. Miss Whister is locked in deadly combat with the widow Sargeant over floral arrangements for the altar. An urgent message came this morning to the rectory (from the doctor's wife, I am sure, though it is unsigned) informing me that the smith is leading the serving girl Catherine into immoral courses, which behaviour is lovingly detailed in full by the letter writer. The squire has penned me a note, little more gracious than the anonymous letter, conveying his displeasure at the overly "thinkful" tone of the last sermon I delivered before travelling to town. This is the gavotte of organised piety.

More dramatic is an affair in which I must play a part. For two years now our village has been the site of a "manufactory," indeed, when I first came here I think I wrote to you about the lunatic scheme for mechanical fabrication of nails then beginning. My dear Snigs, there is method in this lunatic's madness. He is a fellow called Morgan, perfectly respectable in his person, indeed agreeable. His wit has been to adapt a machine which forged rods to the more delicate labour of forging nails, nearly six hundred an hour. The nails are then sharpened in another machine he has also diverted from its original purpose. To run this "manufactory" he has no need of skilled smiths; he can make do with downy youngsters. Nine of them are now in his employ, and these lads have become a source of grief.

No, he does not abuse them, starve them, over-tax them; the difficulty is precisely that youths of thirteen and fourteen have, thanks to Morgan, more money in their pockets than their elders. Were they minded to contribute their gains to their families, all would be well, Morgan would undoubtedly be our man of the hour, and I could devote myself to anonymous letters of filth. But the boys are minded to keep the money for themselves; they talk of saving enough to leave our precincts entirely and strike out for London. The parents cannot control their children; the squire lives two miles out. Morgan has been clever; last year he bought a small rural seat far from Hinton. The rectory is on the village green. I must put the fear of God into the boys, such that, trembling in fear of Divine punishment, the grubby little fists empty their coins into the parents' outstretched hands. This failing, I should convince Morgan to close his works and leave the village, for the sake of the families. Strange as this latter request may appear, consider that a few of the farms near us have been abandoned because the younger generation have simply decamped.

These boys prove themselves deaf to prayer. As for injunctions to honour and obey their parents, they reply, "It is our money," reasonable enough, as they labour ten hours a day stamping and sharpening nails. They are the most industrious boys, indeed, Morgan could find. He is blamed as Satan; in truth these good boys had only to look at Hinton's squalor immemorial and *see* it, which Morgan's money permits. My own parent would be pleased with them.

Soon I shall indeed find in Scripture a guide for us all. They are good boys who want only the proper Words. Moreover, in rising to this occasion I hope to become the *"man* of principle" to whom you kindly refer in your letter. But my dearest Snigs, though at Oxford I argued against the meta-physical egotism of Absolute Doubt, I have failed to ask you a single question about yourself. Is rumour, for instance, to be credited that you have at last found a remedy for your cough? You have always and indul-gently listened to Frederick and myself; pray now be more forthcoming with your own news.

Yours in friendship,
Charles

Frederick Courtland, Esq.   *1 April 1829*
Ecole des Beaux-Arts
Quai Malaquais
Paris

Dearest Brother,

Do you remember the folly Father wished to build for us in Tetfield? The Chinese pagoda folly, its moat a goldfish pond? I have considered building something like it here; the expense would be little, and it would give a graceful note to the otherwise sombre rectory. Recently I have been told, however, that China is no longer fashionable. Can you advise me?

Snigs and I were at Father's house on Sunday last. He quoted us long passages from your missives, whilst all we could return in the way of information were your hurried announcements that you are about to fly to the theatre, or to install yet another piece of elegant iron in the centre of Paris. I regretted so your absence at Easter. For myself, it has been a time of reflection upon the logic of charity, and that of retribution. Snigs pursues Sir Geoffrey Hind, who may well be obliged to leave England for a time. To what end? Hatred and villainy are mankind's worldly por-tion; to see at all is a great gift. I urged Snigs therefore to abandon this revenger's spirit, to cease boiling Father's blood, to thank God instead for the preservation of his vision. I wish my voice had carried more con-viction.

The wound is now occasionally painful, rather than continually so; the doctors consider Father to be recuperating normally. Perhaps once a fort-night he must resort to laudanum, a physic which he resents for clouding the brain in soothing the body. The cheek beneath the eye is still scarred, the stitches having been sewn at first with less than perfect art in Swaffham Prior. Father, I notice, avoids the mirrors in the house.

This year, for the first time, I have known him afraid. There come moments when he suddenly abandons his pen and winces over the table in pain. The other morning a new servant and I had to wash India-ink out of his hair, when he collapsed while at work, upsetting the inkwell. As I helped the servant wash his hair, Father attempted to pass the entire incident off with a stream of witticisms and blasphemies, recounting old stories of drinking with Scrope Davies, while I thought, "There is no need to speak, Father, I will cleanse your hair, you need not speak." Again, this was only proper, was it not? He continued in his licentious vein, becoming ever more crude as the pain jabbed into the innards of the brain, until the servant led him away, out of hearing, to rest in his own chamber.

Let frank speaking rule among ourselves. Of course I envy your foreign residence. In my branch of learning, if learning it be, the French are the most modern. I mean no insult to my brilliant contemporaries at Oxford; Whately is a most cunning analyst of passages from Scripture long considered obscure, as is Blanco White and the young Newman, all these men of Oriel remarkable. You, however, dwell in a country in which the enterprise of religion, if I may phrase it thus, is subject to secular investigation: the uses of faith in politics, the relation of religion to the secular fine arts, which questions interest me exceedingly. It would be as hard for me to return as for you. Need I add, however, that your presence here would give the greatest joy to both your father and

your admiring
Brother

Severus Rood, K.C.   *9 April 1829*
6 Inner Temple
London

Dear Snigs,

The affair of Morgan's juvenile employees becomes steadily more serious, and now threatens my very authority. As a healing gesture, I invited Morgan to join my parish in prayer. Imagine this upright man of commerce, the sustainer of fully a tenth of the youths in our village, singing "A Mighty Fortress is our God" on the Sabbath, the beneficiaries and their families surrounding him in song and in person. The church shakes to the final hymn; when we have finished singing, I am still so sensible to the succession of silence after celestial thunder that the voice of one of these parishioners is like an obscene sally:

"Be it true, Mr Morgan, that you 'bout to open another works?"

The industrialist starts, then recovers.

"Crowther, please remember we are within the House of our Lord."

"Be it true? They say it full ten mile away. Be you thinking of taking our boys with you?"

"My children," I attempt to intervene, "it is not meet thus to conclude Divine Service."

"Be you so minded? They cannot go, we will not let them," this taken up by two or three parents.

The industrialist suddenly rises, his wife rises, his two daughters rise, his two footmen, faces inflamed, rise from the back of the church. There are eighty of us in church, all others sitting except this clutch of family ready to flee danger—danger in God's sanctuary! The footmen traverse the length of the aisle, arriving beside their master. Suddenly we look mutually in horror: the boys who are Morgan's employees look at last to me, Morgan looks from the threadbare men and scrubbed boys to his own daughters, perfect in their bright, starched dresses, the latest hats from London on their pretty little heads. The amazed squire's fat tongue lolls out over his heavy, hanging jaw.

I attempted to master the conflict by alluding to the morning's sermon. "Our sermon today was drawn from the First Epistle of St. John, Chapter 4, verses 12 and 20." Here I think I even raised my arms in a gathering. I said, "This text I chose little suspecting the shameful incident which would desecrate the service today." The Morgan family sat again, as did the others, and I continued, my voice ringing. "Verse 12 tells us, 'No man hath seen God at any time. If we love one another, God dwelleth in us, and his love is perfected in us.' Verse 20 says, 'If a man say, I love God, and hateth his brother, he is a liar: for he that loveth not his brother whom he hath seen, how can he love God whom he hath not seen?'

"Let me emphasise, if I did not do so before, that these are perhaps the most daring words in St. John's Epistles. They tell us we can never know Our Lord, as it were, face to face. We cannot see Him. Yet we can be sure of Him, not merely by the Authority which is the Word but also by our own acts, by the purity of our love for each other." I was in truth wrought to a fevered pitch. "Do you understand? If you fail in love for one another, if you fail in fraternity, your love of God is a lie!"

In succeeding days there have been strong if diverse criticisms of myself, prefaced by universal disapproval of my interjection, "My children," Hinton tending to be Broad Church without any corresponding enthusiasm in prayer. "My children" kept them from attending to my words. Moreover, I am criticised for not saying who was at fault. A letter has circulated, purporting to come from me, blaming the squire for the second manufactory; the doctor's wife hates this worthy because he does not treat her with sufficient consideration in table placement. The letter deceived him not for a moment, yet his own advice to me was, "But you didn't say whom you meant. Tell who is the liar, man! I can't understand a word you say!" Morgan alone has responded to me with civility.

That morning did not end in disaster, though no thanks to me. After I had finished speaking, our good Miss Crater had the inspiration to begin another hymn on the organ. The congregants responded, sinking into the ritual of prayer, intoning the words so familiar to them, "Hallowed be Thy Name . . . For ever and ever . . ." These words they could repeat in their sleep, pushing them farther and farther from considering what it means to treat one another as brothers. Instead, they offered thanks once more to Heaven.

They have healed themselves thousands of times thus.

Charles

Mr Charles Courtland   *19 May 1829*
The New Rectory
Hinton
Gloucestershire

Dearest Brother,

Your letter of 1 April has just arrived after long delay, and in the meanwhile further news of you has come from Father and from Uncle Snigs. Let me begin at the end of your own note. I am as sensible as you of Father's need, yet whenever I have proposed returning to him he refuses. I have discovered it was he, indeed, who in the midst of his own worst pain dictated a letter, via Snigs, asking M. Fontaine to employ me upon what you amuse yourself by calling my elegant pieces of iron. It is important to Father I succeed in this work, and in truth, it has become important to me: this will be the most famous construction of the nineteenth Century.

About your difficulties with our parent I can only say what I have said before, his wit comes from a man whose eye was nurtured in youth by Boucher. About the spiritual difficulties which Uncle Snigs reports I have a suggestion.

You say Paris attracts you as a man of learning. Then come here! Come to Paris. An absence of some months from a village of anonymous letters can do their authors no harm and you only good. It will be easy to lodge with me, as I am just moving to new quarters, quarters of my own in 6, rue de Buci, on the left bank near the river. Did you not once pass a month at an inn behind the church? I have taken this step principally for the light, as the small room in which I formerly lived was so dim it was impossible to work at home. I plan to hang yellow stuffs upon the walls to emphasise the southern light which streams into my new sitting-room; the fabric will be flat on the wall, rather than be folded and quilted, as I would prefer, to reduce the expense.

The chambers in the rue de Buci are commodious, Charles, large enough to house us both in comfort for as long as you care to stay. We can walk in the Tuileries, we can visit the site of my new arcade, we can even, if you permit yourself, visit the theatres. Diversions might clarify your mind.

In truth, I would like you to see what I am making, my own effort of course subsumed in a larger whole. The ground for our arcade is now entirely cleared: level, raked earth, not a trace of the old foetid scenes. I also had moments of doubt of a spiritual order when this work of destruction began, the people who spent much of their waking lives here as though abolished by the carts removing the wood. Yet the throbbing of Paris soon restored me. And I do not mean pleasure, although there is here an abundance of that sure, vulgar tonic for the soul. Sometimes, at my table, I will try to weigh a line which I have drawn, an absurdity but a beautiful one, or I will imagine myself the naked man, arms and legs stretched out within Leonardo's circle, this circle defining the roof line of a pavilion, or in the street, on a good afternoon, it becomes evident how the absolutely transparent can yet have colour and so mass. This is the throb of possibility I mean, and I wish it also for you, my dear brother, I wish this astonishing conviction of possibility to irrigate your soul.

Do then say you will come; write to me directly at my new quarters, where I shall await you impatiently.

Yours ever,
Frederick

Severus Rood, K.C.   *3 July 1829*
6 Inner Temple
London

Dear Snigs,

Frederick's invitation has been followed by letters from Parisian clerics, informing me of various opportunities and curiosities which might interest me, should I choose to honour Paris by a visit in the next few months. Yesterday a ticket for the London–Paris diligence arrived; my brother had booked me into the most luxurious of the carriages.

You also are mistaken. I did not choose to abandon my flock. I was given to understand that an older man might better be able to lead them in their hours of need, that a (relatively speaking) mere youth of twenty-six without children, not to say a wife (and why is that? twenty-six is quite old enough to marry, especially for a stripling with a little money of his own), that such a youth lacked Moral Authority. Moral Authority was their requirement, not sermons on fraternal compassion. Besides, no one understands what my sermons are about. To the squire I proposed a period of mutual reflection, during which I would award myself a vacation —but to Paris! The squire was horrified! He had heard dark tales even of Cheltenham, which was said in point of recreation to be in every way superior to Paris—perhaps I ought consider an indefinite absence, during which both sides would seek other arrangements, seeing that the village found me not exactly wanting; but the place was more appropriate at the moment for an older cleric, who, the squire assured me, will force those children to turn their ill-gotten gains over to their parents. He will take the youngsters properly in hand and teach them some discipline. My clerical error, thus far, is to be too gentle with boys. At least for this I will not blame myself.

I will regret the Chinese pagoda, now twelve by twelve square, roofed and tiled. There are even young goldfish in the moat. The doctor's wife assured me the day before my interview with the squire that it will be a *most interesting* place for my future wife and myself to observe the sunset, advising that prior to my marriage I should plant nothing *obscuring* around the pagoda for the sake of propriety. Father wants the tiles, which came from Peking to his London storerooms and thence to Hinton, so I suppose I might as well have the pagoda taken down. I shall give James, one of the labouring boys, the goldfish, in hopes that parental responsibilities of his own might induce him to remain in place.

So to Paris in the autumn. At least this rupture means I can see you sooner than I had planned. I shall leave by the 1st of August, and remain in Father's house until the middle of October, when I join my brother. In expectation of the pleasure shortly of embracing you, I remain

as ever, your friend
Charles

Charles Courtland, Esq.   *3 July 1829*
The New Rectory
Hinton
Gloucestershire

My dear Charles,

How happy I am that after this extended period of deliberation you have decided to award yourself a Sabbatical. Your father is pleased your brother made the offer, I am pleased you have accepted it. Remark, Sir, that I have uttered before neither a word in commendation or in disapproval of this plan. My entire life has passed in offering opinion, and thus I have learnt that, in momentous matters, the man who lives by the advice of others seeks not aid in action but refuge from responsibility.

Blame yourself indeed! Rather, sir, abandon this flock to its own courses! Fortunately, I know nothing about nature, and thus can summon up in my mind no sufficiently terrible image of what indeed becomes of sheep without a shepherd, nor do I particularly care for lamb. However, surely one difference between the State of Nature and Civilised Society is that, whilst in the savage state we may be obliged to direct those without wit or will, civilisation obliges us to serve only those who engage by their distinction our sympathy. I offer then counsel reprehensible according to the lights of Christianity but edifying for those who seek to avoid a dull, burdened, miserable life. Worthiness has been my principle in choosing clients, and I believe it to be a good one by extension to marriage partners, parishes and similar entanglements beyond my ken.

Charles, perhaps it is no more than the prospect of your liberation from this rectory in limbo, but I feel an immense, lawyerly desire to flood you with Truth, an impulse wholly contradicting the wise nostrum I have earlier advanced. Your father has always had a weakness for foreign views, unpotable beverages and revolting foods. Even as a boy he strained on the leash of the life immediately to hand, and has been saved from folly of temperament only by genius. I have no genius, yet the eye which is not bold may none the less see clearly. I say to you, Beware! Not of Parisian pleasures—these a rational man must taste, I suppose, though London's have been more than sufficient for my palate. I implore you to beware that which I have observed amongst many who have travelled much in foreign parts.

I can only describe it, Charles, as an illusory calm, as though the clock of life had stopped the moment one left England's shores. No indulgent father had the means, and even, were they available, the desire, to launch me upon a Grand Tour, but all I have seen who have been so cosseted return with Memories in lieu of Resolve.

Now you know your loving godparent to surrender only periodically to such flourishes. To me you are dearer than any of the relations a shrivelled old bachelor forms among his contemporaries, and so I take the liberty of speaking to you as a Father, and leave to your kinsmen the pleasure of addressing you in other terms.

As for myself, I have left off treatments of Harvey's Vesuvial Fog, although these vapours came recommended by a distinguished client of remarkably advanced age. I myself have been counselled to quit England's shores during the worst months of the winter damp; however, the wolves prowling these Temples might devour me *in absentia.* In place of the sight of Mount Vesuvius, I thought, therefore, to avail myself of its packaged vapours, but these have proved unacceptably sulphurous, as perhaps the Romans themselves found the mountain's original Eructations. I must stop this catalogue of complaint, as work once more calls

your most affectionate
Uncle Severus

Mlle Mercure   *4 October 1829*
Théâtre de la Comédie-Française
Place de la Comédie

Most Kind Lady,

This letter comes to you from the unknown foreigner to whom you were so gracious last evening at the Restaurant Grand-Véfour. My thanks for your genial presence at our table come coupled with esteem, for it was in assisting at your miraculous performance in *Le Cid,* no matter that your appearance was limited to a single blazing scene, that I conceived not merely affection for your person but respect for your powers as a tragédienne. How well did you combine impassioned speech with the most demure movement, imparting to your rôle thereby a singularity which supported to great effect the more forward rôles.

May I take the liberty, therefore, of calling upon you at your *loge* in the theatre? I should view it as a singular honour were you to receive me. In thanking you in advance for this courtesy, I am yrs most respectfully,

M. Frederick Courtland

Mlle Mercure   *8 October 1829*
Théâtre de la Comédie-Française
Place de la Comédie

My dear Mademoiselle,

Yes, I am the silent English youth, head bent over his plate, to whom you condescended to address a few words some days ago. I thought I was gay; perhaps the sentiments you inspired in me deluded me into believing I had spoken as I felt. Your command "Reveal yourself, who cunningly among the others remained invisible at table," shews you expect court from a man of the world. Now you know me as I am. I had not before written a letter of homage; perhaps the mask of my letter comes from inexperience of flattery, for in essaying we resort most easily to the most worn models. Perhaps also I should not have written, as it is a man far different from myself whom you would have expected in your *loge.* I shall not therefore take advantage of your kind invitation, as I do not want to be a man who had insinuated himself into your presence under false colours. All I can do is thank you again for the proof of your kindness.

Yrs respectfully,
M. Frederick Courtland

Mlle Mercure   *20 October 1829*
Théâtre de la Comédie-Française
Place de la Comédie

Esteemed Thespienne,

Last evening I dined with Louis de Flavigny, whose cousin Marie supped two days previously with you. So my little efforts have amused you! Let us agree on the following points which may impede future gossip but undoubtedly will save your reputation:

1. Your "unknown English slave" is not a schoolboy; he is an architect in the employ of one of the master fabricators of Paris.

2. He is not the heir to an English dukedom. Set your mind at ease therefore; the fear you expressed to Marie de Flavigny that you could become the Duchess of a fledgling Duke need trouble your dreams no longer. Indeed, the young gentleman is in fact five years younger than yourself, that is twenty-three to your twenty-eight if the information he has obtained is correct. True, his flaxen hair and his features give him the air of one younger—men in the third decade of life regret, in general, this impression if so endowed; but regret for indelible youth is a useless waste of sentiment.

Let me assure you that his sole claim to nobility is in the purity and elevation of his regard for your acting.

3. Finally, most superb Lady, he does not haunt your stage door. He works outside it, as the artist's entrance of the Comédie-Française is at right angles to the shed housing one hundred and sixty-six glass panes which, under the direction of your humble correspondent, will soon be inserted into the roof of the new Galerie d'Orléans.

Last week I watched enthralled your *Armide*. Although my French is not quite deft enough to penetrate all the nuances of your voice, I felt you evoke, by silence, by momentary pause, by quiet delivery, that passion which would die trumpeted on display. And does not all great art marshal the unseen, unsaid, ineffable, the absent? This power which you command on stage I counsel you to deploy privately in the necessities of gossip: do not paint me colourfully, but rather let auditors like Marie de Flavigny imagine my infancy, beauty and nobility by the murmured phrase, "I wonder, perhaps it is his carriage, the softness of his lemon gloves, his assurance, but he has an air, that little one . . ."

Artful thespienne, what a debt I owe you! How else should I have learnt, so quickly, that a heart "worn on the sleeve," as we say, is likely to suffer from exposure? Believe me, Mademoiselle, to be one of your most fervent admirers. My only hope is that the arcade we are constructing behind your theatre will cause you to return a modicum of this admiration to

the less mysterious
Frederick Courtland

Severus Rood, K.C.   *10 November 1829*
6 Inner Temple
London

Dear Snigs,

We were ever adept at charades, do you remember? I adored the cunning
stages Father used to contrive for us around the table set against curtains
in the drawing-room, and even then, I admit, my untamed egoism made
itself known; I still recall with pleasure pushing Frederick off the table
whenever the occasion arose for making an important speech. So perhaps
it is meet that my newest impressions of this city are at once of its theatres,
which my brother haunts, and of his prominent place in that other theatre
in which Talent declaims to the Future.

When you, Father and Mother journeyed to Paris, I cannot imagine you
frequented the places of amusement to which Frederick takes me. Near his
works, for example, in the boulevard du Temple, is the Théâtre Compte.
The law fears the aroused passions of the mob at theatres like the Compte;
thus last week we found an obscuring gauze curtain hung between the
actors and ourselves in the audience. The government had decided this
gauzy film would filter those bursts of violent laughter, pity and anger we
would otherwise experience with a clear view of the stage. The actors after
a few minutes of uncertainty contrived to defy this protection, coming close
to the gauze when they wanted to enact an intimate scene, their faces
pressed against it, as though the words of love had always been meant to
be tested in this way. After the Compte, at midnight, we went on to the
Funambules: there one may witness a café scene, the rise and fall of an
empire, the agonies of death or of broken love, all in silence, not a word
spoken in a hall whose audience is correspondingly silent. Here the authorities had deprived the Funambulists of speech; the mimes convert the prohi-
bition into art.

Frederick is frequently occupied with his affairs. I had expected to
attend lectures and to study here, improving my somewhat rusty powers
of intellect in this capital of Mind. But frequently I find instead I resort
alone to these theatres for comfort. I sit up in the "gods," where people are
packed close together on benches, crude people who in England might
embarrass me. At home we have created for the French the vice of miserli-
ness, but up here my neighbours will without thinking offer me the end
of a sausage or a bit of roasted tripe, the food held out in a greasy hand while

the purveyor remains head forward, entranced by the stage. When words are permitted in the theatres, they are only simple words destined for the common people, and these I understand; when words are forbidden, as at the Funambules, then we are all equally deprived. And in this, also, there is a sort of fellowship.

One often seeks comfort in forgetting a nearer past by recovering a more ancient one. Thus, when sometimes my recent failure presents itself to my mind without any softening or self-pity, I think to gain relief by going to the gardens of Paris, the Tuileries, say, where as children Frederick and I often romped during visits, nurse commanding us to return to no avail. Now, her voice has been replaced by a half-amused, half-bitter sigh; this is how men in the gods signify "I understand." All around me they sit for hours, chatting during the long intermissions, comparing the performances of this actress to that last year, explaining one to another the nuances of the action, the actors treated as cunning commentators, the mimes or melodramas as contrivances for contemplation, in play, of the bitterness of life. All is serious, there is no pleasure in make-believe: even in the trained animal acts, my companions in the gods manage to find a political meaning.

My most curious brother understands it all. In two years he has become more French than the French: his accent is superb, his gloves and cravats would embarrass any honest John Bull by their delicacy, and he is passionately in pursuit of an actress who toys with him. In equal measure, when I look at him, I see the same brightness of eye, the same flush patches on his high cheeks, the same ready, wide smile, in a word the same beautifully *ardent* brother who could so easily succumb to tears at his own roles in our domestic pageants. Yet it were a genuinely French laugh he gave that night at the Théâtre Compte, only half of pleasure, when the actors discovered the possibilities of gauze.

We have walked every square inch of his arcade. The new Frenchman recounts who had to be bribed to do what, your English godson cannot keep himself from praising the result. To my untutored eye, it is hateful. It lacks any softness, this iron and glass pavilion; although the volume is enormous, there is no inspiration in the severity of the structure, the arcade does not arouse awe.

I have never dissembled before with my brother. "Give me your frank reaction," he requested of this, his first love. I did not use the words "hateful" or "cold," I rather disputed his claim that this vast structure of the manufacturing age is our modern version of the cathedral.

"Pray tell me," I rounded, "what doctrine or creed is represented by these metal replicas of the columns in the temples of the Greeks? Is it the credo of Endless Repetition—ten, a hundred, a thousand Greek columns seeming the more wondrous in form because they have been manufactured by machine?"

At this my brother silently took my arm in his. My tone had in it the accents of Hinton; I hear them again in the writing of these words. Frederick replied to me with a caress. Still, I will confess to you that I do *not* take pride in the regard with which he is held by the other draughtsmen and indeed by the master architect. I do *not* enjoy hearing others perform the kindness of praising him to me. I resent even the times when he translates rapid French in conversation, so that I may comprehend beyond my schoolboy powers. Why then have I come here? It is a cunning question, is it not?

Charles

Charles Courtland, Esq.   *20 November 1829*
in care of
Frederick Courtland, Esq.
6, rue de Buci
Paris

Charles,

Self, Sir, Self!

Yours,
Uncle Severus

Mlle Mercure   *4 January 1830*
Théâtre de la Comédie-Française
Place de la Comédie

Most Kind Lady,

I believe that, as we are both invited to Adolphe Nourrit's supper tomorrow, prior words between us might make our mutual presence bearable in the same room, if not agreeable. I will apologise, if you will. However, I impose certain conditions: First, at Adolphe's you will be obliged to wear the spray of American orchids which Duclos et Fils will deliver to you tomorrow. Second, we will *not* discuss Miss Smithson's talent. I realise that this estimable lady has caused the theatrical world to revise the opinion it formerly had of the "barbaric Shakespeare" (for shame! for shame!), but the English residents of Paris by now have no new anecdotes to offer about Miss Smithson, and I do not even have the honour of her acquaintance. Moreover, you make us feel even more foreign by asking us only about English matters. I, for instance, should like to speak to you about Victor Hugo. Everyone seems to have decided there should be a large scandal over M. Hugo's new play. In good English fashion I took the precaution of reserving today a box for the *Hernani* first night next month, as that seems to be the designated evening to evince the outrage and the partisanship which those who have not yet read the play already feel. I shall take my brother; he is susceptible to these sentiments. He is older than am I, but also unfortunately not the son of a duke. However, I will prevent you from meeting him; you would certainly bewitch him, and we cannot have two bewitched persons in one family. You, I am certain, will be attending this evening of scandal in the company of the most distinguished persons of the theatre and I am also certain you have in fact read *Hernani*, perhaps even discussed it with the author. You are obliged at M. Nourrit's, therefore, to instruct me in those passages which should lead me to cry out in disgust, and those passages, on the contrary, which should make my blood boil most partisan and Romantic.

There; these two conditions, the flowers and M. Hugo rather than Miss Smithson, they should see us through Adolphe's supper party. Perhaps they may even, some day, lead you to smile, when you look down from the artists' reception room into the gardens of the Palais-Royal.

Your admiring servant
Frederick Courtland

Charles Courtland, Esq.   *19 January 1830*
12, rue de Seine
Paris

My dearest Charles,

It is so long without a letter from you, and I fear the fault to be entirely mine. I have forgotten that youth is a truly terrible age; you face the world without the dread armour of Resignation. I should not have reproved you when you opened your heart to me, though I am equally uneasy,

Sir, that you should take so mild a reproof as a catastrophe for which you must punish me with silence. I am uneasy, only because I wish above all else concourse with you, I wish you never to become foreign to me.

Frederick writes that you have taken your own lodgings, a more convenient domestic arrangement for your extended stay. Have you no word from your various sources here of a fresh appointment in England? I thought Blanco White might easily have helped. I remember the apartments of the Parisians as, for the most part, impossibly minuscule. You may tell me of this, or of any trifles you wish, so long as you write.

Sir, what folly is your brother committing? An amour with an actress? You mention it so casually. Frederick is ardent, true, but he is not foolish; moreover he is not common, and entanglement with a French actress is, surely, an obligatory adventure *Only for the Most Vulgar*.

John has somewhat recovered his spirits. We gave together a large dinner last week, on which occasion he managed to shock several young persons who came out of duty, thinking they would be bored. (He quoted to them lengthily from the most provoking bits of *Don Juan,* to prove Byron's courage greater than Mozart's—utterly absurd!) His work since the accident now begins to appear tangibly as two new structures in Jermyn Street, and is acclaimed. However, his strength remains intermittent; I fear that alone he will be unable to execute the royal commission. I have heard him in his studio several times reprimanding the young draughtsmen for faults of drawing the lads claim are fictive. He will not admit he has recourse to laudanum; the draughts he takes furtively. May I confess that my pity is less, and my annoyance more, at your father's repeated assertions that he sees with as much Penetration as ever? To complete this catalogue: he says the young men who enter the profession of architecture are more mercantile, narrow and ill educated than those he knew in Nash's studio.

I had thought, these ordinary complaints of a man moving past the prime will cease when his son returns to share the burden. But a young man minded to duty who has succumbed to lurid snares? Can you not do something, *in situ*? You *must* make your brother return when the diploma is in hand in July.

My boy, I am pleased to inform you that I have found the most unlooked-for weapon against my cough. It is a beverage labelled "McGurdy's General Restorative and Tonic." The apothecary McGurdy promises to heal ague, catarrh, piles, pustulent excrescences, as well as bronchial tremor; having not sampled this banquet of complaints, I cannot judge of his larger claims, but certainly for the racking coughs in my chest it has proved miraculous—although it must be used with Caution, great Caution. When you both return, you will be witness of the results.

Yrs most affectionately,
Uncle Severus

Severus Rood, K.C.   *28 February 1830*
6 Inner Temple
London

Dear Snigs,

My good and true friend, do not interpret my silence ever as reproof! You whom I cherish! The last two months I have rather sought to spend in the discipline of retreat, contemplating the Word of John, valedictory words for me in England, but which I shall always hear within. These verses have come to me here to seem doubly true, and in solitude I hoped to lead myself back from an abyss.

These months of contemplation have told me quite simply that I wish no longer to be responsible for my father's happiness. Do you remember your own words? You insist on worthy clients. I mean never to suggest him unworthy in any way to any man, save that if he cannot enter into my perplexity, I cannot undertake to ease his pain. John tells us that without love of our fellow man the love of God is a lie. I have also considered that. "For he that loveth not his brother whom he hath seen, how can he love God whom he hath not seen?" Perhaps the Doubt I harbour ever more heavily in my breast comes simply from refusing this ailing father—as I say, it is quite simple.

But about my brother, against whom I vented my spleen, let me tell you that my love for him is stronger than ever, and he has furnished me the most moving proof of his own. He has left me to myself, trusting in me. When at last I signalled to him that I had ended my retreat, he did not ask how I knew, as indeed I could tell neither him, nor you. Instead he rather shyly demanded,

"It is something to celebrate?"

"I hardly know, since I am the same confused creature I have ever been."

"Surely not," said he, but, I say, he made no effort to recombine or recompose me. Instead, he asked what I had most missed during my seclusion—a seclusion passed, for this I can tell you, not only within the dun walls of my little room in the rue de Seine but also in various cafés in the city, in walking about aimlessly, for one fortnight in a solitary trip to the town of Talloires, whose beauties were known to me from Slade's engravings—my brother asked most what I had missed, and I replied the theatre, the peculiar comfort for me here, a comfort I denied myself.

I met him at the Café de Foy, a place of fashion in the Palais-Royal to which he frequently adjourns. "The theatre it shall be then. I shall take you to the theatrical event of the season!" Having your letter in mind, I thought after this evening of renewed and mutual pleasure, I might at least communicate to him your concerns. But I shall be obliged to explain to you our extraordinary outing in detail so that you understand why it has been difficult for me to communicate your wishes. Because I felt so transported myself.

Believe little of what you may read or hear in London of the *Hernani* and its reception. Scandal there was, but also poetry and truth. I have never been so stirred, nay transported by anything like it. The reports spread here by those who have only a love of intrigue dwell on the character of M. Hugo's partisans. It is said his claque consisted of drunken ragamuffins who desecrated the theatre; the scum entered the theatre, it is said, several hours before the curtain's rising, dressed in extravagant and provoking rags, passing the time in the corridors drinking, chewing garlic which they then spat upon the floors, and relieving themselves against the fine silk-clad walls and upon the plinths of the statues which decorate the reception rooms. All lies.

Yes, extravagant M. Hugo's men were: The painter Deveria wore a silk hat *à la Rubens* and a cloak copied from a painting by Velásquez. The poet Gautier, premier among the young scriveners of this town, arrived clad in pale-green trousers and a black jacket with velvet facings. These garments were encased within a grey overcoat, its inner lining of green satin, so that when M. Gautier drew back his cloak in the foyer one was stunned by the dark green of that wrapping against the watery green of his legs, the black velvet of his upper torso seeming to recede and the poet appearing as a creature only of lank lower limbs. But in the lobby, after removing his cloak, he then revised this impression by sheathing his chest, as though he were completing his toilette in a dressing-room instead of in a theatre filled with hundreds of ladies and gentlemen, in an intensely red doublet. Frederick explained this colour as almost one ruby yet with no hint of black. Having completed his entrée, young Gautier ascended the stairway, reciting in full voice one of M. Hugo's poems.

Frederick smiled at M. Gautier: "He has well launched the spectacle."

I wanted to follow him, to see where he was going, if he had further secrets to reveal, if he was meeting someone. There are sometimes moments like this when you are enslaved by the sight of a person. Frederick, however, noticed me staring, and led me within.

We were seated quite near the deserted royal box. Up and to our left was a balcony box in which, Frederick remarked off-handedly to me, the actress of his acquaintance sat. I should never have mentioned this woman to you, I suppose. Honour obliged me after your last missive to reveal to my brother my indiscretion, and since then he has held aloof from me on this subject. Having started matters, let me only further remark that her toilette is demure, almost sombre. She is diminutive in height, too thin, and her face, like her dress, gives one the impression of a grave lady looking sadly at the frantic doings around her. She must be quite an actress, to give so convincingly this impression of a gentlewoman. The eyes I could not see, but when she recognised Frederick, the mouth moved only slightly to smile. As far as I could remark, she was entirely devoid of natural beauty. In any event, you are mistaken: in this amorous passage he has succumbed to no ordinary vulgarity.

She, however, is not the difficulty of which I speak. We did hear from the extravagants above cries of "To the guillotine with bald heads!" It is true that there was a scent of garlic in the air. Only Rumour smelled evidences of a more bodily desecration in the hall. The young men were not bent on destruction, they were poets come to celebrate, they were exuberant singers.

Young and old sporadically traded insults; the real scandal occurred upon the stage. M. Firmin, the rebel Hernani, has like all actors at the Comédie-Française trained since boyhood to enunciate Alexandrine poetry regularly, the voice rising and falling with the line, majestic when the lines are those of a king, but a sound unsuited to the barbaric commands of a bandit-prince. Mlle Mars was better; she understood the pathos of her role, her voice quavered and broke, she entered in declamation the throbbing metric of M. Hugo's verse, but her body did not join her voice. Again it is the training; she stood stock-still when hurling a curse, she sank sound-lessly and decorously to the stage floor when she died. M. Michelot of all was despicable. Imagine Don Juan recited by an elderly cleric; Michelot raised his eyebrows at his own words, spoke rather doubtfully of an ever-hot lust for vengeance, offered cowardly irony in place of refusing M. Hugo's verse openly.

But what poetry! That is the matter! Poetry to equal the blazing colours of M. Gautier's person, as though fire, thunder and ice were made palpable in speech. Never again shall we use the words "barbaric" or "savage" as condemnation: here was the flowing life of the untamed, and we who are shackled by the niceties of modern civilisation, we would better look upon ourselves as degraded!

Snigs, it is so difficult to explain the effect of it. Frederick and I wandered the streets for hours after leaving the theatre, the music of that poetry echoing in our ears. Throughout the night we encountered young men, and women also, whole groups of young people chanting and weeping, and we knew that they too had assisted at *Hernani*, that M. Hugo's flame burned in them. No, it were a mean-mouthed scandal to speak of this evening as scandalous.

In the depths of the night we collapsed finally at a café near the St. Germain market. By then I could not remember the action of the play, but still the rhythms of it coursed in my brain. I turned to Frederick, who had procured us large mugs of chicory-coffee; "Did you expect anything like it?"

"No! Never!" returned my brother, his ardour revived. "Never! Try to imagine this evening in England, a theatre, an entire city inflamed by verse."

Perhaps it was the hour. In any event I said something ridiculous like, "Think of Shakespeare, of Milton, of Byron . . ." at which point Frederick cut me short.

"Charles, the truth about the English is that they"—we were of course speaking in English—"the truth is that they are artistic cowards. Give them guns and a war, there are none braver. Read them a poem in a metre unfamiliar or difficult, they are afraid. They bluster, 'It's all nonsense, it's a sham,' so that they needn't think or attempt to enter into the sentiments of an alien realm. It is the same in music, in painting, in architecture. Whatever you may say of the French, everyone at the theatre, those outraged as well as those partisan, was eager for the evening."

The moment was not auspicious, obviously, to raise the issue of Frederick returning in a few months to his native land, but this speech put me in mind of your letter.

"You ought not judge a People entire. What would you say about the career of our father? Surely there is no one bolder, and he is well received. You would be as well."

"What do you say, Charles, as to the tolerance of Father's clients when presented with an unexpected, charming fantasy?"

I advanced your views as to Frederick's necessary return. He had planned to travel for a year after receiving his diploma, then to decide upon his own future. I revealed what evidence you had given me of Father's failing powers. At this he said he would write to Father immediately.

"You know he would urge only your own pleasure, especially as asking you to return would be to admit his own weakness."

"Then what would you have me do? I cannot simply return to London and appear at the atelier, as if a place there belonged to me at whim. I must ask Father formally."

The subject of his entanglement could not, you see, be raised by me, given my earlier gaffe, nor, as I have explained to you, do I feel impelled to lecture Frederick on his obligations towards a person whom I shall no longer serve—which conviction I shall not discuss with him, or anyone else, but you. Our chicory-coffees had become cold; the coals in the café's grate were nearly extinct.

"And you? Will you return to a new vicarage in England? Surely you have enough money to live, albeit modestly, as a private scholar."

Here is the answer I would have made him, could I have but expressed the ebb and flow of thought within my aching brain, but we had arrived at that point of exhaustion which demands silence.

Hernani is a very long piece; there were moments when the actors spoke so rapidly in the heat of the action that I could understand nothing. Thus throughout the performance my attention made its own entrances and exits; when I could not attend to the burning poetry I looked at those around me. Men called out an oath from time to time, as if to remind everyone that this was meant to be an evening of scandal, each shout causing ladies in the best boxes to agitate furiously their fans, warding off offensive words with turbulent air. At Hinton, as I have recounted to you, we once had a day in church in which the congregants interrupted service also with offensive oaths. My eyes found M. Gautier's box; he was leaning forward over the box rail, his face a mask of concentration, out-lined to the rest of the spectators by the light from the stage. Next to him were a young man and woman, each beautifully long-stemmed and pale, also leaning out of the box, but towards the stalls crowd below, occasion-ally recognising friends with slight nods and smiles. Have you ever seen Texier's painting of the Egyptian twin gods of the reeds? They were like it.

There were musicales once a fortnight at Hinton. I left the playing of the piano to the doctor's wife, the lady of the anonymous letters; although I play much better than does she, one had to be very careful and she was vain of her fingers. We played hymns of course, but also the latest music of respectable character from the capitals of the entire world, from Berlin, Rome and Vienna, as well as Paris and London, all this music posted to us fortnightly by the Rectories' Service of Shands Musical Publishers in Ber-wick Street.

The stench of the thousand Parisians gathered for Frederick's great voyage to the unknown shores of Art: here the women are liberal in the use of perfumes, scented powder is not considered indecent, and men soak their gloves in Cologne Water. Higher up in the Comédie-Française the patrons cannot afford these sumptuous masks; one smells one's neighbour's most recent meal every time he breathes. Perfume, Cologne Water, Garlic and Beer—and of course hawkers parade constantly up and down the aisles during the performance, selling sausages, wines and camphor drops. As I say, *Hernani* is a very long play; the theatre is poorly ventilated.

Before I quitted Hinton, I calculated the household I could support on £184 per annum. Your legal eye will find little to take exception to in these figures: one serving girl, a Cook, a man for boots and heavy work also serving as coachman when needed, a trap, one horse boarded out, rotation of six clerical costumes per annum, coal, produce and other comestibles not provided by decimus tithe, wine daily and port weekly, leaving £30 for wifely expenses whose nature I cannot fathom and so did not reckon in parts.

In the ordinary way, brothers lead their lives in more or less amity and intimacy. This I am sure will be the way of it for us. Some good woman will accept me on the modest terms I have outlined; the firm of Courtland and Courtland will flourish by placing all of England under glass; my children will wait impatiently for their annual visit to their smart cousins in Town; Frederick will make an effort on these occasions to enquire into affairs at the Rectory and the latest in ecclesiastical opinion. At the moment, we are otherwise circumstanced. I came to him, having failed in the first jump towards this future. The little brother who flourishes within his magic circle, so beautiful, so free, he would give me life for a time. Snigs, he has.

Thus in the café I should have answered my brother, "No, I shall remain." This is why I am unable to press your suit.

During my moments of inattention to M. Hugo's art, I sometimes thought of the other amusements to which my brother had led me, I resisting at first because they seemed beneath notice. I thought of the tricks of the trained dogs, walking on one forepaw, chewing their tails while barking, or again of the dead-white face of a Pierrot, which stared at me in memory as Don Carlos and Hernani thundered to each other in Charlemagne's tomb. The dogs and the clowns also have their own consequence. That is the *terrible* fact of this city: flowers out of season, actresses who play gentlewomen, actors who mock their own lines, disputes about the most fashionable colour for gloves this week, the sardonic smile of the man who watches another bribed, the light on the statues in the Tuileries, the statues covered with a century of bird droppings, everything has its consequence.

If one could put these matters on a scale, they might weigh as much as sound views on the nature of Christian service.

We walked back to our separate lodgings as the sky began to brighten, my brother now thoughtful rather than aroused. He will do, and, I pray you to believe, so in the end will I. Frederick will console Father, as my presence never can; please understand why, in the meantime, for a while, I remain here in his place.

Your devoted friend,
Charles

M. Frederick Courtland   *29 April 1830*
6, rue de Buci
Paris

My dear son,

Thank you for your frank letter; there is so much possibility in your future, I wonder not at your indecision. You must put entirely out of your mind "returning" to London; "come" to London, yes, that is a decision *you* make, but the word "returning" suggests you are drawn back by invisible reins. I cannot advise your course; pray know that I have full confidence in you wherever and however you roam.

I own that there pass in London certain stories about your roaming; it is said that you are enamoured of a French actress, this matter detailed to me as proof that education in a foreign land means schooling in profligacy. Rumour, as you know, is the spontaneous combustion of polite society. Your adventures, whether true or false, put me in mind once more of how Sarah and I were circumstanced at your age, long, long ago. Our Courtland relations, you see, had grown so rich from the wars in the colonies that their wealth no longer was considered, at least by them, to have come from trade, whereas some of Sarah's family were still behind the counter.

When I took your comely mother for love, the reason was not reasonable to these handmaidens and handmasters of Mars. For our comfort we escaped our first autumn together wandering through the Tuscan towns, Sarah each day fresh for the revelation hidden in a nave or in the faded apartments of a palazzo. This outpouring of her zest steadied me during the time my mother called our "shameless Gypsy travels." Sarah was always curious about what I could already or might possibly *do;* I had bored the young ladies of my acquaintance by my architecting talk, and also puzzled them; at most they understood the possibility, one suitable for ladies, of water-colouring. During the months we travelled, living little better than peasants on the pittance my parents gave me, Sarah fortified in me the desire to learn the fabrication of solid beautiful things.

Only Snigs appreciated this merit in Sarah; he said to me on the eve of our marriage, "She esteems your capability." Now you are old enough, and perhaps so placed as to understand the true nature of innocence in a woman. A maiden may harbour most putrid thoughts when her eyes turn modestly away from a gentleman. A girl curious about the mathematics of an arch, about the manner of best laying brick, this enquiring woman no matter what her circumstances has more of candour and purity.

I recall this wonderful autumn, not to reassure you that I once was as you may be now, for the manner of love has assuredly changed. Sarah and I held to the usages of the world, whatever the world held against us. We travelled, then married, then consummated. No, rather it gives me licence to question you: does this lady stimulate your capability? Do you wake in the morning avid for the day, impatient for it? If so, her dubious profession, her foreign ways, her age (or is this more but Rumour's soaring?), all are prized attributes of her being. I do not speak in terms of the flush of momentary pleasure. But if you are tied to her by bonds of contest, if there be no sharing of sympathies, if when apart she afflicts your brain yet when together she inspires you with a secret boredom, then end this liaison; it is the love, or rather the obsession of men who do not love themselves. And, were this unfortunately true, then I hope you would come, rather than return, to London.

You will note that I am observing exactly the form required of a Father in speaking for the first time frankly on delicate matters to his Son. I have consulted both Chesterfield and Hervey and find in my manner nothing to which these arbiters of taste in my youth might object. Let me continue with a particularity of which Hervey would disapprove, and Chesterfield accept so long as the style of it proved unexceptionable.

I grew to manhood in an age less prudent than this one; our freedom were of itself no education. To come to it, when Sarah carried your older brother, she was liverish, and we, in our innocence of these matters, thought it required merely the waters of Bath for a cure. The cause, I was later told, could be traced to the sheepskin, which I had used too many times. I cannot give you the physic of it, and if my meaning entirely escapes you, we'll enter into the matter when next we meet; if perchance you are sensible of my discourse, let me implore you to care and cleanliness. I date the origin of Sarah's difficulties to this ignorance.

I know I make sport of Charles, though he doesn't *truly* mind, you know. The boy takes my teasing as a tonic, a tonic I've administered since the days the women coddled him because he was sickly. The serious and insuperable objection I have to his profession is that it confuses, rather than informs, the innocent about the real perils of the world. Clerics, whether Catholic or Protestant, are in the main ignorant of the body. Who better to counsel the young at the high season of fecundity?

Once, when Sarah and I first met, we fell into furious disputation about hedgerows: should they be clipped like box in a Renaissance garden or be allowed to grow as wild as possible? On this momentous topic we heated to madness: I reviled her taste, proceeded from her deficient eye in shrubbery to her deficiencies in dress, comportment, and thence to the general foolishness, vanity and greed of women. She correspondingly reproached my pretensions, my family, my wigs and my moral character. We were in tears of rage; suddenly we were laughing, her brown hair between my hands, whilst our neighbours from the lodgings below pounded on the door in remonstrance of the cries and shouting.

I do not importune you about your private affairs, but perhaps you comprehend that, although you are in another country, never, never have you been closer, never dearer to your father. Upon a further occasion I shall send you news of my doings for the Crown, a demanding commission because my patrons do not know their own minds and I have yet to master my own plan; already, however, it has a few happy touches.

Your loving
Father

John Courtland, Esq.   *5 August 1830*
12 Jermyn Street
London

Dear Father,

Let me instantly set your mind at rest: both Charles and I are entirely unharmed. The confusion led everyone here to exaggerate the danger, and, I suppose, the alarums abroad. It was only an uprising of three days; the first two were indeed violent, danger passing on the third.

Since you have honoured me in the past with your candour, I feel obliged to treat with you in turn candidly, although what I must tell you will, I know, cause you pain. Please understand: I have fathomed your need.

But just now I can make no plans, for I cannot say how we are circumstanced, or in fact if it is the end.

Father, I take up my pen the day after I wrote above. You may think my matter the examinations which are, it is true, delayed a month, but the issue is more to me than a diploma, as I shall explain to you, in detail which may be tedious but will I hope make you understand why I *cannot leave now.*

On the evening of the 27th last, we went to the performance at the Nouveautés; there was a juggling dog and a pantomime verging on the obscene. The Nouveautés was stifling hot, the smell of dog and face paint almost choking, which made it easier to watch the lewd gestures of the clowns without shame, as the audience was panting like beasts. When the performance ended we rushed for the exits and the fresh night air. The doors were flung open, and upon the steps of the theatre the gasping crowd encountered the corpse of a woman, no more than thirty. Gore from a bullet wound in her head oozed out upon the stone steps. Her dress was soaked with blood from the bullet wounds in her legs. Visible under the pulsing trickle of brains was the woman's mouth, the lips drawn back tightly, the mouth open, eating. I must tell you everything. The crowd shrank back from her, save a few, impelled by the crush behind, who were forced upon the pool of her gore and slipped down the steps around her, one gentleman colliding with the corpse and screaming thereupon; we thought he too had been shot.

At the moment he struggled up alone, no one willing to touch him either, we heard opposite little Arago, manager of the Vaudeville, standing on the back of a companion who was hunched over on all fours. From this podium Arago shouted that he had put the woman there; she had been killed by soldiers outside the Bourse. "Close the theatres!" Arago cried. "Hoist the black flag over Paris!" Along the boulevard du Temple crowds spilled out of the other theatres, joining the audience at the Nouveautés. The dead woman multiplied by ten, by a hundred, in the mouths of those afraid to touch her. The street became one surging mass which suddenly ignited, the throng taking up Arago's chant and rushing towards the Hôtel de Ville.

Mlle Mercure did not quit the steps for the street so quickly; she continued to stare at the woman's corpse, almost to study it.

"Come," I urged her, "we must see what is happening."

"But I know already what will happen." She showed no horror of the dead woman. "Look at the lips."

"I have remarked them," I replied. "Why do we tarry here?"

She turned to me. "You think we are missing an appointment?"

I grasped her arm lightly to steer her away from this morbid scene. She shook me off. "My coach waits for us off the boulevard. Will you sup?" I was about to say that I would of course conduct her home safely, but I must have given some sign about the noise ever mounting in the boulevard, where also now there could be occasional shots. "I see I have no call upon you this evening. Take care, Monsieur Frederick, go, observe carefully. My coachman is strong, no harm will befall me."

These words I recount as exactly as I remember so that you comprehend something of what it has been: a woman slightly older than am I provokes me by speaking to me as to a child. Usually, as I shall explain, I return sharply in kind, and then that is the end of it. That night I was distracted at the moment of riposte by the sound of cannon succeeded for a moment by absolute silence. This evidently was not the usual fracas we have, at least once a month, for which the cannon are never brought out. I turned round, trying to fathom the weapon in the darkness beyond the theatres. When I addressed myself again to Mlle Mercure, I addressed the air; I sought her in her fiacre, but it had departed the theatre.

Once you wrote to me that unfortunate love may resemble a contest, "bonds of contest" I think was your phrase. It is not that simple, Father. She falls into the deepest gloom when at the end of a gay evening I or another companion will recount some absurdity of life when we were children; she loathes reminiscence. At other moments curiosity is her mistress, as this evening in studying how a murdered woman looks. I have also seen her prey to the most complete panic from trifling causes; she is absurdly sensitive to insult from inferiors, even servants. From all these morbidities she will rouse herself by attacks against persons near to her, persons who understand her and who answer with correspondent sharpness. I have become one of these persons. Often her attacks are more than a little malicious, provoking us to pay especial attention to her in her need. That evening, however, she did not wait for a reply.

You understand, politics are for me completely without interest. But I resolved for the hundredth time that I was tired of this game, and to distract myself I began to walk the streets.

Within an hour the people had set about barricading. No teacher of architecture could explain the manner in which a barricade, being only a heap of rubble, paving stones, furniture and overturned carriages, manages to become an impregnable wall. By every rule M. Fontaine advances, it should on the contrary fall, yet somehow the crowd, as though the art of it had passed from father to son, knew how to hoist a *fauteuil* up upon the smashed door of a carriage lying on its side so that the delicate chair in turn would support paving. Instead of placing the most solid material at the bottom, they place it at the top. Street urchins scamper above the line of refuse with rocks it seems scarcely credible these emaciated children have the strength to lift. I enquire the reason of this from someone standing by me in the boulevard du Temple and am told, as if I were dim-witted, that of course the heaviest goes on top; if the barricade is assaulted by cannon balls, the mass will settle on the hole blasted through the base. They are also cunning in placement: the barricades are placed in the middle of streets, away from cross-roads, so that soldiers attempting to penetrate the barricade itself must pass in a valley between houses, from which the populace can fire upon their aggressors in even greater security and deadly accuracy than from behind the barricade itself.

I found myself at midnight witnessing the spectacle of this structure arising in the rue de Beauce, near the boulevard. The men and women at work reminded me not at all of the inflamed crowds Charles and I encountered the night after *Hernani*. Despite the occasional, immense thunder of furniture crashing into the street as pieces were thrown onto the barricades from the house windows, the scene was pervaded by an air of calm. At the near corner is the little wine cellar, with a few chairs and tables in front. "You would like to help?" a young elegant sitting over a glass of wine asked me. His blond hair was powdered with oily dust and his gloves were ripped. I said of course I would and added that I was an architect. "In whose atelier?" Knowing the hatred of the Parisians for my master, I was forced to give a false name; the elegant soon disappeared, but my lie to him somehow then held me back from joining in.

The gunshots in the rue de Beauce were fired into the air by the citizens to warn away the government troops—but there were no troops. The members of the National Guard had been allowed to keep their weapons when that body was disbanded a few years ago; it was these citizen-soldiers who now protected the crowd, under the sign of a black chemise stuck upon a pole. As to professional infantry, they had been little in evidence during the governmental crisis of the few days previous, and were commanded by the coward Marmont. So the authorities, whether out of contempt or ignorance, had given the people all means to rebel. I watched, fascinated and, as I say, somewhat abashed, until the barricade was ten feet in height, the work of two hours—whereas it had required three weeks to remove a similar amount of rubble from the old Galeries de Bois.

As I wandered the streets in the hours before dawn, the fruits of this industry gradually became familiar sights, the tantalising fear of violent encounter diminished. I saw a woman cutting linen into strips of bandages near the Hôtel de Ville. The woman cutting bandages rose from her squat position on the street and looked carefully around; as I was near her, she remarked, as though replying to my question, and in the accents of the Midi, "Ah, sir, it's as much as I have the cloth for, and I fear 'twon't do even for my own boys." "You are too young to have grown sons, Madame," I replied. "Foreign, are you?" At this she spat. Such is the quiddity of great events.

I quitted the old woman, crossed the Seine, intended instantly to return to my rooms. But the short distance from Notre Dame to the rue de Buci had become impassable with barricades and skirmishes between what few soldiers there were in the city and the revolutionaries. I was told I must make a circular journey, down to the Luxembourg Palace. I walked slowly; the streets were pitted by many missing stones. Men passed me, pulling barrows loaded with possessions or with refuse to be contributed to the barricades, a cross-current of struggling, swearing carters. Near the gardens of the Luxembourg Palace I was suddenly overcome by longing for home. Certainly I had no place among people who to the sound of the tocsin know how to set about barricading, and my trophies of Foreign Adventure are like the jumble one finds in someone else's box-room. At the Luxembourg Palace itself I encountered a squad of government troops in their finest regimental clothes; I was gladdened by the sight of these forces of order, I who applauded so furiously at *Hernani*. The citizens of the unbarricaded quarter shrank into doorways out of sight of these troops, but I walked before them, unaccosted in the gloom of my first homesickness in three years.

Now the sky began to lighten, and with it my spirits. I thought I would walk just a little farther and, due to my sleepless stupor, did not realise just how far I had come until the dome of the Invalides loomed up before me against a sky in which there was now more pink than grey. After the difficulty about my foreign standing in enrolling for examinations, Mlle Mercure had sent a little note of encouragement which contained the following lines—I have the letter before me, but I could as easily quote it from memory. This note was the first time she alluded to her own past, although, as you will see, the allusion is slight:

"On the banks of the quays flowers now push up between the stones, and also between the paving on the streets, but not such flowers as I saw as a girl in the country. Neither lavender, thyme, nor the flowers of the forest; the city blooms in coarse yellow plants that would be uprooted elsewhere as weeds. Only one place in Paris is there a field which would remind you of your country, as it does me of mine, the field behind the Invalides planted in poppies, miraculous varieties of poppies blooming from early spring to frost. One turns one's gaze from the great dome to look down a broad avenue, the mansions of generals, the barracks of officers on either side, but as long as I look straight down the avenue into the sun's light, all I see are poppies. I come here often, in widow's black, and out of respect for my colour I am left alone. Sometimes I even come at dawn, after a night at the theatre, a supper, diversions, and the officers on parade take the black circles of fatigue under my eyes for signs of grief. But never am I happier than when sitting on a bench in my field, even though it is tamed into an avenue and the poppies must struggle against the yellow-flower weeds which are choking the rest of the city with their life. For I have found in this place a secret peace, and the solitude which my heart craves. Now you are the only one who knows where to find me."

And so I did, although it were not intended but only an accident of upheaval. She was seated on a stone bench, beside her a basket filled with flowers culled from the irregular and ill-planted plot they call here the *jardin anglais*.

"You have denuded the garden," I gently chided her.

"Yes, I came before the others." She appeared still wrapped in her sadness of the previous evening. "And did you see, my Frederick, was it the spectacle you hoped for?"

Again, she was vexing. I replied that I found it increasingly alien. "In truth," I added for some reason, "I want to go home."

Far from ridiculing me for this longing, my friend suddenly took my hand in hers. I must have betrayed some surprise. "Poor boy," she said, smiling slightly.

I rose, fatigued by events and by her tone.

"No, do not leave," she said. "This evening gives me sad memories of the past. You shouldn't have left me."

I began to protest but she went on unheeding, "Did you know that all my brothers were soldiers? My parents pleaded, but they insisted, there were great opportunities in the Emperor's armies. They were sure they would become rich."

We sat quietly for a moment, her hand again in mine. I asked her why she stared at the woman tonight. At this she shrugged.

"My childhood was untroubled by events," I said.

We looked in silence at one another for a moment, so apart in every way; either could have quitted the bench and left for ever, but instead our eyes looked across that distance and we departed together.

At noon that day the unnatural peace of the city was broken, King Charles' troops having arrived from Versailles, but I can tell you little about it. I remained in my room, moving my few pieces of furniture about as though playing chess, and re-hanging the yellow draperies. The flowers Anne had given me I placed in a blue crystal vase on the table; when the cannons roared outside, the water's surface trembled slightly. I also saw again and again a woman early in the morning, staring out the windows; the pale flesh of her arms pressed against the soft, watery yellow silk.

My concierge came up in the afternoon to tell me that, at midday, a furious battle began at the Porte Saint-Martin theatre, actors against a battalion of Royal Grenadiers. Through my companion, I have met the great ones who play there, Frédéric Lemaître and Marie Dorval, have watched them rehearse *Trente Ans,* the one a gambler who murders, the other his heroic wife. The concierge rubbed her grimy hands together at my door, recounting the blood and "good hits" the Porte Saint-Martin actors made, whilst I remembered Lemaître and Dorval in their dressing-rooms after the devastating end of this melodrama, the two popping out from one cubicle to the other, laughing and joking as they wiped the greasepaint off their faces, a fervid band of admirers unknowing and near tears on the other side of the stage door.

My concierge offered to bring me dinner—although the market of St-Germain was closed, she had a friend. By nightfall, I roused myself, and decided to go to Anne. She now lives in an *hôtel particulier* in the quarter known as "Nouvelle Athènes," a charming little house shaped around a half-round court in the rue de la Tour des Dames, a folly built for another actress, who lost her public. It may seem foolhardy, traversing a city in the midst of fighting, but at the time I was oblivious. Therefore my retreat during the day had not prepared me for the difficulties of this journey. By the evening of the 29th, all of Paris was in the hands of its citizens, even the Louvre, which they took in the afternoon—it was this cannonading I heard when the water in my vase of flowers trembled. Marmont's regiments had deserted him. Everywhere, however, the citizens were on the alert; you could not take ten steps without someone challenging you. My concierge had given me the password for the quarter, only after beseeching me to remain in her cubicle off the street, to eat and drink. When I reached the Pont-Neuf, however, a new password was necessary. I was in temporary confusion, I apologised for my ignorance; my English accent became stronger, as always when in a foreign land we are distraught. Suddenly I was surrounded by an angry, suspicious mob. "Where are you going?" they demanded. "Who are you?" You will be appalled, and of course in the ordinary course of events I would not dream of revealing a lady's name to strangers. But it was not my person I feared for, it was my sudden inability to speak, to communicate, that made me stammer out the name of my companion.

"He is going to see La Mercure, the great Mercury," one of my inter-locutors snickered. The other guards along the Pont-Neuf passed her name across the bridge like the password I was seeking. "The young Englishman is going to Mercury," the word "Mercure" becoming fainter as it echoed from mouth to mouth, on to the Ile de la Cité, "Mercure" on the bronze lips of the statue of the Vert Galant in his park, still audible, I imagined, all the way to the right bank. I was allowed to pass, and, avoiding the guards' eyes, my cheeks burning, I did so.

Once on the right bank I was able to move more easily, as the route I had to take from the Pont-Neuf to Nouvelle Athènes went directly by the precincts of our work in the Palais-Royal, and I knew all the little passages and streets here. I arrived in the rue de la Tour des Dames to find my companion's house brilliantly illuminated. At my suggestion Mlle Mercure has left the windows on the first floor undraped in order to conserve the northern light and unite the view from this floor to the gardens of the Palladian mansion across the street. Opening the courtyard gate, I glanced up at these windows. The light framed the face and shoulders of M. Lemaître, who was without cravat and in his shirtsleeves. He was laughing loudly at some witticism being retailed from within. A lady I did not know appeared at the window with him, and proffered him a glass of wine. Another unknown lady, wearing about her neck a collar of diamonds which glinted yellow flecks of light into the garden, appeared beside M. Lemaître and tousled his hair; he was the hero of the hour, as my concierge had foretold.

What should I reply if, upon entering, they asked me for my news—that I had spent the day playing with draperies and measuring the state of the world by the trembling of water in a glass of flowers? I waited till my companion should appear at the window; I would call to her, she would bid me within, and under her protection I should perhaps not be obliged to account for myself. But Anne did not appear at the windows of her home. The laughter and tinkling of glasses continued from within; I ex-pected Madame Dorval to appear, it would have made the scene complete, but only the robust frame and tousled hair of M. Lemaître, passing from one blazing embrasure to the next, his ironical eyes occasionally darting away from some elegant lady to glance out into the garden, his mouth turning down at the corners to smile, as is his way, only M. Lemaître was known to me.

It was cool in my companion's courtyard. I sat upon a bench. How great the transmutations of a day! Scarce twenty-four hours before, I had sat upon another stone seat, in another garden, with a grave lady, one in need when she heard the tocsin sound; now I sat outside her home, listening to the popping of champagne corks. Perhaps she is not within, I thought; this would explain it. But then I heard her throaty voice; her words were slurred, as I have heard other women's when revelling.

"Brave Frédéric!" Was she addressing M. Lemaître or me? She always pronounces my name perfectly, she whose English is superb from her seasons at Drury Lane. But I could not tell because, as I say, her words were slurred. I rose, now to enter. I looked up, hoping to see her at the window.

"Brave Frédéric! And so clever! All the world knows within hours he is a hero! Our Hero himself retired after each volley to bring the news to the cafés! But the world did not stop for you, noble Warrior! Frédéric, if only you could have . . ."

Walking softly on the edge of the grass, so as to avoid making a noise on the gravel path, I quitted the court, closing the gate softly behind me. As on the previous night, in my abstraction I walked oblivious to my surroundings, and evidently my gloom provided me as much inviolate protection from citizen as from soldier.

I decided to pass the next day in the monument to my Parisian sojourn, the only memory of this time I imagined I could later summon without despair. The régime of the passwords was relaxed on the 30th, so it was easier to move; it had become evident to all that no government forces remained puissant within the city. Indeed, among the Parisians there was a great fervour, the Bourse as glad of the overthrow of King Charles as those on the barricades. It was a hot day, people in light clothes. As I walked from my lodgings I had the sensation of strolling in a fête, which seemed unreasonable to me, as I imagined others similarly crushed.

When I arrived at the Palais-Royal there were gathered many prosperous gentlemen, seemingly just passing by this, the seat of the Orléans. From the very first moments of the revolt, the House of Orléans was spoken of as the successor to the Bourbons. These gentlemen near my palace, no matter how nonchalantly they swung their canes, could not entirely disguise their preoccupations, and all the city was uncertain if the Duke of Orléans remained still at his summer residence in Neuilly.

Behind the gate of the Peristyle de Chartres, barring the way to this genteel rabble, stood old Florentin, one of the porters in the Duke's service who had taken a kindly interest in me during the dull days when I remeasured the excavation for the arcade after the accident with the footings. Florentin was in full livery but without gloves.

"Florentin, you are naked," I accosted him.

"Monsieur Frederick, don't have your joke with me. It's as good as my place. The washerwomen have fled."

"Where is the Duke?" I enquired, and at this several of the gentlemen near us who had been idly listening pressed forward. "Come my man, yes, where is he, when is he expected, let me pass for he will surely want to receive me, tell me where is the state anteroom . . ."

Florentin, a servant of the old French school, reserves civility for those who are civil to him. He sneered at these good bourgeois. "I ain't seen you before. Come," he said to me. "No one is working inside, but you'll find everything just as you left it," and with that, I was allowed to pass within, a chorus of cries—"Who is he? Let us in!"—at my back as the gate clanked behind me.

I have never seen anything as lovely as the sight which greeted me in the courtyard. The sky was now overcast, the air close; under this sultry canopy the iron plates stood bolted upright, the iron arches for the roof securing them at top, yet not a pane of roof glass was laid. The whole of this iron skeleton had been painted in its grey undercoat, just before the rebellion. Could you imagine all the columns in the Roman Forum restored, thrusting upward, free of the work of supporting a roof, you would have a part of the effect, but not all; the parade of columns in Rome would be white stone reaching up to an infinite blue, whereas here, the dun colour of our work melted into the metal sky.

I walked down one ghost wing in this dissolving space, then down the central corridor, then back along the other outer answering wing. The foundations had been so perfectly laid, the beams so exactly cast, the marble underfoot joined so square. I began to walk ever more precisely, measuring my steps between the bolted filigree of iron. One completed tour, then another. No irregularity of form betrayed the carpenter or mason's hand, each empty window and door owed its beauty to the brute fact that cast iron is utterly lifeless. I knew exactly therefore what I saw.

Near the end of this tour of the skeleton, I noticed a chisel lying on the ground. I picked it up and cast it out onto the refuse heap which will soon be levelled for the Italian garden. They will take away everything which does not fit. The garden with its geometric network of paths and disciplined shrubbery will be no more hospitable than the new arcade.

Now a third tour, not long really, to walk 65 metres three times, but I no longer thought to measure my steps, for I was sure I had succeeded in dividing each 65-metre length into equal parts with my legs. I felt quite hungry, having not eaten since the day before. I thought I saw Charles at the other end of the garden. He smiled at me. I walked out of the skeleton, it was no cage at all, my pacing exactly what it had been within the frame, I walked down the still-littered path towards Charles, all the way to the Grand-Véfour restaurant, where Charles proved a phantom of my hunger. In their haste to flee the rebellion the Grand-Véfour had left out the chairs and tables in the garden; I sat now, looking at the tightly shuttered restaurant, waiting for food.

You may think I am recounting to you a delirium brought about by exhaustion. Not at all. It was here, in my creation, that I realised I had made a mistake. There was no reason I should have left the night before. I could even have waited in the garden for her to finish her amusing, betraying story; perhaps she had even known I was without. What did it matter? She couldn't hurt me. I should have rung the bell and entered indifferently. Do you understand, Father, I should have done this for myself even though it was playing according to her rules?

I was nearly faint when I sat, and so not quite so clear as I am now, but I know I had made a mistake and determined somehow, immediately, to make at least a gesture undoing it. Florentin let me out, thrusting me among the men demanding who was I, where was the Duke? I struggled through them, and nearly ran back to the rue de la Tour des Dames.

A maid familiar to me answered the door.

"Monsieur, you have missed my mistress by an hour. She has gone to her parents for a few days, to rest." I never thought of her having parents alive. Suddenly I ached for her, a girl playing a terrible, unnecessary game. "It is a pity, for she said she had a note for me to take you, a most urgent note, but in the confusion of departing, she kept it."

That was a week ago; this has taken two days to write. Forgive me for pouring out so intimate a story to you, but I want you to understand the true nature of my indecision. It is no indecision about you. The aid you have yet to ask for you shall have, as soon as the circumstances here are clearer.

Yours ever in friendship and in love,
Frederick

Last Touches

Severus Rood, K.C.   *26 April 1832*
6 Inner Temple
London

Dear Snigs,

I look up from my writing table in my stone tower, gaze across the Lake of Annecy and remark in the distance small boats, a few with blue and white sails, most propelled by paddle-oars, bobbing up and down in the miniature harbour of Talloires. The air here is still chilled by the snows of the Alps. You say the newspapers are shockingly vague, uninformative. If I divert my eyes from the lake scene, it is equally hard for me to see in my mind the city.

This is but a prologue to requesting your indulgence. In Descartes' *Meditations* we read the most complex, abstruse matters made intimate by the author's voice, which is that of a confidant. During the years I have struggled to cast my sermons in literary form, I have often heard the voice of Descartes in my ear. He spoke as a friend while I wrote as a pastor, he proposed gently to me as I expounded with forced conviction to the reader who has remained, alas, entirely hypothetical. So I should like to make an experiment, not that of writing in the style of Descartes, which would indeed be immodest striving, but perhaps in emulating his intimacy of tone. We write letters three or four times a day; why should Christian Meditation be fashioned more pompously than the confidences, comments and understandings we exchange with our friends? This means I shall give you no grand sweep but only close reverberations of events, close to me and therefore, I hope, to you. Please keep this letter for me.

My own Meditation is founded on 2 Corinthians 1:12: ". . . by the grace of God we have had our conversation in the world." In the very midst of the worst days my thoughts were turned to this verse by the report which reached Paris of the audience the Pope granted Messieurs Lamennais, Lacordaire and Montalembert last month.

On the 13th of March, His Holiness Gregory XVI allowed these three, amongst his most ardent servants, an interview of half an hour, although hardly a quarter proved necessary. They were shown into the splendid ante-chambers of the Vatican, and I imagine the Frenchmen, like all others who have entered these halls, must have been blinded for a moment by the shower of gold in the reception rooms of Christ's Vicar on Earth.

Their mission was in theory this "conversation in the world" which the pilgrims hoped to hold with His Holiness. In fact they came to Rome to affirm the next verse of 2 Corinthians 1: "For we write none other things unto you, than what ye read or acknowledge . . ." In our own country, the battle raging round them, particularly M. de Lamennais, seems absurd, for their writings are indeed read by a very, very few—but these few are the strongest thinkers in Catholic France, and the most troubled, seeking in the modern world some adequate reason to remain within a Church sinking under the weight of its past. In any event, the three were received and shown into the presence by the Cardinal de Rohan, a clever decision. No man could have greater dislike of the doctrines of M. de Lamennais than this prelate, whose family's device is "I cannot be King, I deign not be Prince: I am Rohan." M. de Lamennais calls for a fraternal church in which each man and woman is accorded a full measure of dignity; the Cardinal de Rohan takes such doctrine as a personal affront. They say that in his own person he is unfortunately unlikely ever to inspire the dread etched into the family armour, for the age of manhood twenty years ago brought him no beard, left his angelic soprano voice unchanged, and guarded upon his downy cheeks the quick blushes of childhood. "Il bambino"—as the Romans call the Cardinal de Rohan—led the pilgrims to the Holy Father.

Although M. de Lamennais is not a keen scholar of biblical correspondences, and is a modest man, his mission to Rome might have put him in mind of Paul's mission to Corinth. Paul's sought to assure the Corinthians that, as he says in the fifth chapter of his letter, ". . . we know that if our earthly house of this tabernacle were dissolved, we have a building of God, an house not made with hands, eternal in the heavens." Paul's Church amongst all religions is the most dependent upon buildings and their luxurious contents. His eyes must have forced M. de Lamennais to acknowledge this truth in the jewelled, gilded, treasure-heavy Vatican, had he denied it to himself before, but the priest, truly a loyal son of Rome, is certain that his views can do the Catholic faith no harm. He believes that the reflected light of the ante-chambers has temporarily blinded his censors, as the sunlight blinds those Hindoos who force themselves to stare at the sun steadily, unblinking. He has quoted against the ultramontane party another verse of 2 Corinthians: ". . . the things which are seen are temporal; but the things which are not seen are eternal."

Paris is, as all the world knows, a city in which the embroidery of truth is but another name for pleasure. The reports of the ensuing quarter of an hour have therefore to be compared, and truth decided by sifting their common features—since each Parisian reporter seeks to make his mark by adding of his own to what he has been told. I do not, dear reader, set myself above others; but as a foreigner in Paris I have learnt to weigh what I hear, especially ecclesiastic news about what the Pope "really" thinks and does. The points of the interview upon which all Paris seems to agree are the following:

First, the physical character at the moment of the Holy Father. All Paris agrees his eyes are alarmingly bloodshot, that he now stands painfully, a Pope who has received election too late in life to prosecute the war against heresy or, what is worse, modern liberality, a war which in spirit he is disposed to wage relentless and merciless. It is said that one of the most affecting sights in the Vatican this past year is that of Gregory XVI moving slowly through the sun and gold corridors, leaning heavily on the slight shoulders of the Cardinal de Rohan.

Second, all Paris agrees that His Holiness received the emissaries of liberal Christianity standing, girding himself that much for battle. Save that by prior agreement, there would be no battle, no "conversation" about whether or not M. de Lamennais has committed heresy in print with his *Essay on Indifference* or whether or not these three pilgrims would be allowed to take up again their journal called and dedicated to "The Future." They would be allowed to say they had been admitted to the presence of His Holiness; in turn, by agreeing not to speak of their own faith, they tacitly agreed such a subject was inadmissible with Christ's Vicar.

What then did Gregory XVI speak of with Lamennais, Lacordaire and Montalembert during that quarter of an hour? His Holiness offered M. de Lamennais a pinch of snuff, who accepted it with good grace, although he was unable to disguise his surprise at its poor quality. His Holiness spoke of the abbé Vaurin, who has accomplished good works in the hostile climate

of Geneva, and praised the Catholic schools founded in Brittany by the
brother of M. de Lamennais. The Pope gave his blessing to Madame de
Montalembert and her second son. The Pope, the Cardinal and the three
pilgrims spoke of art for a moment, His Holiness showing them a silver
statue on his desk which was a small reproduction of Michelangelo's Moses.
He regretted it could not be given to the pilgrims, for it belonged not to
him but to the Museum of the Vatican. He could, and did, give them
commemorative medals of the occasion, and his blessing in the spirit of
2 Corinthians 1:24, "not for that we have dominion over your faith, but are
helpers of your joy: for by faith ye stand."

It is agreed, lastly, that the pilgrims conducted themselves honourably
—that is, did not raise the subject of their own controversial activities—but
awkwardly, unable to submit themselves gracefully to the sort of conversation they had each led a hundred, a thousand times in their own drawing-
rooms. It is said that the Cardinal de Rohan ushered them out of the holy
presence with an angelic smile, his downy cheeks blooming.

What in this encounter might give any Christian pause for reflection?
One might pause over M. de Lamennais' provocation to the Church. His
doctrine is of *le sens commun:* by this he intends the core of beliefs shared
by all religions, by all passionate believers. His papal audience illustrates
that territory on which men—even of the same faith but shading it according to different needs—might meet, a common ground of tact, politeness
and silence. At least, I should like to propose that religious "discussion" so
often must lead only to polite silences, that in religion there can be little
communion between those who disagree. And if the reader permits, I
should like to illustrate this conundrum, which seems to take us backward
in turn to the intolerance and deafness of the militant Churches, I should
like to dramatise M. de Lamennais' difficulty by recourse to a somewhat
bizarre passage in my own life a few weeks ago.

It occurred shortly after the audience granted to M. de Lamennais. One
afternoon I passed the quarters of my concierge on the way to visit the
patients of the English Hospital. Her door was open; whimpering came
from within. I peered across the sill, seeing nothing, but the faint moans
continued. I advanced within, and finally found her, behind a partition,
delirious.

"Madame Pacquot, where is your daughter, where is your daughter?"
The poor creature was too far gone to tell me anything, but in her writhing
on the pallet she seemed to give a sign towards the rude wood dresser
opposite. I looked through the drawers and found clothes for an old
woman, but none for a liverish spinster of forty. The metal box in which

I have seen her furtively drop coins was empty. Such cases are common enough; often the husband or children simply cannot bear to watch the loved one die, nothing more than that.

In his Epistle to the Philippians, the apostle Paul writes of the "fellowship of his sufferings." Madame Pacquot suddenly called out to me in a clear, if thin voice, "Father, hear my confession." And in his second epistle to the Corinthians the apostle Paul writes, "And our hope of you is stedfast, knowing, that as ye are partakers of the sufferings, so shall ye be also of the consolation." There was sufficient warrant for me, as a man, to comfort this woman, and so I drew a chair beside her pallet, the words "I am not a Catholic" dying on my lips.

Madame Pacquot had, unfortunately, only those words for me. She sank back into delirium and turned towards the wall. Given the current conditions, I knew I was more likely to find a doctor than a priest for her, but set out to find both. My colleague at the English Hospital agreed to come as soon as his rounds were done; I had perhaps three hours to find a priest of her own faith. I tried first the churches in the *quartier*. All of them locked. I ventured across the river to Notre Dame. Here of course there were priests, among whom I was cordially enough received, but I was told, quite properly, that they could promise nothing quickly; she would have to wait her turn, with so many. One of the priests had tears in his eyes at this terrible necessity. After taking the address of our building, they promised to send someone certainly before nightfall.

The doctor had not arrived by the late afternoon. Of course they are pressed to minister first to those for whom there is a glimmer of hope; still, he had promised. Madame Pacquot remained unchanged. I decided to remain with the concierge, therefore, until a priest should arrive. The sun set, with no sign of a priest. "But we had the sentence of death in ourselves, that we should not trust in ourselves . . ." This terrible verse of 2 Corinthians 1 came back to me as I looked at the almost-dead Madame Pacquot who had been abandoned by her daughter, a daughter who, under the circumstances, would not be blamed. There was a slab of butter on a faïence plate, and a stale loaf of bread, both laid out on Madame Pacquot's dresser. The butter smelt sweet. I took out several issues of the *Courrier Catholique,* a *European Church Times* and *La Foi,* all of which had continued to appear regularly, and in which the various accounts of M. de Lamennais' papal audience were given. Although I did not know it until much later, when I was free to meditate upon matters in the beautiful sanctuary of a medieval château on the edge of the Lake of Annecy, in the next few hours I would join the spiritual drama depicted in the pages of these journals.

Towards midnight, the end was clearly at hand. The collection of corpses was scheduled in St-Germain for three to four in the morning; as I had finished the accounts of the Frenchmen's pilgrimage, my watch told me there were still at least two hours to wait.

One always feels when terribly tired that one's mind is wandering, though in fact it is hard at work assembling evidence. I finished the papal columns and turned to various local and diocesan contributions. The newspapers all reported with satisfaction that religion is fashionable again. The correspondents deduced this by counting the numbers of young gallants and demoiselles in bright spring colours who flock to the churches on Sundays, as carefully turned out as for the opera. Any person dining in polite society would have observed the new disposition, for it is no longer an awkward turn in conversation when the subject becomes religion, nor does one see that slight, knowing, tolerant smile on the faces of the elegant. Those who harbour doubt are considered, indeed, a little vulgar, our sceptical parents a little lacking in the spirituality becoming to refined people.

I reflected that these new believers have acquired faith as easily as they might purchase a carriage; they appear to possess a ready fund of spiritual capital. Then my mind, wandering so that my ears might be diverted from too constant a keening for the final death rattle—the shepherd can also be undone by the suffering of the lamb—my mind put these joyful reports next to the news from Rome. What sort of Deity can become fashionable? An ordinary mortal's place in the fashionable pantheon depends on previous engagements in response to most invitations, a salon frequented by a small circle and a general air of inaccessibility. God, however, cannot become popular by seeming so exclusive. For God to be fashionable, He must garb Himself in a mantle of affability, He must be convenient. The reasons for this M. de Lamennais has unwittingly revealed.

Consider: The *European Church Times* correctly reports this return of the young to the churches as a phenomenon in all Christian nations, not merely in those countries where the young have cause to fear untimely death. Its very universality is a sign that those of our age are seeking not a particular faith, but faith. They believe in believing, and this is the source of M. de Lamennais' great appeal. In his *Essay on Indifference* he tells us that the germ of religion lies in "what has always been believed, everywhere, by everyone," this fundamental truth humanity shares at prayer, no matter the names of the God invoked, or the doctrines of God's relation to mankind. The difficulty is that he claims this to be the essence of Catholicism —he is "catholic" in our English and liberal sense of the word. M. de Lamennais is a Christian; that is, he believes his own religion is the best among all the varieties of faith. Only Christianity, he says, compounds the spiritual elements of "unity, universality, perpetuity, sanctity and the highest degree of authority." He is a Christian, he is also tolerant. In his sermons he has quoted the Koran of the Islamites, the Talmud of the Hebrews; indeed this member of the Church of Rome advocates liberty of belief for these infidel creeds and the separation of Church from State. His infrequent sermons are marked with a fervour of utterance, a colour of imagery, a force of declamation; his figure is imposing, his voice reverberant. His creed offers Pure Inspiration without demanding any sacrifices. Thus I say that while M. de Lamennais abjures fashion, he cannot help constituting it.

The difficulty faced by M. de Lamennais is how he might reconcile his superiors to the faith he inspires in a kindly, affable God. In England young elegants in church more easily gain the consolations of prayer than do they here, for the Church of England admits a certain latitude of creed. The capacity for truly ardent devotion appears to M. de Lamennais' superiors, on the contrary, to arise from true doctrine. He went to Rome to convince them that his appeal to the young contained in its liberality no heresy, and they were much too wise to be seduced into debate. A doctrine subject to "conversation" is no longer a doctrine.

Nearly asleep, my mind took me so far. But, unbeknownst to either of us, Madame Pacquot and I were about to have our own talk. I had hoped Father Foult would be sent to the concierge, as he is one of the few Catholics I have encountered who speaks of his faith and its rules without garbing himself in the armour of impenetrable mystery. Neither he nor another priest came, however, although I know that each morning Madame Pacquot went to early Mass at Notre Dame before returning to the St-Germain market, and thence to her quarters to make coffee and awaken her sluggard daughter. The undertaker's cart passed at four in the morning; I went out to inform the men that an old woman within would soon be theirs, but they cautioned me they could wait but a few minutes, as they maintained order by finishing the collections before many people were about the streets.

When I returned to Madame Pacquot she suddenly gave me cause for hope, as she began to stir upon her pallet. She called for water. The urgency is usually such that one cannot be nice in administering it; I drew a brimming glass of water from the jug, poured the liquid onto the lips of the supine woman, in hopes some of it would be taken into the throat; some was, but more soaked the bosom of Madame Pacquot's black dress. I could never remember when she had not dressed in black. This icy water roused her for a moment. Her face was burning with fever spots, already the eyes were milky and clouded, like those of a sick dog; however, she said to me, clearly enough, "Now. Give me them now."

And so I began to administer to my concierge the last rites of a creed which was not my own, she dying in the belief she would leave this world properly attended by a priest who would speed her journey from pain to eternal rest. The Latin formulas of the Catholics came at first haltingly to me, and I feared, in my unworthiness, that Father Foult might suddenly enter the hovel, discovering the old woman soaking in water, the room filled with the incense of butter, attended by an impostor. Still no one came, my memory of their sacrament became more assured, which confidence must have found its way into my voice, as Madame Pacquot, although hardly conscious, suddenly thrust her hand into mine.

That is how she died, some minutes later, her left hand between both of mine. The years had encroached upon the wedding band so that this token of her womanhood was now buried in flesh; the fingers were hard and the skin rough from a lifetime of scrubbing. Madame Pacquot's head lolled to the side; still I could feel her hand moving slightly, as if restless. Then came the moment when her nails bit into my palm; the nails withdrew, the hand ceased its uneasy fluttering. I closed the eyelids, placed both hands upon her wet breast, a crucifix from her dresser between them. And then I continued the prayer for the dead, in the form the Catholics prefer, I continued as her priest even though she had already passed infinitely far from me. I have said many funerary prayers; none moved me more deeply than these words I disbelieved.

Paul tells the Corinthians that true Christians "have renounced the hidden things of dishonesty, not walking in craftiness, nor handling the word of God deceitfully . . ." (2 Corinthians 4:2). I intend no irony in recalling this verse. Imagine that I had told Madame Pacquot my convictions were those of the Church of England, and, further, that she was in fit condition to understand. Would she have been reassured that she was received into the bosom of God because consoled at the end by someone of faith, if a faith not quite her own? I think not. When we are at prayer, the slightest change from the "correct" way to kneel, the "correct" order of service, the "correct" manner of taking wafer and wine breaks the spell.

M. de Lamennais has written against indifference. Could it be that he might himself be accused of what one might call "modern" indifference? His desire to pray so strong that he would share the rites of Hindoo, Mussulman, Hebrew, and Roman? In joining together, his communicants avoid questions as to whether the Supremacy of God includes His power to do evil; such a total Being is not affable. They eschew too seriously considering the plight of a crucified God; pity for this Crucified One might raise too many insoluble questions about the utter uselessness of His suffering. Better a pantheon of God-possibilities, all inspiring prayer: the matter of faith is believing.

By the curious route of considering how unsatisfactory is this ecumenical Deity, this Supreme Being on excellent terms with Signor da Silva and the Vicomte de Greffulhe, I was led in the early morning hours, after the burial wagon had finally carted Madame Pacquot away, to take the side of the Pope—this sounds too pretentious. I understood why the Pope resists M. de Lamennais. What indeed divides this *sens commun,* this shared longing for God, this aching for Him which invades every believer, what divides it from my imposture? I know, my story is more complicated than a reproach to religious liberalism. By mouthing the words of a creed I did not believe I surely satisfied Madame Pacquot's need for prayer and, after she died, my own. Yet we had no "conversation" such as the French pilgrims sought with the Holy Father.

In reading over this meditation, I indeed observe that what began in my mind as an odd conjunction between this public event and the conclusion of a private history has ended as an accusation. To attack M. de Lamennais would do him a great disservice: his aim is to restore religion by the practise of an open charity, and he does so with a knowledge of the darkness of the human heart. In a moving letter to the Baroness Cottu (recently made public by the Count d'Haussonville), Lamennais wrote more than a decade ago:

> Happiness does not attach men to each other. They must suffer together in order to love each other, as much as men are capable of this love. In the arts, in literature, in society, *joy* is sterile; sorrow creates almost everything men admire. Virtue, which inspires in us the strongest feelings of beauty, finds its perfect form in suffering. This is the doctrine of Saint Paul.

Why should one then impugn the faith of those who seem to be, in Paul's words, "giving no offence in any thing, that the ministry be not blamed..." (2 Corinthians 6:3)? Even in a lie there can be beauty, and release.

I conclude this meditation, therefore, with the suggestion that our religion is in doctrine at odds with the compassion the doctrine inspires. The Pope who received M. de Lamennais and his friends well understood a fundamental precept of Saint Paul: "But if our gospel be hid, it is hid to them that are lost..." (2 Corinthians 4:3,4). And yet Madame Pacquot and I met as two Christians. In no other religion could this travesty pass into the realm of Grace. Madame Pacquot and I met as Christians, but we communed, the dying woman and I, not through the understanding but rather through our hands.

Charles Courtland,
Château de Duingt,
Duingt

Post scriptum: Snigs, please send me your comments on this. In connection with the death of Madame Pacquot, something else happened which I cannot relate, and I fear the story I have given is truncated because incomplete. But honour binds me to constrict the facts to what I have given; these are entirely accurate as far as they go.

John Courtland   *1 May 1832*
12 Jermyn Street
London

My dear father,

I must repeat to you what I have written ten times over. I have commitments; these are real to me, if to no one else. Sir, I mean you to take no offence. Why, however, should the conduct of life in difficult circumstances prompt others to counsel flight?

Now I have the leisure to respond to your plaints. No "madness" possessed me, nor had she put me "in thrall." Indeed, she was another one of the persons who tugged at my coat, imploring me to leave, as though the work of three years meant *nothing*. Very well, she is not an artificer, but you, sir, are. You should have sympathised, or at least understood.

To remove the first of your misunderstandings: the conversion was in fact quite simple; were my task merely mechanical, I could have been in Jermyn Street a month ago, dining out on my observations. The plates of glass in the shops are clamped to the iron panels, which are in turn bolted to the frames cast as Doric columns. Since no leather bushing lies under the glass, the plates can be taken out simply by relieving the clamp pressure; then, when the panels are unbolted and removed, the galleries become a set of cubicles open on the sides. It was thought that the light and air of the gallery would be salubrious for those who shewed, after a few days in hospital, any signs of surviving. Once the arcade was stripped of its interior partitions, patients were quickly moved into the old shop spaces and easily ministered to by doctors and nurses. The attendants walked up and down the corridors of the galleries just as those shopping did.

The technical side was thus trivial. You, in company with almost all who know him, have an ill-disguised contempt for M. Fontaine, and I shall not attempt to defend him; I have my own reasons for disappointment in him—that I shall recount in its proper place. But you reduce the man to his defects. He is at least loyal to his buildings. M. Fontaine argued heatedly with representatives of the government against this plan—the first time I have seen him contentious with those in power. He is now aged to the point of incapacity, he wants to preserve monuments to his genius in their original state. Surely one can sympathise with that wish. M. Fontaine lost his struggle, first with the Ministry of Health and then with the royal household itself. He was assured the changes would be temporary, his work not permanently disfigured, but he quite naturally disbelieved these assurances. He had given similar ones to the fabricators of several buildings in Paris, then entirely transformed these during improvement. As a sop to his distress, however, the government allowed him to appoint the person who would oversee the changes, and he chose me.

Your letter asking me if I had "taken leave entirely of my senses," reminding me that "every man has responsibilities to those who love him," even that our courageous, beloved mother would have insisted I be "rescued"—this letter arrived the same day M. Fontaine came to my table in the atelier and looked at me steadily before saying in a quiet voice I had never heard before, "My dear Frederick, I cannot face this desecration myself; I refuse to help them in any way. But someone must make the changes. Would you? For me?" And he ended this affecting speech with an appeal you might laugh at: "Trick them whenever you can!"

I recommence a day later. Know, then, how I saw it first during the second carnival of Lent; I mean that literally, I saw, rather than read about it in a newspaper in a club, as did my putative saviours, or all but Charles. The news from London, Rome and the East had the whole city in the greatest anxiety. Musard, who manages the Variétés, had organised a series of wild masked balls when the Lenten season began. At these fêtes both men and women performed a new dance from Algeria which appeared last year as an abandoned rite among the poor but which no respectable man or woman would have thought to enact; the partners knock against one another, kicking their legs in the air, the men holding the women by the shoulders while both writhe in ecstasy until they can hardly stand. This year La Battut induced Musard to organise this dance at his theatre. The ladies and gentlemen who frequent the place were indeed thirsty for it; exhaustion took their thoughts far from the impending doom. Young women of fashion, their faces running with sweat, their bosoms heaving, flung their legs so high that anyone could gaze straight at their mounts of Venus; everyone was so minded. The police interfered once with this display at the Variétés, and then were given money.

I went with Anne once to the Variétés. She did not desire this obscene relief, mark that, but she was curious. Everyone begged for Mlle Mercure to can-can; Anne only shook her head, smiled slightly, and continued her inspection. I must confess I did find it a release; as brown, golden and black mounts appeared momentarily to view, I was arrested, such possibility of colour, hair and fleshy lips. Noting my heightened colour, Anne turned to me. "You are amused? Why not join the dancers?" But still the habits of England held me back, as though I were restrained by an invisible chain.

February passed into March and still it had not come. When I wrote in early spring that we had been miraculously spared, I reflected the common sentiment of everyone here. The weather from the middle of March onwards was so fine that it made the reports seem like gossip, the air so light and clear, the almond trees in bloom, their scent mingling on the quays with the premature flowering of the first iris. At sunset the city was a haze of yellow, blue and white. On the 26th, I decided to take Anne's little Adèle, who had just celebrated her eleventh birthday, to an altogether more innocent masked ball in the open air near the Porte Saint-Martin theatre. There we found a passable quadrille in progress, the quadrille square formed by dancers in costume; they were attended by hawkers of ices and sweetmeats, and few of the hectoring band of drunkards who often blot the edges. Near midnight, a harlequin, tall and robust, suddenly burst from his companion's arms, gave a strangled cry and tore the mask off his face. It had turned blue-black! This was the plague.

I drew Adèle away from him; indeed, everyone shrank back so that the harlequin stood alone in the middle of a stunned, horrified circle, he emitting little cries like a dog whining in pain. I had no idea it struck so fast. Then another of the dancers, thank God on the opposite side of the circle, broke into the same whine and fell to the ground. All of us at this moment began to run, as fast as we could, anywhere to get away from the square. The band of musicians were hidden under an arch and could see little; they continued to play the quadrille air as we ran until one of the crowd shouted "Plague!" to them and they dropped their instruments, joining the fleeing revellers.

Evidently, the plague had erupted that day all over the city, but I did not know that; I thought we were the first exposure. By a circuitous route I managed to return Adèle to her mother's home, avoiding all congested streets in the city, but by the time we reached Nouvelle Athènes rumour had flown before us. Anne was pacing before her windows, wringing her hands, waiting. We flung open the lower doors, servants rushed to us, stripping off our clothes with their hands in heavily camphored gloves; we passed stark naked into an ante-chamber thick with more camphor fumes from flaming vessels and, after choking on the fumes for what seemed ages, were led out into the hall, given robes and conducted to the salon. Anne flung her arms around Adèle, and then turned upon me in a rage. It was my fault the child was exposed.

To gain a moment's peace, I informed her I never argue when naked, and left her to put on fresh clothes in a little dressing-room I have established at the top of her house. There, on a silver salver which Anne gave me to celebrate the first year of our friendship, I found the first of your letters telling me I "perhaps did not realise the gravity of such a situation," that my circumstances in youth had been so "salubrious" I could not perhaps recognise the seriousness of plague, etc.

The discord between us on this occasion I shall not further retail. Injustice towards me and love of her children are inextricable. I shall complete my description of the domestic scene that evening only that you understand a constraint upon me, one I can reveal without indiscretion.

The time allotted us for recrimination was short. We spent the rest of the night and the early hours before dawn carrying out plans previously contrived. Cécile was fetched from the governess in the little annexe round the corner. The girls were put into a fiacre with a coachman and footman in front, both armed with pistols; these stout servants, long loyal to Anne, were willing to shoot through, if necessary, were they challenged at the Neuilly barrier. (This proved, as it happened, an unnecessary precaution —the guards fled that night, and the throng of carriages was impeded only by a complete collapse of civility, each carriage refusing to give way to any other at the gates.)

Let us leave the house, you and I, for a moment. The next afternoon, it appeared the midnight voyages might have been precipitous. The authorities officially announced that no cholera cases existed in the city; Harlequin and his companions, who had been taken to the Hôtel-Dieu, were pronounced suffering only from exhaustion, of which they had unfortunately died. Anne decided that she would continue to perform, but as a precaution, the girls were to remain in Normandy. Within a few days this proved more than wise; the hospitals began to fill to overflowing. There were no more official announcements.

Within a week it was hard to find enough hearses for the dead; the police commandeered huge carts normally used for furniture removal or at the quays, and piled them up with coffins. A fortnight ago, even these could not bear the traffic. You often found the dead simply wrapped in a sheet, thrown into the street—or worse, into the river. You could see the bloated bodies gradually floating out of their windings, huge putrescent objects bumping against one another like logs in the ebb and flow of the Seine current.

Have I sufficiently indicated to you, Father, the conditions under which a man will agree to become the undertaker of his own art? Or can you adduce a contrary reason why a building has the right to be spared? M. Fontaine is near his time; a few months more of eating and sleeping mean little to him. The preservation of that geometry made tangible in glass, iron, leaf and gravel is his last connection to the world: the architect miraculously endowed squares, circles, parallel lines with the capacities of life. He little imagined—why should he?—that this geometry could therefore die. In any event, I was distracted by my domestic life, and resistance would have been useless. Your suggestion in one letter that a Grand Tour of German Treasures of Art and Architecture might be instructive as well as enjoyable was not quite the solution to these difficulties, of which, of course, you were completely ignorant.

A few months ago I saw her cast a look of pure hatred at M. Lemaître when he accused her of denying him the pleasure of seeing the girls. Cécile has just followed Adèle into the Sisters of Pity, in the rue de Grenelle, a horrifying strict convent school, in my view, but Anne would have nothing less. When they are at home, she is ever vigilant that no loose talk such as is common among persons connected with the theatre should reach the ears of the children. Sometimes she rules the house by anguish; the servants become agitated by her irrational outbursts at them, at the children, or indeed by the bitter reproaches she heaps upon herself; they begin to fight amongst themselves and her ménage is reduced to chaos. Thus the preparations for the departure of the girls from Paris were decided upon by me; Anne had hatched a thousand plans, contradictory and elaborate and impossible.

Perhaps you think, Sir, that I receive a manly gratification in ruling over this famous and disordered woman and her brood. I will tell you only that for a period of months I did, and then I realised that my resolution also has its appointed place; when distraught, I must be her "rock." My own disorders are negligible in her eyes. I shall draw back the curtain on one more domestic detail. I am afraid that on a few occasions I have had to deal with Anne more roughly than I might have wished, which severity disturbed the little girl, but, I also fear, unfortunately gave her elder sister a perverse pleasure; once I saw Adèle smiling faintly when I slapped her mother's cheek. Enough; you know now in sufficient measure why all those appeals to come "home" seemed to me irrelevant if still a sweet, an ever so sweet music. No, Father, in truth I am not angry with you, at least for caring.

Well, let us pass on to what you could not read in a newspaper. In the shops where one is known, the flower-seller or breadman will place his wares on the counter, the customer will pick it up from the counter only if he is willing to risk touching a foreign object; the traditional shake of the hand is annulled. No one would think of buying from strangers—this lacks sense, since one eats bread or fruit which has at some point been held by unknown hands, but such it is. In the streets people are careful to keep a sufficient distance from others to avoid touching inadvertently; in those places where crowds are unavoidable, the mass spreads out so as to thin itself, each man a little island, everyone carrying handkerchiefs raised to the nose and mouth, the entire city in gloves. I found the city during the Revolution curiously silent as people set calmly about their uprising; now Paris is pervaded with another silence, the silence of mutual fear; there can be no great stir of Fraternity amongst Citizens when there reigns the horror of skin touching skin. To slap a woman across the mouth is, shall we say, the plague's caress of love.

Charles. I am obliged now to tell you about your other "orphan," although this sobriquet is hardly fair to me. Let us not go over this again.

Once affairs in the rue de la Tour des Dames were more in order, and Anne was reassured about the condition of the children in the country, I sought out my brother. He lives well enough on his income when in the country, as he has told you, and, as perhaps he has not, in retreat he feels less the sting of failure in his calling. In the last year his caustic for this sting has been ever more a bitterness of tone in speaking of the worthies who, through intrigue, dullness or accident find themselves published in Paris.

My dear father, attend with caution the man who speaks of "my insufficiency," or "my inability." No man passes these words easily through his lips; he can only pronounce them in thinking to himself, my insufficiency is not my fault. Sometimes Charles lashes out at me, which lunges miss, and will ever miss, the mark. I know by now even when the attempt will be made. We pass an evening in company of distinguished persons, a dinner at Foy's, for instance, with the coming painters and poets. These persons depart, Charles proposes a last glass at Vier's; he speaks genuinely of his admiration for the poet X or the philosopher Y and then, as though he does not hear the words himself, he says to me, "I do not think practical arts such as yours can ever attain the dignity of those dependent solely upon the imagination." From anyone else, I would receive this as perhaps provoking but certainly worth refuting. His tone precludes discussion. However, if I take no offence, it is as if he had not spoken, and we go on as though there had been but a silence. Once, in Anne's home, he made a wounding innuendo addressed to her—yes! our sweet kinsman! to a lady!—which made her draw up as if bitten. I have found the best course in general is to keep them separate, though he, when he returned to his senses, was sensible of and overcome by remorse for his lapse. I have ventured to say to him, "Why do you pain yourself by association here with persons who are likely to make you bemoan your estate? For you do seek them out, these persons of extravagant character. Then you reproach yourself for your own contrasting virtues of modesty, sweetness and sobriety." His response is that, had he wanted a modest, sweet and sober life, he would never have left Oxford, laughing a bit at this in a satiric voice which rings to my ear totally false. Yet the little of his sermonising I have read is instantly recognisable as the voice of an estimable parson, his *true* character. Failure, I say, is the most deforming of man's tribulations.

To resume: Charles had been this time in the Haute Savoie, at Duingt, but was due back by the 10th of April, when he had, I know, another appointment with yet another publisher about his truly orphaned essays.

I sought him out in the rue de Seine, discovered his chambers inhabited but vacant, descended, and searched out his old concierge, whom I found moaning, evidently in her last throes. Shutting the door to her hovel, I mounted again, and left a message for my brother to quit this pestilent building and come to me instantly at Anne's. Emerging into the rue de Seine I encountered an English doctor, who had been sent at the request of the senior doctor at the English Hospital to Charles' lodgings. There was some confusion here, as my brother was out. I led the English doctor away to a café still open across the river, as I wanted some further information about chills and draughts before tackling the difficult problem of ceiling ventilation in the galleries. The English doctor was unable to help me, and I could not experiment once the patients were moved inside; but I mustn't get ahead of myself. I hadn't found Charles, our medical talk lasted some time, fruitless as it proved, and it was only late the next morning that I could return to fetch my brother. Him too I encountered outside his lodgings, shambling up the rue de Seine, his eyes black-rimmed from sleeplessness, his shoulders sagging.

"I sought you out yesterday, but you were abroad."

"Yes," he said in a heavy, heavy voice.

I began to insist that he leave his rooms, as our part of the city is higher and nearer the gates, with Charles nodding, as though a sleepwalker, until I added,

"By the way, when I was here yesterday, I came in the street upon the

English doctor, the young one from Bath, and took him off to enquire what is requisite in circulation . . ."

As though I had slapped him, Charles suddenly shook himself alert. He stared at me wide-eyed.

"You took him off before he reached the house?"

"Of course, you being absent, and I needing to know . . . what is the matter?" I broke off, as his jaw now hung and his eyeglasses were left askew at the edge of his nose.

For a moment the naked eyes continued their wild stare. "We just missed one another! I must have turned in from the rue de Tours just as you met the doctor at the rue de Seine crossing—" Then he mumbled something indistinct, pushed his eyeglasses back up and, abruptly announcing "I must leave you," fled down a side street.

You may imagine that I feared for his reason; at dusk that evening, however, I received at Anne's a messenger with a note from Charles, writing in a firm hand and coherent, indeed somewhat cold manner, informing me that he was removing himself once more to the country, and would remain there until the plague had subsided.

Do not judge this strange behaviour of our kinsman as cowardice. Few duties of a pastoral kind really bind Charles. He only occasionally preaches. Moreover, as I have explained to you, his literary difficulties are great. Unfortunately, many of his fellow clerics, those still with flocks, did number amongst the crowds which jammed the barriers the moment the town-criers chanted, "It has come! It has come!" It is some religion, this Romish Christianity, when one can be surprised that a spiritual leader has as much courage as the secular members of his congregation.

In any event, these familial and conjugal alarums made me almost relieved to begin, a fortnight ago, the destruction of the Galerie d'Orléans, destruction at least of its ideal form, its purpose and its elegant detail. Has defined volume alone sense? Not even the primitive Egyptians believed so, as the rude, immense geometries they built are lavishly decorated.

We were obliged to exit and enter the Palais-Royal under cover of armed guard. This is because, in the last fortnight, there sprang up in the popular districts the rumour that the government started the epidemic so as to kill off the poor. As evidence for this absurd idea, the poor point to the fact that no one on foot is easily allowed to leave the city; one must have the means for a carriage to escape. They adduce sightings of persons leaning over wells and cisterns, dropping mysterious packets within; these are said to be the King's poisoners. The Prefect of Police has foolishly tried to extinguish these suspicions by officially denying them, which has only convinced the common people that they must be true. And thus there have begun the series of killings—the poor seizing some unfortunate gentleman who had the misfortune to bend over a well as he sneezed, hanging him with their belts from a near-by post, another knot of rabble taking a soldier who lingered "suspiciously" in front of a wine shop and strangling him. Yet even as the mob exacts this illusory vengeance, the executioners are careful to keep enough distance from one another so as not to inhale their fellows' breath; it is said the strangled soldier was killed by two gloved men who kept their arms outstretched and held him between them. It is said that the hospitals are also places where poor patients are starved, or, another popular version, that water is denied to poor patients so that the ordinary people die hideously of thirst. And so we had to be guarded.

It is the time this disease requires which most perplexes. There are quick deaths, and there are deaths which take days. Sometimes the blotches on the face disappear after an hour, and the victim believes he has had a lucky escape; the next day he perishes. Other times, the marks appear, but nothing else happens; the sufferer lives in a prolonged agony of suspense, the death sentence seemingly immutable by the presence of the blue-black marks yet stayed.

It took only four days, as I say, to accomplish the work. There is a ventilation ridge along the roof apex, which top ventilator is too small to be effective, and side ventilators which at least circulate breezes from without. The remaking of the side panels went according to plan, and quickly. The neat removal of further roof glass proved beyond us, in the time we were given; the glass panes tended to crack if we pulled hastily on the leather edges. I had the seemingly good idea to expand the air vents around those already existing in the end walls, but the leather bushing here also had so hardened and bound the glass that terrible cracks opened in adjacent panes. Do you think we allowed too little expansion space between iron frame and glass panel? I gave up; we could not proceed in the roof, as open holes in its fabric would spell disaster below at the first rain; I decided that the cracked openings on the walls would have to serve as sufficient enlargement to the vents designed for a structure holding one tenth the number of inhabitants we were about to receive.

Now I want you to understand how this matter of ventilation caused me to come to grief with M. Fontaine, the fault more of the building than of ourselves. From the time the plan had been agreed upon to the completion of our labour, the number of cases the Hôtel-Dieu proposed sending to the gallery had steadily increased, so that when the ambulance wagons started to arrive, once we had filled the cubicles, the litters of the plague victims overflowed into the corridors. By the end of the four days it required to transport the patients from the Hôtel-Dieu, we had lined the corridors on both sides, leaving only a two-foot wide path down the center for the attendants, and making access to those in the cubicles a matter of stepping over the bodies of those outside.

The last day the patients were transported, M. Fontaine came to the Galerie d'Orléans to see what his arcade looked like. I do not know what I expected of the bent, wrinkled old man—shouts of rage, tears of grief. The moment he entered the Galerie, from the visitors' end (the Comédie-Française end it used to be), he stood absolutely still for a moment. Then he remarked to me, "There are too many bodies in here for the ventilation. Have some of these people removed." Before I could explain that the plan on paper had been overturned by events, an overworked nurse came up to him and asked whom he wished to see.

"No one," he said, "I've just come to look. I—" but the good Sister would let him go no further. "Out, then, get out you filthy prune! Come here to watch people die, imagine!" and she made as if to push him. Whilst I explained to her—and in the circumstances there is no sense in berating people who momentarily lose their tempers—M. Fontaine fled his building. I made my way around the archipelagos of new bodies (it takes time to lay them exactly in line, neatly), and recovered M. Fontaine in the street. He looked bewildered. For a moment my heart went out to him, and I began to describe the technical work so as to take his mind off the affront without pretending we had no reason to be there. I advanced several sentences when he burst out at me, "I allowed more than enough expansion space between the frame and the glass! You must be breaking the panels because you are clumsy!" This ended our interview.

That evening I received a note from Charles, once more happily ensconced in the Château de Duingt, telling me that he forgave me for not knowing what I did, or something like that, concluding by imploring me to leave, to come to him and to reflect. By now my temper had worn thin. Evidently I was committing suicide, selfishly, by remaining in Paris. I must tell you that in fact Charles *hates* Anne; in place of my imminent death due to sensual thraldom, he offered some sort of Christian consolation in his friend's château, if I would only abandon the witch and her brood. The letter didn't say this, exactly; it was all couched in lofty invitation to retreat and meditate, but like his seizures in the Café de Foy, it was best ignored.

As a final touch to our original plans, we installed within the gallery gas lamps of the sort which appeared on the city's streets two years ago. In the open air, the fumes from these lamps are negligible. In our gallery, even during the times when a throng of fashionables paraded through it, the slight smell of gas troubled no one. The air vents have cunning fins extending from the walls; these fins trap the fumes which the movement of the strolling bodies circulate upwards. But when a mass of supine bodies carpets the galleries, the gas becomes noticeable; one can breathe but remarks the smell each time one makes an intake of breath. To this unanticipated stillness of air there is added the smell of cholera; some victims have an outpouring of diarrhoea, but in the majority of cases gas issues from dry bowels. It is heavier than the gas from the lamps, so that when one bends over to clean the bodies of the ill, one is assailed by their stench, and as one rises, one chokes slightly on the fumes from the modern convenience.

When M. Fontaine conceived the Galerie d'Orléans, he anticipated that his invention would encounter one defect not present in the old Galeries de Bois. Iron and glass more poorly absorb sound, he knew, than the jumble of wood and dirt which enclosed the structure before. This defect remained in the actual construction; ladies and gentlemen in promenading were obliged to lean close to one another in speaking; only within the shops was the din stilled. By taking away the front and rear panels of these shops to make room for the ill, something most strange occurs. The victims of the plague do not cry out in pain; they make instead those dog-like little whining noises I have described to you. And these cries of men and women mortally parched float out of the cubicles, up through the layers of gas to the protective glass ceiling, and there rebound echoing, a steady, light and above all distinct music of pain, the yelp of each audible to everyone, so that the ears remind even the victims who keep their eyes protectively fixed on their own bodies that they are surrounded by death.

The day after M. Fontaine fled the arcade Anne and I spent quietly, together, dining alone at home. The cries and the smell of the arcades tormented me, I was revolted by hot food, and the sight of water glasses on the table made me want to gag, although Raymond had placed the unopened bottle from the spa actually on the table so that we would be reassured. The hot food! Now that the children were safely away, however, my work done, Anne was calmer. The rue de la Tour des Dames is on a hill, and that night the breezes were fresh. We went up to the roof terrace, perhaps foolishly taking the air, but the few lights in the city winked, there was not a sound, one could hardly believe this was the peace of a capital in plague.

My nerves gradually steadied. We drank from the same glass a rough Calvados, we always finish the evening drinking from the same glass, it is a little habit of ours; but in the circumstances, people afraid even to breathe where others have breathed, that night it was a token of union. On the terrace, sipping the Calvados, we forgave each other.

The next morning Raymond placed on the silver salver your last letter, which we will pass over. The evening before, Anne wanted to know how comforting is our construction to those in the final hours of life. I did not want to upset her, but I will tell you.

The new tenants are beyond compliments, and to die here is surely better than to die in the street. Our construction is not perfect enough to adapt to the smell of death, while the acoustics of pain are better in it than the acoustics of pleasure. But the light, the light the structure floods on the sea of pallets, buckets and sponges, it is the light to which our victims respond. Indeed, this experience of light has prompted in me all manner of ideas about vertical glass columns, arcade towers.

The dying look up through the clear glass panes and believe, as one day I fancied, that there is nothing above them, the building melting into the sky. In their pain, this union with the heavens is not a conceit of fancy, and they cry to be taken indoors, for they do not want to die like animals in the open air. To comfort them, we have arranged a system: those most cognisant of their surroundings are placed in the cubicles, those closest to death are placed in the corridors. If a victim's condition deteriorates, he or she is moved out under the full light; if it improves to consciousness, the patient is moved into the comforting shelter of the cubicle. This means a good deal of work, but is not entirely a matter of spiritual accommodation, for in moving the pallets we have the opportunity to clean under them fairly regularly, an absolute requisite of common sanitation. But I have thought, in watching or helping with this changing of the guard, how wrong is the commonplace of "the shadow of death." Light, union, immeasurable space, these are the afflictions of those who can see death; in their terror they want darkness, cover, the sheltering cave. It is certain that the light here exposes man to the final cruelty, penetrates his last illusion of comfort. Do you remember that I once wrote to you about shafts of light as forms? During these days they seemed like knives.

My work was done. The arcade in the Palais-Royal had become a hospital, the same scenery serving comedy and tragedy as it often did in the Comédie-Française. That theatre was shut, along with all the others. Now Anne begged me to depart Paris, to fly with her to her daughters. I closed the circle: I refused also her. In the end I do not know why I put Anne alone into her carriage last week, she angry once more. Not love of the building, not exactly: instead I had the nagging conviction that there was a solution to the problem of air, vexation about the gas flow, matters of that sort. The only time I have been in danger is, indeed, after I remained alone in Paris, finally trying to make the structure work.

There really was no reason to persevere. The last few days have seen an abatement in the delivery of victims to the gallery, reflecting a more general subsiding of the scourge in the city. As the corridors become less crowded, it is possible to imagine the panels of "Richard et Larbier, Chocolatiers" bolted again on a cubicle which was the scene of a score of deaths. Once we re-bolt the panels and clean the cubicles, *there will be no trace* of the horrors which have passed here. Indeed, this is one reason perhaps why I do not "love" this building, if one can so employ the word. Iron and glass architecture is too plastic, the form easily bending to changes in use. In an arcade the object of one's love is never constant—and what is the beauty of architecture if not the reassurance of solidity, the promise of enduring, of the eternal?

In any event, yesterday a woman grasped convulsively at my hand, as the victims do when the final moment arrives, seeking in human touch a last impression of life. Before, I never returned the gesture, since the hands of those with plague are unclean from involuntary contact with the mouth or nether regions. It was insane but I was so exhausted that caution had fled before invading fatigue; I afforded this expiring creature her last impression. We touched but for a moment; a nurse remarked it, shouted at me, the woman rolled over and was gone, the nurse plunged my hand in a bucket of the acid called carbolic with which we have just begun to wash. The acid bit into my flesh.

When I saw Anne that night I described to you, during the July Revolution, the night she regarded dispassionately the dead woman on the theatre steps, I felt an incomprehension such as I had never before experienced. Last week, however, when I took the dead woman's hand, I was momentarily curious what impression the limb would make; perhaps the palm held a message for me. One spends week after week avoiding something as simple as touching hands; the desire to do so becomes overwhelming. I felt her dry palm and miraculously, in this place I had helped create, had destroyed, and would remake, the power of a sick body did not harm me. The volume and light in the arcade transmuted the woman. Her death— you understand there had been so many—her death was nothing to me. But I felt I understood Anne better.

Enough; I shall not read this endless letter over again. Know that I am

Your son and friend,
Frederick

"One Amongst Many"

An Article by Charles Courtland
in The International Courier
19 June 1833

Gentle reader: this meditation is dedicated to my father. It was he who doubted, in a letter sent me several months ago, that Paris could hold many charms for a person such as myself. He meant that a serious young man, given to study, whose recreation is advice, would find little congenial here. My eye for pictures is deficient; all wines caress my nose equally and indifferently; I have no need to lounge in Freyer for cravats, as I employ a clerical collar, nor do I essay the dog-skin gloves of Martine, as I wear cheap English cotton; my shoes are those I have owned since coming down from university. The pleasures of Paris so alien to me, my parent was perplexed I had remained here so long—it is now four years.

His enquiry was couched tactfully; my father has never hectored me to return to England, as do sires whose elegant scions frequently mislay themselves during the Grand Tour. Yet I hesitated at that moment to reply. For, two days before his missive arrived, I had sent one of my own to England, informing the proper authorities of the Church of England that I was no longer to be counted amongst its clergy; I renounced the pleasures of dispensing advice in the name of Authority, (and receiving a modest stipend in the name of Scholarship). My father, I knew, would receive this news smiling. He would chafe me that Freyer and Martine had proved more powerful than Newman and Pusey; now he could certainly solicit my opinion on obscure claret. A gentleman of the Age of Light, this triumph of Paris over religion would amuse him, if he also found it perhaps familiar, the plot of a frivolous evening, he seemed to recall, at the Drury Lane called *The Traveller's Surprise*.

I knew I should have to make an effort of correction. If my sojourn indeed has defeated my last vestiges of faith, it is not the twinkling of the city which has called me from prayer. Nor has my passage been the stuff of farce. However, I stayed my hand in reporting to my parent; how frightened are we when called to explain to a father! Mine, moreover, does not like to hear the thumping of a breast beaten. So I began some weeks ago to write, in order that I might better know my own mind. I rewrote this letter several times, my explanation becoming sometimes too convoluted, sometimes too clear. But as I laboured, I came to think I wrote not for myself and my parent alone; I wrote also for you: to you, if you have mislaid your sons; in your name, if you feel that the ordinary course of piety is likely to cause you to mislay your life—there, the clerical voice is not easily stilled.

I wish first, Father, to paint for you two scenes. One represents a Parisian promise, the other a danger. My decision comes from navigating between these two, the ebb and flow of the city; after several years of navigation, I could no longer remain a priest.

The scene of promise I shall paint you is the Café Turc, near the Palais-Royal at no. 29, boulevard du Temple, its immense garden fronting the street. Tenanted round the clock, the Café Turc draws its clientèle from the theatres on the opposite side, as well as from the denizens of Paris seeking air, noise and other forms of relief from the propriety of the neighbouring arcades. In 1780 the grand Oriental décor of the Café Turc seemed to its creator—who I doubt was an architect—to require a ceremonial green space before the entrance. History and man's need for man replaced the green with tables, kiosks and illuminated shows in the evening; now this terrace gathers the most diverse physiognomies in the entire city.

The Café Turc is so familiar to most visitors, as well as to Parisians, that its true genius has seldom been remarked. Consider: M. Bonvalet, the proprietor, informs me that never in the last fifty-five years has it been necessary to call a guard or soldier to maintain order in this vast swarm.

People speak, of course, of the charm of the place. Within there is a smell of spice, upon one wall a painting of the father-in-law of M. Bonvalet, a man who wore a garland of lavender atop his wig at family christenings, burials and weddings. The mélange of tables, stands and umbrellas without is also colourful, but décor alone reveals not the secret of the amiability here.

From dawn to noon to dusk to dawn, on all but the worst days, hundreds sit at the tables of the *terrasse* studying those around them. For instance, if you buy a pear at the fruiterer's kiosk, you may be sure that after the sale is completed someone at a near-by table will turn to his companions and remark, "The Englishman paid too much for his pear." No one would dream of warning you before that you might pay less. People do not interfere with one another. On the other hand, the comment is not offered as criticism; the man knowledgeable about fruit may smile at you if you betray that you have overheard. He but observes.

Occasionally a marital or other dispute erupts which seems to require the police. A wife pounds the table upon learning her doltish husband paid five francs—think of it, five francs!—for a new pair of gloves, when any idiot could have them for four francs eighty at the Marché de la Cité, and the wife will soon be a widow with a fat old pig like him wheezing and puffing, and where will she be without any money? Perhaps the table overturns under her assault. "Ten centimes, Madame, for the broken cup!" a servant of M. Bonvalet calls out, and the shrew's anger, like a great river suddenly changing its course, pours out upon the waiter the wrath formerly cascading over the husband. "Ten, criminal! Six, seven at most!" Around her, the inhabitants of the *terrasse* of the Café Turc by the most light and deft of swerving motions upon their chairs assure that not a drop of liquid bespatters them, then take up the theme: are gloves really four francs eighty at the market on the Ile de la Cité?

It is here that moral judgements of a weightier kind are suspended. The women of the town come to the *terrasse* to rest their feet. They permit themselves to smile at the friendly banter men direct to them. A fact incredible to any English visitor: these "ladies," while never allowed to speak to respectable women, who of course would never dream of addressing them, these "ladies" are yet permitted to be seated in the garden near families.

Even the poison of France, political intrigue, is rendered a little less deadly. Counterpoint in debate is to be heard on the *terrasse*, however unfashionable this practise has become in the concert halls. Political arias, so to say, are never sung in unison, nor is there a main melody at the Café Turc with supporting voices, but rather true polyphony, the political songs of all managing miraculously to interweave in perfect time, so that once one singer has dropped a particular subject, others also drop it and commence new counterpoint on the changed theme.

You suspect, Father, the city begins to twinkle before my eyes? I merely adduce the substance of one fact: in this place, it has not been necessary to resort to force in the last fifty-five years. Why? The *terrasse* of the Café Turc induces its scholars of the price of pears and gloves, its resting whores, its political Malibrans, to consider themselves one amongst many. Life so various: they observe, they argue. Life which marches on of its own, if they do not interfere. Even during political clamour: no one antagonist hopes for absolute victory, for then this Beethoven of debate would sing into . . . silence. Each one amongst many.

This *terrasse* embodies what I should call an architecture of irony. True, the human compass is modest, its movements small, its matter forgettable. You may say I describe to you mere diversions, inconsequent in the shadow of revolution, war and material striving. Inconsequent? Here men and women tolerate one another, in this city which has known the guillotine, religious persecution and a ruinous thirst for European conquest. Which shall we say is the more worthy, the more precious: domination or tolerance?

Dear father, neither of us is minded to abstruse adjudication. Once at the table next to mine, men were engaged in a game of cards. A player was obliged to part; another asked if I should like to join them. It was an evening in which I had been prey to the most profound melancholy. Indeed, in answer to his request I produced, "My soul is too full." He shrugged; "Suit yourself, Monsieur." In this little place where each person feels one amongst many, I learnt, slowly, to smile at myself.

I have said that the decision to abandon my calling came as a result of navigating between this scene of virtue in Paris and a contrasting scene. Do not be alarmed! I did not lose myself in a den of vice. I sought out the place in Paris where the normally sceptical disillusioned people of this city are ardent and faith-filled.

I asked you to imagine the crowd outside the artists' entrance at the Comédie-Française after a performance; the door gives off one of the gates to the Palais-Royal. Thirty or forty gentlemen wait there, meticulously attired, each carrying a little spray of flowers in his hands, perfection in the tailor's art marred perhaps only by the small box an admirer has secreted in his pocket, the box containing a jewel, a cameo, a locket of hair fastened in silver and gold.

At a certain moment, this crowd of admirers will part in two, like the Red Sea, as the actresses of the Comédie-Française issue from the portal which has earlier ushered them within to the sacred precincts of Art. The actresses will emerge, and since this is the most dignified haunt of thespiennes in the world, each of these ladies will descend the steps slowly, like queens condescending to meet the populace, each lady lightly clutching the arm of a particularly favoured admirer or long-entrenched *cavalier servant*. Then the gentlemen in waiting will press forward their bouquets. The elderly gentlemen who have haunted the artists' entrance for decades will, like boys offering sweets at holiday time, modestly hold out their hands; the youngest will thrust their presents forward aggressively. A thespienne queen may ignore any offering of course, but if she deigns to accept, she will do so only by indicating to the escort on her arm that he may accept the present for her. Depending upon their intimacy, these receivers may also, by a subtle glance or movement of the mouth, influence the queen's decision. If the admirer is successful, he hands his flowers or his little box to the *cavalier servant* who by the end of the procession may sag under a veritable bushel of exotic flowers.

I may remark, not all these favoured retainers of the thespienne queens are elderly gentlemen, widowers or hopelessly ugly. Some actresses at the Comédie-Française have managed to snare handsome young men as their loyal escorts.

The doorkeeper at the Comédie-Française has one explanation for this ritual of homage. He is an ancient creature who has kept nobles of the *ancien régime* at bay, as well as Citizens of the Revolution, generals of the Empire, then nobles again during the Restoration, and now gentlemen of the July Monarchy; the entire modern history of France kept at bay. Thus he remembers the time—it must have been in the 1780s, not later—when the suite of admirers remained in carriages. The persons crowding the artists' entrance (then called the stage door) were the servants of the admirers; a servant would listlessly announce that the Duc de Nestor awaited Mlle Vaux in his carriage with a ruby worth a hundred louis d'or. Manners, the doorkeeper says, "is better today." In offering this, he snickers.

He is mistaken. The gentlemen of the present day have not applied a polite varnish to what is essentially a financial transaction with painted women. No; these actresses have become figures of real repute, of admiration in Paris, and the gifts offered to them are disinterested acts of homage. Thus there has even come into fashion the card attached to a bouquet written as follows: "M. and Mme Blanc offer their compliments to Mlle——." Nor may the *cavaliers servants* be presumed to enjoy the favours of these artists.

Some say that, in this age when political life evokes amongst most people only disgust or resignation, the actresses along with their male counterparts have taken the place once occupied in the popular imagination by ministers and generals. People speak of Mlle Mars, Mlle Mercure, M. Lemaître and even the mime Deburau with more lively respect than they speak of their rulers. Perhaps this honour is at the expense of other public figures, perhaps not. What matters is its very existence. The persons Parisians believe in, passionately, are those who enact the passions professionally, those who have become specialists in simulating vivid realities. Here we may include the extraordinary musician like Paganini or Liszt as well, men who provoke adulation of their persons when they play. That specialists in simulating strong feeling are so honoured is a perverse form of faith.

It is unique, I believe, to modern times, and is a disease to which those inhabiting cities are particularly prone.

I ask you, Father, to consider a peculiar fact. In Paris the actress is not called upon to become a respectable person in order to win these favours of respect. Indeed, she seems to enhance the regard in which she is held if there is some shadowy secret in the wings of her life, perhaps a natural child or some other scandal. Consider, Father, that there is reputed to be an actress here who is said not to know who is the sire of her own children. This sorrowful creature is taken thereby to be acquainted with tragedy, and is routinely offered the most sombre and elegiac rôles. In the very abandon of her life there seems a guarantee of her art.

What is the connexion between scandal and these, the most tragic rôles a woman can play before the public? A woman so abandoned need not disappear from sight because of these violations; she has only to marshal her disordered forces, to continue, her head held erect as though she were contemptuous of any possible sneer. Perhaps at first there were a few rude remarks, but after a time her public began to admire. Something about her gave her the force to go on, despite all; her very strength must be due to her life. Then they began to find the art more touching, they said her troubled history has given her the knowledge of tragedy in art. Entirely illogical; there are thousands of fallen women who could not recite one line, but the artist's public now endows her with these powers because she is everything they fear they are not.

This age for which all dreams of Justice and Right are soaked in blood; a monarch who encourages his people to enrich themselves rather than dream, uselessly, once more; a city Petronius would scorn, avaricious with no redeeming gluttony. The sensual abandon of the thespians seems proof that they are *free*, unlike the quietly tailored men in the boxes who hang upon their words, which are abandoned words, the flames of Don Carlos, Hernani, and all the fevered rest. The public hungers for sensual impression.

You see, they are not content with the little pleasures of the Café Turc, and neither, I confess, am I. The word "daily" is ineradicably associated in our minds with "dull." Once, when I sermonised in the English countryside, long far away, I spoke in my youthful wisdom of Virtue shining, an enormous outsize figure like M. Delacroix's "Liberty Guiding the People." But now we know her, Virtue, to be no larger than ourselves, to be exactly the size of "daily," to be contained within the ironies of an evening of cards and the placid rejoinder, to a man whose heart is too full to play, "Suit yourself, Monsieur." You reckon by the eye, and here are the dimensions of virtue, Father: too small to give the soul room. But my colleagues at cards, myself bent over a cup of coffee, M. Pierre reading his newspaper, M. Bonvalet in the kitchens—for a sense of greater room we do not turn to crime, to flesh. No, we seek out people who can *safely* make us feel life larger than ourselves, safely and cheaply.

It costs three francs at the Comédie-Française, fifty sous at the Variétés. We feel "what it would be like" to be a corsair, a great general or the most angelic monk; the women we have paid to see also arouse in us, as though passing from wall to wall in a room of mirrors, images of desperate longing or murderous rage. The francs or sous of freedom spent, we return to the streets, to family prayers, to the careful keeping of accounts, to the virtues of living one amongst many. Have I explained? The light of our longing plays upon the performer's mask as it does in the mirrored reception halls of the Vatican, reflecting from one surface to the next to yet another, so that we no longer know where the image began. Her secret lies buried in the insufficiency of our virtue. I too have gazed rapt across the barrier of the footlights.

Four years spent, as I say, tacking from one side to the other, now smiling, now rapt, passing from virtue to faith and then back again. During this voyage I continued the priest's recreation of giving advice. I sought to advise myself what virtue and faith might imply, if anything, for the conduct of my own life in Paris. Matters might have been solved, of course, had I left during the July Revolution, as did so many of those concluding Grand Tours with finishing months of Parisian gaiety. I should have left during the cholera of '32; foreigners were not wanted then. Indeed, the paucity of my resources meant that for months on end I have been obliged to live far from this capital; I have lived in the mountains, whose air the noble Sénancour recommends as the only ether fit for a free man, and in the depths of the Touraine, rank with pollen. I have lived within my means during these rural retreats, yet always felt the draw of the more ruinous city. How should a prig—let us not shy at the word, Father!—how should a prig make his way amongst the most bitter, credulous, impulsive, miserly people on earth?

The answer I found had always been to hand, staring straight at me from atop my writing table. On this much-abused surface I have two framed engravings.

One is after Menil's portrait of the young Pascal, the present from my tutor. This likeness does not at first glance appear to be that of a young man quite, since the eyes are creased at the edges with crow's-feet. But then one looks at the space between the eyebrows and sees the skin wrinkled in concentration, which in turn reveals that the creases at the sides of the eyes are not marks of age but the tensed effects of thought. My tutor made me the gift when we read together the essay which confirms the likeness, Pascal's "The Mystery of Jesus." It is a meditation upon the sufferings of Jesus, particularly upon His absolute loneliness in the world of men, a despair bred of loneliness until even His faith is shaken at last and He cries out to His Father, "Oh, my God, why hast Thou forsaken me?"

My tutor gave this essay to all his charges so that they would be prepared for the numerous outbursts of grief, despair and hopelessness which the practising clergyman encounters on his rounds. Though no prelate, Pascal seemed to my tutor to have coined some excellent responses for these moments, sentences fortunately free of all Romish colour.

We received instruction in this terrible and perplexing moment in the same spirit of utility. In his solitude Jesus is about to lose faith, but it is only a temptation, only a moment: the mystery of Jesus is that even when utterly abandoned, utterly lost, in His pain upon the Cross He is able to reach towards God.

Pascal indeed contrived some excellent sentences about this consolation afforded Jesus, but the mystery is Pascal's true matter, a mystery which escaped my tutor. On the Cross Jesus is at last alone. Men cannot *do* evil alone, for its essence is dominion over others, society appearing to Pascal like a pool filled with carnivorous fishes, each creature hoping to eat before he is eaten. But, unlike other celebrants of monastic life, Pascal also emphasized the risks of solitude; he thought of loneliness as a terrible gamble. Only in solitude can man truly test his faith. What will remain to us if the cry of Jesus is our final word? What if, at last alone with ourselves, we keep company with Nothing? Thus the portrait on my desk of a young man, afraid of contamination, afraid he might lack the courage for faith, withdrawn, his face lined and furrowed, aged beyond his years.

For a long time I had no doubt I could, in Paris, come to resemble that engraving. The easy manner of my writing would disguise, as did Pascal's, an isolated and uneasy soul. Sometimes I perverted the portrait, hardened Pascal's narrow skull, burning eyes and thin tight lips into marble. I would become the man who had acquired the courage to see through illusions, both his own and other people's. What a fine man I would be! Strong and cynical. Nothing could hurt me—except myself.

Father, year in, year out, notes of rejection came from academies, from publishers; the latter often returned my manuscripts with the wax unbroken, though the accompanying notes spoke of the excellence of my prose, the clarity of my thought. I was refused admission to the English Academy at Geneva, to the School of Moral Sciences at Aix. Friends asked, why did I submit to these indignities, why did I struggle to gain a purchase upon the world through writing—there are quite enough writers. They asked in the kindest manner. But discovery of what is possible and impossible is a knowledge given to us in part by other people. I do not say I depended upon others, but I was not indifferent to them. Armour against life is no source of pride.

Finally, when my fortunes turned, I could publish an essay here and there, the occasional communication of news from European churches; still, I did not think of my professional independence, modest and precarious as it was and is, as a safe-conduct pass which would permit me to withdraw at last within myself, to plumb the cavernous contours of my soul. Nor did this growing independence seem to solve my questions, my doubts. I have need of other people, even though they hurt me; I have applied once more to the Academy at Aix. Why? This I do not know. But I know I do believe myself one amongst many: staring at Pascal's portrait, I saw in time his life would not guide mine. He is a true Christian, willing to risk all in withdrawing from the world. I contemplated his tortured portrait ever more intently in France; finally the time came to write to my superiors in the Church of England.

The other portrait on my writing desk you must surely remember. When Dr. Innes awarded me my Pascal, you remarked it upon your very next visit, commenting that the modelling was remarkably free. At the time, such criticism meant little to me, who saw only words. Later in the day you presented me with a drawing you had found in a shop of Westall's portrait of Byron, an even better example, you thought, of ease in modelling a head; I kept it, of course, since it came from you. They make a provocative pair.

My Pascal shows a man strained and burning. My Byron shows a person of similar age, his shirt open at the neck, his hair ruffled, his eyes looking quizzically at some person or thing in the passing parade. It is the fashion today for posed poets to gaze dreamily downwards, lost in contemplation of some inner conundrum. Westall, like most of Byron's portraitists, reports his eyes alert. Pascal had found an answer by the time of his portrait: withdraw. Byron was painted by Westall in 1813, just before the poet's trials in public were to begin, his private griefs already racking. Byron had no solution to his own suffering. Yet the portrait shows him with a clear brow and no tensed lines at the edges of the eyes.

Before I came to France, the verse of Byron's which most often recurred to me was, I confess, a fragment from the "Vision of Judgement" which we thought so wicked at school:

> Saint Peter sat by the celestial gate:
> His keys were rusty, and the lock was dull,

So little trouble had been given of late;
Not that the place by any means was full.

I thought him a light if pungent spirit, his death for the cause of Greece misadventure. In the prig's world, a man must furnish continual evidences that he is "sound"—if a poet, edifying, worth re-reading, a good investment of time. Byron's menagerie of parrots and monkeys, his drinking of wine from skulls, his half-secret liaison with his half-sister, all convinced me in my prighood that his poetry would not be "worth my time." I found modern poets in general, save for a few like Gray and Southey, to be dubious. Still, since it was your gift, Byron's face greeted me every day when I sat down to write and gradually we began to speak. I plumbed his sufferings, I attended to the alert, released expression upon his beautiful face.

The answer to the question, "How shall a man live, who has lost faith and who feels confined by virtue?"—Byron would have such sport with this query!—is none the less the inadvertent subject of the letters and journals of the poet, published a few years ago by his friend Mr Moore. For it was indeed a question the poet himself had to face, once he was sent into exile twenty years ago by my youthful colleagues Respectable Opinion, Outrage and Fright. Earlier in his life, whenever restless or world-weary, the poet had journeyed, and he had been consoled. The exile, he was to learn in 1816, loses a traveller's refreshment in foreign climes; to savour the foreign, one must be sure of a comfortable, cosy hearth somewhere one can call "home." Byron learnt this hard lesson in crossing the Alps.

The record of this crossing in the autumn of 1816, which Mr Moore seems to have rendered intact, commences as if Byron were once more on his adventures. There are related his various dangers on steep mountain paths, his narrowly avoiding a slide of rocks, his roving eye for beautiful shepherdesses, etc., etc. Sound or not, I never found this corsair spirit attractive in the man's poetry, and unrelenting bravado is little more interesting in a life. But within a week the mask of high spirits cracked. On the 23rd of September Byron writes, "Passed *whole woods of withered pines, all withered;* trunks stripped and barkless, branches lifeless; done by a single winter—their appearance reminded me of me and my family." The poet has thoughtfully underlined the best phrase in this account to the half-sister Augusta, as in his prior correspondence. As the voyage progresses, this manner disappears. More and more the poet permits Augusta to glimpse his pain; the avowals of his love to her become more heartfelt; he becomes more distracted; within a further week Nature can no longer "lighten the weight upon my heart, nor enable me to lose my own wretched identity in the majesty & the power and the Glory around, above, & beneath me." Byron, his detractors maintain, passed his entire life with his heart worn on his sleeve. Perhaps, but this journey transformed the poet's effusions. As I came to read him, I saw it was the event through which Byron first spoke of his own suffering without inviting pity of self.

Before his exile, the young lord was avid for fame—which he thought to earn in his person by swagger. Fame, our cheat of death, fame assuring us our work will outlast our body, or simply that we are persons worth remembering. After 1816, the poet famous for his words and infamous for his life felt neither to be a guarantee of endurance. Christian morality predicts he ought to have become a chastened man. But not at all. This is the revelation of Lord Byron's last years.

Although delicate with his books, his pets, his costumes, he was often callous in regard to human beings; he exploited his *persona* as poet to take advantage of women and excuse himself from the ordinary courtesies due to men. The adult no better than the swaggering youth. Recent revelations of his friend Mr John Cam Hobhouse add to the documents collected by Mr Moore. The report of his friend is, rather, that exile made him wary; he learnt the limits of his swaggering power. No force of genius cunningly deployed would overcome the revulsion his erotic tastes inspired in others; most men abandoned him and declared loudly they had performed that virtuous act. Though always cynical about his critics, Byron in his travels became increasingly sceptical of himself. By 1822, Lord Byron finds rather boring his own lists of the number of bottles he had drunk in a night, the number of kisses he had bestowed on serving girls, and the number of his witty sallies. By the time he was ready for the fatal Greek adventure he knew his callousness and his contempt had also, rightly, disposed men in England to revenge themselves upon him when he faltered. But he never apologised. A defiant irony sharpened the sword of wit: surely later genera-tions will judge *Don Juan* a comic masterwork, the sallies in it more mor-dant than those in *Childe Harold,* because the ageing poet spoke in a cool voice, and his art was equal to his hurt. Disabused of himself, doubting of the world, deeply pained by the solitude he felt amongst foreigners yet as deeply interested in how these aliens arranged to live, when last glimpsed by the English visitors in Italy Byron appeared a man who had, finally, contrived his own sort of peace.

Embarrassing as it may seem, I found the poet's story as recently re-vealed in these documents to be an inspiration. No, I did not dream of piloting a ship to free the Greeks; no, I did not imagine myself to drink wine from skulls. Indeed, I did not suppress the prig's impulse to derive a moral of good value from another man's story: I found in this Byron gradually being revealed to us a more serious lesson, a more extreme example of living with a sense of one's limits, one amongst many, than that afforded by the Café Turc. True, he would have been at home there; throughout his life details arrested his attention—the angle at which a Venetian woman holds out her hand to be kissed, the early signs of moulting in young parrots, the differences between crusted and true vintage port wine. He found these matters absorbing without being assured they were worthwhile, and thus he would have found companions at the café. But the story his friends are now allowing us to learn is of a man who strengthened his *individuality* through learning his limits. Byron became more of himself the more he acknowledged he might be, justly, cast into shadow. I began to ask myself, what peculiarity might be concentrated into my essence, what fracture gave my life a specific weight? For so long, you see, I had thought if only I could become like other men I would become stronger.

Perhaps you do not see, for I have again indulged in the pastoral ruse of providing a moral without indicating the manner in which it comes to seem reasonable. There was, indeed, an occasion when the portrait you gave me stiffened my resistance to returning permanently "home," armed me to continue an independent journey here.

Last year upon visiting our country briefly I held an animated conversation with an elderly gentleman; it was he who expostulated about my future.

"Sir," he argued, "the divines of my youth celebrated Christmas, Easter Sunday, and other sacred occasions before masters more inclined to raise their own heads in search of wild fowl than glimpses of heaven. In France, the aristocracy haunted boudoirs rather than hunted birds, these terrestrial pursuits hardly more edifying. Did the prelates thereby lose heart? The best of them did not! One found priests who indeed doubted that such a disastrously confused and clanking place as the world could be the result of a mere seven days of Celestial Meddling, or that a truly beneficent Creator could blame his first two human creatures, naked and in ruddy good health, for disporting themselves as would anyone in a warm climate during a late afternoon without the distractions of court gossip or lawsuits. These divines doubted, they preached to their half-listening patrons, and got on with it. They wrote their books; they did the odd good work. Sir, you are greedy! Must you also enjoy the luxury of telling nothing but the truth? How dare you presume?"

By the time he had stopped speaking, I had already packed the few objects I owned in Paris, disposed of my cat to a neighbour and booked my passage. The elderly gentleman at the conclusion of his tirade exploded in a bit of coughing, an interruption of our discourse which was fortunate for me. While he coughed it occurred to me I might reasonably respond, "The conditions of society are not as they were in your youth."

"A lame excuse!" he gasped. "My boy, have you no shame—to answer reason with truism?"

"Still you would judge me lame, were I to admit to you that my highest aspiration in life was to go on living as those before me lived."

"But why this thrusting? Why wallow in your disillusion?"

Suddenly I experienced the headiest moment of my life! An observer would have noticed nothing, nothing at all. We continued to sit in our quiet corner in the new club in Pall Mall. The passing servant would only have heard me remark, "This wallowing, as you call it, makes me ever more independent in spirit," and then noted I dropped whatever embarrassing subject we had been discussing and more properly enquired after the health of my elderly companion, who in turn roused himself from youth's indulgences to give a complete and graphic report. But to me, this moment when I could change the subject was an amazing revelation.

The prig, you see, is ever ready and always able to *justify* himself. He lives his life waiting to be called to account. But I was free! If this neatly wigged gentleman felt I wallowed, then, so be it, I wallowed. Free, even, because I could not justify myself. In that single moment to understand that "wallowing" was indeed the manner in which I lived as a thinking, sensate being. I do not recommend doubt to others; it is my way only. When I cudgel my brains about Lamennais, Charles Courtland does so. How ludicrous the baronet in Venice would find an ex-priest inspired in Paris to worry about Obedience versus Service. I worry; this is what I do.

I sank deeper into my leather chair in Pall Mall, attending the horrific catalogue of my elderly friend. At this moment my brow, I am sure, began to clear. Lamennais' dilemma seemed ever more intriguing. My brow, I say, cleared, even as spiritual struggle continued painfully. Each of us, gazing into the face of another, finds something radiant in the loved visage, beyond their understanding.

Whatever the combination of causes, the modest spiritual crisis I have recounted has abated. I returned to France; the streets of Paris were as foul, the Tuileries as quiet, as when I had left; the King's Chamberlain continued in his researches for a suitable livery for the household of the new régime. It is a curiosity of Egoism, however, that when some great event occurs to ourselves, immediately we re-colour the world, as a painter who has stared and stared at a half-finished canvas might suddenly, one morning, go to his brushes without a trace of hesitation, shrugging to himself slightly that he was a fool not to have seen it before. When I returned to Paris I, having heroically changed the subject to my host's health in a Pall Mall club, I saw the city in an entirely new light.

Scepticism is the most aristocratic of virtues. The superior sceptic must be endowed with confidence, for he lives without assurances. Aristocrats in drawing-rooms often evince a kindred ease; they have passed beyond caring that others know "who" they are, and so seem to talk on occasion with becoming, deceptive humility. Any man is of their number spiritually if capable of exclaiming on his deathbed, "It was all so interesting!" This ease has usually a darker side. Pain exists for the true sceptical spirit as the dukes and duchesses of the old régime imagined the ordinary people of Paris: ever ready to be of service.

When I returned to Paris, I saw we might make an entire city in this manner, a more aristocratic city, a sceptical city. I would not close the theatres, nor give M. Bonvalet licence to sell Turkish coffee on every street. Indeed, the essence of my plan derived directly from the sudden revelation that I need not defend myself against "wallowing." Could we make a city in which men and women did not feel on trial for their lives, in which they were not continually assayed by where they came from, the quality of their parents, their present fortunes, their future prospects? This ravening desire to determine the value of other human beings, so to place them in a fixed landscape, this is the Platonic essence of the prig; rather than a prig's city, I thought, let us imagine a more fluid life, men and women more discreet —it is not a dream: ancient Athens forbade its citizens to invoke their family lustre or their wealth during days of political discussion. We could make social life more political in this ancient sense.

It indeed seemed necessary, timely. The constitutional monarch of France has laid an injunction upon his people: Enrich yourself! Some Parisians have profited from the opportunities afforded by their liberal King, finding careers open indeed to talent, and trading upon the Stock Exchange throughout the week. The majority of our citizens, however, watch from afar these few successful ones, fine gentlemen in English suits, ladies in bright silks; in the new order the enriched have lost all fear of displaying wealth. The ones who watch are moved, of course, by resentment, yet also by shame. There but for fortune, and my cunning, go I. Several of the King's ministers are in trade, the Exchange accepts all bidders. Under a liberal régime, the ordinary man judges himself more harshly than in the days when law forbade him a carriage, custom denied him the right to imagine changing his station in life; matters were beyond a man's control. How could a footman imagine the place allotted him in society was somehow his just desert? In this liberal era, you discover in the eyes watching the vulgarian carriages of the newly rich pain, hatred and also unease.

When I returned to liberal France, it seemed to me that this shame of subordinacy might at least be tempered in Paris. Lyons, like Birmingham, has been reserved for Progress; Paris, like London, is too sprawling to be thus confined. Here, it seemed, those who move in crowds might be rather less exposed to invidious comparison; men and women who give themselves up to the life of the city might feel freed from the terrible conviction that their own persons were on trial.

We speak of the Parisian accent as being "characterless," just as we are rather amused by the still surviving little marks of Burgundy or Belgium in the r's and g's of the slippery habitués of Fomor's Casino. The more Parisian a young man becomes, the more he prefers neutral black to colour. A cassoulet in Paris has less garlic than a cassoulet prepared in Toulouse; lavish suppers in Lyons begin with thick slabs of *foie gras;* in Paris, with a few grains of caviare. From the provocations of diversity, the threat of the unknown, the man of the city seeks the protection of neutrality, of imperceptibly fitting in, of anonymity. We know the more anonymously he can conduct his life, the less he is prisoner of his past; this gift his mask makes him. Once released from the prison of the past, he may fortify himself even with a lie, like those gentlemen who having conquered the Exchange suddenly discover a "de" before their names, this *particule* found lying in one of the streets leading to the Tuileries. Others simply forget, forget themselves as they were, suffocating from village gossip at dusk. Only a madman demands of strangers: justify yourself! Thus I have begun to think the key to freedom today is to become lost, one amongst many, in a crowd.

No one in it might notice, unfortunately, that the face of a man wearing a mask is contracted in pain, that his heart is heavy; Pascal did not take sufficient account of this fact. He thought one had to flee to a monastery to find solitude. But to feel truly lonely one needs to find a sufficiently dense mass of human beings, and to plunge into their midst whilst under the spell of great sorrow or great joy. If by chance a man tells strangers of his grief, they are at best likely to reply with a polite murmur and pass on. The crowd itself makes this mask against pain for everyone, and the sufferer pays the price for the freedom of all.

In the rue de Beauce one evening I came upon a woman seated on a bench. She leant forward, held her head in her hands, the picture of bereavement, abandonment, despair—one could not know. Still a provincial, I went up to her, but she waved me away, either from fear or because I was interrupting. Twenty steps beyond her was a café, where I seated myself and watched, afraid for her and unoffended at my rebuff. I drank a coffee, she continued immobile. Dusk fell; I began to be bored, in truth, but the early evening was pleasant, and I ordered a second coffee, no longer attending. As I was in the midst of my own reverie, the unknown woman passed me by. Though her eyes were red from tears, the tears had dried, and, as she passed, a smile flickered upon her face for a moment in recognition. She entered a shop, where I saw her, as I made my way home to feed my cat; she was trying on a scarf. She could have gone, instead, to confession; in a village the cause of her tears would have been known to everyone; in the rue de Beauce she was left in grief to herself. Pascal imagined that in solitude we might finally come to know God with a pure faith. Within the solitude of a modern city, we may instead become better acquainted with the just proportions of our pain.

You, a man who conceives and executes buildings, reach for the pen on your drawing table, you lift it, you turn your face to mine, hovering with interest next to your chair, you ask politely, "And now?"

You are relentless, in your gentle way.

"Tell me, my dear Charles, how to draw a building which promotes a spirit of one amongst many? How might I thus relieve our fellows of the oppression of being judged? Come, Sir, I am ready to perform this good work."

I say I had not quite reached my conclusion, which is that creatures freed of being judged might be less inclined to judge others, or even to require rules of judgement. You nod equably, the pen poised still above white paper. I urge you to grant that anonymity might be thus the secret of modern agnosticism, that in learning to live thus one amongst many we surrender our need for metaphysical reassurance.

You sigh, your pen lowers to its resting place. "I grant all that."

At least, Father, I think I could prevent you from drawing a mistake. Consider that architecture of iron and glass, the architecture we celebrate in the name of Progress: consider the arcade.

The arcades have spread their tentacles throughout modern Paris, radiating from the Palais-Royal to the north, east and west. The Passage des Panoramas, the Galerie Vivienne, the Galerie d'Orléans: these have become glass capillaries of the city. London has its Burlington Arcade, its Royal Opera Arcade; more primitive in construction than many of the iron and glass creations in Paris, yet also triumphs over water and cold. One hears of plans to place the centre of the Eternal City under glass; the broken columns and fragments of ceremonial statuary would indeed then become eternal, no longer citizen-objects in nature.

The *terrasse* is open to the elements, as are the old squares of the city.

The fabricator of arcades may by contrast point with pride to his glass roofs which keep out smut and smoke. He invokes fashion: a lady in the Galerie d'Orléans promenades without fear that her dress will be grimed. He invokes more serious advantages: an infant in his perambulator breathes easily in an arcade, without choking on coal dust.

The lessons derived from Nature by the Great Romantics have no application in this building. Man, far from suffering at the hands of blind Nature, laughs at its terrors. The arcade nullifies cold, its brilliant lighting erases night; man admits into this architecture of control only what is pleasing—tropical plants, for example, to decorate the corridors of his life under glass.

This abolition of rude Nature suggests to the inhabitants of arcades that they may similarly rule or revise their own lives. I mean nothing cryptic. Last year I attended a re-dedication of the Galerie d'Orléans for commercial and sociable purposes; it had been previously converted to a shelter during the cholera epidemic. The Mayor of Paris spoke. Before a great throng of elegant ladies and gentlemen gathered in the central aisle of the arcade, surrounded by a bevy of other dignitaries in white and blue robes, the Mayor proclaimed:

> Consecrated in pain, this arcade is once again a temple of pleasure. Never shall we forget the terrible afflictions of those unfortunates who died here, but this little palace shall not remind us—it cannot, for its light and airy canopy suggest only peace, its aisles only the most refined intercourse, the precincts enclosed here containing objects made with the most devoted care . . .

Official events invite a good deal of wheezing. Other robed figures used words like "temple," "devoted," "consecrate" in connexion with the place of commerce. I took it all seriously. The arcade re-made to its original form, all marks of history abolished, as though the months of plague never occurred. The church no longer a believable site for prayer, the shop counter now an altar, man praying to the products of his own labour, praying to his hats, his gloves and his chocolates. Like the building, he manufactures these objects of his own devotion.

My request is that you stay your pen until you consider what might happen to the soul of an artist who is the provisioner of these icons. Unlike Faust he has no need of the Devil. By mechanical invention he has accomplished one of the great tasks of traditional religion. He has armed humanity in its struggle against Nature, armed it with glass rather than prayers. Is he almost, then, a god?

In general fabricators may be capable of anything, great exploits, yes, but also great horrors. They cannot imagine discomfort or pain implacable; they have lost the fear of nature, removed from the tempering influence of storms, plagues of smuts, foul air—plague itself is an erasable memory, like a mistake of drawing. Whenever they want to work or to amuse themselves the world is available. These sanitary men may become innocent perpetrators of the most horrible outrages, unable to imagine the pain they inflict.

I grant this is extreme. Let us say, then, that the creator of arcades faces the conundrum of the actresses at the artists' entrance to the Comédie-Française. Both are threatened by believing too much in themselves, the architect triumphing over wind and rain, the actress rousing thousands to howl and weep when she pretends to be an Egyptian queen. Such extraordinary conquests must influence any heart regarding itself. The prig is not well disposed towards men and women in the arts; this pair, however, can furnish him with whatever proofs of strength he may require.

Aristotle tells us that drama, and by extension the other illative arts, requires a willing suspension of disbelief. The practitioner of these arts must know, on the contrary, how to suspend *belief* in himself or herself. It is this suspension which allows a man or woman to enter into another life, absorbed in the part played. Franz Liszt has declared, "The concert is . . . myself." Surely not. A musician must also surrender to making music composed by someone else. An originating artist, a romancer, playwright, poet must possess the power to create distinct persons, none his own simple reflection. To look into a glass, expecting it to be a mirror, and to discover it is a window—this is the peculiar surprise for the artist, the irony separating his intentions from his acts.

A truly great actress is in need of this gift. Once so endowed, confronted with the outstretched arms of her admirers at the stage door, she might smile to herself and at herself for having provoked the scene. Indeed, because she is not swept up in the adulation of her person, she looks out *at* this collection of men; she distinguishes amongst the fripperous, the quiet and unhappy, the lecherous, the distraught and the resigned. Because she is looking at them when they are caressing her with flowers and gifts, somehow, someday on the stage she will make use of their hands, lips and eyes. Her face might recall Lord Byron's portrait at this moment; looking outwards will clear the brow.

I want to conclude my homily—yes, I admit it! another homily—by maintaining that the architect must regard buildings as a writer his characters, an actress her public. Even more than these artists, he needs to be able to look outwards, look for difference, acquire that capacity when gazing in a glass suddenly to discover it is a window, not a mirror. For his art is most of all concerned with the vast field of physiognomies, characters and oddities gathered in a city. These faces in the crowd are the words in his dictionary. How shall he display them, combine them, compose them within volumes of glass, iron and stone to speak the city? An architect who can see only reflections of himself will deploy these human forces in space so that his work will become ever more like a signature, the "words" always spelling his own name.

I would not presume to tell you how to draw. I do not know what the following phrases suggest even to your eye: an architecture of irony, a building responsive to complexities. Those of us deprived of artful eyes can at least recognise this living architecture once it exists—in the Café Turc, modest as it is, for example. Could you conceive a space grown out of it, larger, bolder, more Byronic? Those of us who are your peculiar "words" would know you had spoken in our names.

I imagine this might be particularly difficult at the present time. The architect is more flattered, more seduced than any queen of tragedy. His is the only necessary art. And yet I left the Galerie d'Orléans with a sense of foreboding. This time the original signature has been retraced; the architect who takes such care to sign his name can expect, however, that people will have little regard for preserving what he has done, since he has little interest in reaching out to them.

In more magical times, when the gods seemed to dwell on Mount Olympus, leap from rocks to heaven, appear in the world only to quit their own dead bodies, in these more credulous times the errors of religion could justly be attributed to man's sense of weakness. In his frailty he sought to make of his religion an engine of compensatory strength. Today creation has replaced creed. Man has finally the means to believe in his own works, and thus he can in turn believe in himself. Will this faith become a vice? Faith in himself become indifference to others, masterful indifference? Will there arise a new order of solitude, entirely opposed to the desperate spiritual withdrawal risked by Pascal? I suppose that is the moral of my own story. The temptations of faith are greater for those better endowed than am I, endowed especially in your art. The tempted no longer live one amongst many.

In the Hôtel de France

From the Diary of Anne Mercure
November 1836

3 November 1836

What a daring evening! I had hardly thought she could show herself in Paris, the family is so incensed. But then, no one would think to receive in a hotel for provincial merchants, and with the exception of Liszt and the Dudevant woman, she received no one anyone knew. This Hôtel de France is not positively vile; large, clean rooms, and although it is on the commercial end of the street the noise is tolerable. But the furniture! Little white lace bits everywhere on horsehair, on horsehair settees, horsehair rugs, horsehair tables for all I know, an entire stable draped in lace. In the sitting-room the enormous mirror, that enormous mirror over such a miserly small fireplace. Perhaps the mirror led her to the rooms; Marie always did like catching glimpses of herself. How could I ever forget that day she dressed in M. d'Agoult's uniform, pacing restlessly back and forth before the big mirror in the boudoir at Croissy? "That's what I needed: trousers and a whip!" She was beautiful then, a lion tamer, and after all her sufferings she is still a beautiful woman.

We spoke of baby Blandine, to whom I urged Marie to give her own name, as she is still legally bound to Charles; anyway a baby named d'Agoult will cause less comment. I encouraged her, and she, once so proud, clasped me to her bosom. It was a beautiful time, that house party at Croissy, the pear trees were in flower, the sea smelt so fresh; I think I wore organdy that year, no, organdy was '20, '21 was crêpe and my best one was a brown Chinese crêpe with white panels. All the world paid us

homage, Normandy so *far* from Paris, I was the friend of the granddaughter of a Duchess, far far from here amongst all those shy, tall men, but when
she called me "my dear Anne," I was obliged to curtsey. "Your Ladyship."
Poor Marie! She has found we are something more than playing the old
game, she with her bastard baby. Also urged her to contest any move for
an annulment of the marriage, although she wishes to submit to the annulment as a demonstration of love for M. Liszt. "My contempt will be proof
against all insolence!" When she gave way to this foolishness I saw for a
moment again that young lady, flicking her whip before the mirror, hoping
for lightning.

Nearly dawn. It *was* organdy. Organdy was '21, and I wore the powder-
blue dress with the answering shawl in grey. Sometimes I wonder if there
is any remedy. Think the following:

Stop worrying about money. There is enough money.

Take more interest in Frederick's upright pavilion. Tell him it is
brilliant, it will make his name.

Punish Cécile for playing with Adèle's powder. Adèle very angry
over this.

I was early in the "salon," as I suppose one has to call the dainty stable.
We plunged into the story of her trials, her children, her etc., as soon as
I came, the master of Suite 3A of the Hôtel de France still about in the
streets. Then Marie was flooded by a swarm of extras she had chosen to
furnish her return from Geneva—that is the trouble with these modern
rooms, they are so small you think five people is a crowd. There was a
"Baron" d'Eckstein who droned on about upholding the Church against
the "infidelities" of Lamennais—*such* a felicitous expression in the drawing-
room of this hostess. How can these people cross the street? However, the
man of the waxed moustaches is no Baron and very much, unless I am
mistaken, a Jew. A fat deputy called Berryer came in, Marie evidently feels
genuine affection for him, he is a Legitimist. Returned; he took her hand
easily, no long communing looks. On his heels there was that gaggle, it was
probably ten or twelve, of people she barely knows, I nor the world never,
tumbling in to meet the famous pianist who remained elsewhere. Marie and
I were the only women present in this rag-bag until the entrance of Madame Dudevant—who insists now on being called by her writing name, so
that only two-and-a-half women were present. (Nota bene: Cook has served
turnips two nights running.) She was no stranger, this Sapphist, she is the
one who entranced Marie Dorval a while ago, the one I came upon clasped

in deep embrace on Dorval's couch at the Comédie. Evidently "George Sand" remembered me, as I could not help laughing then at these two ladies disporting themselves like little girls, for tonight she blushed and then turned away coldly.

Madame Dudevant was surrounded by the little men who gabbled at her, and I suppose Marie was provoked by the stir caused by the entrance of the authoress, but, although ill becoming a lion tamer, Marie now assumed her spiritual-seeker face, speaking vehemently of *Obermann* by Sénancour. The invited moths continued to swarm around the other flickering flame, the light of a famous as well as infamous candle (nota bene) and I was obliged to remind her that she had spoken to me of this volume for the last three years, and that although I had not yet read it, I was fully aware of the story and the profound changes it had wrought in Marie's own life, and further, that as she was fully occupied now, I would leave her. She was far too distracted by the silent, and I admit, powerful presence of Madame Dudevant to feel the barb of my malice, which I thought would recall her to her senses. In the presence of an emphatic personage we should offer the alternative, pleasurable relief; let the Sapphist point a finger to make an emphasis, we will roll the wrist languidly—this is the way to manage moths, if one could even bear to think of the lepidoptera as pets. In any event, she bade me a warm farewell, asked me to return soon with Frederick. Madame Dudevant in the midst of her admirers noticed in one flash of her eyes my leaving, then draped her hand on the arm of her chair more gracefully.

I really must stop and I have hardly begun. It was a wasted evening, as I had wanted to speak to Marie about Adèle, who must do something, anything. Marie could easily take her as a companion on her travels. Although the company Marie keeps is hardly prim, still there is her name, and the fame of her lover more than makes up for the breach of decorum. I am sure Adèle would find a suitable husband in one of these foreign places, Marie would help her; Adèle would simply be the tall, fair girl with erect carriage and proud manners attached to the suite of the Comtesse d'Agoult. Yes, it would be best for her. And also for me. That is the sad truth—and also for Frederick and for me.

siesta (nota bene, Spanish)

Sister Agnès came for Cécile then at ten, but she had promised for eleven. I measure even the hours for my little precious one, who also wept. Cécile shrank back this time the moment Sister Agnès came into the room, crying "Maman, do not let her have me!" The little one hid in the folds of my crinoline and would not come out. She is too old to scratch or bite, of course, and not at all such a girl, but still too young to hide her grief at parting from me.

Sister Agnès has cheese-breath. Adèle, who was also in the room, advanced slowly and presented her forehead to be kissed. When Sister Agnès leant over to kiss my girl, Adèle sniffed and shuddered slightly. How graceful my girl! And this shudder, it made me see, her breasts are large enough to tremble, already.

We three paused in the room together, Adèle, the little one buried within my dress, and the fat, odorous virgin who was to conduct Cécile to school. I suppose I know why at eighteen there are no suitors, eighteen, already I was carrying her, already here and yet so often it seems one is here only on a visit, shortly to go back, all undone. Adèle spoke tartly the words which brought Cécile to release me and to emerge. You see it in that wonderfully straight carriage, her stare is withering when she is displeased.

Frederick came in half an hour after Cécile had departed, thinking he would hand her over to the Sister—if only! All would have been calm with my little darling. But it was just the three of us, and so another, longer, more terrible silence, which Adèle finally broke by leaving the room. This moment has absolutely determined me on her joining the entourage of the Comtesse d'Agoult, even for a few months, that is all we need.

Of course I have no idea really of how Marie lives—indeed, we can be told a woman has aged twenty years in two, that our seamstress is now the mistress of the King, that an old château has been re-decorated top to bottom, we still see it as it was. Instead of reclining on horsehair chairs (I should have thought of it at once: the little lace doilies cover spots from the greasy heads of commercial travellers), I saw Marie in her old home, not her husband's country house but the wild, tumble-down manor of her own grandmother Flavigny, perched on the sea coast, damp salt air you could breathe so freely, the pine fires which always smoked in the grates, nothing ever dry. This is where Adèle would go. She would find a good husband, and she would come to her senses.

At luncheon I told Frederick of my plan. I said that perhaps we might send Adèle to Marie the next time she travelled. My friend suddenly vanished. "That would be to acknowledge her accusations." Mr Prig did not look at me, he looked at an invisible person sitting at table who I imagined would reply to him, "What a horrible girl! To accuse you of indecency. She will pay for this!" But I was the only person dining there that day, and she is my daughter.

So I threw a little temper, not entirely feigned. "It is enough that I do not believe Adèle on this point—my faith in you should be enough. She has never wanted you in the house; now, you understand this, you must, now that there are no young men for her, now she wants to drive you away, just as before she wanted me alone, or not to have anyone . . ." My temper overtook me, and I wept, I wept once more, cursed with fountains of hot burning water overflowing my eyes, and he cannot bear to see me weeping, it upsets him so he cannot work. Once more I imagined Adèle and Frederick in the drawing-room. She hisses, "Don't ever try to touch me again; isn't Maman beautiful enough any more?" That was his word. I cannot, I will not hear my daughter hissing. At luncheon I rounded on Frederick, "Think! It was not you she was attacking. About this accusation, the only person who matters is *me*. I know you have always behaved with the utmost propriety towards her, towards everyone."

Then a calm sensible voice told me, "To send Adèle away is to admit to her, at least, that she has disturbed us, that we cannot bear her in her mother's house. If she is unhappy here, her duty is first to apologise—to you as well as to me."

There is some justice in this; I saw Frederick's face again. However, it is my daughter's future, not his pride which matters. As always when there is a scene, I had driven him to seek repose. He has left the house without taking coffee.

Passed the afternoon blocking the *Phèdre*, which took too long. I apologise for calling him Mr Prig, which I have never and will never call him to his face.

Saw in the morning the last of Cécile for two months, fought with Frederick at lunch; it was only proper that Adèle should pull one of her sulks at tea-time. This was due, evidently, to her lesson with Nourrit. Adolphe presses her to master the sudden pianissimo and equally sudden fortissimo, without which there is no good pathetic style; she claims Adolphe is too demanding of her. I explained once more that an effort with her voice now will be repaid a hundred-fold in purity and endurance throughout her life; listen to Malibran, or the father, old Garcia! Adolphe only follows their example. So of course she sulked.

At last I have relief here, in the dressing-room. Vignolet's have sent two more heavenly rice powders, one scented with primrose, I think, the other made in flakes which you crush in the hand. I powdered Pussy with the primrose; we looked quite smart, especially when we flopped our tail about, releasing little clouds of powder all about us. How Cécile would adore it! What else? Yes, I also took the dogs for a walk in the Bois, the strangest fashion, but everyone has taken to it. You hold the dogs, English-style, by the end of a rope; I've stolen a wonderful silken cord used in the strangulation scene of *Malatesta*, and tied Max and Pierre at each end, myself holding them by the middle. They (and, I may say, I) are adorable in procession, as the tassels at the ends of the cord hang down under the knot tied beneath the doggies' chins, jiggling as they romp. I decided to wear the beaded white muslin for the walk, with the light blue shawl with beaded fringe; just a little echo of the dog tassels. Max bit Madame de Suze's poodle today.

One thing I've forgotten to add about the soirée at Marie's, perhaps the strangest. Mademoiselle Le Normand was there! Without her cards naturally; Marie would never permit any form of cards, even for a séance, even in a hotel room. I know this: whatever happens to Marie, should she run away with a bear, should she take up the polka, or Poles, she will do it as the daughter of the House of Flavigny. Mademoiselle Le Normand was present in her private capacity, though the shameless old thing let drop her "services," to the Duke of Wellington after the attempted assassination, to La Beauharnais, of course to Marie herself. As a further advertisement, Mademoiselle in company wears the square-cut bonnet of the mediaeval abbesses which serves as her peculiar professional costume in her own rooms.

She leant over to me to confide, the bonnet enclosing my face in its immense visor, that she had predicted it all to Marie in '34, "her entire destiny." It is a divine conceit, to bury the face of the confidante in one's own hat, so naturally I asked who is her milliner, and Le Normand, the silly old sow, pouted.

Well, soon she was more than furious, it was when Major Pictet came in. The Major has taken up Zoroaster "definitively," he says. I enquired who is M. Zoroaster, as it seems all Paris has gone mad for Arabs, and they are so hard to tell apart in native costume without further information. The Major launched into an explanation which became an entire lecture, for Marie had prepared a rum-and-lime punch which was brought while he talked, and of course the dear thing had a few cups which emboldened him to tell all about Zoroaster who was indeed an Arab but an ancient one and quite attuned to the mystical harmonies of the universe and so on. The Major discovered him last month in a book left behind in the Hôtel de l'Union in Chamonix.

Well, Le Normand evidently felt the Major, a mere amateur, menaced her borders. She marshalled her forces, stared into the blue flames dancing above the punch (nota bene, which Marie knows how to keep alight for the longest time, find out the secret), stared into the flames, threw up her hands in horror, very well done, and exclaimed, "I see the ghost of Zoroaster!" At this, a light, boyish voice behind asked, "You do?" It was Liszt, who had suddenly appeared, and he was taking the whole thing seriously, clutching his hair with his hands at the sides of his head, his eyes eager, he who of all of us, a colleague as it were of Le Normand's, he should have known better.

"Yes," the old frog laid it on thick now that Master was home, her voice trembling, "the ghost of Zoroaster is in the room at this moment, an astral force hovering, warning, blessing. He says . . ." At this moment the alcohol in the punch was providentially exhausted and we were plunged into darkness, only Madame Sand's cigar glowing. Marie whispered "Warning, blessing!" Madame Sand sniggered, and a hotel servant marched in unbidden with large candelabra in both hands.

Perhaps it is my age. They thrill to ghosts, to horrors, to faint voices, to portents, to the abyss, to the sublime, to poetry one must shout, can't speak, to the infernal, gobble, gobble, my heart is bursting, aching—while outside the slop man is carting away the contents of the Hôtel de France chamber pots, the windows are open, and one is choking from the fumes while groaning over the spirit of Zoroaster. When I was a girl we wanted to be *amused*.

Were Marie's adorable Franz to fall in the public imagination she would fall much farther, from the Mistress of Genius to slut. Wasn't she that awful woman who left her husband and one daughter, a year after the other died, to live with Franz Liszt? Before Thalberg came he was considered quite something; whatever happened to him? Marie admitted last night her uncle will no longer receive her, as he has taken up Thalberg. There is much she can do to guard her position, however, about which I had hoped also to speak to Marie, until the advent of the "George Sand" and the visit of the spirits prevented it. Soon: the first months of scandal are the ones which require the most adroitness. Establish yourself as wronged, or convey the impression that you have chosen dishonour in the eyes of the prudes to avert a greater familial shame, as we did, and opinion will gradually settle in your favour. Marie has, I think by accident, chosen the perfect moment to return; by the time the winter season opens, she can contrive a *reason* for her conduct, and the burden will be upon d'Agoult, the poor puppy. Yet she clouds her mind with all this morbid spiritualism—the ghosts, the mystical union of their love, its immortality, his celestial this, her astral that.

Well darling, to be amused you must be amusing, and at your age to be amusing you must feel rested and look pert. So to nap.

4 November 1836

Frederick has had bad news from the man Birkenshaw. The beams or whatever they are, like the rails of the steam carriages, cannot be made long enough for his vertical arcade, so he will have to think of something else. He has no word from the other one, Fairburn, but is also afraid this Englishman will steal his idea. I tried to divert him at supper by suggesting the livery for the men who operate the pulleys of the stage—and that at least is clever, it is so fatiguing to walk up even two flights that men who hoist you up on a platform four, six, even eight storeys would be a great boon, especially in the evening when all movement is dangerous to one's costume. Anyhow I told him these servants must look different from footmen, since they are in any event arm-men (nota bene), and leaning over in britches to turn a wheel or crank or whatever would be hideously uncomfortable, as well as soon deforming to the nether garment. So I have the idea to dress them in *Turkish Pantaloons,* bright red Turkish pantaloons like the eunuchs in harems, billowing and gathered at the ankles so that the haunches are enormous but the legs tapering to Turkish slippers with upturned toes; the torsos could be white blouses with answering leg-of-mutton sleeves perhaps. Men on each side of the platform, rising up and subsiding with the turn of the wheel like sea foam, so divine! so stylish! One ascends one's glass tower with these silken servants below, ever smaller as one ascends; by the time you reach the top you cannot even hear the swish of silk. And perhaps the attendant on the platform could be dressed in a silk burnoose of white, to complete the effect without overdoing it.

Well, I did manage to amuse Frederick with all this, though he talks about how practical it all is, a matter of homes and offices in the sky, so there could be twice, three times the number of people there are now in Paris in the same space. I don't like to say it to him of course, but I don't quite see why this is such a good idea.

6 November 1836

Last night at the Grand-Véfour Adolphe provoked me by all his talk of the moral labourer, the good family man in our decadent, effete world. Adolphe of all people! "Lemaître," I said, "created Robert Macaire on a whim, by accident. You argue another character because you are jealous. And I know you have a secret rôle you keep from us, The Hero of the Sewers, The Prince of Carters which you prepare by singing and dancing with the riff-raff."

Until last month Adolphe's enthusiasm kept him within the temple erected by the followers. They have taken a charming old house in the rue de Payenne for their rites, or congregations, as I believe their chanting and praying to the spirit of rational industry is properly called; and how can one object, it is perfectly harmless and perhaps even in its own way pleasant. Moreover, I know my Adolphe; he carefully waited for the summer heat to end before taking up the call to spread M. de Saint-Simon's promises to the people at the barriers and markets, and so brilliant to think of a choir composed of waifs, strays and drunkards. He claims Music and Saint-Simonianism together are infallibly reforming, and it merely happened that this choir of socialist regenerates has attracted a certain notice.

I am sick of turnips. Dinner has made me positively bilious.

Sweet Adolphe! He gazed last night at the table so sadly and said, "Is it quite our place to look down, I mean from the moral point of view, on the family life of these poor labourers?" and then he raised out his hand to me in that Egyptian way he learnt for *The Pharaoh*, the palm turned up in appeal. Well, I wasn't having any of that! The others in the party got between us, it all was straightened out, and my part of the apology was to go hear the chorus sing this morning.

We left the house just before noon. Nota bene: the green hat goes back tomorrow morning to Gallet. Timing is important. He assembles his forces at the hour reserved for the midday meal allotted to the few of them who labour; but they sing before drinking anything, for Adolphe says that after one glass he may lose them. We calculated the exact time my brougham needed to arrive at that little street in La Villette from which we would walk down to the Canal de l'Ourcq. How had he managed in the first place?

"I thought, choose either one of the barriers or the canal, because that's where I'd find gentlemen at leisure. Although the Canal de l'Ourcq stinks" —which explained why so large an eau de cologne atomiser at his feet in the carriage—"it has more children, so we could have a balanced choir of high and low voices."

I said that this didn't really answer my question. How did he *do* it?

"Oh, darling, I just arrived at the edge of the canal and asked, 'Who wants to sing?' Wasn't that clever? Of course I was frightened, but it was thrilling, and I do mean thrilling, rough strong menacing men who looked so surprised that several asked at the same time, 'Sing what?' That started me off. Now, Anne my pussycat," he said, "you must treat this very seriously and, please!, we are very respectful towards me, the Maestro. I am to them a man without past, friends, money—simply a great artist."

We alighted at the little square in La Villette at twenty past noon. The five minutes on foot to the Canal de l'Ourcq seemed like an hour to me. I had dressed entirely in brown. There was a single plank down the very middle of the path which I had to negotiate like a tight-rope walker at the Variétés in order not to trod in the filth on both sides of the plank, filth oozing slowly down the street towards the canal sewer. No one tried to push me, but the bare-foot urchins cavorting in the sewage shouted threats and curses, hoping I would lose my balance. Mutton-fat Adolphe of course tight-roped perfectly easily over the wood boards, the atomiser held out in one hand and for balance a silk handkerchief held in the other. As really I was becoming rather distraught, to divert both the urchins and me, my friend struck up popular airs from *Le Roi d'Italie*, in the last street changing to the Kyrie from a Gluck Mass. This did delight the little beasts: church music from a fat man trying to keep a lady balanced above slops.

Well, we arrived. Where, you ask? We arrived at the planking over the newest canal sewer hole! M. Adolphe Nourrit's Workingman's and Popular Choir practises in the air on the roof over the ordure of Paris! I tried to imagine taking a big breath for singing a long line. However. Nearly a hundred people waited in the square to go through this ordeal. Adolphe has arranged matters so that the choir turns away from some sort of vile pipe coming up through the boards of the pit; the artists face him to the south, where there is that little pothouse. The proprietor of the pothouse has lent Adolphe a barrel to stand on as podium. When Adolphe later spoke of this man as saintly, I was confused, until my cunning Machiavelli explained that not only was Maestro Nourrit blocking the entrance in so placing the podium, but that the good man within had assented to this loss of trade in lending the beer barrel. Saintly, or even more deeply clever than my mutton—surely this hideous part of the canal would otherwise not be so populated, and after an hour of hymns and songs, all great artists need liquid refreshment.

As we stood on the construction over the sewer Adolphe was greeted warmly if with little ceremony by the older men (how the old jou-jou glowed being one of the fellows!), and I was presented. The workers shifted their feet, suddenly embarrassed, even ashamed; they were going to sing in front of a Lady. Adolphe had presented me as his "cousin," since the word "friend" to these deeply moral people means "mistress." I saw they might all just drift away, indeed some were already making excuses or heading for the pothouse before the barrel was put in place, so I declared that not only was I the Maestro's cousin but also his pupil and that I would wager any man present that I could sing louder. Great applause! Clever, clever me!

In any event, the same creatures who tried to make me fall and who laughed at the Kyrie now had their hideously grimy little faces turned up towards my turnip-thick friend standing on the beer barrel. At first it was droll; Adolphe had assigned some of the older men to sing the accompaniment, bupp-bupp-bupp, poing-buppy-buppy-bupp, while the younger ones and the high-voiced did the melodies. They started with "Man will ascend to Progress," and badly; whatever pleasure the dear late Comte de Saint-Simon may offer in the library of the rue de Payenne he has a tin ear; one really *couldn't* sing "Man will ascend to Progress." Adolphe had them start with this, which is the elevating part of his work, while they were fresh, and then fed them as a reward what they really seemed to like. "Gentlemen, the long one!" he announced.

This proved to be "Jesu, Joy of Man's Desiring," a beautiful tune if strange for us to sing. But what, when you think of it, should it matter to these creatures whether it be a Protestant or a Catholic hymn? The boys! One saw on those faces such ardent, passionate surrender as Adolphe led them through "Jesu, Joy of Man's Desiring." A great wen oozing pus on the cheek of one, a red bandage over the eye of another, all of them with the blackest fingernails, all the hands hanging at their sides, hanging down to puny thighs covered with rags soaked in urine, their own or others, these boys belong to God more, for the few moments they can spare, so much more than the little blond choirboys in their short robes who sing in the church where the Sisters chaperone the girls. These take to Adolphe, who is, when all is said and done, absurd because he makes for them a moment of peace, these the abandoned of God.

Of course I began to sing as well; the tessitura of this hymn happens to be good for me. I rose above them and soon some of the men were clapping, while the boys continued to sing with me. When I finished the second stanza, I noticed my jet bracelet was missing. They had moved on to sing together the Kyrie Adolphe had chanted as we moved down the street. This was too hard for them, so I had to help again, and in leading them through the notes I forgot my loss—which amounts to little anyway.

"Don't ever try to touch me again! Isn't Maman beautiful enough any more?" The fear of the abyss! It's not Marie-twaddle!

All the old longing to hold a little one warm flooded me once more, I wanted to clean the running sore of the little boy with the wen. It was magic, it must have been just after Cécile had come back from Nurse, to return home alone and go up to their room, to sit in that wooden chair beside their cribs, listening to them breathe in their sleep, the thud of a drayman and his horse every so often outside, sitting next to them until I, too, would doze, the three of us all breathing together. It was magic. Adolphe saw I was moved; when we finished, only a few of the children scampering round us as we moved back to the carriage, I heard him say behind me, "I knew you would understand, Anne, I knew you would." But I have nothing to say to him.

10 November 1836

Frederick has again received more news, making him impatient once again for England. The man Paxton has caused the Duke of Devonshire to begin an enormous conservatory on his estates, this Duke being evidently so rich that the man Paxton can follow his fancies without a worry about the expense. Frederick burns to return, push aside Paxton and convince the Duke to try a vertical glass tower. I went carefully; I remarked only that the countryside might not best show off his tower, that it would be more impressive built here in the middle of Paris. His visitor told him there is much money now in England for improvements, more than when Frederick's father began. Then the visitor said there is money for the stations for the steam carriages, inflaming Frederick further, as these too will be created from iron and glass. I diverted conversation to the character of Paxton, whom they dissected gleefully as only the English can do it.

As usual I'm ahead of myself. This visitor is the Mr Rood who is Frederick's godfather. He did not tell Frederick these things to entice him back to England, and he did not come to Paris because mere letters had failed to tear the adored son away from the wicked woman. It was really so different than what I thought it would be, though I could not have done it without a little champagne and also a very long, hot bath first. The bath especially. Pussy came to sit on a chair next the tub, and I petted her while Arlette washed my hair. Then I dismissed Arlette and sank deep into the hot water with Pussy purring louder beside me.

One had two strategies to win him over for the evening.

1. Assume he is an invalid, as indeed Frederick says he partially is. This means a grey peau de soie skirt, perhaps a white bodice, and definitely a heavy, tasselled shawl, suggesting matronly comforts and requiring a complimentary cream soup, much roast fowl, and no cheese. If only Frederick

were a little more fripperous (frippered?) and would allow me I would dress him to suit, large sagging pantaloons in dark blue, I think, with a peau-de-soie flowered waistcoat and a heavy grey tweed jacket. The combined effect would be a mixture of sick-room and hunting lodge, yes you will get better, you feel most robust already.

2. He is an important man of affairs, again true. This makes more for a gaberdine and linen evening. In this case, a pannier skirt of light blue linen, a blouse either the cream silk from Lyons or, even better, the cream and black Chantilly silk with bouffant sleeves, and no shawl, with the high pearl choker, the one from Lemaître when Cécile was born. How dreadful. Anyhow, Frederick would be entirely in gaberdine—black, preferably. Turtle soup, sole with figs, lime sorbet, venison, late peas, definitely cheese, and two pies.

Frederick was as nervous as I before. Of course he said his reason was different, his concern for an elderly gentleman making a first voyage abroad, the inclement weather bad for his chest, etc. and so forth. We heated the salon and the dining room to near boiling and sealed every possible source of draughts. We spent so much time searching for draughts, which Frederick suddenly thought of when I emerged from my bath, that I had no time to do more than throw on whatever Arlette had immediately to hand, and of course Cook had gone her own way as usual about dinner, including those unspeakable vegetables yet once more, so it was only passing flights of fantasy anyhow, although I do like the idea of matching food to clothes. Anyhow. Frederick's worry was really the same as mine: what would the family friend and counselor think? Six years. We could have had a little boy already out of skirts by now.

We sat in the salon waiting for the sound of his carriage, both Frederick and I fidgeting and moving about the room distractedly. I heard the sound of gravel crunching and thought it must be Arlette or Cook in the garden for some purpose. But it was Mr Rood. Raymond announced a dusty frail old man with the most lustrous brown eyes, his dry skin blushing. He had forgotten the French words for "hansom cab," for "parallel to the quays," which is how Frederick told him to come from his lodgings, and so had walked, all the way from the inn next the law courts! Well, of course we have worried so much what he would think of us, we had forgotten that he was worried what we would think of *him*.

"Madame, a thousand apologies," he stammered out in that amazing French the English people speak, "I came to you on my feets, according to . . ."

I put the poor thing out of his misery by speaking English to cut him off, but this only made it worse.

"To think that my first night in Paris, I commit this solecism"—Frederick explained this and many other English words used by Monsieur Snigs, as I soon was bidden to call him—"this solecism which has undoubtedly ruined your dinner."

Frederick said that not at all.

"Please, my boy, do not spare my feelings with polite fictions, for it is undeniably," and here he withdrew from his waistcoat a watch concealed within a small silver turnip, "it is undeniably past eight-thirty."

I explained that in Paris no one supped before ten in the evening, at the earliest, and that he should feel no alarm. Monsieur Snigs transferred his stare to me.

"This, surely, is to subject the digestion to an extreme, if daily trial."

Frederick led the family friend away to wash. When they returned, Monsieur Snigs immediately returned to the subject of supper hours; hoping that I did not take his last remark in bad part, etc., but that "foreign manners" were difficult for him to imagine, having never travelled, and so, "it unfortunately is a condition of the human mind that what is unfamiliar appears unreasonable." He really does talk this way, and I wager he has always talked this way, even as a boy. I was charmed, entranced, seduced.

However, I was also rather stupid. I asked if Monsieur Snigs had ever discussed philosophy with Charles; it was nerves and having no one else we three knew, and the father is out of the question for Frederick.

"Madame, I have." A complete silence fell.

I think, or I thought, "This old one is still on the side of Charles, or I have reminded him that he ought to be." And if so, I was definitely stupid but the vibrations, as Mademoiselle Le Normand might have put it, were different. Spots of colour appeared in the old man's cheeks again, and then he broke the silence by saying,

"I came to maturity, Madame, in an age in which Resolution was all. Resolution and Discretion!" He could have been rebuking me or it could be entirely the other matter, whatever, I had displeased this testy man in stumbling upon a painful subject, but his courtesy is great; it was only a moment.

Frederick gradually became younger in the presence of his godfather. Soon he stopped speaking of "we" in discussing the work of the atelier; he began to dream aloud of what "I" want, "what I shall do," all the boyish infection of enthusiasm, of despair, of ambition which at first bound me to him: beginning again, the dream which is our greatest dream of pleasure and which he dreamt this evening for Monsieur Snigs and for me. At a moment when Frederick told of the making of the new embassy at the end of the rue de Rivoli my eyes met the eyes of Monsieur Snigs, his eyes shining from love and regret, as were, I know, my own. It was the communion of a moment's glance. We both loved Frederick for his poetry of beginning again.

At table Frederick told Monsieur Snigs all the curiosities he could think of for the old man to visit, with the same mounting flush. I whispered to Raymond to hold back the roast as long as possible; the spell was our house, our house of safety in the unknown city. The candles burnt lower in the dining-room, Raymond built up the fire and brought me my Spanish shawl, which Frederick made a great show of placing round my shoulders. I said nothing, the old man dozed momentarily, then smiled awake as Frederick explained now this street, now that habit. I who know a Paris Frederick cannot begin to imagine, I . . . no matter.

At midnight we called for my carriage to take the old man back to his lodgings. After his outburst at Charles, he had said so little, just a word or question now and then to prompt Frederick further. There was only one curious moment. Frederick had interrupted his own flow to ask me to describe Marie's evenings this autumn, which have become the talk of Paris. I feared the old man would find an exact description of the rag-tails in the rented rooms re-awakening suspicions of our own loose existence. But not at all. He was quite curious about Madame Sand's (as I suppose one must call her) cigar and clothing, and even more about Adolphe. "Having been weak-chested all my life, the power of singers naturally fascinates me." Of course this is his idea of what Paris should be, salons filled with cigar-smoking women, revolutionary singers of great physical power (!), so close and yet so far away from the room panelled in dark walnut in which we sipped cognac as the logs burnt into coals. Here is a thought: most of Marie's crowd are also tourists: Poles, Hungarians, Jews from Prussia or young men up from the provinces. They may have for years in imagination been rehearsing the parts they are now playing to universal comment. Monsieur Snigs asked me, rather hesitantly, if it would be possible to visit the Hôtel de France. I assured him that nothing would be easier; no cards were necessary.

"No cards! Astounding!" I did not explain. The old advocate has, I suspect, seen much, but her open house, her circus—it diverts our pleasure-seeking public, they do not too loudly condemn her ménage, because one cannot visit the house of a woman one has vehemently branded as immoral, a point of Parisian life which Frederick did not make to his godfather. Still, she is in no position to demand *cards*.

As Frederick has also expressed a desire to visit Marie's cenacle, we agreed to go in five days' time, on the sixteenth, together. I hardly credit it, which is why I promised to Monsieur Snigs at the carriage door to bid the revolutionary Adolphe also to attend.

It is beginning to lighten; once more diary has robbed me of my beauty sleep. Only to add that I gave myself to Frederick tonight as though we too had begun again, no ugly rumours in the house, Frederick, whose arms smell of pine-soap. I cannot bear the thought of anything being different, even if it means he cannot quite have everything he wants—who, after all, does? There is enough work for him here in Paris.

12 November 1836

Adèle was presented briefly this morning to Monsieur Snigs. He treated her as though she were a person who had no relation to myself. He said in English, "Young lady, it is a pleasure to meet one so pleasing as yourself so early in my sojourn to Paris. Although ignorant here, I know London as well as any man living, and would be delighted to answer whatever questions you have about that equally strange city. Madame Mercure, would you have the kindness to translate to Mademoiselle Adèle my salutation, if perchance her English resembles my French?"

She behaved passably, replying briefly, but in his language, and that effort was enough for him. Indeed, her countenance softened at thus being addressed as a woman in her own right, and she permitted her back to sag a little.

In the afternoon there was a tea, the two brothers and the godfather, which the last rehearsals kept me from although expressly invited. They went to the tea-shop in the Place Dauphine, not the place next to the Madeleine which would have amused Monsieur Snigs, everyone wearing hairy tweed, which is uncomfortable and will never last in fashion; you *cannot* feel chic if you are obliged continually to scratch yourself. They "took tea" (why do the English "take" something which properly one drinks?) near the law-court lodgings, as the old one swears he will walk until he learns to speak. Frederick says there was a "scene."

"Tell me!" I commanded him, crawling more deeply under the covers.

"Oh, nothing, just one of those family things, but Snigs became heated, and it was embarrassing, in the middle of the tea-room. It was nothing," says Mr English who dies of shame in "scenes" involving himself but loves all gossip about other people's quarrels.

"Frederick!"

"If you really must know, it was about my money. I have done as I promised you; today I spoke to both of them about it."

Promised me! I Never, Never wanted a centime! I kicked off the covers, jumped up, anger kept me more than warm enough. I began to accuse him of making me truly a harlot in their eyes, but Frederick pushed me roughly back into the bed. Our usual recoil, and he continued as if nothing amiss had happened.

"Snigs thinks legally about legal matters. He simply commented that we might encounter a problem in revising this sort of legacy in favour of a foreign national." I will never understand these things. "We were quite mistaken. It was, you see, Charles who brought out 'What will Father say?'"

Monsieur Snigs evidently became annoyed at this point. Frederick's money from the aunt was passed by the aunt's own solicitor; Monsieur Snigs was not consulted. Now this good sum can be disposed of outside the family again, even though traditionally these free accounts stay in families. Monsieur Snigs said whatever their sentiments the practical fact was they were not in control. Frederick rounded on him; Monsieur Snigs spread out his hands in apology, saying it had nothing to do with Frederick and me, it was some foolishness between the father and the mother's sister, and in finishing his gesture knocked over the salver with the tea-pot and the cream. Waiters in the English tea-room evidently hovered uncertainly, not quite understanding what was happening, since the family spoke in English.

If I understand, at this point Charles said the family must remain together somehow. What a man! He talks of the future of the family, he, who has begun to *dress* as carefully as Adolphe. He actually said, "What about our own children, if we have any?"

"I informed Charles I already have two daughters."

Once when Marie and I were walking beside the sea, it must have been just before our first dance at Mereuil, I remember that I kindly explained to her that the more you love, the clearer things become. They say Frederick is ambitious, he is spoilt; even before Adèle lunged I suspected he had become bored with me, why not, after six years it would only be natural; then he thought nothing of proposing we remove to London the moment he heard about Paxton; it is true that I have begun to wrinkle. "I informed Charles I already have two daughters." Frederick and I looked at each other for a long moment—the only thing I could think to ask Frederick is how the two of them took this.

"Here is where matters truly began to boil." Now that he was over the hard part, the embarrassing part, which consisted of no more and no less than affirming his love to be honourable, the love of a gentleman, Frederick sunk in with relish to retailing the embarrassment of the others. "When the waiters had cleared away, Charles leant forward, staring at the floor as though it contained an important message. It seemed they were not quite understanding, so I told them,

" 'You both are not understanding. I propose to give to Anne the money which comes to me from Father only in case I die. I have no intention of giving it to her now, nor do I suppose she will outlive me.' " Only too true. Frederick then went over the top. " 'By that time, Charles will no longer need my money, as he certainly will be a famous writer on his own and well established. This is all about the distant future. You will continue to receive your stipend from me, Charles, of course.' "

At this point, Monsieur Snigs evidently regarded the bowed head of Charles, then said to him quietly, "You continue to take your brother's money even after, and despite my great inner reluctance, since you are of an age to be your own support, I convinced your father to resume your allowance?"

This awoke Charles as though he had been stung. "But that surely is my own money!"

Monsieur Snigs riposted, "How can you be so stupid about practical affairs?" and the maître of the tea salon now came forward to ask the Englishmen to leave—rightly, as it is after all no place like the Café Turc. The three Englishmen were suddenly ashamed of causing a scene, and so began apologising to one another. By now, in listening to this tale, I was happy under my comforter again; I prodded Frederick, "And did you also apologise to the patrons at neighbouring tables, for it was they whom you disturbed?" He scowled; they are a strangely humourless people. In any event, Frederick asked me what I thought of the whole complicated matter. Well, I am in no doubt, and I did not hesitate to tell him.

"What a philosopher! We thought we were his sole defence against the poorhouse. I salute him!"

As usual I have wronged the brother. "You cannot understand him. He of course believed the little I give him from my practise is an addition to money entirely his own. He knows little about the world, you yourself told me he is innocent of women! On the pavement, he instantly instructed me that he would take nothing henceforward, and he asked Snigs to enquire if he could draw upon his own capital to repay me, at least refund something. Snigs was stricken, miserable."

A man should believe in his brother, of course. I have essayed for the last time on this subject.

"My pet," were my final words, "Monsieur Snigs is without doubt also innocent of woman, yet he can tell a pound from a franc. Here you have before your eyes, not twelve hours ago, another proof that this man—he is thirty-five years old? it is remarkable, is it not?—this man wants to remain the sickly little boy others will care for. You hover upon a great success with the invention of the vertical arcade, but for the moment you have barely enough for your needs, and he *does not notice.* He does not notice that in London there is delay, confusion before money comes, and that it comes directly from the father's account. I do not speak of his undoubted brilliance, I speak only of the fact that this one wanders the streets, he has been seen in the worst part of the Tuileries, he dresses in rags and suddenly he is immaculate in linen, probably a 'gift,' and he speaks of writing which no one reads. I have seen him watching you and me together. I accept that when he looks at me he sees a woman for sale, her wretched dress hanging in rags from her grimy shoulders, a breast naked to the eye, I, no let me go on, I accept this, even though he is polite, absolutely and unchallengeably polite when we must meet, but I do not accept how he now looks at you. He knows you are not the innocent, seduced brother, not now. It has gone on too long. So instead he thinks that you, too, have a touch of harlot, a spot of whore on your soul, yes, and his eyes burn when they fix on you with something which is other than brotherly love. Tell me one thing about this afternoon: at your parting, did this brother, who has taken your money in blindness if not under false pretences, did he say in parting so as to convey a healing, 'I so look forward to see Anne in a few days' time, it has been so long,' or other words that might have been a *recognition* of the truth of our lives? Did he reach out?"

These are my final words on the subject of Charles. I think they have gone home. Frederick by force of habit pushed the matter aside—"I didn't have time for long farewells, I left for the atelier, Maurice has mucked up some drawings."—but I could see in his eyes that my words have taken root, finally.

16 November 1836

This evening we will go to Marie's with a large party, but I want to write down this afternoon right away. For some reason I was glad Frederick was occupied with the pavilion; it would have been blurred with him there. (Nota bene: probably the blue jade choker; Marie is calling it a grand evening.)

Adolphe claimed he would not go to the Hôtel de France, so I bade him to come here for tea. It amused me, the idea of Adolphe, atomiser in hand, scented cloths up each sleeve, those eyes always moving to judge the effect on you, Adolphe "taking" tea with the advocate. Monsieur Snigs came early, at precisely the hour I had named, Adolphe at five with Pixis. I was at first put out by this uninvited guest, as he might detract a little from the scene I imagined.

Well. Monsieur Snigs in two minutes had us all deep in it, as, hard upon the introductions, he asked Adolphe if Waldron's Acidulated Vapours were known in France.

"Known?" Adolphe squeezed the bulb of the atomiser.

Like a connoisseur of old wines, the amazing Monsieur Snigs sniffed the air.

"The formula, if I am not mistaken, is weaker than that sold in London. I ask myself, Sir, if you are not in possession of Vapours prepared for the export market, rather than the true, robust, domestic product."

Pixis speaks not a word of English, nor is his French much better. He resorted to me, in his slobbering thick German, to find out why they are squeezing and sniffing Waldron's Vapours immediately upon meeting. I explained the old lawyer's condition, at which Pixis exclaimed, again *auf deutsch*, that nothing compares with Harvey's Vesuvial Fog. The lawyer makes out the name and exclaims loudly,

"But they are disgraceful, Harvey's, the penetration is nasal only, altogether avoiding the lungs."

Before I have time to translate, Pixis has read the lawyer's frown, and to prove the superior virtues of Vesuvial Fog he pulled out a bottle of it secreted in his frock coat, uncorked the stopper with a flourish, and pushed the bottle under the Englishman's nose. Adolphe, not to be shoved off centre-stage, puffed on his atomiser again. Pussy quit the room, just as the tea-party was becoming fun.

"Gentlemen," I said to my visitors who were now babbling in their own languages. "Gentlemen, you are all mistaken. Do you," I said to Pixis, "teach chest tones in the same fashion to every student?" As I spoke English, I was obliged to answer for him. "Of course not. Nor do you, Adolphe, make the same gesture of despair, night after night, at the end of *The Huguenots*. My friends, just as we adapt our expression to the needs of the evening, so must we adapt the treatment we give to the body. Just as no two performances of a song by Mozart should be the same, we must treat the throat differently in winter than in spring, in the afternoon differently than in the evening. One must have a veritable library of lozenges, of sprays, of the robust domestic Waldron as well as the more tame, exported Waldron. The art is to know which to choose when, just as a great writer knows which book in his library will provoke his own Muse."

I was superb. I continued, "Gentlemen, we are all professionals," and at this the lawyer with his cough glowed with pleasure as though he had been received on Mount Olympus. "We know that the voice of nature is too frail for the demands of modern art. The throat must be enlarged, yet at the same time the pressure of air through the nose repressed; we strain to fill our chests with enough air, and there is never, never enough air for the new music. If a vapour revolts the nose and opens the chest, as I confess the Vesuvial Fog affects me, so much the better: this is our particular tribute to Meyerbeer. If our cheeks tingle with oil of ginger rubbed on them, so much the better for the articulation of Rossini."

I had certainly no purpose in coupling these two names; Adolphe's eyes, however, rested for a moment on me contemplatively. He turned to Monsieur Snigs and said quietly,

"You know the music of these composers?"

Monsieur Snigs confessed to knowing only Rossini.

"A pity. The role of Raoul was written for me. This year, in the new opera by Meyerbeer who is, sir, a great composer, greater than Rossini, the equal of Beethoven . . ."

"And who now," Pixis interrupted in French, having caught the drift from the names, "is writing a new opera for M. Duprez."

I *wished* Pixis would leave. This was cruel, not at all a joke as I made to Adolphe at the Grand-Véfour. Adolphe's eyes moved to the side to regard Pixis, although his head remained fixed towards Monsieur Snigs.

"I am afraid my French is too weak to follow you, Herr Pixis." The lawyer had understood, intervened, and waved the fly away. "Tell me, kind Madame," and he rolled out the question as though at last, here on Olympus, we professionals could talk frankly, "what is your view of the moral character of tragedy?"

Adolphe's eyes returned to their centre, and he cut through the old man, "You will understand that in art, as in commerce, competition is often thought stimulating. My colleague Pixis refers to the invitation to a certain Duprez, given this autumn, to come to Paris to sing the Italian repertoire at the Opéra—so that the burden would not fall solely upon myself. The invitation, Pixis, was made by Duponchel with my full concurrence. Well, my dear English sir, Duprez has come, and with Rossini's help he has conquered, Rossini who is jealous of Meyerbeer, the Meyerbeer who wrote the rôle of Raoul in *The Huguenots* for me." Adolphe gave a little puff on his atomiser and struggled forward. "Duprez has conquered. That means he sings certain rôles I used to sing. No matter: some say he sings better, some say worse, but all are rôles which were made for me, and so in this matter he is in my shadow. Now, however, the young composers fight to present him with new rôles of his own, a music more dramatic, more barbaric, shall we say, than the bel canto style with which my name will be for ever associated."

Then the fat neck creased, the full head as well as those sad, vigilant eyes favouring Pixis. "It is a little like Liszt and Thalberg, my friend. Last year you composed a concerto for the one, this year for the other; last year you told the world Liszt was immortal, this year you declare Thalberg supreme. Next year you will have forgotten Liszt and the music you wrote for him, Thalberg will move from supreme place to the immortal position, and a new man will receive the garland of your current favour. This is the edifying result of what we call competition in art, a competition more truly for reputation, in which only one person must appear to triumph at any moment. But what sort of supremacy has an artist? Not over himself, not over his art, that battle is never won, but rather a victory over your indifference; he conquers your attention. Any artist who engages in this combat is like a child wandering into a den of wolves. Your hunger for new genius, your boredom with the artist whom only yesterday you crowned as supreme, these capacities for betrayal in the name of competition, in the name of knowing what is best, who is best, they are overwhelming, ravenous. All one can offer is the honest practise of music."

Pixis, understanding not a word of Adolphe's beautiful English, and recognising only the names, smiled uncertainly at the singer, and then at us. I was deeply moved, as I had been the four or five times before I had heard Adolphe make this speech in the last month, since his humiliation before the public, the dreadful hoarseness which prevented him from completing *The Mute Woman* early in October.

Monsieur Snigs rose from the larger armchair under the north window, in which the cushions had nearly buried him. So did Adolphe, from the elegant Louis Quatorze secretary stool he has always insisted upon taking, though these days his haunches lap over the side.

"Sir, I have been given to understand by Madame Mercure that there will be some person present at the soirée of the Comtesse d'Agoult this evening who may be distasteful to you. I, who have spent a lifetime in jousts, although with pen and paper rather than the lance no less brutal for that, I would like to make a suggestion to you. Never avoid meeting your enemy in society. Smile upon him. I therefore trust we may see you once more this evening."

"At all events, I am so utterly bored with these intrigues."

Now, darling, wouldn't you have just a little to add to Adolphe's speech of your own? You would say, there comes a time when one can no longer say to others one is "resting between engagements," one must use the more spacious, "I am waiting for just the right rôle."

And is it not true that the lovers of the world divide into two camps? In one camp are the consolers, how awful for you. And in the other camp are those, to revert to Saturday, *who do not notice.* They see just the two of us, withdrawn from these petty affairs and these vermin. Of course, it is not amusing listening to an actress complain who has been so long before the public that no one bothers much what she is doing in November rather than, for instance, January. But it would be nice, very nice, to have someone to whom each night you could complain and sigh. Your boy, perhaps out of absorption in his own affairs, counsels you to condemn the great public, they are all boors. Enough of this: the great evening is before us.

20 November 1836

After four days still each moment demands attention like a child tugging at one's skirts. Curtain up in my hall: Frederick, blond hair brushed back, black eyebrows also brushed, cheeks flushed, his square mouth smiling wide, the neck wrapped in a blue-and-white-only Paisley silk scarf, blue-black frock coat, white waistcoat with blue horsehair buttons (a present from me for the evening, to match Marie's décor), black military trousers cut tight to show off his high carriage, blue slippers of the softest patent leather. Next to Frederick, Monsieur Snigs in *powder* (yes!) on the few long strands of hair on his head (moreover he predicts the wig will return for gentlemen, "as part of the rational progress of society, Madame, wigs in these modern times will be manufactured by machines, and constructed with insulated linings"), pince-nez on a red ribbon ("customary in my country on festive occasions as a modest exhibition of male finery"), the dry withered skin of the face as flushed as his godson's, and then black, almost all black; a black frock coat buttoned up to his chin ("my adversary, the evening draught"), dazzling white silk shirt showing only at the cuffs, black trousers shiny from long use but beautifully pressed and creased, a pair of over-the-ankle black boots with heavy laces, which were, I think, fashionable at the end of the last century, the shoes also well cared for. Then Adolphe, a symphony of scents, powders and pomades. If only the workmen at the sewer could have seen him that night! On top we were pomaded with Vignolet's Extra Lustrous. We had plucked and pomaded our eyebrows, powdered our cheeks with the same rice powder that Pussy loves, but we had also been very, very naughty and rouged. Perhaps a lip cream had also delicately darkened our lips, for they were certainly very, very ruby. Then we offset the face with a manly, indeed revolutionary neck, a black kerchief tied bandit-style on the side, a kerchief which, however, if one looked carefully, betrayed some very intricate needlework as its edging. Our pear-shape form was yellow, a yellow cutaway frock coat braided in black rope, the palest yellow silk Moor's blouse, and military yellow trousers almost as tight as Frederick's, but whereas Frederick's seat is firm, ours jiggles; the pantaloons were dreadfully tight, the bulbous thighs squeezed into a garment meant for men with thighs like tubes. We completed our toilette with yellow peau-de-soie pumps and black buckles.

These three went into the first carriage. I gave them the four-in-hand; Frederick, in the style of Lord Seymour, held the reins himself.

In the second carriage, a large brougham rented for the evening, I shepherded the extras. These were a lady and two young gentlemen, who spoke casually of "Marie" and "Franz" and "George" without, I am sure, having ever before been presented to the Comtesse d'Agoult, Franz Liszt, or their circle. The young lady was passably pretty. Mouse-brown hair done in an aureole of ringlets, a little too long but only a little, sensible white pumps, which looked like début shoes and were a fatal error in the company she was about to keep. In costume, you must know how, like Adolphe, to go much too far if you are going to go in that direction at all. (nota bene) This young miss was married to one of the men, who in figure and form was nondescript.

The other, my escort, is Frederick's "colleague" at the atelier. One never knows about an evening whether it is good to invite the enemy as though he were a friend, disarming him, or to exclude him to show one's own power. In Frederick's place, I would have shunned this one, since the soirées of Marie's already have a certain allure, but Frederick thought the oaf would make a fool of himself in front of Rohault de Fleury, and then Frederick could present himself for the greenhouse work at the Jardin des Plantes. Well, the man on first sighting certainly repelled *me:* he has that terrible habit of running his hands through his hair, hair which was combed back, a gesture and a coiffure which they all think is best Brummell. But could Brummell, would Brummell ever offer a lady either a glove or a bare hand sullied by hair grease? Or hand her into a carriage without a slight, courtly pressure on her fingers?

It is as well I found these young people without interest, for they certainly found me so; I don't think they took in who I am. My escort even made a barely veiled joke about glass towers. The men thus passed virtually the entire journey in gossip about the atelier, several useful titbits of which

I was able in turn to pass on to Frederick. What fools ambition makes of young men! They calculate how to use this under-minister, what will please that client, which is to be the next fashion in doorways and stairs. Yet they imagine that some day, once they have triumphed over all the others, as Adolphe would say, they can begin to practise their art just as they want. The slime through which ambition has dragged them will not stick to their skins. These young architects, each thinking of whom he would meet tonight, what was the quickest way to arrive at the place occupied by the late Fontaine (lamented of course but his death had, as one of my companions observed, made "room" for new men), these boon colleagues made one concession to me, who deserved something as I had rented quite a smart brougham, with cut-velvet seats and walnut panels. My escort put me in the know by informing me that "George" had seduced Chopin but found him impotent, only yesterday.

Now then, to my own toilette. As early as last year I predicted the death of the leg-of-mutton sleeve, but although many have agreed it ill suits the flounced skirt, the question has always been what should take its place. My own niche in history is assured by finding the answer. I found it a few weeks ago in a costume book from the time of Molière; *the garden sleeve,* which is moderately wide and open at the end rather than cinched-in like the leg-of-mutton. The old actresses wore them provokingly; no garments underneath so that if the arm were stretched outwards to the audience, the groundlings could see up the costume. Now, even for Marie's this would be too much. So I wore the simplest lace camisole underneath my blouse, which Forstier's cut directly from the picture I showed them in the book. I was sensational! My hair was in plaits, giraffe style, up high, with a crown of blue-jay feathers; my face in the dead-white powder from Floris, *one pearl* mounted on the thinnest gold chain to emphasise my swan's neck, dead-white silk blouse with those revealing garden sleeves with which I teased everyone all evening by frequently extending my arm, to emphasise a point, to let myself be kissed—it's heaven, when you are seated the gentleman is standing, the arm is raised upwards, he bends over to the presented wrist and his eyes are prisoner, following from wrist to forearm, then within the garden sleeve, all the time the gentleman is weakly smiling, saying anything, babbling, as he stares into the sleeve, his eyes defeated by the camisole. Yes, one must know how to go too far, which means order, focus, logic. I therefore wore the simplest three-panel skirt, trimmed modestly in not very interesting Alençon fringe, that all attention be focussed upwards.

I was as beautiful as ever I was, more so because riper, more assured, more daring. Perhaps the events of the evening came from no more than that. Yes, from no more than elation.

Our carriage arrived in the rue Lafitte to a scene of chaos. When Marie said a grand evening, she meant at least a numerous one; carriages filled the street all the way to the smart end. Two ahead of us I could see the house carriage of the dukes of Flavigny. Marie had triumphed! But if Marie had enticed her family to the hotel suite she shared with her lover and their illicit babies, then it was no evening for companions such as I had in my carriage; the family virtually owns the Jardin des Plantes through Urbain's department now, and these young sharks were hungry enough to force their way forward against all obstacles. I resolved to find a means to pack them off as soon as possible, no matter how Frederick protested. Perhaps that part was indeed my fault.

The moment we entered the room, panting from the climb up three flights, the ladies obliged to hold their skirts up, which were heavy enough, so as not to brush the not-quite-clean stairs, the moment we entered Marie's hotel suite, I saw that Marie was in trouble. The room was filled also with not-quite-clean men, with obvious mistresses, with the sort of dignitaries who haunt the artists' entrance, leering men who breathe heavily through thick wads of hair in their nostrils. In the midst of this crowd, all screeching, was a small knot of elderly, obviously aristocratic persons speaking quietly amongst themselves, their good if worn clothes immaculate; these relatives of Marie looked discreetly out from their little island and then smiled from time to time to reassure one another. It was so bad that the Dowager Duchess of Flavigny greeted me warmly when we were presented; I was at least someone whom she had once known well, though never since I had come alone to Paris has this patron of my father deigned to recognise my existence. She was standing next to the door, poised to flee.

"My dear Madame Delsart, what an evening! As Général de Beauséjour said of the Battle of Waterloo, 'The noise! And the people!' "

I was confused that she called me by my own family's name. Was it to deny that I *could* be known by her as I was known to all Paris? But then I was distracted from the possible insult when her hand trembled and dropped the little silver herb cage she had been clutching. The ornament belonged at one of the hunt balls in houses perched on the sand of the Atlantic, Mother's fichu a snowy halo echoing her grey hair, the smell of the soap with which we had been scrubbed nearly to death, the sea lapping outside in time to the scraping fiddles and flutes. All this rushed back as I picked up the dowager's little silver cage for herbs, the chaste way a country lady scented before the Revolution. No, it was no insult, she needed to remember those names which made her feel secure. Holding the little box out to her, I was afraid I would give way and that my eyes would brim over.

"Thank you, Madame Delsart, there is such a crush a footman, were that such a personage here, could not have performed the office for me. Who amongst those you know here would it please you to present to me?"

Together our eyes scanned the sitting-room. The hotel had opened an adjoining boudoir for the occasion as well, so the space was in fact quite large. The horsehair objects were pushed against walls, and Marie had contrived some species of decoration by placing both of Franz's grand pianos in the very center of her sitting-room, vases of flowers piled on top of the pianos. In the further room there was a buffet without attending servants. (Marie tried to pass off this crudeness as "service in the fashion of St. Petersburg.") Only my trained eye was able to separate the scenery from the surging masses of men and women who filled the place, chinked glasses, and bumped into neighbours behind them when they attempted to bow. Several of Marie's guests had nonchalantly placed brimming glasses of champagne on the ebony lids of the pianos of Franz Liszt.

"There is, next the piano," I replied to the Dowager Duchess of Flavigny, "the leading poet of the hour, Théophile Gautier. Seated at the piano is . . ."

"I no longer see distinctly, my sweet child. Who is the great poet?"

"The tall man dressed entirely in green next to the larger black piano."

"Oh, I don't think I could be presented to an entirely green gentleman. Who else?"

I went through the list of those I knew, with much editing. Berryer wore a determined aspect, a man who had known Marie all her life and was letting it be known he would always know her, (perhaps also he would always be a little in love with her). Madame de Flavigny knew him but he was too far away. There was Madame de Créteil covered in dove silk, jet beads and strings of rubies ("Pass on, Madame Delsart, the 'de' appeared in the name when the husband became Commissioner of Salt"), there was Adolphe, but of course that would have been impossible, there was a sinister young man called Sainte-Beuve, who wrote articles and whom I distrusted ("Then I also distrust him"), and so on and on, queens of salt and culture who would give anything to be received, even if contemptuously, in the rue de Grenelle; worst were gentlemen whose eyes never stayed fixed upon you as they spoke, always scanning the room to see who else had come in. Among all these were the rulers of this bohemian world, the musicians, poets and painters, whose smell of turpentine, whose ink-stained palms or manicured, neatly clipped nails were as much patents of nobility as the standards carried by the mediaeval ancestors of Marie's grandmother. (nota bene)

"I do not see M. Liszt amongst his guests," I had finally to remark to the dowager, as it would have been absurd to pretend in this company he did not exist.

"You do not because it was part of our agreement, Marie, her mother, and me. The family can attend because, in the absence of M. de Liszt, it is a Madame d'Agoult who receives us."

"If I may be so bold, Madame, it is a pity that M. Liszt is absent. Among all these people, he is one of the few truly distinguished by greatness of soul, and genius in art." I felt honour-bound to say this for Marie's sake.

The dowager added another wrinkle to the many on her forehead.

"The personal merits of M. de Liszt hardly enter into the matter. And who are the party with whom you came?"

Hovering behind me, the friends of "Franz" and "Marie," the news-agents of Chopin's impotence last night with "George" all wore the modest and hopeful smiles of nice young people who would consider it such an honour to be presented to my friend, the Dowager Duchess of Flavigny-Mereuil. They looked at me, their familiar and dear companion, encouragingly. The one who ran his hands through his hair even had the effrontery to touch one of my bare arms.

Little fools! In that whisper which has penetrated to the very last seat in the balcony of the Comédie-Française, I replied, "I was escorted by the assistants of my great English friend, Frederick Courtland. Indeed, here he is, with his brother and his godfather. They are people to whom I can present you with both confidence and pleasure."

I began the introductions, but unbeknownst to me, Gautier was steadily advancing upon our little party. By the time I had reached Charles, the poet stepped next to him in our little circle and said, "M. Courtland, I am Gautier. You are Charles Courtland, are you not, author of *Intimate Meditations*? Then you are the author of the only honest essays on religion I have ever read. Particularly the essay in which you write as if to a father. I want to make your acquaintance. Pray excuse yourself from these people, who will, I am sure, understand."

Madame Flavigny perceived that the green gentleman had forced his attentions upon a member of the only presentable circle in the room. She rattled her herb cage.

"But Monsieur, I also would like to make the gentleman's acquaintance, and was just to be presented. Will you yield me the honour? It will oblige you to spend but a moment in the presence of Mr Courtland's friends, and then you shall be free to leave, instantly."

So saying, the Dowager Duchess turned to Charles, waiting for his bow. Gautier appeared thrown in some confusion by the old woman; she had forced him to remain amongst us, as it were, a courier who would soon disappear in carrying out instructions. He stammered, and of course we others were hardly more talkative as Charles paid the obligatory court to Marie's grandmother.

Frederick said to the great poet, "I have admired you ever since I first saw you at the first night of *Hernani.*"

Gautier pulled on his earlobe.

"You know Hugo?"

"I regret I do not."

At this moment the poet recognised me.

"Ah, dear Mlle Mercure, my vision was for a moment clouded. Good evening, good evening." He turned his back on Frederick and Snigs, who made the listless conversation of snubbed persons. "They say, Madame, that Hugo might appear tonight, that Sand and Chopin might, and have you heard? It is too delicious! They say . . ."

"But Gautier, I do not know any of 'them,' whereas these English gentlemen, who are the brother and godfather of the man you so admire, are my dear friends."

Gautier darted his eyes around looking for other geniuses. But Monsieur Snigs had already commanded with a glance the one waiter with a tray of champagne, the waiter homing to him obediently; Monsieur Snigs indicated the poet should be first offered champagne and for the glass the poet was caught.

"His brother?" A sip.

"Your admirer and also his brother. The essay of which you speak is indeed addressed to our father, who read it with great interest."

This was handsome enough of Frederick, considering. He might as well have given our names—Charles claims these personal touches are merely a way to enliven otherwise dull exposition, that an actual life is but the clay of art, he claims the usual. The *Moniteur des Modes* defends itself with similar arguments against libel.

"Surely an actual father matters little when a man summons the muses in addressing himself to the character he calls 'my father.'" As I say, the usual. Then Gautier conquered Frederick's courtesy.

"What indeed does your admiration mean?" Gautier quaffed the rest of the champagne at a gulp. "Must a poet be loved by unpoetical persons to hear the voice of his muse?" Already at this moment I knew we were in for it; Gautier was going to profit as well as flee by making one of his celebrated scenes. "Is it love of you, Monsieur, whoever you may be, which prompts me to dip my pen in ink, or, on the contrary, is my reward the terrible satisfaction of earning your contempt? One might say that I have failed to be a poet, a truly terrible poet, at once condemned by the world

and in the grip of *terribilità,* of the powers of dread, as they say of Shakespeare. So I in despair accept your compliment. 'Thank you.' (This in
English, enunciated slowly.) But when I praise your brother," Gautier
spoke now more rapidly in our own tongue, "it is because a great philosopher, unlike the poet, truly has need of the world's admiration, and is never
demeaned by praise. His object is to convince, to arrest, to throw the minds
of his readers in confusion from which he then rescues them. The philosopher is in truth no artist but a prophet in the Hebrew mould, uttering oaths
to whose power we attest by signs of submission and fealty. Such is your
brother."

The space in the room around us was now silent, the company witnessing one of the great entertainments of Paris in our times, M. Gautier
possessed by his spleen. Monsieur Snigs could not follow the rapidity with
which the poet spoke, but knew from Frederick's colour, and the down-
ward smile on Gautier's lips, that something was amiss. Charles and the
Dowager Duchess had stopped speaking. He was spellbound, staring only
at Gautier; the grandmother stared at Marie, drawn to the outer circle by
the commotion.

"Your brother is a sage, but I have not yet explained him to you well.
He is a Hebrew prophet come down from the mountain not with the word
of God, but with the laws of Baal, or rather the writs of scepticism, the
iron-cold truth. You must learn to honour this genius amidst your family
circle for what he is, you must sacrifice yourself to his voyages into the high,
thin air of solitude, receive the messages of his forays into the black night
as once you no doubt received the sermons of your pastor. I know, I know,
it is difficult when a family contains a genius, his light casts the others in
ever deeper shadow. Still, prostrate yourself before him—"

"The astral signs!" Mlle Le Normand suddenly intoned from the outer
circle.

"My dear sir," Monsieur Snigs began to remonstrate in English.

"Théophile," Marie called to the poet as if bidding a child in from play
in the woods.

"You ridiculous fool," Frederick burst out when Charles touched his
arm.

"It doesn't matter. Let's not have another scene."

At this, Frederick turned his head from the poet who stood before him,
relaxed and swaying on his heels, as if resting contentedly after singing a
difficult Rossini aria, Frederick turned slowly to the side to look at his
brother. In the last four days I have come to understand these moments.
The words of praise could be shorn of their barbs if Frederick withdraws,
if he is a "good sport" when insulted by the ever so "difficult" poet; this

was Charles' solution, "let's not have another scene," Charles who should have defended his little brother. Frederick must have felt in his soul this betrayal. The head returned to Gautier and spoke English.

"Thank you for your advice. I must tell you that I long ago learnt the true dimension of my brother's genius, and I have been supporting him ever since, in every manner I know how, and indeed, even in ways of which I have been ignorant."

Monsieur Snigs gave a short bark of breath.

Even the witty souls who would dine out on this scene for a day or two, with suitable embellishments, at the moment perceived matters had gone far enough. A dozen voices began to cover, the Dowager Duchess leading off Charles of the sympathetic parson's manner whom she perceived in some dim way to have been insulted by his own brother, Marie bustling forward to take Frederick by one arm and the wife of his colleague by the other to meet a personage, the men of my carriage following behind.

A natural danger also assisted us at this point. The "Humanitarians," as Marie's circle style themselves, permit smoking on the part of both men and women. It is another fashion from Arabia, though how women can, I don't know. The singing Humanitarians naturally must withdraw when there is cigarette smoking, to a corner or even to another room. Now, in the wake of the scene, several people lit their cigarettes to calm their nerves. Monsieur Snigs began coughing ("It is nothing, or rather, a souvenir of London smog, no matter, do not bother yourselves"). But Adolphe did bother. Quite gently he led the old advocate away to be presented to a blond youth, the understudy of Frédéric Lemaître, a blond youth in whose melancholy Adolphe takes a deep interest. I spied Duprez looking around with that idiot leer on his face; I hurried over to warn him the Humanitarians had begun smoking.

Half an hour passed in which, although there was a constant racket of talk, people began to be bored. None of the great names was there, except Gautier who had already performed for the night; no one save the family and me knew why Liszt was absent. Marie let drop to me that she had also "banished" Chopin, Sand, Vigny and Delacroix; they were amused and understanding, and also they were upstairs drinking in Madame Dudevant's room if I cared to join them, which I did not. So below a hundred pairs of eyes gradually grew fatigued, too long watching, waiting, sometimes staring within the piano as though the great geniuses might be hiding there. The Brummell architect happened to be standing next to me while the rest of the atelier murmured and simpered to the ministerial personage whom Marie found for them; Greasy began to pay me court, having witnessed my intimacy with the Dowager Duchess.

At first it was merely to talk of himself. Having gathered my relations to Frederick, he explained that in his view the new methods of making buildings could extend them either upwards or outwards, and that, as he was interested in the outward, he worked in perfect harmony with Frederick, although my friend had not quite yet found the secret for erecting tall metal skeletons. Quite in passing he asked me if I had seen M. de Fleurie in the rooms, and then, since I did not pursue the opening, he essayed gallantry, but with no real art. We were both to understand he was only passing time.

Well. I thought, we shall see how long you can keep up these insolent compliments. I extended my arm to point to some imagined figure of interest in a painting high up on Marie's wall; the garden sleeve fell slightly back, and I had him! He began looking along the arm, his head and neck pushed forward from his spine like a vulture. I drank another glass of champagne. I began to demonstrate to him the difference between Taglioni's dancing in *La Sylphide* and the way the little Grahn girl dances it now for Bournonville, not dancing myself, of course, but waving my arms just to give the young gentleman the idea, and the dear thing raptly followed my lecture, hoping in the course of it I would be obliged to raise my arms high again, high enough this time. Suddenly, as though I had the second sight of Mlle Le Normand, I knew someone behind me was watching who was not amused, turned, and found Frederick staring at me as he had stared at Charles.

Now our little nightmare began swiftly to turn. God punished me for my wickedness! I wanted to go to Frederick, to explain I was cat-and-mousing, but he was far away, next to the buffet in the inner chamber. No matter, I would make my way around the pianos to him. At the big piano two persons were talking, one of whom I think I vaguely know, but only vaguely. Neither of them acknowledged me, their heads were bowed together. The man I could not place was smiling to the complete stranger.

"Yes indeed. She tolerates it. After all, at her age . . ."

I slowed and turned my head away slightly, so missing something from the unknown man.

"Yes," said the other, "the little one can't be more than fifteen."

Now I almost staggered forward to Frederick. My ears burned! It could not be true! As though some terrible sea tide battered me, my forehead throbbed, my body heated. I will not here, I shouted to myself, not here in front of these babbling, horrible fools! We will leave, we have to leave this party and then I will kill him! If it were true I swore I would kill him.

By the time I could have reached out with my garden-sleeve arm to touch Frederick, but didn't, he had already bid adieu to Marie; she glanced at me and gave proof of her superb tact. Whatever she saw in my face made her turn away, as if negligently; we could escape her rooms without arousing comment.

On the first stair below Marie's landing, he began to accuse.

"You act like a tart before my colleagues! You, who say reputation is all—what must he think of you, of us, seeing you virtually naked?"

The landing of the second floor. The fire in my cheeks would surely bake my cream and rouge to a crust.

"Yes, I amused myself." We were racing down the stairs, we passed little knots of people still climbing to Marie's great evening, racing down as if we were falling. "I toyed with your 'colleague,' as you call this nobody, your little world of nobodies, but tomorrow his thoughts will be elsewhere, the most harm will be he leers when he next sees you."

The landing of the first floor. Our breasts were heaving. We both stopped for a moment to gather ourselves.

"A nothing. But you? You repeat my daughter's fancies, you give all Paris a topic for scandal, delicious scandal, for days, for weeks, for always!"

Frederick looked at me amazed. He sought to grasp my hand. But I moved forward and down ahead of him. Through the windows of the Hôtel de France, a crowd of gapers came into view in the courtyard. Slowly, almost stately, I walked down the last flight of stairs, as if preparing to receive them; Frederick was one step always behind me, just as if he had rehearsed perfectly, and whispering to me urgently, "Anne, I never, no one could have learnt from me, you know I would not . . ."

We were on level ground. Instead of the bleary night porter, the Hôtel de France had laid on a footman, powdered and in livery. He opened the door. Frederick took my arm, which I allowed, as the crowd parted to let us pass through to the brougham which was just opposite the hotel. Raymond flung down the stair, Frederick handed me in and then threw himself next to me. Raymond tucked in the stair, climbed up next to the coachman and gave the order to depart. The horses were cold, they wanted to move, they immediately jerked us forward.

The shutters, stone and paint passed nearly in a blur, horrible gaslight, until suddenly we rocked to a stop at a crossing. The lamp outside played a trick with the glass, and in the carriage I stared at a mirror. Here is what I saw, just for a moment: a crown of blue-jay feathers, a casserole of ringlets, a high, clear brow, eyes cracked at the sides by little lines, cheeks streaked by tears, no rouge visible in the yellow light from the gas, a mouth turned down at the corners because it was clamped tight, and then the beautiful ermine stole Lemaître gave me, over the collar of the blue satin shawl I have had since I was a young girl, far away in that place where women adorned themselves with the scents of herbs carried in silver boxes, where sea storms frequently made polite conversation inaudible, and under this cape, the cunning dress which had entranced and enticed so many during the glittering event. An entire lifetime reflected in glass.

The carriage jerked forward again. "If you did not tell, who did, then?"

Even as these words left my mouth, I already knew the answer. He was the only one who could possibly have penetrated Frederick's guard. I looked at Frederick. He hesitated before this final step yet the very silence which fell upon us by the time we arrived home, the gentleness between us in the days since, shows that in forgiving he also has accepted the answer to my question in the carriage.

There, I have spent the evening in reliving.

21 November 1836

Adolphe came this morning with the account of Marie's soirée in the *Journal des Débats*.

> The Duchess d'Agoult gave a brilliant evening recently in the Hôtel de France, where she has established herself temporarily for the season upon her return from the Swiss mountains. The Duke d'Agoult remains in Angers hunting, but, although his absence was regretted, several members of the Flavigny and d'Agoult families were able to attend, lending a pleasingly domestic air to the evening.
>
> Prominent among the guests were the Dowager Duchess of Flavigny, the Andorran Ambassador, His Excellency Xavier Rubellesc, and several notables from the Republic of Letters, the Principality of Painting and the Kingdom of Song. These included Madame George Sand, the incomparable Franz Liszt, Théophile Gautier, Eugène Delacroix, the singers Adolphe Nourrit and Samson Duprez. Of special note were several architects from the studio of the late lamented Pierre-François Fontaine, among whom we remarked M. Guiraud in particular. This young man dreams of iron and glass palaces double, triple the Jardin des Plantes. Truly, it is astonishing, those who build are today the masters of the modern

imagination; this demanding work attracts the most ethereal, or the wildest youths, as well as practical young men. Unlike those who dream of glass towers thrusting up like needles or of zoos in the sky, M. Guiraud is clear sighted and competent. It hardly surprised us that the Comtesse d'Agoult, a connoisseur of the future, presented him to the most knowledgeable public in Paris! He was accompanied by his charming wife and other members of the Fontaine studio. Also present were the actresses Mlle Biron and Madame Mercure.

There were several delicious moments during this glittering occasion. M. Gautier was able to display his rapier wit. M. Liszt followed him with a remarkable group of variations upon a theme supplied by his friend, Frédéric Chopin, who, along with the entire company, sat rapt in awe of the Master's art.

The music concluded with a short selection of songs in which the voice of Duprez moved everyone to tears. The Comtesse d'Agoult's prize spoke forcefully to this correspondent of the need for a new architecture in Paris, a modern architecture reflecting the new spirit of enterprise under the influence of our great Monarch. The Duchess d'Agoult's circle has acquired the name "the Humanitarians," a sobriquet well merited if a humanitarian is a person in whom the love of genius and the grace of the best society are combined.

Adolphe encountered Monsieur Snigs on the way here, and showed our visitor this example of Parisian journalism. "He is a charmer," Adolphe says, "like a ferociously loyal lap-dog. He is outraged, he says everyone present will write to the *Journal des Débats* to protest that almost none of it was true. I felt I rather lowered myself in his eyes by remarking that almost everyone there wished it happened as it had been written, and so are unlikely to complain."

We calculated that Guiraud must have paid at least fifty francs for his part, although I think for the *Journal des Débats* now it must be at least ten francs more. Also, Greasy will have paid something extra for the mention of his wife, an unnecessary expense I hope she will take as a token of affection. What will the effect be on Marie's position? I maintain good, because of the mention of *both* families. Adolphe says bad, because no one hunts in d'Agoult's part of the country at this time of year, so the excuse is transparent—but this is too subtle a point. Adolphe claims both Duprez and Gautier were shown the piece. If so, it is curious that Gautier let the hack treat him so airily; perhaps our poet was too cheap to buy the word "devastating," or perhaps he had only enough money for "rapier wit" and supper.

I found I had to tell Adolphe about our scene at Marie's, which meant explaining Adèle's little story. He gave me all his attention. Adolphe's tastes have taught him to listen with a clear brain to tales others would find too sordid to contemplate. For it is sordid! She soils herself repeating it, even once. Anyhow he listened well, not moving or commenting until I had finished.

"Poor Frederick."

"Poor Frederick? What about me?"

"Anne my delicious." I thought that was all he was going to say, but he was merely preparing to move. He rose from his chair, waddled over to my settee, and sank into the cushions beside me, then taking my hand. His is baby-soft.

"Anne my delicious. You would like my advice. Now you and Frederick have been together six years. My passions, except of course for you, last only a few weeks. It is too exhausting, feeling as much as I do, and so I must save my strength by not feeling too long. Really I cannot give you advice. But, if I were Frederick, after six years, I would begin earnestly to hope that you, darling Anne, would stop counting."

I let go his hand. "Adolphe, when you are profound I don't know what you are talking about."

"You do, you know," he replied. "You think thirty-five female years are at least two times thirty-one male years. You worry that now, every day, you lose a year of beauty, you think that men do not need to worry about growing old, even a person of sixty can have young girls . . . Oh, so often I have heard women say this, but if you *only knew* how we search our faces for lines, tug our hair constantly in fear one day we will begin to pull out bunches of it, how we worry about the terrible, ever-larger rolls of fat around the middle . . . well I haven't the heart to pursue, my precious Anne, this sad subject. I only say, worry enough in your misguided female way and he will correspondingly begin counting in flattering male years. After a while in love one should stop keeping score."

"You think I treat him like a boy?"

"No, not at all," Adolphe replied and surprised me, for others have accused me of this. "No, I mean you are constantly seeking to dress superbly, to flirt, to *prove* how desirable you are. In this affair of Adèle; has he not shown his loyalty to you? And could you not prove your trust in his manhood by, shall we say, being more calm, more demure? There, that is my advice. Now I want to tell you the most revolting thing about the great Duprez. Last night he said to Véron . . ."

Finally an evening to myself. Only Monsieur Snigs, for tea. His great adventure of a fortnight ends tomorrow: "Labour and duty call me once more to London, thank goodness; after two weeks of idleness I began to think, with regret, of the alarums and skirmishes with which my days have been filled for forty years." I asked what he now thought of Paris.

"It is quite different from the city in my mind. Rather less disordered than I feared; more alien."

"We are lunar do you mean, sir?"

"I had not understood—and I say this, kind Madame, to you as almost a member of the family . . ." he coloured deeply and broke off, squeezing his wrinkled hands together tight.

"No, you have not offended me, Sir, you could not. Pass on; you had not understood what?"

The hands unclenched.

"I had not understood, for instance, what could have brought my other godson to publish what is patently thinly disguised autobiography, what is tantamount to naked revelation. In my country, Madame, Tact and Discretion are supreme virtues—"

"As they are here."

"But not in the same way. Let me continue with the instance not of these writings, but of the most unusual soirée"—the French word Monsieur Snigs brought out with considerable satisfaction—"of some days ago. I have been able partially to forgive myself my Gypsy Adventure by conducting some business with officials at the Ministry of Justice. One offered me condolences on the troubled family relations I am also obliged to deal with on this, my very first visit to Paris, etc."

Monsieur Snigs pounced and found that "all Paris" was saying he was trying to starve Charles back to London, all Paris knowing this from a remark the Dowager Duchess made to Madame Morin—at least the Dowager Duchess said to Madame Morin that her granddaughter had the English Voltaire at her evening, and also had invited relatives from abroad pursuing the English Voltaire, which delicious mixture Madame repeated to Monsieur Morin who repeated it to the official at the Ministry, who put two and two together when Monsieur Snigs mentioned one of his godsons in Paris wrote atheistical tracts, for how many English Voltaires here can there be? Word had also circulated of a violent argument among English people at the best English tea-shop, the police called in, a window broken, in which a writer was mentioned in some accounts.

I asked him how the Dowager Duchess of Flavigny should be so well informed, and he took one hand in the other, but lightly this time. (Nota bene: you could use it for the revealing trick in the last act of *Malatesta*) It is however quite clear to me. I credit Charles with no direct maliciousness; I am not in the habit of exaggerating, especially when there is no need to. When the elderly lady took him off, after Frederick's riposte to Gautier, Charles simply did not correct the impression that his brother and godfather were persecuting him in some way. In any event, Monsieur Snigs said now, briefly,

"Yours is a city, Madame, in which the coins of social life are more freely exchanged in public than they are in London. So I have merely understood that my other godson has become, in his own way, French."

Monsieur Snigs rose. He looked at me keenly, searchingly, I feared he was going to make a declaration, but it was not that. He frowned in concentration when he took my hand, and departed with these words: "Come to me if ever you are in need."

This strange English farewell frightened me more than any of Le Normand's stories. But with him it has been triumph, and besides that, I shall miss him.

"The Suicide of Adolphe Nourrit"

An Article by Charles Courtland in
The Free Thinker *June 1839*

The singer Adolphe Nourrit, born at Montpellier the 3rd of March 1802, has died in Naples on the 8th of March 1839. The authorities of that city determined, and the family acknowledges, his death to be a suicide; M. Nourrit threw himself from the fifth-floor window of his lodgings.

Usually, one hopes, faith will erase memory. In time the bereaved may efface the terrible images of discovery, leave off their own sorrow and their anger at the suicide, surrendering to the Lord's consoling Power. But in the case of M. Nourrit, one cannot in charity draw a shroud over memory, at least not now. His death was as public, as theatric, as his life, the falling body menacing a thick crowd in the square beneath his hotel chambers and narrowly missing two young children when it landed; the reasons for this homicidal suicide remain hotly in dispute.

The most common explanation of why M. Nourrit should have threatened the lives of so many others in taking his own is that his professional disappointments had driven him insane. Once the leading tenor of the Paris Opéra, he had come to Italy to master the new style, found he could not reign abroad, again, as he had reigned before at home. On the evening prior to his death, the 7th of March, he had given a charity concert in Naples to benefit the cause of Saint-Simonian Socialism; he was convinced that he heard amongst the warm applause the Neapolitans vouchsafed him also hisses and cat-calls; previously he had taken the clerical interdiction of a performance of Donizetti's *Poliuto* as a personal attack of the Pope. Finally, on the 8th, crazed, he threw himself in a rage into the square of Italians whose modern music defeated his powers and who had produced in the person of Gilbert Duprez his nemesis at the Paris Opéra.

This common explanation is literally so; it demeans M. Nourrit to a man obsessed by ambition. It fails, moreover, to explain why a supposedly ambition-racked singer should be giving a concert in aid of an unpopular cause, or why a schemer would tangle with the ecclesiastical authorities in that country where they maintain the strongest grip on artistic life. Indeed, few of those who have advanced the thesis of a disappointed career championed it with much conviction. As so often happens, what we cannot explain, we cannot forget.

The facts of M. Nourrit's life are these: Adolphe Nourrit was the son of a singer who himself occupied an honourable place at the Opéra of Paris during the time of Napoleon. Nourrit was trained by Garcia, but described himself as more inspired by Talma, and indeed by the style of the controlled, shaped, smaller phrase enunciated in a pure, uncoloured voice which Talma so well represented. Her singing recalls the age of Mozart; one irony of M. Nourrit's career is that while his political opinions were advanced, his artistic tastes inclined him to the classicism of the *ancien régime*, its marble stateliness, its solid architecture, M. Berlioz indeed having exclaimed upon hearing the young Nourrit that he possessed a "heroic exaltation."

In 1821 Nourrit made his début, singing with his father, at the Paris Opéra in music by Gluck. Rossini, much struck by the powers of the young singer, began to advise him, helping Nourrit even then to soften his powerful voice with the suppleness characteristic of the Italian theatres. Thus began one of the most fruitful artistic associations in the recent history of French music, M. Nourrit coming only in his last years to calumniate Rossini, believing the composer had abandoned his old friend for Duprez. Indeed, it was M. Nourrit's performance in the rôle of Neocles, at the première of Rossini's *Siege of Corinth* at the Paris Opéra on the 9th of October 1826, coupled with the retirement of his father that same year from the stage, which pushed Adolphe Nourrit to the forefront of French singers.

I shall not repeat the list of his subsequent rôles and triumphs which other memorialists are better able to impart. I adduce these facts about the early life of Adolphe Nourrit to remove any impression that here was a young man struggling to make his name known in a hostile Paris, and so disposed to dwell on place, having hard earned his reputation. Not at all. Nourrit entered Parisian musical life as though entitled to that leading position which his gifts indeed justified. We cannot explain his suicidal despair as that of a man who fears he is slipping back into the abyss.

In the next decade M. Nourrit was to marry, to become himself the sponsor of young singers, indeed a champion of young artists of all varieties during the high season of Romanticism in Paris. He was unusually generous for so sought-after an artist, and the influences at once fraternal and paternal which animated him have more pertinence, I believe, in explaining his tragic disappointment at the end than vulgar jealousies. It was M. Nourrit's love of the young, of the Future, which brought him to grief.

Some of my readers may recall a famous scene ten years ago. A month after the Revolution of 1830 had put Louis-Philippe upon the throne as King of the French, the Opéra re-opened, the new King and his family in attendance. The opera was *The Mute Woman of Portici*, in which M. Nourrit sang the male lead. When he finished the great aria "Sacred love of the Fatherland," M. Nourrit suddenly gathered the artists of the theatre around him, began to lead them all in the Marseillaise, and unfurled a tricolour flag which he had concealed within his costume. The tenor came centre stage forward and knelt, chanting the Marseillaise, holding the tricolour flag in his two hands outstretched to Louis-Philippe, who in turn rose with the rest of the new Royal Family in the Royal Box, the King paying tribute for the first time in so public a place and dramatic a manner to the flag of Revolution.

People had previously said of Adolphe Nourrit that his rounded form and feline gracefulness ill-suited the heroic cast of his voice. After this moment no one doubted; the young flocked to him. I was one of this throng.

Before the re-opening of the Opéra, I had listened admiringly many times to M. Nourrit's singing, but had never thought to approach the singer. His courage that evening prompted me, as it did so many young people, to seek him out. The aftermath of the July Revolution had disgusted us. The old régime fell swiftly and ignominiously, but the new régime substituted vulgarity for credulity, money for prejudice, whilst the revolutionaries muttered about yet another upheaval which somehow would put everything right. Disgust fouled the air of Paris. M. Nourrit appeared, declaring, "I am the worst coward, I cannot stand the sight of blood," even as by his wits he forced the King to pay tribute to the flag of Revolution. M. Nourrit with his atomiser of scent, his gaily coloured squares of silk held in his hands as he sang, his piping laugh which often rose to a shriek: this *vivid* man inspired a more attractive vision of the future than did the grim men fighting amongst themselves in the political cafés about who would rule the world re-born.

Overcoming my native shyness I became, as I say, part of the entourage of Adolphe Nourrit, though I was the least poetic of his circle. In his presence melancholy seemed a perversion rather than a consummation of life; this conviction was the gift he made to me, as to so many others. I hope that my friend, for such I have the honour to call him, received from our talks some steadying influence. His usual hours were impossibly late for me, for like most artists of the stage he was a convivial creature of the night; he had also various familial obligations. Usually I met him in the late afternoon; I was the companion with whom he took constitutional walks along the *quays* of the Seine.

Though we spoke of ideas, his was not a philosophic temperament. Rather, the moment in which he and the King of the French both paid homage to the tricolour inspired in Nourrit a political passion which lasted until the penultimate day of his life. His was not a passion for an explanation. It was for a more fraternal life than that which is possible now in the vicious striving of the modern world, a politics of fraternity precisely *against* the grain of ambition. It may seem preposterous in this cynical era to maintain that a man's ideals can unbalance him.

Nourrit was first an adherent of the Count of Saint-Simon, that proponent of industry as a new religion. The Count's catechism: the factory is a cloister whose labourers are the modern equivalents of the monks, strenuous labour is inherently dignified, pure, moral. The religious trappings of Saint-Simonism often caused a smile to light the face of Adolphe Nourrit, as one witnessed upon several public occasions. However, just as the hymn to God is a necessity in church, the new priests of industry believed that music, like all the arts, should be united with everyday labour, even of the simplest kind. "The singing labourer," said Saint-Simon, "is happy in his task." This political dimension accorded his profession by the Saint-Simonians pleased Nourrit. He conceived the idea of teaching even the most ignorant of the common people how to sing; the pleasure street louts and urchins derived from learning how to sing would pass easily to the pleasure of other forms of disciplined work. Thus was born Nourrit's famous chorus of workingmen, which aroused so much hilarity among the rich and the complacent.

The doctrines of Saint-Simon never sufficiently provoked M. Nourrit's imagination, however. After the July Revolution he became also a partisan of the more extreme views of Fourier. M. Nourrit confessed to me his conversion came from observing Fourier in the Palais-Royal. Until his death in 1837, Fourier could be seen each morning wandering from the rue Montmartre to the palace of the Bourbons. The elderly gentleman carried a yardstick in his hand; in the course of his journey he would often stop, press the yardstick against the façade of a building, and mutter, "It could be altered, it could be done." This calculation meant little to his retinue, a body-guard of a dozen cats whom he fed from caches of food-scraps in his pockets and inside his shirt. For twenty years he had shared his meagre portion thus; it is said that the cats of the *quartier* were quite loyal to him, generations of felines having grown old in his service. Or at least he claimed so; once he was seated in his customary chair in the middle of the Palais-Royal, the cats nestling round his feet, their loyalty seemed no less wondrous than the other enchantments he sketched to any who would listen, his arms raised, trembling, as if in supplication to the gods, his eyes raised, the whole arthritic malnourished elderly body seeming to strain upwards towards the source of his visions.

Nourrit was one of the artists working in or associated with the Comédie-Française who would pass through the prim, proper passage of the Galerie d'Orléans out to the gardens of the Palais-Royal to be entertained by the old madman as a fixture in the daily parade. They came to smile; after a few days of his Mesmerizing gaze into the future, they left him convinced. Surrounded by the actors, singers and by other credulous persons, as well as his cats, Fourier foretold a future of pleasure, pleasure which machines created; this new world, unlike Saint-Simon's, was one of leisure rather than labour. The people in this new society will be at ease because machines give them powers we cannot even dream of: the power of one man to make a thousand carriages in a day by pressing buttons on an automatic forge, the power of another to perform mathematical calculations in an instant on a machine no larger than a tea-chest, calculations which now require several clerks days of grinding labour—the old man's delusions were endless.

Nourrit, I say, was one of the ones to fall under his spell. But this was not just because he liked to listen to stories. Fourier, much more than Saint-Simon, emphasised the profundity of the co-operative impulses. Fourier explained that intrigues, jealousies and cabals flourish not because of personal ambition but rather because of social organisation: rotate in a theatre the parts allotted to the actors, give everyone a chance to act leading róles at least once a season, and you will diminish intrigue; the actors will treat each other with more friendly respect because they are on a footing of equality.

I remarked that my friend lacked the philosopher's passionate attachment to ideas, a lack which may make the proposition seem all the more absurd that this extravagant could not bear life when it disappointed his ideals. However, his fraternal sensibility was far greater than any Jacobin who had deduced and declaimed fraternity. Once M. Nourrit directed our afternoon steps to a graveyard; it was a dull, cold day and I thought he sought in our path some correspondence to the weather. Suddenly my friend stopped before a small limestone mausoleum, executed as a miniature Greek temple, and smiled.

"Who is it?" I inquired, thinking the little dwelling contained the bones of someone he cherished.

"There are two of them within."

"Both your friends?"

"No, I knew neither of them. But this is a happy grave. It contains two architects, Percier and Fontaine, who chose to be buried with each other rather than with their separate families, as a testament to the art to which they jointly devoted themselves. A beautiful thought which always cheers me."

Such was Nourrit's sensibility. Moreover he had, as a musician, a practical experience of the ideas of the supposedly insane Fourier. François-Antoine Habeneck's Société des Concerts du Conservatoire, although it commenced two years before the July Revolution, embodied them. Habeneck taught his musicians to play together, for instance to push the bows of the stringed instruments up and down in the same way at the same time at the direction of the conductor, where before each player pursued his own, often illogical fashion. Similarly with the breathing of the wind players. Habeneck contrived those clever gestures in the air which continue to delight us, signs which to the audience signify little but to the players allow them to express their various parts in co-ordinated fashion. Everyone says the Société des Concerts du Conservatoire has the greatest *esprit de corps* of any musical body in Paris and perhaps in Europe. M. Fourier, in his *Treatise on Universal Unity,* compares a good society to just such an orchestra—a comparison to which Adolphe Nourrit often alluded during his frequent battles with other singers, capricious musicians in the pit, or management.

Nourrit, a highly strung, passionately dedicated artist, worried about everything on stage, not merely his own part, his own effect. In the rôle of William Tell the real Nourrit was revealed: the strong, almost harsh voice demanding liberty; in the heat of singing this rôle Nourrit would sometimes forget or simply efface the usual decorations so that the line of melody thrust itself out, irresistible to his auditors, cut cleanly like the stone of his favourite grave, Nourrit demanding liberty in the name of the united people. To those who knew him best, there seemed indeed something ascetic in his taste for direct and uncluttered expression.

I believe Nourrit calmed himself during the inflamed and intense labour he performed every day in the mire of Paris, that he salved his spirit with that vision of the future revealed to him by the prophet Fourier. Preposterous—of course. We "know" men contemplate political visions only because they are avid for power. Perhaps Nourrit's madness lay in the fact that he had no desire to rule anyone; he had instead a need for love.

When in 1837 he lost his balance and fell into the mire of Parisian ambition, intrigue and scheming, he found that his ideals no longer gave him courage, or even solace. His comrades turned against him; the young no longer wanted to hear the story of Louis-Philippe and the Marseillaise. During the humiliating last two years of his life, he who had formerly reached out to others, he now gradually turned against them. He began to hate mankind as only a man does who despairs of himself, whose ideals have been stripped bare as illusions. Such was the man who determined to throw himself, a deadly projectile, from a window five storey up into a crowded Neapolitan square. The suicide may have occurred, as one wit has it, because Duprez opened the window in Naples and Duponchel, then director of the Paris Opéra, pushed him out it. The attempted murder occurred because, to complete the figure, Fourier urged him to climb to such a wicked height at all.

Consider what happened behind the scenes of those lurid events in April of '37: for months previous we have all Paris anticipating with glee the duel of Duprez and Nourrit, perhaps in preparation for the war between the nations of Thalberg and Liszt. Nourrit, yielding to a momentary impulse, turns one night in the winter when he is singing in *The Mute Woman of Portici* to the box in which Duprez listens and makes a provoking gesture. Duprez responds by having an article published about how quickly older singers can lose their vocal instrument (Duprez is all of four years younger than Nourrit). On the 4th of April Nourrit finishes his season at the Paris Opéra, on the 17th, Duprez makes his official Paris Opéra début—in *William Tell*, the rôle which Nourrit has made so particularly his own. Duprez's voice proves more penetrating, but also capable of more colour; his decorations are elaborate and faultless, his range is four notes higher than the older man's, and these high notes are sung effortlessly. If Nourrit is an architect of song, Duprez is a painter. Paris is bored with architecture, which ceased to be fashionable when the Jardin des Plantes was completed; Paris decides in favour of decoration.

On the 20th of April, Nourrit attends a meeting of fellow Fourierists. Here he has always been honoured; these are his "brothers," men committed to Fraternity. All we know of this meeting is that on the 22nd, a list of artistic personalities engaged to sing a concert to benefit the cause of the Phalanstery does not contain the name of Adolphe Nourrit. In May, Nourrit revives his Workingman's chorus at the Canal de l'Ourq, and one paper reports the event, only in a paragraph, noting that several of the workingmen are now demanding payment for their services.

In June he is engaged to sing in Marseilles, the city whose revolutionary sympathies have always guaranteed him an especially warm reception. On 13 June, in a performance of *La Juive,* he loses his voice in the last act, and the red Marseillais boo him as enthusiastically as they would any unknown who had failed them even for a moment. It is at this time, his friend Bouffe has revealed, that Nourrit begins to plan his suicide. The singer tells Bouffe on the 14th: "My friend, how vicious men are. Before they carried me on their shoulders, perhaps today they'll drag me through the mud! And how stupid architects are! The one who designed the Grand Théâtre makes you climb three flights to arrive at a window from which you can throw yourself so that you die infallibly."

The singer then leaves France. He hopes to re-learn his art in a more modern fashion, by study with Donizetti. All reports are that Donizetti was kind to the broken singer attempting to start over at the age of thirty-five. In Italy Nourrit does have a momentary triumph in the Bellini *Norma;* however, he has ceased to sing the French repertoire abroad, or Schubert, whose name he made in France and whose songs he made seem French; "I am a man without a musical country," Nourrit confides to a colleague, the strongest of the fraternal bonds broken. In Italy the foreign singer is honoured, but, like all exiles, expected to conform to the usages of his adopted land. Nourrit, the lion a year before of the Parisian salons, a hero to its workingmen, adored by his strong, handsome lieutenants, Nourrit now struggles to make himself understood in Rome. His compliments often seem absurd to the Italians, the police keep him strictly to account because his political reputation travelled with his musical fame, the singer is obliged to review his activities weekly at a police station, and all because another singer has sung plangently a rôle he had himself once made his own.

The Romantic heroes, the men who fashioned the dreams of our youth, suffered from a fatal disease of the imagination. They believed that the time of living is like the passage from night into day, life so hurtling that in a matter of hours the whole world can be transformed. Their taste for revolutions was no different than their love of ghost stories, in both the ground of life suddenly violently trembling and from the depths a dread dark Power appearing. Not by chance is *Macbeth,* less subtle but more violent than *Hamlet,* the favourite Shakespeare of the Romantics. In their terrors, so in their dreams. The lunatic Fourier cast his spells in the Palais-Royal over cats and men in equal measure; he promised a change of life as total as the difference between night and day, and as rapid—if only men have the courage. The Romantics, ever avid for immediate sensation, have never lacked for courage.

I call a man's imagination diseased when it is formed around sudden sharp contrasts, when living time, the time of human history, is measured in the mere hours of night and day, the mere minutes of storm—I call this man's imagination diseased because at the slightest sign of distress he begins to gird himself for catastrophe. Indeed, he does not believe he is truly alive unless he is risking all. He may force the most petty incidents into earth-quaking upheaval; then they matter. Pain appears to him inevitably the prologue to despair.

Such a diseased imagination has no resources to cope with the reality of living, historical pain—the slow grinding of the wheel of events. The man of storm, darkness and radiant light lacks the spiritual armour which permits him to wait. The diseased imagination is incapable of irony, our only true solace in the face of history.

Adolphe Nourrit suffered from this Romantic disease. Its tell-tale symptoms appeared in that side of his life men took least seriously, his visionary politics, his desire for the bold gesture before a king, for a plan ready-made and entire of a new fraternal régime. It could all happen, he believed, if only men would take their courage in their hands. These dreams are no different from the wild metric of Hugo, from the stunning sounds of Thalberg and Liszt, indeed from those seemingly practical men who want to build the city twenty storeys high or a hundred miles wide. The word which obsesses all of them is "suddenly." But "suddenly" has terrible associations; it implies "totally" and "totally" is the emblem of life-or-death.

When pain came to M. Nourrit, he magnified it to a life-or-death struggle, which he lost. No triumph in Italy could salve the wound of his bitterness, nor did the thought of retiring gracefully to live upon his substantial fortune appeal to him. He recognised the genuine virtues of Duprez and the Italian School; after defeat he wanted to re-make himself, to become a new artist, to start fresh as though it were indeed a new day. The terrible paradox is that his art was not Romantic in the inflamed sense; his voice harked back to a more stately, sober era. This is why I maintain, when the vulgar claim that Duprez opened the window and Duponchel pushed him out, the truth to be much sadder. M. Nourrit began to prepare for his suicide the day he knelt before Louis-Philippe and forced the new King to rise. He launched himself upon the fatal seas of "suddenly." A sadder truth than the vulgar know and perhaps also more frightening. For if Fourier urged him to climb so high, it was only that in the final moment, his dreams shattered, the singer might seek revenge, jumping on complete strangers. Throughout our era, suicide has held for Romantics a place of honour, one might almost say, of prestige: the ultimate, decisive stroke. But this taste for suicide may conceal beneath its lurid raiments something far worse. When life fails to conform to the laws of our imagination, we may turn into creatures of murderous rage.

The evidence for the sad, terrible truth of Adolphe Nourrit's last days lies in their sequel. The body was not yet cold when those who had laughed at his hoarseness, or dismissed his Schubert as old-fashioned, when these persons suddenly remembered that he was a great artist whose life and work meant everything. The body was returned to Marseilles, where in the Church of Notre-Dame-du-Mont on the 24th of April Chopin played at a memorial service for Nourrit, performing on the church organ one of the singer's favourite pieces, Schubert's "The Stars." The church overflowed, and it was said that men wept freely in the rudest cafés on the waterfront.

Here in Paris there was also a sudden re-discovery of the greatness of Adolphe Nourrit. The Opéra closed for a day. A mass was celebrated at which Gilbert Duprez sang, painting the entire Madeleine with the tones of his exquisite grief. Liszt, who was a constant friend to Nourrit through all his trials, preached a sermon which I believe both pays tribute to the singer and is a symptom of his disease: Liszt said,

> He was a noble artist, at once passionate and austere. . . . His dreams were of art; he dreamt with all the fervour of a monk of the Middle Ages of a regenerated future of pure beauty, a glorious future of immaculate beauty! In the last years of his life he refused to lend himself to situations which were common or superficial, in order that he could serve his art with a chaste and enthusiastic respect. . . . He considered art as a sacred tabernacle whose beauty forms the splendour of truth. Dully undermined by melancholy passion for this beauty, his face in these last years seemed already to compose itself in marble coldness, under the fatal shadow. The burst of despair always explains itself too late to men.

Let us pray that Adolphe Nourrit will be the only one to die of the illness from which his age suffers. In taking this burden upon himself, may he rest in peace.

II

The Crystal Palace

A Future of Our Own

Letters of Adèle Mercure,
Frederick Courtland and John Courtland
May–July 1843

Mlle Cécile Mercure   *13 May 1843*
3, rue de la Tour des Dames
Paris

Dearest Sister,

I'll tell you frankly what I think. A gentleman of twenty-seven is not old enough to serve as deputy chaperone when you are riding out in Madame Nourrit's carriage. Two or three dances at a ball do not justify it. This is why you would make a mistake to allow him to escort you to the Dufresnes'. Other young men will keep away, even if they do not think you formally engaged. I am writing to Madame Nourrit; such a generous young charge she has!

I heard from a friend of Laguierre who has come to London for the horse sale that old Dufresne is now worth another million; you can be sure Nicole would not return to a pauper's hearth. By the by, you do not tell me anything of the fortune or prospects of your admirer; we have high hopes for you dearest, since my price becomes lower with each passing year.

Today Maman was at me again about the fall of my crinolines. You see, if only Madame Véry can execute a perfect pleat-turn callers will throng the door. We have wasted hours in pinning and unpinning. This morning I said, "Maman, if I die from asphyxiation, I shall certainly make a pretty picture in my coffin; I prefer life and a thicker waist. What? You are not amused?" We were about to have a scene when Monsieur entered her boudoir. He took my side, which is something. He does not like, I think, the many evenings Maman spends husband-hunting for me.

He is, by the way, engaged in business which may bring him to Paris next week, but it is too brief for Maman or I to return with him, so you two will be alone in the house. It would be only proper for Madame Nourrit to be frequently in your company. I must say I have become quite fond of Monsieur's Papa. He now takes me to the theatre for the rest of Maman's season, pays me compliments which flatter rather than embarrass me, talks interestingly about paintings and buildings. Were it not for Mr Courtland I would have to ask one of Madame Vestris' friends to accompany me to the theatre, and these women are mainly interested in what the other ladies are wearing.

What else? To recompense him for the evenings, I have begun to read to him in the afternoon, as his sight is weakening in the remaining eye; I read from French books, attempting the English translation as I go along. This is difficult, but wonderful for my English. The books he asks me to read him! *Adolphe* in running translation! And I believe the cunning thing knows full well what he is about in choosing M. Constant's novel of incitement. Time otherwise would hang heavily.

Maman's own season is quite good. Last night she dared to play Constanza, and was cheered. She can make herself the most believably young girl on stage, still; it is you two who could pass for sisters. Maman is in such high spirits, indeed, that she has done up her boudoir in a blinding tint— she calls it "heavenly outrage blue."

Do not fail to tell me everything about the Dufresne evening. You are an infuriating correspondent: you say everyone was "charming," the evening was "ever so pleasant," and I never know what *happened.* My darling, lovely sister, I long to embrace you, and shall very soon.

> In the meanwhile, love from
> your adoring
> Adèle

To:
His Grace, The Duke of Devonshire
in care of Arthur Cudlip, Esq.
Coutts Bank
Charing Cross
London

May it please your Grace,

I venture to write you on behalf of gentlemen architects whose work, our mutual acquaintance Sir Rodney Hulls informs me, is already known to you. Sir Rodney has further and, I trust, not indiscreetly, indicated that your Grace considers doing the Metropolitan Association for Improving the Dwellings of the Industrious Classes the honour of serving as its Patron in a new scheme for residences in the East End of London. I take the liberty of proposing our professional offices to your Grace.

My father, Mr John Courtland, R.A., has long been considered a master of his art amongst men of taste, as I perhaps need not tell your Grace, *primus inter pares* in this elect and necessarily small circle. Recently my father has honoured me by inviting me to form a partnership with him for the joint practise of architecture, the erection both of individual buildings and of larger ensembles. This latter, more urban, design is the branch of our work which will be my particular concern and, as I am as yet unknown in this country, I have made bold to address myself to you, who I hope will not take this advertisement to be a sign of immodesty.

My particular claim on your good offices lies only in the circumstances which have long kept me from my native country. I was sent to France to train at the Ecole des Beaux-Arts, receiving my diploma there in 1831, under the direction of M. Pierre Fontaine. It was my great good fortune to learn from him the most advanced French methods of the construction of iron and glass structures. He created the Galerie d'Orléans in the Palais-Royal, justly called the most elegant arcade in Europe, its patron His Majesty Louis-Philippe, King of the French. I had the honour to assist in this building; indeed, I seem to have become its curator, charged as I was by M. Fontaine in its alteration to a hospital during the Great Plague of '32, and then by the Crown offices to restore the Galerie to its original form in 1833. This arcade since has served as the model for the Jardin des Plantes, for the new Passage Jouffroy, and other structures of exceptional scale.

Until 1841, when a wave of chauvinism swept their Government, and so decreased the opportunities for foreigners, no matter how long resident in France, to receive employment upon official commissions, until this unfortunate turn I served as draughtsman, as under-architect, finally as senior architect in a number of projects deriving from this original work. Most notably, I was associated with the design of the Gare St-Lazare, Paris' first railway terminus; I provided technical advice on the iron-and-glass roof, and was amongst those who created the arcades of bookstalls and cafés adorning the sides of this edifice. May I say that, unlike those who had the designing of the Kew Garden, my work has sought to fit these large iron-and-glass structures so that one structure may be put to a variety of uses. Such are my qualifications, such my experience; should it please your Grace, I would devote these to your service.

As no plan exists as yet for the East End housing, might I make so bold as to suggest at least a possibility, a possibility drawing upon one of the great assemblies of building already known to man?

You are undoubtedly familiar with the town of San Gimignano in Italy, its needle-like stone towers ringing a central square. As one journeys up the hill towards San Gimignano, one is stunned by the sheer drama of these towers, whose original purpose was simply that of posts of observation for the protection of the city. Later the towers became places of sport; from them the nobility of San Gimignano rained arrows, oil and stones upon the hapless population in the squares below. These allied towers, however, need not in form serve only crude usages. Somewhat expanded in size, both in width and in height, they could provide the most extraordinary form of housing: a high density of population, such as exists in the city of today, could be accommodated upwards, the families in each tower enjoying light and fresh air, rather than the terrible crampedness of our streets, the common square serving as a place of fraternal association as well as economic provision. I propose to you quite simply that we build an iron-and-glass San Gimignano in the East End of London.

When I advert to this ancient city, I do so, of course, only by way of illustration. In Alberti's treatises, we do find the most rigid specifications for the construction of towers; he rules that rectangular towers should be six circumferences in height, round ones four. I do not suggest following such rules; indeed, San Gimignano lacks an exact geometric, just as the great individual towers of the Northern Gothic were irregular, and even the great campanile of the Cathedral at Ferrara, though seeming but one storey after another atop an identical base, in fact is most varied in proportioning and detail.

If I have learnt one thing since my early days as an apprentice, it is that the mass manufacture of windows and doors from a substance like iron must not dictate a tyrannical uniformity; modern materials can be used to provide the greatest variety in form—if used with taste. For over a decade, I have sought to explore this relation between the regularity of parts and the individuality of wholes. May I say that, in restoring the Galerie d'Orléans in '33, I realised that, however admirable as a demonstration of elegance in uniformity, my future work would have to bear the stamp of my own vision, were I to call it mine, a future in which I dedicated myself to play with proportion, to contrast between the uniform and the unexpected. In short I came to understand that today one may create the most individual structures by architectural geometry, a geometry inherently reacting against, even as it derives from, mathematics. My explorations are thus far mostly in the form of drawings.

Forgive me for trying your patience. In introducing myself to you, I thought it only fair that I introduce you to how I see. This housing, following the model of an ancient city yet embodying an individual composition derived from manufactured elements, would mark a decisive turning-point in the practice of architecture. It would be economic in construction, adaptable to the needs of the poor, whatever these may be, perhaps in time so striking that more fortunate citizens of London would find aerial living attractive. It would be a thoroughly English architecture in result, combining our industrial prowess with our long care of individuality. May I say I thus appeal to you in the name of principle?

With the greatest respect, and entrusting this missive to the good offices of Mr Cudlip, your agent in London being as well my father's old and dear friend, most of all hoping that the matter I have set before you will excite your curiosity even if you deem others more worthy to execute it, I remain, your humble servant,

> Frederick Courtland
> Courtland & Courtland
> 12 Jermyn Street
> London

Mlle Cécile Mercure   *2 June 1843*
3, rue de la Tour des Dames
Paris

My Dearest,

She managed my introduction two days past, at an "evening" of Madame
Vestris and Mr Mathews, who are now husband and wife thanks to a tour
they made to America a few years ago, although they remain most devoted
to one another. The grandfather of Monsieur escorted me to the slaughter.

He is a discharged bankrupt, (I mean Mr Mathews), which perhaps
accounts for the lavishness; we dined upon delicate game birds out of
season, fillets of beef stuffed with oysters, and drank jeroboams of champagne. This "evening" was in truth a ball in miniature given by the couple who are afraid of being thought presumptuous and so snubbed if they
issue cards. Still, the Mathews engaged a small band of violins, footmen in
livery and some quite good furniture "rented for the occasion," according
to Maman. There were at least eight young ladies on display, most of
whom, I am happy to say, looked as wretched and worn out from their
fittings, crimpings, etc. as did I. The happy parents discoursed mainly on
how the new theatre law would affect contracts and tours; Maman, abhor-
ring evenings of such talk, deployed what we all admit is her exquisite,
indelible charm on these people who were hardly attending to its rainbow
colours.

Except of course the father of Monsieur. He had the courtesy to call for
us in his large landau. I believe the old gentleman's eye was painful that
evening, although with him you could never know, he is not given to
complaint. He handed Maman in first! Perhaps that is why, when I took
the place beside him, Maman remarked, "Adèle looks extraordinarily fetch-
ing tonight, does she not, Mr Courtland? Madame Véry has contrived a
most complimentary frock for her."

"Your daughter is ever in beauty." Maman then spoke of the danger of
steam locomotion.

At the moment both she and Monsieur advance that "the Future lies in
England," a principle evidently applicable to all. Why an old maid should
have more of a future in London than in Paris may not, perhaps, be
immediately evident to you. I have met persons at the British Library, most
knowledgeable and kind, but they are invisible in their insignificance to
Maman. Or rather, she accounts them not because my interest seems to her
no part of feminine accomplishment; indeed, I have taken up antiquities

only to further vex her, as my dresses become filthy within the precincts of the Library. I promised, however, I would make a real effort this night.

Madame Vestris is the one who abolished the shilling gallery at Covent Garden, who has the reputation of "respectable evenings of quiet smiles" —she it is who extracted an annuity of £700 from poor Mr Gore and whose fame rests on exposing her legs in breeches! We were introduced; she greeted me kindly enough. I too, because I could think of nothing better, asked her about the new law. She said it did not address the real problem of the English stage, which is an insufficiency of income due to low ticket prices, and then spoke of the great achievement of "my husband and myself" in ridding Covent Garden of "the vulgar." It is "our gift to British theatre."

We passed from Madame Vestris to the person evidently singled out for me by Maman. He is a slender, sleek protégé of the great Dion Boucicault to whom I was also presented. "Great," Mr Mathews remarked quietly of the playwright, in promise, though he has done nothing really since *London Assurance,* and "promising," remarked Maman equally sotto voce of the protégé, in that although he is three years younger than myself, his connexions have already made him a coming man. You have met Mr Boucicault many times, though usually he is older than Dion. He is the attractive and diplomatic personage at dinners who asks you flattering questions about yourself, delivers graceful opinions upon current topics, who leaves you with the impression that he has never passed so agreeable an interval; a minute later you cannot recall a word. I was presented, rich and ripe meat, to this lion of the season, by Maman as follows:

"Dear Dion, I should like you to meet my daughter, Adèle Delsart, who has kindly come to London to see me through the season."

"Then you do not come to us from Mercury?" Dion purred and bowed.

Maman answered for me. "Unfortunately. I had hoped to retain the name of my husband on the stage, but when I began Mlle Mars had set us all the example, and we became distant stars to her nearer planet." Maman trilled the silver laugh and then composed her face into wistful recollection. "However, 'Delsart' was fine enough, quite fine enough. Manners have changed, dear Dion. Today the 'stage name' seems foolish and crude, does it not? But in those days, in France, one played by other rules, one's domestic life hidden."

At this old Mr Courtland's good eye twitched; I turned away. The protégé of Mr Dion Boucicault, either from exquisite tact or insensibility, accompanied my turn as though we two now could consummate the desire to speak to each other which had grown so lively in the last few minutes.

1.   He, Mr Thomas Waller, complimented me on my excellent English

and asked how I had learnt to speak without an accent. Instead of replying that Frederick and Charles Courtland had taught me whilst both lived in Paris, one of them in the house, I replied I had studied in school and Maman was an apt conversationalist. First step towards Delsart.

2.   He asked me if I were acquainted personally with the great actors of Paris, as he was sure my Maman knew them all professionally. Did I know Frédéric Lemaître, Marie Dorval? I replied that of course I had met these persons but knew, really, no more than the public at large. Second step towards Delsart.

You will ask, why was I walking in this direction, towards yet another of the great lies Maman tells when she is ill at ease? The answer is simple. Maman and I this evening communed in unease. Within my tilting crinoline, under the weight of ringlets both natural and culled from the heads of others, my gloves held tightly in my palms to absorb the disgusting dampness exuded when my head and heart are agitated, the imperfect confection that was me cried to itself amongst the rented furniture and gentlemen actors and tardily married actresses, "This is the best you can do, this is your last chance, now or never!" Had not Maman told me that in France I would be "difficult" to place? Argued the advantages of husband-hunting in a foreign country?

It has come to me, usually in the D room of the Library, that about matrimony Maman and I think ourselves to be like lions prowling a farm where the sheep, goats and dogs have never seen such large pussy-cats before. Of course this might only be our illusion about English people. At Madame Vestris' evening we were thirty; perhaps each one addressed all the others with his or her own "Delsart." And then there has been rented furniture from time to time at home. The best I could do; I am twenty-six years old.

3.   Mr Waller smiled with a very London assurance and asked did I not find the city dull after Paris. "We imagine your town as wicked, filled with schemers and impostors and crazed revolutionaries and I know not what. Then we meet a person such as yourself"—for a moment, dearest, I was amused, for how could he rescue himself from his quagmire of words save by contrasting this Paris to the dull creature in front of him, and indeed he faltered, but only for one moment—"and we realise there is another Paris hidden behind the life of the streets, a demure, elegant Paris whose denizens must surely find us a simple and credulous race," and so forth, but Bravo! I was beginning to enjoy myself.

4.   Suddenly the charming young man proved himself not quite so ignorant. "I have heard that M. Liszt has left the Comtesse d'Agoult for Marie Pleyel, that all Paris seethes with the news. Ordinarily I would not

take the liberty of discussing such a matter, however delicious, with a lady, but I know in your country manners are frank, and I make bold to ask you, what do you think?"

Now I was forced to take a final step towards Delsart. I told the smiling young man that Papa and Maman had raised us almost in seclusion. I well understood that behind the smile he was testing me. Had I given the slightest sign to the delightful protégé that I understood his allusions, we would have continued to chatter ever more gaily, yet his smile would be tinged with just the slightest leer. However, since I know nothing, I understand nothing, I am the sort of girl he could pursue with propriety. We might now speak of the Queen's ever so gentle greeting to the Duke of Wellington this afternoon in Rotten Row. Indeed, Maman should have been proud of me. After displaying my complete ignorance of the sufferings of Aunt Marie, I turned on my heel in a huff. That a Delsart had been approached on such a subject!

To have a future, we must be very careful about the past.

Macready dropped in for a moment; he is well-known, it seems, to hold Vestris and Mathews in contempt, which he deserves to, as he is an infinitely finer actor than either of them and a true gentleman. He came straight to Maman, Mr Courtland and me after paying his respects, which he did punctiliously, to La Vestris. He said not one word about the theatre act; he omitted any reference to his own triumphs of the moment; indeed, miraculously, he said not one word about himself or any other individual present, talking exclusively of poets and their promenades. This subject engaged both Maman and Mr Courtland in a discussion wherein they had the pleasure of discovering they knew more than they had imagined, Maman speaking of Victor Hugo's hatred of certain mountain vistas, the old gentleman of the art of the Renaissance gardener in contriving promenades as dramatic excursions—for some minutes the room vibrated with that play of words Maman so cherishes at home, until Macready was obliged to leave for his long journey to his own house. Most of the guests had gathered round us by this time. Macready parted with the warm exhortation to Maman, "Please give Frederick my very best wishes. Your evenings in Paris redeem a thousand trials. Does he well? Together," Macready now turned to Monsieur's father, "together you shall rule the building of London, I am certain." Then he kissed my hand, nodded briefly to Boucicault, and vanished. How heavily, I wondered, did her—our—lie weigh in the balance against Macready's esteem?

In the carriage she burst out, "Why did you cut that nice young Irishman?"

I looked at the old Mr Courtland, now sitting across from me in the brougham. In place of the usual black eye patch he had worn a blue velvet one. At midnight he looked a very tired pirate. I said only to Maman, "Because he was forward with me."

"That is generally how young men make their attentions known to young women." At this moment, my dearest, I felt I would not stand for any more, and I am sure you will judge me entirely in the right.

"He was forward with me as 'Mlle Delsart.'"

Mr Courtland took her hand in his. He looked at me whilst holding it, then smiled faintly; the eye closed and he dozed with his hand still in Maman's.

If Maman wishes to remain in England at the side of Monsieur, no doubt she can contrive a fitting story here to re-touch the tale begun with her marriage to the estimable Delsart. Do you imagine I enjoy the sensation of being constantly at war? Does that conduce to make me a good daughter?

I embrace you in touching this page to my lips.

> Your most loving sister,
> Adèle

Frederick Courtland   *4 June 1843*
3, rue de la Tour des Dames
Paris

My dear Son,

I trust your crossing has been smooth; in my day, it was a veritable journey whereas in yours it seems a mere jaunt. Will this speed of locomotion render us eventually unable to distinguish where we are, Paris agog with the latest scandal about Lady Jones, all London knowledgeable of the best fruits and viands to be had each week in the Marché de St-Germain? I introduce this subject not for the purpose of philosophic concourse between us during your brief absence, but rather to indicate to you, my dear boy, that the future, if this be it, is not at hand. I refer to Paxton.

Yesterday Brunel burst into my inner chambers. Dame Gossip told him you had written to the Duke of Devonshire, the good lady chortling in Brunel's ear that you proposed to supersede Paxton. I know in France to call oneself an "architect" is to declare one's love for the blood-soaked pageantry of the mediaeval ages. This is not the English way, which obliges us to varnish our dealings as highly as our boots. Brunel's storms are familiar to me, however. I assumed that you, ever an adept pupil, would have learnt —or re-learnt—the pretences of your countrymen within six months. To re-assure Brunel that you had done no more than make your existence known to this August Personage, I asked Smallbone if a letter to the Duke had indeed been composed, and your clerk-slave indicated that he possessed a copy of a missive already sent. I hid my surprise, and then recouped, thinking you had sent the Duke of Devonshire so modest a note you did not bother me. Smallbone now intimated it would be improper to expose the communiqués of a Member of the Firm to casual scrutiny. I intimated to Smallbone—you see how this little passage has already roused my jousting blood—I intimated to your wizened rodent that the name of our partnership, in which one Courtland is no more prominent than the other, made it perfectly appropriate for him to reveal to Mr John what Mr Frederick wrote on behalf of both.

It is fit you be acquainted with these particulars, that I be acquitted of the charge of meddling. I respect the Entente Cordiale which reserves to you the lofty Switzerland of the Future, while I superintend the more spacious, if flatter, Burgundy of the Past. This matter concerns, Sir, the connecting Grenoble of the Present, whose commerce pays both for your dreams and my memories. To wit: the Duke of Devonshire is the most prestigious client of architecture here apart from the Crown, in my view even more Enlightened than Prince Albert himself. To offend the Duke would be the ruin of any man's reputation, no matter what the sum of genius under offer. And one would offend him, were one to challenge the patronage he has extended to Joseph Paxton; he *made* Paxton, raised Joseph from gardener's boy to premier inventor. Thus I had no scruple in extracting the letter from your guardian canine.

We retired to my inner office. Smallbone, pursing his lips into the oval of disapproval which so regularly disfigures his face when in my company, shut the door of the inner sanctum after us; thus our commentaries upon your prose have not reached the ears of the draughtsmen. Perhaps you will charge me with exposing your draught to Brunel; however, he came from affection inspired by long friendship—for us both!—and you know him to be discreet. In the event, the letter startled me but quite sobered our colleague, who declared it was even worse than he had heard.

"I venture to write to you on behalf of gentlemen-architects whose work, our mutual acquaintance Sir Rodney Hulls tells me, is already known to you. I take the liberty of proposing to you our professional offices." I have remarked that the Bachelor Duke made Paxton; I mean he lavished upon him the care, and furnished him the opportunities, any loving father would upon a son—perhaps the more care, this adopted son rising from the lower orders. Thus your phrases "gentlemen-architects" and "professional offices," while perfectly unexceptional in themselves, can only give the Duke offence. It is as good as writing, "Your Lordship employs a mere gardener, the son of a common labourer, as the architect of his estates?"

Since you left, men of industry have entry to the most exalted houses (often, indeed, as prospective purchasers). In this confusing condition we are perhaps more particular about forms of address: this letter refers casually to "you." Of course one used to say simply "Duke" in speaking directly to an aristocrat of this degree, there being no question of familiarity; now you must remember *consistently* to write "your Grace." It is confusing, is it not? The manufacturer enters boldly by the front door while good manners oblige a gentleman to speak like a servant.

"We have worked with the most advanced French methods for the construction of iron-and-glass structures." Do you mean to imply that the extraordinary greenhouse Paxton has built for the Duke is *not* advanced? "The Arcade we constructed has served as the model for the Jardin des Plantes, the new Passage Jouffroy and other structures of exceptional scale. Unlike the designing of the Kew Garden [a solecism, my boy, which would not endear you to an aristocrat who dislikes the Hanoverian accents heard at Court], our building aims at fitting these large iron-and-glass structures for a variety of uses." Very good, save that the Duke and Joseph Paxton were said to share a little joke at the opening of the grand Chatsworth Conservatory: "Where will this end, Joseph?" demanded the Duke. "Plants tended under glass, the new steam-rails housed under glass—will mankind soon sleep, dine and converse under this transparency?" Paxton, they say, replied, "No, your Grace, these industrial buildings are not a fit habitat for us, their makers, who still require the primitive materials of stone and wood for comfort." Of course, this was in 1836 or 1837, when you were out of the country.

Your missive harmed us in its unintended arrogance. Yet as well it intimated an unjustified contempt. I refer not to your abilities, but to the implicit comparison with those of Paxton. He is pursuing a less adventurous course than you in his designing; this does not mean it is less honourable. No one could fail to be moved at your declaration that we must find an art equal to the new techniques of building; Brunel himself applauds your repeated attacks on cast iron poured into Rococo moulds, the fluidity of the material perverted into ever more elaborate ornament; one wishes you God-speed (if our Creator is capable of rousing Himself from His evident sluggish melancholy in contemplating the world today) in discovering not merely new buildings but entire new city landscapes for metal and glass. You seek the opportunity from the most enlightened patron of architecture in our century. Your letter, *in itself,* is a model of decorum, exhibiting pride in past work without flourish or boast. In France, no government official could resist a cordial reply. Here your admirable document constitutes an attack on the Duke's social principle, on his sagacity and of course upon the capacity of his protégé, your letter implying that you are now ready to supply the visionary art so far lacking in the labours of the Duke's architect. No wonder this letter has created a little affair.

May I confess, had you consulted me before penning your note, I should have told you that, even were it feasible, I should sooner have taken work from any "gentleman" than from him. The Conservatory, like the landscaping, like the workingman's housing, is honest—if not particularly interesting to view once one overcomes the shock of the scale. No matter; I follow our colleagues in admiring his prose.

Frederick, I am perplexed that you could have taken so momentous a step in your career without consulting me. Why? This indifference is so unlike you. Why? Please think well on this matter. I thought in writing to you I might relieve my pique; I have not. Perhaps we ought retire for a few days to the country when you return, to regain in repose a mutual confidence.

Your loving
Father

Since the letter I wrote yesterday evening, a cooler brain has revealed to me how aptly you might have cause for offence.

Sentient men of my age measure perhaps too neatly provocation. We all grew up during wartime; the entire period of your childhood there was war. Then consider that in '34 Snigs and I discovered his valet to be reading his mail, copying confidential passages enclosed to him from old clients, embellishing these in the copying, and then causing the result to be printed in an incendiary tract issuing from a hole in Clerkenwell. One of my draughtsmen in, I think, '40 assisted the police for several days in their enquiries into the matter of a bomb placed, but fortunately unexploded, in the Strand. I am no avid judge, but from simple prudence have practised what Snigs and other cognoscenti of economy counsel: effacement of provocative display of rank. The lower orders must be accounted. In the matter of Paxton, he deserves accounting. Do you know what Snigs claims? The jovial John Bulls at their groaning boards, speaking sharply to the servants, from whom so nearly and recently they have risen, are the greatest revolutionary force of our time. Would you by inadvertence lend Dame Gossip a hand, so that she might wickedly count you amongst the guests at this suicidal feast?

Perhaps you remain unconvinced that these large matters justify me in rounding on you. I seek only to save you, who reveal yourself a foreigner, from being further misunderstood; there are no other grounds for what you might disown as excessive sensibility. Surely you cannot doubt my esteem for your work, my love for your person and my gratitude for your return.

John Courtland, Esq.   *9 June 1843*
12 Jermyn Street
London

Dear Father,

This morning's post brought your letter. May I begin at your conclusion? With entire justice you reproach me for sending this letter without regard either for your sentiments or for your correction. I will offer you no excuse, for I would demean neither of us thus, nor can I give you in truth an explanation. I draughted this letter carefully in our rooms, not in the atelier; that effort seemed to exhaust me. Once draughted, I gave the letter to Smallbone to copy out, and signed it barely attending to the proofing of his fair copy. I am not even sure I expected a reply, at least I did not think strategically what it might be.

Now I ask myself why I did so, since I am not, could never be, indifferent to *you*. I had forgotten how much our profession depends upon the circumstances of pleasing; I know little of the current gossip which inspires fellow feeling; our colleagues refer to persons or events in their youth which seem to me not only foreign but trivial. They speak of some fracas in a club as though the very heavens had parted, or about drinking a bottle of brandy each in an evening as a great adventure. Manners, you say, have changed; very well, but these are persons my own age, nearing the middle of their lives, to whom nothing has happened. When well in their cups, they may confide to me, "Frederick, the slut I found in '35, what charms, what good times!" or "We sent the draughtsman X packing a few years ago, a sullen fellow who never played cards, he spoilt an evening with his talking, talking, and he had thoroughly unsound views, but as I say we sent him packing, and did I ever tell you about White's dog fouling the blueprints for . . ." Can you think how interested they might be in Gautier's recent poetry? I have taken some account of our colleagues, Father; they will never discover me superior, but one feels the solitude of it. Anne does not seek out their wives, but think, if she did, what would these gentlemen architects say of her? These, my brothers in arms—so well established, the commissions pouring in upon them, more money in this country for building than in all Europe combined! And then it is hard, you must realise, for a man my age to be presented everywhere as your son who has returned home, as if from school.

Perhaps it was this, no more than a misguided desire to establish my own footing. In the event, the letter is good; if the Duke of Devonshire is displeased, it must be but a momentary annoyance which, reported somehow to one of our colleagues, has then passed ever louder, furnishing in magnification from mouth to mouth, from glass to glass, this week's illusion of life. And, in the event, the "little affair" will do us no harm; my work commands respect; I will make my way.

Your just rebuke does not prompt the unease which this letter causes me. It is rather the revelation of your insufficient belief in, even understanding of, my work, which you so lightly refer to as my Kingdom of the Future.

This pleasantry betrays a much more deeply paternal prejudice. If you truly believe us to be colleagues, you will "joust"—to use one of your words—on the terrain on which I propose to commit our firm. Do you accept that commitment? Does it excite you? If your answer to these questions is affirmative, then the questions of strategy we can easily share: your superior experience becomes *our* ally rather than my corrective. What is the very sense of the word "partners"? Men have work which they want to do together, work which is better for the collaboration. Your letter betrays not one sign that you take co-operative effort on these terms at all seriously.

I meant what I said to you six months ago: even with the changed attitude towards foreigners I would have stayed in France, for Anne's sake, had she not refused this sacrifice, categorically, for my sake. Of course the immense wealth of our country was also a lure. I chose to return to you because I respect your work; this is the compliment of a colleague, not a son. If I thought it were better for the furtherance of my buildings to work with Brunel or Stephenson, or to have joined the Metropolitan Association, I would have acted differently. If now, after six months, you do not feel the need of my work to do your own, let us dissolve a partnership in name which does not exist in fact.

In this connexion I would like to request you to cease from the suggestion, in explaining my absence to our colleagues, that I sought the pleasures of life abroad when they could no longer be obtained at home. I wish to give them no such impression, indeed no impression at all of a reason or an excuse; sometimes I think you more than half believe this pleasantry yourself. The familial life I led there was more demanding than would be any marriage in London, and I made my way professionally only by a constant exercise of will. Do you imagine Anne finds it convenient to pass some months each year acting in a foreign country whose dramatic standard is infinitely more debased, more vulgar, than that of France? Leaving Cécile alone, at a most tender and dangerous age? Think: you and I, Sir, have not embarked upon a jolly lark.

This brings me again to the matter of the Duke of Devonshire. In the next year, we *must* find a sponsor for at least six cast-iron towers. From inattention—forgive me, Sir, but we are at last speaking openly of matters which familial love and mutual politeness have covered over—from inattention you have not grasped the urgency of time and the necessity of scale. Indeed, the more I have mulled over the plan, the more I should like to advertise twelve, but this indeed might seem a dream to those whose imaginations have never conceived a vertical city, and so I will restrict our plan to the practical minimum, which is six.

It *is* practical. Yesterday I dined with Perrey. We discussed conducting pipes for heat, which they will deploy just beneath the floor tiles of the Passage Jouffroy. To build a sufficient degree of enduring steam in the pipes requires a boiler burning steadily at 110 degrees centigrade, the boiler lined with sealed tile, clad in 1.89 centimetre-thick cast ironstone. The efficient volume of bituminous coal for such a container—even this inferior grade can be well utilised at the scale we are speaking of—is $+/-$ 4.4 cubic m. *an hour!* Ponder that; it is cheaper by a factor of nearly 2 to heat one passage 100 metres long with one boiler than to heat five passages each 20 metres long with five ordinary boilers. I calculated with Perrey, who might come in with us, that the economy of scale in heating six towers jointly, assuming buildings (in our measures) of eight storeys, 82 feet in total height, each storey 1,600 feet square, the cost of heating these six together is a third less than heating two groups of three towers and half that of heating six structures separately.

You advance that great plans terrify most clients by the initial expense; the moment the Passage Jouffroy is completed, I predict on the contrary that capital will be attracted by the demonstrable savings. Recall that when Neilson first injected hot air into the blast furnace, everyone was sceptical because all the old ironmasters "knew" the injected air had to be passed through ice-pack pipes. They knew it, until he cut consumption of fuel from 8 to 5 tons per ton of iron. When Mushet availed himself of hot-blast to smelt Scottish ironstone, everyone "knew" it would fail; now the Scots need not import their ore from England. When men invoke the word "practical," they mean to say, "I am afraid."

Walk along the King's Road: what strikes your eye? That all the gardens and fields between the old clumps of buildings are filling in. The value of a level-standard square yard has doubled; it is the same here, a level-standard square metre now Fr8.79 in the *quartier* of the Champs de Mars, a decade before Fr4.92. As a horizontal space becomes dear, we must colonise the air; air still is free. Were it possible, we should indeed advance plans for sixteen storeys rather than eight; the higher one rises, the more economically one masters space.

The greatest impression I have received from this removal to London is that time is short, very short. For if you and I do not find the capital to begin immediately to build, Stephenson or Brunel surely will. In erecting iron-span bridges, and, even more, iron rail termini, they are already preparing in iron, like musicians practising; all that is required is that one day, with a start, they will realise that the immense iron members they have learnt to cast horizontally could be deployed vertically. Suddenly they will mentally turn their bridges through ninety degrees, thrusting them up into the air rather than over water or land; the abundant English money will follow them, as before, in this new revelation. Again I speak very practically: consider the outside main ribs and bracing frames which Stephenson contrived for the Chalk Farm bridge over the Regent's Canal. Stephenson has in these criss-cross X ribs and bracing a workable template for building up; he need only stack X over X over X to go as high as he likes. How long will it take Stephenson to realise that this template could establish him as the most revolutionary builder in London? A year, a month, or tomorrow?

Thus you may comprehend that I am not much impressed by the amiable exchange between Joseph Paxton and the Duke of Devonshire, the worthy Paxton assuring his patron that mankind will never enjoy life under the same structures which shelter the Duke's collection of exotic plants. We are not considering an idle whim, we are confronting the logic of technology and economy. Or rather, this logic confronts us, and we dither. When Stephenson or Brunel begins construction of a building which transforms the modern city, will it be enough for you to say to me ruefully, "I'm sorry, my boy, evidently you were correct in your surmises." And will these words issue from your lips in a year, a month, or tomorrow?

No, the Duke, his Grace, Duke—as you prefer—is not the only patron capable of comprehending that mankind is about to take a remarkable step of Progress. You, one of the few architects welcome in the most distinguished houses as a gentleman, know others; if your judgement suggests alternatives, let us pursue them; we will be eclipsed if from nicety of sentiment we walk slowly.

Last month I complimented Stephenson on the superb outer main rib on his Hampstead bridge for the London and Burlington Railway—you know it, the triangular rib within which is inscribed a diminishing row of circles; I told him I found this rib so graceful, recalling some of the hidden ribbing in Palladio's villas, and I asked him if he had indeed the master in mind. Stephenson stared at his boots; there was a pause. Has he ever journeyed to the Villa Rotunda, for example; had he perhaps ever seen a picture of it? Like a child, Stephenson asked me to explain my appreciation, and when I began to do so, invoking the tension between the weightless circles and the massive enclosing triangle, the suspension of depth so brilliantly achieved by this drama at the vaulting's outer edge, Stephenson again stared at his boots. I do not, Father, take pleasure in another man's ignorance. But in the urgency upon us, it is an asset. If Stephenson becomes aesthetical, he will probably succumb, like the other engineers, to disguising his drain pipes as Corinthian columns, or to casting rain gutters in imitation of the tablature friezes banding the Parthenon. We must advertise what we can do, you and I: deploy art to realise the inner beauty of this engineering. We shall make ironwork the more powerful, as all materials become when will and judgement replace blind manipulation.

Often you seem to speak of yourself, as in your letter, as if your day is past. I have seen the drawings you made when you were under Nash; they have the boldness of Soane without his eccentricity; you knew, you still know, how to make an unexpected door or a room of exceptional height flow into more usual spaces. You stimulate rather than disorient. This, my dear Father, is what you might in substance bring to our collaboration. Consider well San Gimignano. Unlike my teachers, I find it more than a matter for curiosity. Here is the most evocative quotation I can give from the past building of cities to exemplify the city of the future. Perhaps your eye suggests another: Lucca? It is as colleagues we might discuss this, not as companionable kings of adjoining realms called Past and Future—do you not now feel how *demeaning* this conceit is to *yourself* as well as me?

A few days ago, in going over the drawings I made last year, I saw something I had not remarked before—saw it in memory, not in my drawings. During the course of the solar circuit, the proportion of tower shaft to piazza floor in San Gimignano ensures every corner of the Piazza to be at some time entirely sunlit, and at another moment in the day entirely in shadow. This distribution of light by the tower masses had the beneficent effect of making all open space equally valuable; the eye is teased to explore every cranny of this complicated square. Height is the hidden stimulus of horizontal enquiry. This is the practical aspect. We must also argue that these stone needles reaching into the sky prophesied sheer thrust, walls rising straight, great height freed of buttressing or spreading mass at the base, the drama which can be contrived from placing one iron X above another X above another. The needles of San Gimignano gave humanity its first intimation of the vertical absolute. Now this intimation can be reinforced, the towers higher in modern London than in renaissant Italy, this vertical absolute in its turn a new principle of economy and efficiency. This is what we must say.

I do not pretend to be an ideal partner for you. Snigs, for example, could he but draw a straight line, would have furnished you more daily pleasure. And, to be frank, I should have wished ideally for a colleague with more technical expertise than yours, my own in engineering seeming to me deficient. Limited creatures we are, and as such we must take one another; we can contrive, if we share a common, serious purpose. Perhaps this Affair of the Duke's Letter is the moment for you to judge whether the companionship which you long sought in imagination is the partnership you wish for in fact.

Be assured, therefore, of my genuine respect; do not fret over the possible slight to my feelings. Only decide. Our labour, once we are launched, is likely to be intense, immense, exhausting—at least I hope so. I would prefer The Courtland Partnership to do this work, but if I must do it alone, I will. Until next Saturday, then, best wishes from

> your colleague
> Frederick

Mlle Cécile Mercure   *2 July 1843*
3, rue de la Tour des Dames
Paris

My dearest Puss,

The greatest news! Maman will allow me to travel to Greece! She will even pay for everything! I have been included in the expedition of a group of most eminent scholars, all from the Library and from the University of Oxford, to whom I shall serve as secretary. My English remains deficient, I think, though they find it passable; as we shall join French persons engaged in excavations on Delos, I trust I may prove my worth. Another English lady, wife of one of the scholars, will also come, serving as my chaperone—though it is hardly necessary! We go to Genoa, thence by sea to Athens.

It is uncertain whether we shall remain in Athens more than six months; that period is reserved for the classifying and crating of statuary and vase fragments retrieved from Delos. As far as Maman knows, this is the work I shall assist—though I have hopes to be allowed to survey sites. Once I am there, I plan to make myself indispensable! During this season I have made excellent progress in Greek, and another three months should, my tutor at the Library assures me, make me truly fluent.

There is a great deal further to tell, the most important of which, sadly, is that we shall not see each other until I return from Greece. I do not accompany Maman back to Paris next week but will remain here to study and to prepare for the journey. It is all so sudden that I've taken a room in the house of a dreadfully dull lady near the Library, someone who would drive one frantic with her talk of expenses and domestic cares, but I had need of a perch and she, Mrs Hargrove, is overwhelmingly *respectable*.

Maman relented partly from pity. My triumphs of the Season consist of three tea visits (and for one I was merely the occasion for a young man hopelessly ensnared by Maman's charms to call), and a few warm glances at balls, which could be either politeness or interest. I have not heard again from the delightful protégé. The Season. It is strange for us to employ this word of respectable society; there are so many occasions which Maman avoids because she knows that she will be snubbed. It is not like Paris, you see no women of fashion in cafés, which they call "pubs," and they are very canny, these English; in half an hour they have your entire life history. And then the women care so much about reputation, which makes them dull, I think, all of them very dull. Maman had to make do with the Season of persons like La Vestris, absurd persons whom *we* would scorn at home for their pretension and their want of poetry.

Before the Season commenced, Maman drew me one day to her in her dressing-room; ever so softly she said, "You will make some man happy, not just anyone, but a very special man; he will remove the bitter pain in your breast, and then you will make him the most excellent companion." My dearest, I believe her. I am certain there is someone whom I could please, if not the man she promised, and if only I could recognise this creature perhaps equally submerged in a crowd; his distinction will hardly be signalled by a bright waistcoat or carefully tended hands.

Of course your fevered imagination has already conjured him as a travelling companion. My darling, they are all ancient! Or if not ancient, delighted to tell you everything about their admirable sons and daughters. Nor do I think to meet Lord Byron's last companions.

You will have a veritable army of admirers from whom you will choose, I know, the best, if not the handsomest. But I have come to see that they wish me also to settle myself—soon. From fear of scandal, as I say, Maman and Monsieur seldom went out when invited by his schoolmates who knew nothing of their old friend for fifteen years, these notes to Mr and Mrs Courtland coming at first in a steady stream, and then dwindling, Monsieur replying as Maman suggested that he preferred to establish himself before plunging into the social round. When lively, they saw mostly friends of Maman's whom they already knew. She declares they will live a more dedicated life during their time in England each year, they will escape the intrigues of Paris, she speaks of learning entirely new rôles. After a few months I felt a little sorry for Maman. But you will find her changed, Cécile. Instead of filling the house with visitors, now they like to dine and read alone; they want, not to be rid of us perhaps, but they draw into each other. She let me go when she could not marry me off.

I wish, Puss, all I would need write is that Maman sends me to Greece because it makes me happy.

Byron was often invoked in the small supper Maman and Monsieur gave last night, intended as a farewell for her; she returns in November, though she says she may advance the date a month—note this please, as you will be obliged to change your plans with the Dufresnes. It was meant as a farewell, but thanks to my good fortune, Mr Courtland made it a celebration for me as well, somewhere procuring bottles of Greek wine, which is flavoured with resin and is impossible. Mr Courtland and Mr Snigs were there, also Mr Macready, whom Maman has forgiven.

Everyone was sad at Maman's departure, especially Monsieur. As usual, however, his own affairs counted for him most. An English duke whose patronage he sought for a vast building has asked instead for a drawing of the town of San Gimignano. I must say that Monsieur made an effort for me last night, posing any number of questions almost as if he took a vivid interest. There came a moment when, having gleaned from me all I knew of the placement of shrines in Delos (and a little bit more than I knew, I confess), he exclaimed, "If only one could see it laid bare!" and then relapsed into silence.

They were, I will also say, truly lovely together. They spoke of the days when we were growing up, especially about the house, dwelt in talk of the new roses, or the day the roof collapsed. Mr Macready enquired about Uncle Adolphe; Maman looked at Monsieur and he took her hand, silently, which was the answer to the question and an answer the Englishman understood. This is what I had imagined it would be like here.

Mr Courtland asked that I undertake *Le Paysan parvenu* in English, as he has a great love from his own youth of Marivaux, and I agreed; I said I would practise in Athens for the entire next six months. The old gentleman was tender with Maman as well, and seemed a little on guard with Monsieur, deferring all talk of buildings and paintings to him.

Maman later delivered one of her remarks: the old gentleman feels it is his fault she returns early to France—she was in her midnight bath in the blue boudoir, and inserted this into a lengthy and learned lecture on face creams to be used for protection against the sun.

"Why you?"

"It is absurd. I meant nothing. Pass me that jar of salve, darling." You know how she is, but I had her cornered and I care for Mr Courtland.

"What has he said to you?" She saw she would either have to leave the bath, reeking of something she calls "Houri d'Algérie," or answer me.

"It is this voyage. He thinks I am unhappy here, and came only for Frederick's sake. I have assured him it was equally for your début . . ."

How she could speak such nonsense!

". . . but there is also trouble between him and Frederick."

"Mr Courtland has been troubled by him?" This was as diplomatically as I felt I could put it, but she understands perfectly well when she chooses to.

Maman was quite firm. "Frederick received this absurd request from his duke, and they differ about the reason."

It did seem odd to me that an architect should be asked for a drawing, and I said so.

"Well, the duke claims this town of San Gimignano is one of his favorite places in Italy. I cannot explain it, really. Mr Courtland thinks there is some scandal, and this commission to be an insult. Frederick says the duke was afraid of the building he proposed; it was too grand. I am sure that is it; Frederick is an artist of the largest ideas, his work demanding an exceptional patron, though this Duke of Devonshire must be one of the richest men in England."

At last we had spoken the truth. We had uttered the word "scandal."

I asked her gently, not gently perhaps, but with care that we speak honestly to one another, which is all I have ever asked of her, I asked her, "So it is to this English duke that Mlle Delsart owes her voyage?"

Maman turned so sharply to me that water washed over the side of the tub. "Not at all! You understand nothing. We do not enter into it! We are nothing here."

At this moment, Puss, I felt sorrier than I ever have for Maman.

At least the farewell party ended beautifully. At the end Mr Snigs proposed a toast, pouring out the wine from the Greek bottles for all but himself. Mr Courtland protested he spared himself.

"Truly, John, the sulphurous beverage you have provided would be for me suicidal, and I cannot claim for myself the wisdom of Socrates to justify the imbibing." (He talks like this at home!) Then he rose, holding a glass of water into which he had mixed one of his medicines.

"My dear Adèle, when I was a boy, no one thought of a woman travelling to exotic realms in search of knowledge. How times change! Now you are to travel to the very seat of ancient learning, to Athens, a future of your own as a scholar rebuking those irrational prejudices of my youth which only Lady Stanhope dared to brave." He raised his glass of brownish medicine; we raised our glasses of resin wine. And everything he said is true! He turned to Monsieur and Maman, stared at them for a moment, raised his glass again after repeating, "a future of your own," giving them the most wonderful, steady smile. Finally he turned to Mr Courtland. "You, however, could have done with a great deal more of restraining, irrational prejudice!" They looked at one another in mutual satisfaction and then all the visitors vanished, after quickly kissing Maman and me farewell, these moments of embarrassment overwhelming the English and driving them from a house.

This was the end of my Season in London. I have not begun to describe to you in detail my itinerary, which I shall save for tomorrow's post, as it is nearly two in the morning. This note I seal instantly with a kiss.

Your adoring
sister

Licit Loves

*Letters of Adèle Mercure, Frederick Courtland
and Severus Rood
October 1846–April 1847*

Charles Courtland, Esq.   *2 October 1846*
20 Milner Street
London

Dear Charles,

Please excuse the familiarity of address, which seems odd to me in the writing; I have known you so many years, have called you by your first name for so many, that this friendly form of greeting seems natural, even though we have never really known each other well enough to deserve the title of "friends." I hope most earnestly this will change.

I believe you were rather taken aback to see me at your lecture on "Paganism," courteously as you hid your surprise. I frequently attend events at the English School, and would not dream of missing an occasion upon which you were the honoured speaker. Moreover, as I told you, for the past three years I have been a diligent student of antiquity; perhaps Maman made light of my studies to you; at times I wish *I* could make them lighter.

Let me take the occasion of this brief note to thank you for a most interesting lecture. Your audience was rapt, and not at all bored, as you feared, by a consideration once more of this subject. Several persons remarked that the connexions you make between ancient and modern theology are quite fresh. The attention you commanded was compounded of this admiration and pleasure in your manner of expression; more, rest assured that all French people who attend the English School lectures go there to hear these in English; you need not worry at speaking your own language in a foreign country, though I have always found your French excellent. Will you consider it no more than a continuation of this respectful attention if I offer to you a few comments?

I was quite taken with your notion that Protagoras of Abdera "discovered" atheism, just as I appreciated the distinction you draw among discoveries, some uncovering what has always existed, others inventing new things or ideas no one had thought possible before. Yes, the first savages probably were theists—the ones in the Old Testament, even the most barbaric, were—so that the discovery of atheism by Protagoras falls in the second category, it is a creation of the human mind. Only, was Protagoras truly the first to invent atheism? You have evidently forgotten the passage in the *Odyssey:* "Then you are still existent, you gods on tall Olympus, if truly the suitors have paid for their unseemly wantonness." The shadow cast by the "if" is certainly long in that poem. Also, much of Aeschylus' *Persians* takes place under no divine sign, enacted by characters for whom the real is bounded by each other.

Surely you are correct that "agnosticism" trifles with the seriousness of doubt; the moment we are uncertain we have already judged God or the gods to lack omnipotence. However, you did not translate quite correctly the opening (and, my dear sir, the *only*) sentence in Protagoras' fragment "On Gods"; if I am not mistaken, in your language an exact rendition would be, "About the gods I cannot say either that they are or that they are not, nor how they are constituted in shape; for there is much which prevents knowledge, the obscurity of the subject and the shortness of human life." In English, "obscurity" is not quite the same as your word "doubtfulness," or am I in error? If not, then Protagoras, as a good, and truly the first, *sophistes,* may have been drawing attention to his own incapacity rather than the gods' unreality.

Finally, this quotation put me in mind of a poem, which I would not dare to translate. It is by Musset: "L'Espoir en Dieu," and I wonder if you know it:

> *Que me reste-t-il donc? Ma raison revoltée*
> *Essaie en vain de croire et mon coeur de douter.*
> *Le chrétien m'épouvante, et ce que de l'athée,*
> *En dépit de mes sens, je ne puis l'écouter.*

This expresses, if I am not mistaken, the temper of many of your auditors: their minds are revolted by tales of murdered gods, risings from tombs and the like, while their hearts revolt equally at the dry, measuring little men incapable of fable.

If it should please you, I would be delighted to correspond on this, and whatever other intellectual subjects engage you. It is a pity, I think, that we did not before discover that we shared interests apart from our quasi-familial connexion; I shall certainly make an effort to obtain your volume of essays, which to my shame I confess not yet having read. With sincere esteem and cordial wishes, I remain

yours,
Adèle Mercure

Anne Mercure   7 February 1847
3, rue de la Tour des Dames
Paris

Dearest,

I have staggered into this royal apartment—at least Sir Leslie pointedly smiled at me in saying to the man with my bag, "The old king's quarters, Mason," a sitting-room gravid with its timbering, a bedroom whose bed declares that whichever old king it was, was huge—I have staggered within my royal precincts to recoup from the banquet they call a simple Sunday dinner and to consider in the cold light of luxury an offer of marriage. Perhaps you would like me, my dear Anne, to explain?

Didn't I tell you I made a plan recently for a combined railway terminus, ironworks and coal pens? The idea came to me when encountering Sir Leslie Parkin in the Garrick, he remarking he lacks the first, possesses unmanageably the second and is ever in need of more of the third for his establishment in Leeds. I remarked that I "went in for that sort of thing." He, alerted by my excellently off-hand manner, and mindful that a gentleman does not talk of affairs in his club, proposed to provide me a more suitable occasion in inviting me down to his domestic establishment in deepest Surrey, an Elizabethan manor called Frotham containing the old king's quarters to which its new chatelain has kindly consigned me.

Very well. Yesterday we walk the grounds, which are indeed quite fine, though hardly by Capability Brown, as Sir Leslie hints by uttering that name simply, splendidly as we stand admiring the view from a hill. We return, dress for dinner and are presented to the family. This allegiance we receive from Lady Parkin, quite an excellent old thing who regards with indulgence the squirearchical practise of her husband; Miss Sarah Parkin, spinster, accomplished on the clavier, at the easel, prodigiously informed; Miss Susan Parkin, clear of voice, when at song, that is, otherwise demurely, wisely silent, her complexion, freshened by the country air, speaking for her; Master Edward Parkin, sullen, fat and destined to break his good father's heart. It seems, my dear, that an eligible, if ageing, unmarried person like myself could have my choice of them—Sarah or Susan, I mean; Edward was not on offer.

Though Sir Leslie has the repute of a ruthless master and man of business, the air, if not the wisdom contained in the library included in the purchase of Frotham, has taught him not to push relentlessly in the more tender negotiations of the heart. Thus at dinner Saturday, yesterday, he and I spoke of "reform," that word accompanied each time he uttered it by the blackest of scowls; I had only to don a similar pugnacious visage to keep him company in his fulmination. With the ladies, a lighter touch of course. Miss Sarah Parkin spoke comprehensively of the landscapes on view at last year's Royal Academy exhibition. Miss Susan Parkin asked if I had heard of the strange saddles used by Americans and I stunned her, I amazed her by confessing I not only had heard of these saddles, I possessed one, and I exposed myself upon it daily in Hyde Park. Lady Parkin asked me, quite worried and I believe ready to act the moment I gave her a sign, had I been long troubled by my throat, and I forbore to explain that the cigars we smoke in Paris remain an addiction to me in London. I enquired of Master Edward what were his current pursuits, and his look answered, the most painful death he could contrive for all assembled. "We are thinking of sending him abroad for a period of travel and study," his father later confided to me. "Would you advise it?"

This was our first confidence, over port while the ladies retired to a chamber perhaps a mile distant and the heir to Frotham quitted us without a word. I replied I had no experience of boys, and my own youth passed in the most strenuous fashion. Nodding approvingly at the latter portion of my rejoinder, Sir Leslie smiled and assured me that my lack of experience could be remedied. It was at this moment I understood that I might have been invited to Frotham for reasons other, or at least more comprehensive, than my skill in designing.

Joining the ladies, we were treated to Miss Sarah's rendition of Thalberg's 24 Variations on a theme of Blavet, then a group of Mendelssohn songs uniting Miss Sarah and Miss Susan. I made one error. In subsequently complimenting Miss Sarah on her digital prowess, I happened to mention that Thalberg always seemed to me to listen for what he could take from others, in words or music. Since the whole adventure began to seem to me more to my father's taste than my own, I think I even permitted myself to say that Thalberg is the thieving magpie of music.

"Then you are acquainted with the artist?"

My admission that such was the case raised me enormously in her estimation, while earning me a "reform" grimace from her parent, as evidently the persons creating the music performed by his estimable daughter were acceptable when printed names, but suggested as living beings disorder, the mincing steps of dancing masters, etc., the knowing of such persons in turn suggesting a want of discrimination if nothing worse. However, the hour was late, and sleep soon came to soothe away Sir Leslie's qualm.

The next day, that is, this morning, he and I retired after church to the library to work. This again heavily timbered room has been carefully furnished; it gives the appearance of intense literary labour, books everywhere upon long tables, not a trace of dust upon them, of course; to find a space upon which I might make some drawing we moved several heavy volumes in Greek which I am sure would have been instantly recognisable in content by Adèle, if neither by their owner nor by myself. I asked Sir Leslie to give me some rough idea of the physical dimensions of his ironworks at present; to my satisfaction, and not entirely to my surprise, he gave me better, an exact measurement, betraying that he has indeed and intensely studied that building. Thus it was possible for me to suggest where a rail connexion and storage sheds could be added to greatest advantage. My own precision, I believe, made its impress upon him. We were thus able to speak of possibilities in realistic terms, and did so for two or three hours.

Anne, I will confess to you that at moments I had to hide my hand in my pocket for fear he would see it shake. The promise I made you not to lose my nerve I will myself to keep, but one mis-step and he could go to anyone else. Do you understand that even a retainer by a figure such as Sir Leslie would attract the others who have so far held back, his name worth as much, to be crass, as his building? My will cannot control my hand.

Lunch then called us. Miss Sarah now favoured me with a disquisition on recent tendencies in French music. Without the comedy of Frotham could I have sustained my will? Evidently my interview of the morning assured Sir Leslie that my acquaintance with Thalberg betrayed no deeper unsteadiness of purpose; still, my will suggested I listen while Miss Sarah explained. The nerves were still on edge, but as we could do no more today, I gradually surrendered, I could hold my glass steadily. Miss Susan was content to look from Miss Sarah to myself. I suppose it was then decided that, as I was endowed with powers of intellect, and as Miss Sarah and I are the closer in age, she would be the more eligible of the two; at least Lady Parkin looked also from one to the other of us with a most benign expression during this repast.

The afternoon we spent individually. At the simple evening meal to which I have alluded, I believe some devil possessed the younger daughter. She made up to me outrageously, declared how thrilled she was to meet someone who had both been to Paris and rode upon an American saddle in Hyde Park, chastised the butler for not serving me the very best piece off the joint, all this accompanied by knowing little smiles. Miss Sarah looked grim. I did my best. Lady Parkin was at first alarmed but, evidently a liberal spirit, left the decision to me. Sir Leslie sees only a radiant girl in looking at this daughter. Master Edward consoled himself for the horror of our company by holding out his glass frequently to the butler.

As I say, my perplexity is which to choose. Could you advise me?

Frederick

Mr Charles Courtland   *2 March 1847*
20 Milner Street
London

Dear Charles,

People are finally going out again, the weather has become warmer, unseasonably so, the influenza departing with the cold. Maman has been deep in preparations for a grand ball tonight at the Hôtel Lambert, which the Czartoryski family from Poland are now to purchase from the Comte de Montalivet. Tonight's ball is, they say, for "practise" in using the mansion. In seeking to tempt me to the Ile St-Louis, when I said I had passed the age of balls, Maman declared, "Well, I am becoming a wrinkled old walrus, and even I shall have fun, walrus hide and all." It was true; she dressed with not one attempt to disguise her throat or arms; that is Maman of course, just outrageous enough to be stylish but never so much as to offend.

Having declined to attend the ball this evening with my mother, my sister and her good husband, I began reading the novel Aunt Marie writes under her name of Daniel Stern. She calls it *Nélida* and publishes it in serial, since last month in the *Revue Indépendante*. It occurs to me: would you like me to send the issues of the *Revue Indépendante* to London? Or perhaps it is not worth your while, it is a trifle.

I confess however I spent the evening hours entranced. Aunt Marie is clearly her heroine Nélida, with dyed hair, M. Liszt the lover of Nélida in the guise of a painter, Guermann, disguised only by a moustache, M. d'Agoult is called Timoléan de Kervaens (!) and so forth. I cannot identify many of the others but have read avidly to see if we, too, appear, and so far, not. The plot twists and turns without the events in any way changing the characters, especially herself, who as Nélida has been from childhood a noble soul sacrificed on the altar of male vanity, her very nobility blinding her to the wickedness or weakness of the men who are constantly falling in love with her.

Perhaps, indeed, I shall send you the novel, as you knew so many of the circle; you could make more sense of it to me. Of course, when I was a girl, I saw Aunt Marie as the great lady whom Maman envied, who received us with a certain condescension. I have just finished a scene in which Guermann-Liszt beseeches Nélida-Marie to leave her husband. Finally she agrees and her lover is surprised, taken aback by her responding boldness.

"Would you have such insensate courage?" he asks.

"I have enough courage for anything," she answers him, "except to live a lie."

During the seasons of Aunt Marie's great Romantic evenings, I cut the pages, with trembling hands, on a hundred such ringing declarations. The scene occurred usually in the middle of my book, so that in the conclusion the heroine might be rescued from her folly. We in France are less alarmed than you English by the wicked stories you call "French novels"; if only you would finish these tales you would see that after the woman shouts to the world the truth she then, as it were, returns to her sewing.

I hear my family downstairs returning from the Hôtel Lambert. I must hastily conclude, as while they permit me to abstain they do not permit me to remain ignorant.

I write to you about this silly novel to answer a question you asked me in some letter, I can't remember which. It is a sillier novel to men than to women. One doesn't find all the details in *Nélida,* but how one feels the indubitable anguish of Aunt Marie in becoming the victim of M. Liszt's ambition! Shall I tell you what I admire? I think this open admission is Aunt Marie's final and greatest act of loving M. Liszt. She declares her passion, whereas—they are calling up to me from the salon, I must immediately lay down my pen.

This is the next morning. The legation offices are closed today because of some misadventure in the rue de Varenne; they have sent word that I am at liberty the entire morning, which I shall fill partly with the pleasure of further discourse with you, most contemplative of correspondents.

One would think the temptation would have been almost irresistible to her, but no, she never claims Nélida to have been a genius nor her past glorious. Noble, courageous, wronged; never Guermann's equal. Nor does Maman succumb to exaggerated claims, she who talks gaily of her walrus hide and flaunts it. Nor do you. Indeed, you seldom speak of your youth. Yet you arrived here with your brother.

It does not turn into an ordinary French novel, the reasons for which perhaps answer your delicate question, which nearly missed me. Of course, over the years, both Cécile and I have asked Maman why they have not married, and been given various and quite conflicting answers; I am sure when you or Mr Courtland have posed the question to your brother, you have been subjected to the same confusion. The distinguishing mark of Aunt Marie's novel is that when others, seeking to help Nélida in her plight, suggest to her marriage, returning to M. Timoléan de Kervaens, who has never ceased to love her, in the later parts of the novel she repeatedly scorns this "unworthy solution." So I had only this thought: Maman, who after the great troubles of her early years remains ever alert to the regard of the world, has made for your brother an exception. Why he has not sought to marry her, I do not know, it being hardly my place to ask. All I can tell you is that Maman is most disposed to lie when she wishes to protect a secret very precious to her.

Charles, do you realise this is truly the first confidence we have shared —after all these letters?

Perhaps, then, you will give me leave to pose a question to you. Explain to me, please, the great excitement you report in your last letter over the Mr Newman who has become a Catholic. Why does this matter? I address you. You tell me that people everywhere in England have begun to convert to Catholicism, which does not surprise me, as your "High Church" seems to lack only a Pope—which, considering the current one, might be fortunate. I am of course interested in this, but I am engaged when you then, after much crossing out in your last letter, which despite all my arts I cannot decipher, you add "I understand them only too well." Do you "understand" as Musset did? He once said of his poem that the most important thing was the rhythm. This is the only untidy letter you have sent me. If you would like to write to me upon this subject, I would be glad to receive your thoughts.

This afternoon I shall take Cécile to another of the lectures at the Collège de France with which I dissipate my youth. This one is on "The

Lessons of the Marbles lately Rescued by Lord Elgin"; we shall both think of your country, and I shall think, with affection as ever, of you.

Yours in friendship,
Adèle

Mr Charles Courtland   *23 March 1847*
20 Milner Street
London

My dear Charles,

Your letter in reply to my last has just come. A shadow has fallen over us —my enquiry vexes you, the formality of your words betrays you! There is more. You say that perhaps you "erred" in confessing these "private, if surprising, sentiments about the absence of prayer in my life." Charles, you never so far confessed yourself to me, unless this is what you scratched out. I had no idea.

Certainly I have no wish to pry into your private affairs; whether you wish this correspondence to continue on more impersonal subjects is entirely up to you.

Yours,
Adèle

Madame Anne Mercure   *3 April 1847*
3, rue de la Tour des Dames
Paris

Dearest,

You cannot be serious. I have no intention even of going down to Frotham again in the near future. He has asked me for some preliminary estimates, for a general plan, some rough elevations; the next step is a retainer negotiated by Snigs, not yet another round of French song, horse rides and bracing walks with Master Edward—think, I have given nearly my entire social calendar for a month over to them. I am ready to labour in his behalf on the Sabbath, and have called in people who can assemble the large model for him and his investors; once the retainer comes, we can have it done in a fortnight.

As to the suggestion that I not "discourage" Miss Sarah, I ask you: are you indeed proposing that I marry her for the sake of the fattest fee, the ultimate commission from Sir Leslie? It disturbs me sufficiently that she favours me with that now rather trembling smile, and that her eyes *do not leave me,* unnerves me to talk to her mother or attempt to do so to her brother and feel those eyes ever upon me, staring. The steady eyes, Anne, and a shaking hand.

It would be the height of cruelty to treat this woman condemned to spinsterdom one jot differently from any other person on the penumbra of my affairs, and to advise me to be "politic" is absurd as well as cruel. This is no affair like the imbroglio with Paxton and the Duke of Devonshire. Sir Leslie is a resolute person of business. He esteems capability.

There are times when I wonder how much you do mine. I need not become a scoundrel to make my way.

Frederick

M. Frederick Courtland   *26 April 1847*
3, rue de la Tour des Dames
Paris

My dearest Frederick,

Sir! These abrupt flights abroad are fatal to the rational conduct of affairs. You must warn me when you feel the urge to leave, or, as I should say, to return home. Please convey expressions of esteem and my best wishes to Madame Mercure. Whatever my locution, your absence is a fact which at this moment I deem most unfortunate.

A fortnight ago I received a courteous note from Sir Leslie Parkin, inviting both of us to retreat with him to his estate in Surrey for further deliberations. Previously, I had deployed the very slightest and subtlest of pressure upon him to come to terms about the retainer; slight, because there must be not the least hint that you are in need, which is amongst us to say, nearly greatly in need, of two thousand pounds. Since you had so precipitously fled, all I could tell him was that, at the moment, you were at your Paris address, but that I could fully represent you throughout the negotiation in Frotham. The Knight of Industry then began to evince behaviour of a most erratic character. He demanded of me:

"His Paris address?"

Of course, Frederick, I would not dream of giving clients' private addresses; if nothing else, the other party may seek to avoid lawyerly protections by dealing directly with the uninformed and therefore vulnerable client. However, Sir Leslie's mind seemed bent in another direction. I told him you maintained your old quarters in Paris as well as those in London, and only that. To which he demanded,

"There is some reason for him to live in Paris?"

This seemed at best no contribution to the arrangement of a fee schedule. I said only that after so many years you had interests in France as well as in Britain.

"What sort of interests?"

"Sir," I replied, "we have fully disclosed to you our capabilities in regard to this program of building. Fear not that the press of business in another nation will keep us from it."

"But I do not understand why he continues to live there." A familiar enough sentiment among your countrymen, of course, to which I myself was once not entirely immune. The consequence of this negligible exchange was that first he postponed the date of our conference until you could return—perhaps courteous enough—and then a few days later (20th April) I received the following from Sir Leslie's secretary: a note informing me that the negotiations are forthwith terminated, a demand for the return of the detailed plans of the present plant, a threat that he will take action against us if the drawings for the proposed plant are in any form published or indeed if we invoke his name in any connexion. It was a note the character of which I have draughted only when dealing with swindlers. Judging that Sir Leslie laboured under some mistaken supposition or false information, I wrote to him (21st April) a reply which left him a graceful exit from his own aberrant missive, to which (23rd April) I received an even more insulting communiqué reiterating the initial demands, to which I replied (23rd April), now not as a negotiator, but as the defender of a client whose honour has been impugned. All of this correspondence will be in your private drawer when you return.

This untoward turn of affairs places the Courtland Partnership in difficulties which now must be dealt with by reckoning what is in hand rather than opportunities which might be grasped. In 1829, after the horrid misadventure which came upon your parent in Swaffham Prior, I told John I would supervise the practical affairs of his firm—though serving as his counsellor, nurse and confessor financial has taken me beyond my depth—only if he would honour my wisdom as well as pay me for it. On the whole he has been obedient; certainly you have been since I drew up your articles of partnership. Thus, when Sir Leslie turned his back on us, I felt it incumbent as well as legitimate, even in your absence, to intervene in coping with the most pressing of your financial woes. I write to you because in doing so, I became aware of a deeper and sadder Conundrum to which I would like you to devote your most serious attention, and which we must face together upon your return.

At Easter last, you and I were vouchsafed certain signs worthy of more careful analysis than we gave them. Conjure before your inner eye the wine glass falling from John's hand at Easter dinner: the glass falls to the table, the wine spills from the table's edge into your father's lap. I seek to right the glass, you to stem the flow of staining liquid. What neither of us remarked accurately in this minute passage is that your father flinches not for a second at the moment of accident, indeed continues speaking to Madame Mercure throughout our ministrations. You may have thought this was his usual, imperturbable politeness. I am now convinced otherwise: he simply did not sense an accident to have occurred, even when the wine began to soak his trousers. Politeness there was: he decided not to notice whatever had stirred us. This, my dear boy, is how it often takes old men: the sensate brain ceases to function, while the higher powers, such as those devoted to civility, continue vigorously.

Now, then, yesterday I betook myself to your offices to review this crisis in finance with your father. I discovered your father in the nether sanctum bent over his desk, that enormous sketching pen held high above the paper.

"My friend, put down your quill. I have come to render you assistance."

"As the Lord so rashly recommends you aid all your fellow creatures," your parent returned, the pen still poised for its strike. I quote this badinage to show you that, as I say, the higher powers are alert.

The moment had come to set before him the financial difficulties you face, you must face. I will let John mortgage nothing more on his properties to provide for the expenses of the partnership; I thought it unwise to mortgage those houses in the King's Road, and you have forced me, again, to release Consols for sale at an unwise moment. Of course you have extraordinary expenses, living in two countries. I calculate that your remaining personal assets amount to some £7,500 and that John's are in the order of £26,000 to £30,000. You, my dear boy, will also inherit something from me. These sums are not as reassuring in operation as on paper. The *total* income from your partnership for 1846 was £3,760, the total expenses £5,125; after dipping into capital, you had only £4,098 in reserve. Mortgages might add £8,000, but if you keep on at the present rate this will be gone in four or five years. There will be no mortgaging.

To be fair, your father's numeric understanding in 1828 was no better than it is today. But I expounded once more as simply as I could; he set aside his pen. When I described the strange withdrawal of Sir Leslie from this most excellent and extensive project, he wore a face of woe, though his only comment was that he was surprised in the first place that someone like Sir Leslie could be encountered in the Garrick. I asked when you would return. He too has no idea. I asked what idea he has to reduce expenses. He sighed. I posed questions so that we might together arrive at a *modus vivendi*, not knowing your plans. I pointed to the many idle draughtsmen seeming about the place. He told me you had taken them on in anticipation of Sir Leslie's work. One immediate solution to reducing expenses was therefore evident: these men to be let go. I knew you could not object. He knew it. Would he dismiss them, then?

"Snigs, I have never dismissed anyone." True, only too true. "I cannot dismiss my son's helpers." I pointed out that they were redundant. He only shook his head. "No, they stay until Frederick returns."

My dear boy, I set myself against this Irrational Nicety with the result that I assumed the task of dismissing the workmen you had, may I say, rashly employed. Having reached this unpleasant resolution, for I too dislike serving as the bearer of bad tidings, I rose to do my duty. Your father rose. His hand brushed the inkwell, which spilled over the draughting table; the Easter accident again. When I started, John remarked only, "Have no fear. If I have unwisely succumbed, Frederick will put it right. Or you may." The ink soaked his leg, while he waited for me to exit to the draughting room.

I shall not recount to you the speech I made to the three draughtsmen; I cannot. Suffice it to say, I gave them no cause to think ill of you, nor, I hope, of myself. I salved their hurt and mine by giving them two months' wages. I asked them to be gone in a week, knowing that dismissed men are hardly bracing companions for those spared. What resolved me to write to you was the scene confronting me when I turned from the tables at your end of the draughting room to those where your father's lads are employed. Of course his boys had heard me. John pointed with a pencil to some detail of a drawing on the desk of a flustered youth, John behaving as if no more than a casual visitor had imparted an inconsequential piece of news to the young men seated in dejection twenty feet away. This boy was seated, your father standing, the draughtsman's eyes level with the soaked trousers which now clung to your father's legs; while that melodious baritone voice rose and fell, the good fellow sought to keep his eyes on his drawing, once looking desperately at me for a clue as to whether something should be said. I shook my head. Not only was your father unable to feel his own damp body; the dismissed workers had fled from his mind. Elderly people who come to my chambers to draw up wills often forget, the moment they are alone, even people who have served them faithfully as friends for half a century.

Dame Perplexity, as I say, came to visit subsequent to this event. Usually when a man is ready to retire from a family enterprise his children lift the daily cares from his shoulders while reserving for him labours which bring him intrinsic pleasure; recently, for example, an old Eton friend of ours surrendered the reins of a firm of printers, save direction of a series of pamphlets on gardening. (It is my conviction that men who enjoy rooting about in the earth were as children overly indulged.) For nearly a half century now it has been I who have steered the one and then the both of you from solid land through the perilous straits of Practicality out to the open sea, where I have been content to leave you, the sickening waves of the empyrean little more enticing to me than the muck, odour and thorny plants of a garden. However, amazing as this fact may be to both of us, I shall not live for ever.

How, then, shall we lighten the burden on your parent?

You might dissolve the partnership, he to retire to his clubs, you to form a new alliance with another, more prosaic partner. I consider that this would be the death of your father. I speak plainly. Ever since you were a child, he has dreamt of your union—it matters little to him, in the end, that your defects reinforce one another's and so your appeal to the public is narrow. (Of course I do not mean to impugn your immense prestige, I am merely stating fact.)

You might add a partner. This is subject to the same objection as dissolving the partnership entire: it would sunder the union of hemispheres.

If nothing can, as it were, come between you until the full measure of his days is expended, I can think of only one manner in which you might relieve him of care. Here, I admit, I tread in ignorance, or, to continue my conceit, I steer my own small pilot craft out to sea. However: would it be possible for you to dream *smaller* dreams? The two of you have invested nearly £1,700 of his personal monies on plans, experimental casts and models for a metal city. You have incurred a further £660 in building a large-scale model of works anticipating Sir Leslie was yours. I say your father is cognisant only that he must do whatever is necessary to feed the art of his son. Could you—forgive me, my dear, for speaking thus—could you be less greedy at his table? His tranquillity turns truly upon your restraint.

Further than this I cannot go. In my little boat, surveying the horizon of your watery realm, may I say only that good ideas keep; indeed, they require long ageing to develop. In the law we are blessed with certain principles which have required three or four centuries to reveal, finally, the clarity of their essence. Risk, yes, one must always be willing to take risks. But surely, also, one must face the present calmly.

Well, this rambling missive has cleared my mind; perhaps I should have destroyed it, sending you pithy recommendations, but Policy from which the twisting marks of cogitation are effaced fails to arouse conviction. I mean not to end my letter on a critical note; candour comes from my love of you. Whatever signs you can give to your parent of your sufficient contentment within the modest scope of your present resources will lighten him. In your special art, as in any practical endeavour, one must practise a certain restraint to be kind.

On this uplifting note, so worthy of our times, so rejuvenating, I close affectionately as your

> devoted
> Uncle Severus

Mr Charles Courtland   *26 April 1847*
20 Milner Street
London

My dear Charles,

First I would like to thank you for replying at all, and so generously. Second, I would like to apologise for my coldness; I often seem cold when I am distressed. I have thought all this past week how I can honour your generosity, and it appears to me I can best do so through candour.

May I say that much of what you reply must have been imprisoned within you for a long time. I was struck particularly by your reading again the *Obermann* of Sénancour. "I begin to understand Obermann, his desire to climb to so remote a place that he could discover at last the greatest peace imaginable, the peace of dwelling where his life was a matter of perfect indifference to all around him—'life' upon a glacier." Your dedicated correspondent asks herself, what is the great and terrible matter from which Charles flees, from which he seeks respite up in the clouds? The dedicated correspondent is fairly certain you have not murdered, you have not swindled, you have never been false, nor malicious, nor indeed cunning, envious or insulting. These are the matters for which men feel shame, if they can. There is only one explanation left. You are lonely. And like all of us who suffer from this affliction, you believe the answer to loneliness is flight; you wish to run for comfort as far inside yourself as you can go.

Do you remember once asking me if the other girls in my convent resented my capability in studies? My dear friend, I cannot begin to tell you how I sought to join the others in chatter about dance, about dress; still, they saw through me and tortured me for my origin. I have never told Maman how horrid the girls at this most exclusive convent school could be when they set their minds to it! Malice made them perfect ladies. After a time, one hates oneself for raging and dreams only of escape. So I may say, I understand your taste for mountains all too well.

The lecturer at the English School hit upon one of the little sayings which the nuns and priests held up to us as wisdom. Do you remember? I can quote it to you exactly: " 'Just as I do not know whence I come, so I do not know whither I am going. All I know is that when I leave this world I shall fall for ever into nothingness or into the hands of a wrathful God, but I do not know which of these two states is to be my eternal lot. Such is my condition, full of weakness and uncertainty.' " Then Pascal asks, "Who would wish to have as his friend a man who argued like that?" You answered Pascal that we have no choice but to know him, to know him all our lives, for he is in each of us, the true friend who refuses to demean our pains or sufferings by saying, "Don't worry, it will all come out right in the end." Every intelligent French person among your auditors was quite cheered to hear you on "Pascal's Friend."

Do you remember why you exposed this nonsense? You brilliantly connected your two notions of discovery thus: our minds *create* when we revolt against the gods, so that we might be strong enough in spirit to *uncover* the reality of solitude, solitude in a world where nothing is or-dained, guaranteed or certain. Is it now that you fear your own discovery?

No, Charles, I am not trying to waltz before you. I evoke our happy meeting because to me now you say Newman's conversion aroused the aching love of God which overwhelmed you in youth, he who speaks so quietly and unashamedly, and that it seems "absurd to argue in the presence of his sanctity." You look back through the gates of memory; you see your life as a priest surrounded by dullards in an isolated village; then the easy successes of your brother, his charm and beauty (though your manner is uniquely distinguished); and to your sadness in these scenes of absence, of lost time, you put a name: the love of God. I thought of the words Catullus gives to Attis, *ego vir sterilis ero,* shall I be a barren man? Twenty years later, a voice opens these gates once more. "Come with me." It is a voice promis-ing comfort. "Come back with me." But now it is twenty years, and so the voice does not say "comfort" or "happiness"—you and Newman have seen enough of life for these words to arouse suspicion; instead it says "sanctity."

I have thought a great deal about this the last week, and about you, and I am sure this is right.

What I found saddest in your letter was that your worldly achievement seems so empty to you at this moment. Of course I have said nothing to

Maman. But I did ask how you were thought of ten years ago by other writers. She told me, Charles, and this with genuine respect, whatever are your mutual difficulties still, that you persevered admirably to attain your present editorial eminence. I too have by now seen how hard it is to find employment which gives one independent scope, men as well as women, though it is much worse for us, about which I have more to say. However. You write to me, "Reading what is so far disclosed of Newman's conversion, his willingness to give up everything for the sake of his Faith, arouses in me a sentiment of hopelessness. Tomorrow I shall edit another article, next month I shall have an entire issue ready of *The Free-Thinker,* and then it will begin again, this endless harvest of Reform and Freedom." Forgive me, I said I would honour you with candour; when I read these words first I thought, How sad for you! My poor Friend! The grim reaper a respected editorialist, burdened with the gathering in of ideas in which he believes, for presentation to a civilised and erudite public. This terrible task, when instead he could be singing "Ave Maria"!

Charles, I have had little experience of life, and shall probably end my days in the small circle in which I at present move. I knew this even in the convent, and I do not allude to my "stain," as the nuns kindly used to call it. I shall never glitter like Maman; this quiet life suits me. Still, thanks to your writing, I could answer a modern Virgil who demanded from his country estate, "Why, why do you remain in dirty, dangerous, clamorous Paris?" You make me tolerate those who madden me, their demands, provocations, their false starts clashing against my own; all of us are here like singers in a confused opera upon which the curtain manages none the less to rise and fall regularly in five acts each evening; this madness makes us human. (Do you approve my literary conceit?) This usage of disorder you discovered for all of us, your readers.

Do you not see, there is something false to your own achievement, unworthy of your own struggle, in envying the new Father Newman?

This is all I can think to say to you. I confess I don't understand why despair would come to a man like you in his fullness, only witness that it has, which pain arouses my sympathy, Charles, but no pity, no pity.

Well, I have read this letter over and have scratched nothing out!

With the best, the most
emphatic of good wishes,
from your friend and correspondent
Adèle

At Last We Are Brothers

Letters of Charles Courtland,
Frederick Courtland and Adèle Mercure
December 1847–January 1848

Mlle Adèle Mercure   27 December 1847
3, rue de la Tour des Dames
Paris

My dear Adèle,

A letter from me must be, after so many months, unwelcome. I have written to you many times in my mind, but submitted myself to a discipline of silence. At first it was for my own sake, that I might better know myself before involving you—though an undoubted and generous friend in another manner yet a stranger—before involving you in my inner confusions. After a period of some months, I realised I was keeping silent for your sake. I determined at last to write to you when my brother intimated, gently, without prying, that you blame yourself for trespassing. Adèle, my silence was for you.

In one of your letters you remarked that in my loneliness I but took my place at the family table of man. If only that were so; the solitude of a decade is in truth estrangement from my family. I cannot console myself that loneliness happened *to* me, though I have sought from time to time the comforts of self-pity; I estranged myself. Ten years of solitude measured in three sentences. The most shameful sentences of my entire life.

Do you not understand? That since I met you they have become a torment to me?

When I returned to this country in '42 to take up *The Free-Thinker*, I confided one evening in a friend from Oriel days. By then your mother and I were on wary but speaking terms, as I was with Snigs, and with my father. I confessed to this friend, a cleric, the terrible allusion I had made to your mother in my essay. He re-read the essay. In seeking to lead me spiritually, he said that the allusion would mean nothing to my readers; the sin was in my willing the revelation into being. In '43, my publishers proposed collecting my early essays. I omitted "One Amongst Many" from the bundle I delivered; they asked why, and I put them off with some excuse. A young man in the firm went to the effort of looking up the Geneva newspaper in which my essay appeared; I suppose my manner betrayed my excuse. He confirmed the prediction of my Oriel friend; it was a perfectly good essay to him. When I said, But it contains a libel of the most terrible sort, he looked puzzled. Still, I insisted: "One Amongst Many" has never appeared again; no one today has the slightest memory of the *International Courier* of 19 June 1833. Time has effaced my sentences. The paper of the *International Courier* is crumbling. Even in my family, time has done its work of healing through forgetting. No one vividly remembers except me.

Yes, my publishers might have quoted to me, had they known, from 1 Kings, "There is no man that sinneth not." I might have replied to them from Romans, "What then? shall we sin, because we are not under the law, but under grace? God forbid." By law I had not sinned, by all the laws of mutual regard and memory in common. But I lived hardly, therefore, in a state of grace. For within me, without need, I willed this memory to live. When my volume of early essays appeared without "One Amongst Many," your mother moved a step closer to me; then I was able to assist my brother covertly through the connivance of Snigs in contributing certain royalties to the partnership; Snigs took a step closer to me. Good acts, yes: but I performed them because the memory of the three sentences was alive within me.

Finally, Adèle, you entered my life as a friend. When you wrote, "I must confess I have not read your volume of early essays," a wave of relief swept over me; perhaps no one had told you, and now you would never know. But then I thought, this can hardly be; her mother must have revealed that I, like the nuns and priests, alluded to her "stain" and yet she writes to me with increasing warmth, as though the law of memory had been suspended by her, of all persons, suspended by her. Once, the time you wrote to me about the Dorian inscription you had deciphered, the letter full only of your enthusiasm, I was rapt only by this other wonder, the wonder that memory might be verily destroyed, which would be our state of grace.

A few nights later this refuge was taken from me. I believe I have told you that I have great trouble in falling asleep; hovering, I half-dream. This night I received a phantom visit from your mother. No! Do not smile— it is the phantom which may impose upon man waking desolation! Your mother came to my rooms in Milner Street, her first time there; we sat side by side, the window open to let in some breeze from the mews and gardens opposite. "What is a girl to think, when suddenly showered with the intense and personal outpourings of an older man? You are not a schoolfellow. You are a bachelor nearly fifty years of age, flooding this young person with your religious musings, your literary opinions, your memories, all these bursting like a torrent over a dike. Permit me to be frank, my dear sir, I say it again, you are a bachelor nearly fifty years of age pouring forth your heart to a young woman: what is she to make of this affection?"

That is just what I thought she would say. I could not defend approaching fifty.

I said instead, "Ours is a friendship; I have made no demands upon her." Even as I heard myself say these words, I realised they were far, far from the point, that I was lying even when on the edge of sleep.

I repeated my lie. "You comprehend that ours is a simple, honest friendship?"

She, your mother, even then, gave generously to me. She took my hand. "No, it is, as I have said, a dishonest one. But I understand your sentiments are honourable."

It was at this moment that I began what you called my religious "crisis." What you say about Newman is of course true; with my brain I knew it, and was revolted. Yet I imagined that he, in his heart, had also suffered so that the reality of sin, absolute, finally demanded of him an act of faith. Little was known of the reasons for his conversion, leading me to believe that surely, this figure whose name was synonymous with chastity, with purity, had within himself carried sin requiring an act of desperation. For Newman, the change of religions was a desperate act. For me, editor of *The Free-Thinker*, editor of an edition of the anti-clerical writings of Thomas Paine, etc. etc., the admission that I needed to pray was a desperate act.

And this admission I made to you, only to you, causing your mother again to whisper to me, "You are leading my daughter on, you of all people."

I should judge that, of those in my family whom my three sentences drove away, my father has been the slowest to return, and he has taken the most cautious steps, urged on, I believe, by the actual congress which has become more frequent between your mother, Snigs and myself, yet he is courteous only. He cares for you greatly, as you must know, he esteems your lively intelligence and your goodness. I heard him also in these moments of courtesy protecting you. Your very goodness moved me to pour out in letters my heart: how could I know that, once more, I was committing a sin, seeking from you absolution, while you offered me a larger love? Like layer upon layer of silk was sin in me. I could know myself, and cease folding you within those luxurious, stifling pleats, only if I disciplined myself to silence. Such an effort your protectors finally roused in me. Let her breathe. Duty obliged me to cease writing to you.

Days passed in my rooms, the town empty, the affairs of *The Free-Thinker* delegated to others, while I attempted to think about the discipline to which a bachelor of fifty should submit. I could hurt you by failing to observe the discipline appropriate to this spiritual condition. Frequently I attempted to pray; the words of Scripture are hardly strangers to me, and I could summon favoured passages in large blocks at will, from the Epistles of Saint John above all, the patron saint of those in doubt. For a week, these acts of piety seemed to me so shaking I needed to recover for hours after each prayer of some few minutes. Yet even then, I should have known; never did I feel the impulse to take myself to a church, to share this piety with others. I sought no brothers in Christ. So that, after some days in this fevered state had passed, I rose from my knees. Still I had no desire to return to work; I rose from my knees to pace my rooms, to walk in Hyde Park and to read.

As I believe I told you, Newman was renowned in my youth for the houses of retreat he established. In these, young men and women of the Church of England withdrew, in order to contemplate, their prayers directed at transforming themselves into celibate persons. There was no whiff of Roman Catholicism in this, at least I believe not. He simply sought to make men and women purer in spirit through the purification of their bodies.

Now during these weeks in which I kept to my rooms I chanced to read an essay of Newman's on the "illative faculty," by which he means the imagination of ourselves in the place of others; it is no original essay, as Keats and other poets long have spoken of the need for this faculty if a poem or other work of art is to contain more than one character, but Newman seized upon their idea to show that the imagination thus has a moral dimension, the act of imagining oneself in the place of another the very essence of Christian charity.

As I perused this essay, it occurred to me that I had discovered what I sought when I stopped writing to you. Occurred not all at once. At the time I thought only, This essay cannot accord with his Anglican monasteries: how can we put ourselves in the place of others by withdrawing from them?

By this time, I had received three letters from you, which lay unopened upon my desk.

The illative faculties of bachelors: the bachelor may establish the most rigid order in his daily affairs, demanding his morning tea at precisely the same strength every day, regulating his hours of exercise, labour and leisure to the minute, demanding of his servants a mechanical exactitude in the management of his household. Yet, unrestrained by the demands of spouse and children, behind this orderly exterior the bachelor may give free rein to his illative powers, his life in imagination rich, even riotous, whilst he anxiously takes the first sip of tea to make sure it is just right and frequently consults his watch. Gradually, by this means, he loses the capacity to enter sympathetically into the lives of others; his routine protects the bachelor from his fellows, or, perhaps, he invents their lives wholly behind the shield of his own isolation. Thus the illative faculty ceases to be a largely artistic power and degenerates into mere egotistical fancy.

Now I know, since the time my beloved cats died and I replaced them by those more demanding household pets, the wayward Scotch terriers, that even the most prosaic alteration of the domestic scene in favour of conjugality alters as well the balance between order and egotistical imagining. The dogs must be walked, and in walking them, one is forced to pass amongst one's fellow beings and cannot help observing, noticing and engaging.

I grant this is a little absurd, but only a little. Since one cannot decree all bachelors to keep dogs, there must be found some other way to discipline the spiritual indifference that the bachelor's routines cause, I mean there must be found some way to bring his illative faculty to heel. Newman's answer is not mine, apart from the boredom I came to feel in praying; I will not submit my imagination to any other man's direction. Could one somehow will other dreams?

This, my dear Adèle, is my own convoluted way of saying simply I realised I had failed to put myself in your place. This is what bachelors commonly fail to do.

At first, when I essayed this substitution, I heard only your voice blaming me, "How could you?" After a time I did not hear you speaking to me at all, I imagined rather you speaking to yourself. I heard you wonder if, perhaps, were one to risk less, one would hurt less. You would write no more, you would attend your lectures, labour ever more diligently in the mission where you—a woman!—were beginning to be treated with consideration. You would do that fine, that rare thing, conduct a life of self-sufficiency, on a modest scale, to be sure, but, as you had written to me, it is a life entirely of your own composing.

I imagined you thus, and realised that still I took you as I took myself; I had made you into a spinster. Your instinct, however, is to reach out. Thus I imagined you anew in Paris, receiving one of Anne's missives after my own relapse into religion had passed, and I invited her to Milner Street to erase the dream-lie. "I have seen Charles in London and we have come to an understanding"; these words would chill, perhaps even terrify, you. I began to understand your writing to me again, felt the spirit you poured into these renewed efforts, that she might not stand in your light.

My heart went out to you. I realised that I myself had been too accommodating to your mother in our interview, but having forced myself into your place I now knew she spoke the truth. Our very correspondence was creating in you the ardour she had spoken of, each candid sentence of mine arousing you—do you not see the reason of this? Anne has been our constant if invisible companion in this correspondence: your correspondent her ancient antagonist, you in possession of his confidence and confidences, the excitement of a relation violating not merely her love but her ambition. She who even taunted you once with Cécile's handsome, rich husband. This is your mother at her worst, and we are two beings who do not glitter. There is no great subtlety in what I perceived by putting myself in your place: violation and ardour are so often companions.

I now sought to be more honest with myself about my own motives. You know how curious such self-searching can be; one always looks for the reason which robs the action of its intrinsic value, or I do: I say to myself I quarrelled with some person because I felt dyspeptic, or I was unhappy; rather than because he deserved to be quarrelled with. In these latter days I found myself frequently walking in Hyde Park, going round the Serpentine until I was ready to drop. I looked at the oily water buoying up the ducks and the children's boats; I watched the familiar scene, asking myself, "What happened?"—about Paris, about my brother, about this religious seizure. It was a curious relief from asking "Why did I do it?" Do you understand a man might well pose these questions about his soul's history whilst witnessing ducks fight over bits of bread, or children contend over whose boat finished first?

What happened is that I contained my sin quite nicely during all these years. It would be dishonest of me to say that each day since "One Amongst Many" I have been nagged by my violation of your mother. Relative to this, I have got on quite nicely in my illative condition; it would be dishonest to claim my estrangement from my family was causing me daily intolerable pains. What happens in general is that people get on with their lives; once, in my priestly days, I visited a poor fellow in gaol, condemned to a year for poaching, whose thoughts dwelt principally on how I might increase the quantity of beer they allotted him weekly. I have been in truth more fortunate than merely to get on: when I write I am the airiest of men, I am blessed with a sufficiency of friends. The most self-indulgent moment in my letters was the one you seized upon, when I reproached the estimable *Free-Thinker* for the unhappiness of its editor. The editor of this review would indeed be the most glittering of souls, had he managed to *ruin* his life in three sentences.

Rather, the truth is perhaps that sin has been the shield of my bachelor-hood. I wonder if by chance you have any idea of what I am talking about? Nothing preserves a man in his own ways more than his conviction that he is unworthy; then those who reach out to him are either fools or their declarations suspect. In Hyde Park I understood this to be what my friend from Oriel meant by saying I willed sin into being. What has happened: I have preserved myself as a bachelor these fifty years. You are the first woman to have touched me so deeply that I laid down my shield. It is in that sense I mean that ten years of solitude can be measured in three sentences. It was a sin to write them, and a continuance of sin to use them. I ask your forbearance; I have produced nostrums because the instancing of these truths would cause you to shun me, for ever.

But I might be less obscure, my dear friend, in explaining to you the dénouement of this "crisis" (and do you not know, ardent translator, that this word derives from the Latin for "decision," not "suffering"?). Recently I had a long conversation with a younger friend who has entered the priesthood. I asked, How do you minister to families these days, you who have taken the vow of chastity? For in my time, Adèle, an inexperienced clergyman in the Church of England could console himself that a knowledge of life would eventually be vouchsafed him upon his own marriage and that, until then, God might inspirit him with the right words for those in need. My priestly friend replied simply that he sought to forget himself entirely in listening to another. That, you see, was the way he put himself in the place of his brides, grandfathers and expectant mothers. Yes, I pursued, that is what one is meant to do, but, I asked him, how do you *minister*? Equally, he replied, I try to forget that they are about to gain carnal knowledge, or to bury children, or to give birth. I put myself in their place and ask, What Word from God do they need to hear, the Word which is not of my composing nor theirs; I recite the Word, that they take it unto themselves.

I resolved to wait a few months, then to try again to know you. I hoped we might resume in a more selfless way. This is why I sent your unopened letters back to you; they would be the culmination of a correspondence which was for both of us too laden, too interested. I knew it would cause you pain. The priest would have tried to minister to this, even though he could not pretend to understand, the Word furnishing him your balm. But now I had done with the Word, with charity. I caused you pain. Having put myself in your place, I sent back your letters as a disinterested act, so that you might be free.

I thought your ardour would cool, you would understand, eventually you would go forward. Then, a few weeks later, I learnt from Frederick that, instead, you blamed yourself. It was time to write. Blame is unworthy of either of us.

Charles

Madame Anne Mercure   *8 January 1848*
3, rue de la Tour des Dames
Paris

My dearest,

Please forgive the stream of inadequate courier messages. It was all quite sudden, though he had a premonition, I believe, when we opened the atelier after the holidays. I feared at first between us yet another alarm; then it was too late. That morning the sun beat so strong into the atelier that the ice outside the glass melted, water spreading the light prismatically, the reds and yellows especially vivid. My father and I arrived at the atelier within seconds of each other, and paused beneath this radiance. Do you remember in Nîmes, you disbelieved me when I said a glass prism measures the thickness of light? You would have believed it in our workrooms.

Under this winter sun my father turned to me and said easily, I thought in the spirit of the moment, "Pray come to my inner chamber; I will not detain you from your table long."

There, where the skylights face absolute north, the sun had not penetrated and it was cold, very cold; I lit the fire, still of wood, which he preferred to coal for the colour. He said, as I busied myself over bits of kindling, "Frederick, why not take this room for your own?"

Father had worked in it since 1824.

I turned to demand his meaning, found he also had turned away; he stared at the little copy he had made of David's "Madame Récamier."

"David has made her as glacial on canvas as they say she was in the flesh. It is time for you to have this room."

"I am content with mine."

"But I designed this in all its pomp to be the senior partner's chamber. The place is empty three days each week; surely a void makes no favourable impression on clients."

If only there were a daily crush in need of pompous impressions! I contented myself with a sally: "Ah, but you are present even when you are invisible." You know how my father loves this sort of badinage.

He worked steadily through the day, on a sea-side villa. We had luncheon sent in from the Black Cock for everyone, the sun now passing beyond direct penetration of the draughting room, but its warmth still so reverberant that all removed their palm gloves. The light somehow retained the red, though this may be an echo in my mind of the first impression. The luncheon passed merrily; whilst my father drew in the morning I had calculated: we have in sum five months of work in hand—more indeed than I had imagined—and I informed the boys of the fact during our repast. At five the carriage came as usual, he left in the usual way, ragging the draughtsmen ceremonially before departure. He was wont to remark that the sight of an employer leaving without a word for home, bath and dinner is never encouraging to those who must stay behind to execute his orders. Thus ended one of the most cheerful days we had passed together in some months, and I drew well in the afternoon also.

I remained with the boys, who need constant direction in the articulation of the I-beam skeletons. At perhaps half past seven, Philpott flung open the door.

"Mr Frederick, your father is taken something horrible!"

The six or seven of us in the atelier jumped up. I demanded from Philpott his meaning as I hurried into my cloak; the idiot could do no more than stare, as though one might read everything from his bulging eyes, Philpott being himself, I suppose, at least five years older than my father. Fortunately, a boy thought to query him about a doctor, and it transpired that Philpott had called our usual man, sending the atelier card. I therefore left with this hopeless servant, whilst the boys awaited the doctor, to speed him instantly to Father's house.

Biggs had worked hard in Father's rooms during Philpott's absence. Though the bedchamber reeked, my father was under clean white sheets, and the fire blazed; we discovered her bent over him, wiping his lips and chin with a cloth soaked in rose water. Biggs turned to me as I closed the door; she whispered loudly, "Sir, I put the best linen over him I could find."

"Not so fast, Biggs," a weak voice came from behind her. Startled, she turned, and dropped the napkin on his face. The perfume of roses evidently revolted my father; he started upright and retched over the linen—attend, Anne, these particulars are important and I must try you with worse yet. At this moment, however, the crisis seemed ended. He sank back, still conscious though exhausted from his purge. In the quiet of the next half hour we were able to wipe him clean again and replace the sheets.

"I seen many a man what would sicken himself, Mr Frederick, 'specially it being his own father," Biggs commended me.

At this moment I was holding Father up so that Biggs could pull the soiled undersheet away; it escaped me without thinking: "I have dealt with worse, Biggs, much worse." You know how errant words like this suddenly stir one. The old fear of touching those who have vomited seized me, and I dropped my father. Biggs gasped, he moaned slightly, but it seemed I did him no harm; I had dropped him a few inches into a down bed.

When we had laid him again in bed, I sat down, angry at myself for this lapse; of course this only made me think more about it. Fortunately the doctor arrived at this moment, and, hard on his heels, Charles, to whom I had sent Philpott the moment after we had gained Father's house.

(I tell you the following only because it were no real account which omits weakness.) Whilst the doctor began his examination, Charles came over to me, and put out his arms to embrace me. I had hidden my hand in my coat, to keep the shake from showing; the spasm lasted no more than a minute, but I couldn't stop it in the middle, and this is when Charles sought his embrace. I burst out, "I don't want to be touched."

We heard the doctor far away. "The attack is inconsequent, however painful. Your father is suffering from indulgence in oysters, which I have expressly forbidden him. The disagreement between man and mollusc will end, shortly." Biggs, who had evidently followed her master's bidding for supper, stared angrily at her accuser, who returned the anger. Now Charles comprehended, from the smell. He patted my shoulder, though by then it mattered not.

The bustling of the doctor, who was at school with Father and Snigs and whom they call Don Bartolo, returned us to management of the sick-room in Jermyn Street. We accepted his orders and indeed for two days these seemed efficacious, which is why I saw no need then to call for you. The digestion calmed, my father slept almost without interruption. Once, when awake, he retailed stories of his old comrade's medical incompetence. "Why do you retain him?" I asked obligingly. "My dear boy, there can be no greater pleasure, and thus no more bracing tonic, than witnessing Fatuity parade in the gown of Science." Before dawn, however, I heard knocking at the door below my window, and I knew that we would now require Don Bartolo to do more than amuse us.

He was there, when I arrived in the bedchamber; from the colour in Biggs' cheeks I could see the doctor had ministered to my father by blaming her again. This time the sheets were unsoiled, the room smelt only of the wood fire. My father complained of cold, so I laid on more wood; he mumbled as I placed the logs, attended by his schoolmate, who sat at his bedside, important and stupid.

Charles came; Snigs came, bundled in his scarves, his fur cape and hat, his woollen mittens. Without removing these protective garments Snigs advanced upon the bed, giving Don Bartolo one look which dislodged the doctor from the chair—I imagine Snigs had looked him out of his path thus at Eton; furred and mufflered, Snigs peered at my father, then announced, "I suggest the company seat themselves." As we did so, my father's breathing became more fitful.

Now, my dearest Anne, I will record the following exactly—we owe this duty to the dead.

My father withdrew a trembling hand from under the covers, the hand moving towards his head. He grasped the strap of his eye-patch and slowly began to pull it off. My brother and I, the doctor, the two servants were mesmerised by that slowly crawling, grasping member; Snigs was not. He bent forward, clasped my father's wrist and firmly if equally slowly reversed the movement. The hand retired beneath the covers. Once again the sick man presented only a somnolent face at the edge of his linen and wool mound; against this irregular horizontal was the furred vertical of the other old one. My father then spoke, his eyes still closed.

"Charles?"

"Yes, Father."

"Come closer. Take the chair."

Snigs yielded his seat as my brother moved to the edge of the bed, but withdrew no farther; he remained vigilant.

"Do you remember when they felted my eye, Charles?" The hand was restless beneath its covers. "You were a good nurse, then." This effort was tiring him, the words came slower and slower. "I have given Frederick my table. Why, though, did you come?" He lapsed into silence.

At this Snigs jabbed an outstretched finger first at the doctor and then at the servants, swinging this sabre from them to the door. The doctor made as if to protest; Snigs put a finger to his lips, and the doctor followed the servants out. We three retired to a corner.

"Having attended innumerable such scenes, I am in no doubt the end has come," Snigs told us in a low voice. "The body will soon sink with the wits. His affairs are entirely in order; thus, there is no need for my presence. You may with entire propriety ask to spend these last moments with your parent alone." I believe Charles was as dumbfounded as I; Charles took the hand of the man who had played hide-and-seek with our father; Snigs' chin trembled. Then he managed to smile weakly. "My dear Charles, it is what form and tradition oblige, family being everything and I not a blood member of this one. . . ."

"Charles," we heard from the bed, "I have thought of something." We turned to stare. My father had succeeded in removing his eye-patch.

By the light of the new morning we could see all too terribly; at the rim the skin was pink, almost raw, where the edge of the eye cup might be irritated by errant hairs from the felt cover. Behind this, there was ever darker red skin, not a trace of any white matter, and at the very back of the eye socket there was a blue-black spot, like a scab, where the optic nerve was seated. Father turned his head slightly towards us, who were rooted to the spot. By the slight change in angle I could see more clearly into the eye—the cursed habit of examining deserted me not even in this moment! Just to the side of the optic scab there was a slit with the marks of three stitches; so far had the tip of the whip penetrated. And I was so pleased with myself for seeming to amuse with Paris prattle when I returned after his attack, so pleased at provoking his laughter.

Staring straight at the corner, my father spoke once again to Charles. "You were a very good nurse, then. But more recently you seem to have lost the art. People are so busy these days, though, I know, so busy. Busy boys." He turned away to rest his head on the pillows, mercifully diminishing our sight of his face.

"Do you remember, Charles, how you pounded on the door of our quarters? It afflicted Sarah greatly, that pounding." Charles, pale, made no attempt to speak.

Father for the last time turned to stare at us three again full in the face. "I hope I have never tried you with complaint of my condition?" We nodded dumbly. He flushed with effort. "I hoped not. After all, with the merest cosmetic my loathsomeness has been converted to dashing. Somehow, I thought of those touching little scenes often, when I was alone in this room, the door locked, at last free of the cover to my face. You see, the door was also locked, but now there was no little boy pounding to be let in." Father began to claw at the counterpane, like a dog digging. "I have thought of something. Come to the bed. We will try to pray. . . ." Anne, he smiled at Charles.

At this moment an obscene vision loomed before me: my brother kneels beside the bedside of his dying father; the son bends a knee, he intones the words of "Our Father which art in Heaven," asking for forgiveness of sins. The wretched old man seeks mumbling to follow the son's lead, struggling to remember words which last issued from his lips when he was a child.

Charles moved towards the bed. He stood silent at its foot. He did not kneel. Nor did he seek to replace the eye-patch. He stood silent and straight and he left our father alone.

This was the matter of a minute. Father sank again into sleep. In these last moments, he had thought not of me, but of the son from whom, for years, he had held aloof. I who have shared with Father my life.

We moved to our prior places. I begged Snigs to remove the fur cape, which he did, revealing himself rather hastily dressed; he resumed his chair. The servants and doctors re-appeared at the door; I dismissed the servants, so that my father's eye could remain uncovered, as he seemed to wish. Charles and I wandered the room aimlessly for perhaps an hour. Suddenly we heard the rattle in my father's throat; we crowded to the bed. Father looked at me, at Charles, shook his head; when he found Snigs, he smiled again, this time a radiant, wonderful smile and he chided, quite firmly, "*Tiens!* Snigs! You are even more dishevelled than am I!" Then he rolled over and was gone.

There were no tears, oddly. Charles took Snigs by the hand, who asked only if he could go into the drawing-room to sit alone for a moment. I saw them out into the hall, then returned to my father's chamber. I discovered Philpott placing a sheaf of lilies in a vase (which he must have procured when he went out for the morning's shopping), whilst Biggs and my brother spread a fresh white sheet over the corpse, all the usual unseemly, if reassuring, funeral bustle in a house. I lifted the sheet to see again my father's face. "Sir," Biggs intercepted me, "I fixed it soon as I came into the room. Looks just like he always was." And he did.

Returning for a few hours to my lodgings, I intended to write to you straight away. A sudden reverie of love forestalled me. I thought of how your lips part ever so slightly when you are intent. I remembered the first time my father escorted Adèle alone to Bonnet's, the waiters, he said, exchanging knowing looks. I thought about the day we nearly burnt the house down in the winter of '39. Then the list of our worries began aimlessly parading in my mind, each item increasing the ardour of my love for you—the debt last year, the appalling gossip of La Vestris in '45, the day in Paris when first you asked "Did you draw today?" and the day in London when you learnt to cease asking me that question—even these painful moments sweeping over me increased the tide of my love. Then I thought of looking together at those small Vernets, about the fuchsias from the Jardin des Plantes which seemed determined to die, no matter how we watered them, I thought about the tiara of rhinestones Devarria made for Pussy the First. These memories so crowded my brain I could not take up my pen. Indeed, I think my father would have understood, the flood of life a better homage than mourning. Perhaps that is why he said nothing.

After some hours alone thus, I was obliged to return to the house in Jermyn Street, for the visits of condolence. There is nothing to tell of them, save that there were many, far more than we had expected, so soon. I determined once more to write to you, but now, having heard so many speak of him, I began to hear the silence and to fear it: I would never laugh with him again, he would never chide Snigs, nor even ply Charles with respectful questions, which had become their manner together. I wanted to fill this silence: speaking would bring him back to me; my brother had our entire lifetime. So I did not write. I invited Charles back to my rooms for a light supper.

Although it was reminiscence which I hoped would soothe me, more urgent words seemed to come first. I remarked to him, "I was afraid you might kneel beside Father's bed."

"Yes, you were." He then rose to carve again at the sideboard (Maurice will assist Philpott until the funeral). Clumsy as always, Charles succeeded in dropping the bird to the floor, and we had a business of restoring the duck and its garnish again upon the platter. "I won't tell if you won't." I used to say this when we were boys; it surprised me to hear the words in his deep, resonant voice, as he handed me the bird. Even during the visits of condolence this afternoon men offered him opinions, and he received them, as if they were engaged in judicial deliberation. My editorial, consequential brother now said to me, "I won't tell if you won't," before reverting to my question, which he answered lightly enough rather than in the Charlesian manner. "I saw you watching us, my dear Frederick. But you needn't have worried. Even had he meant it."

We, who were meant to be afflicted, passed an evening which I'm sure would have struck a visitor merely as two brothers indulging in the pleasures of memory. I learnt of little incidents in our early days in England which I had not known, or remembered, or which had seemed inconsequent to me. For instance Charles told me that Father had at least liked the sight of Charles in red and white when he became a chorister; Father sketched in the chapel many times. Charles told me of singing that first day, of the voices pouring out together; evidently the choir inspired him with religious stirrings long before he comprehended the words of their hymns. Amazingly, Anne, he said that the singer whose timbre and purity most recalled to him "boysong" was Adolphe. When I asked, But why did you not advert to this in your obituary notice?, Charles said he thought of so doing, but that the warmth of the boys' singing together would not fit the intentions of his memorial. For a moment silence fell upon us, the editorial *gravitas* hardened my brother's face, and I was afraid he would stop, that we would end the meal in intolerable silence.

Certainly Charles and I had not spoken as intimately in many years. I trimmed the wicks; I mentioned I ought to write to you more fully than brief messages of news, but he would not let me go. He asked after you, after Cécile, even after Adèle, and I suppose I could have told him the entire history of our new garden; he was afraid this night, he also, of silence. Indeed, the débris of supper before us, the room warm, each of us exhausted, he turned to me with an earnest air. "May I ask you a question?"

"Anything."

"But it is none of my affair. Yet I have always wanted to know. Even before we two could mention her name easily to one another."

"If you did not think it fit to enquire, you wouldn't." Do you hear my parent? After all these years I could ape every pause, even every twinkle just before his parry.

"Why have you never married Anne?"

You will understand, my darling, that the circumstances made me, if not indiscreet, at least disposed to make him *some* answer. I did not break my promise to you. It was simplest to give the reply I made when Marie went on so about it.

"It is remarkable we did not marry."

Unlike Marie, he looked blank.

"It is remarkable we have trusted one another so long."

It was entirely foreign territory to him, Anne. The hour began to tell upon me. "The senior partner's room," a designation he never used before, before its gift. Little fragments lodged in my brain dully, heavily. I would explain as much as our promise permits.

"Of course, the children entered into our connexion; there would be, it seemed, none of our own, while Cécile became quite attached to me and Adèle was passing through a . . . difficult period." I stopped briefly here. He may have thought it was to spare him, but I was thinking of the day my father first met Cécile—you remember?—she had the beautiful Spanish comb in her hair.

"In these years, yes, we did think to marry, my prospects seemed quite bright then, too, but also it was a time, it was in the middle Thirties, when we frequently irritated each other and intensely." Charles looked at me with surprise and I found I had a happy formula for him. "You treated us as a datum, my dear brother, whereas in fact we were conducting lives." These strokes came to *him* so naturally, I had heard them pour forth like his music since he first took me for walks.

"Sometimes such trials give one strength." Charles produced this with a sincerity which obliged me to nod my agreement. Evidently the loss of our father was beginning to weigh upon him as well, the machinery of his mind had shut for the night. So it was simpler.

"Yes, such trials may give one strength. There came a moment many years ago when our difficulties became acute." I nearly mentioned that he might recall Snigs' first trip to Paris, as it had been an evening of such reminiscences, but I was able to hold back. "We left Paris, and in the country—we were in Brittany together—there we overcame these . . . difficulties. We had renewed our affections, they were stronger than ever, if calmer. As a man and woman who trusted each other." I am sure these words are exact; I know I never mentioned Adèle's name.

Indeed I believe my speech all he needed to hear, he had his map, hard enough for him to read, he who has so little knowledge of life, as we know. It is a very English type, these innocent men. They imagine every person, every event in a *radial* relation to themselves. But I do not mean to speak against my poor brother; indeed, his innocence was shortly to cause me to feel ashamed of myself.

As I say, I stopped before revealing anything to him of those days of our walks by the sea. Perhaps grief began now to etch itself even upon that plate of memory—whatever, I stopped, I was no longer lulled by the sound of my own voice. I asked him to give me a glass of brandy.

He went to the sideboard for me.

It may be that I felt the machinery of memory still spinning, it may be I hoped his voice, my brother's voice, once again might lull me. I asked if he indeed would ever marry, although I knew the answer; only to keep us going I said the condition of bachelors puzzled me, if no more than on grounds of health.

"Again chaos is spread over your board."

It was a stupid, a cruel question. Even this evening the word "boysong" was his. He had knocked my glass of brandy over a Stilton.

"I fear I have rendered the cheese inedible."

"Quite." The best I could manage was, "I mean that you are quite tremendous and difficult as you are. The thought of you mirrored, of a horde of scribbling Charleses, would overwhelm not just me but all of England."

We were now both standing next to the sideboard with its wet cheese, its duck bone in deranged aspic, its low candles. We could no more. I took him in my arms, we kissed, and parted for the night.

When the door closed below me, I retired to my chair to rest for a moment before writing and woke to the sound of a milk cart. It was morning, all the rest of which I have occupied in this letter.

How often have I felt you a precious friend, a friend above all! you to whom I have ever looked in hours of need! My first thought of the longer term is that now, perhaps, at last our disorders might cease. I shall arrange what work there is in London according to the life we alone lead, together. This will help. Do you remember another promise, the one I made you at the old Flavigny house that spring? Yet you will never let me redeem my pledge. I would, a thousand times! And do you remember what I promised when first he asked me back? That also I would redeem; even grieving for him now I tell you I would promise it again and keep my word. But you never called me back. Never. You have asked only for love, and even this, even love, it is you who have taught me to give. My dear, you are terribly unfair. Still, as I told Charles, it is remarkable, is it not? We shall eventually indeed become ancient walruses, hoary old beasts, splashing and snorting about together.

I go to Father's house; Charles and I are to arrange the details of the funeral, which we are agreed will be entirely simple. We are agreed—how sweet that phrase. I shall write again in a few hours.

Frederick

Charles Courtland, Esq.   *14 January 1848*
20 Milner Street
London

Dear Charles,

During this, your time of mourning, I wished to write to you only to tell you how much your brother and you have my deepest sympathy. Mr Courtland was a kind friend to me during my times in London and, I could see, a friend to all who knew him. He could, with his gaiety and wit, bring life instantly to all upon whom he granted the privilege of his company; though I know nothing of his art, those who do now speak of his houses with the greatest respect; how fortunate that it is an art which endures. Moreover, I am sure that at the end he found solace in you, and that the memory of his love will come to be for you the memory of him you cherish.

This note of condolence is hardly the occasion for me to reply to your earlier letter, which I left unanswered from a need of reflection equal to yours, and from an equal love. Let me tell you only that once, long ago, I did your brother an injustice; I mistook him, and harboured first the consciousness of injury and then of my mistake within me. He did me the great kindness of acting as though he had not noticed; it took me many years to accept this kindness; I could not until, in fact, I had gone to and returned from Greece. I only hope, Charles, it will be briefer, sooner for us.

Again I send to you my most heartfelt wishes in this time of loss. Know that you are ever in the thoughts of your most

devoted friend,
Adèle Mercure

Count Dunin's Man of Steel

From the Diary of Anne Mercure
June 1850–May 1851

3 June 1850

We have taken the most extraordinary house, number 20 of Paulton's Square. Like choosing a pot by number: 20 holds three servants below stairs, there is hot running water throughout the house, room also for three children to run, space for more servants in the attics. All planned minutely by the builder. Frederick will work up there, in the attics. He finds pleasing uniformity in the façades of the new houses around this "square," at present a rectangle of mud; evidently the geometric proportions of new brick to mud rectangle are also excellent. I find our situation daringly rural. How many of our acquaintance will attempt so fatiguing a journey? Requiring an entire change of costume, riding boots, spurs (chased silver if possible), rain cloaks for the ladies and the black Spanish broad brims for the gentlemen, intimating one embarks on a Mysterious Voyage, the selecting and fitting of which may take until dawn after an evening's work—how many will essay it?

We disposed this afternoon our pieces about the house, and such of the articles of their father as the boys kept, which means we have everything in our keeping, Milner Street serving as an annexe to the British Library and otherwise filled with those hideous, hideous earthenware teapots and teacups Charles has begun to "collect." However, I was firm: not so much from Jermyn Street as would make visitors, or either of the boys, think they were living once more in their childhood home.

How I hate Turkey carpets!

I shall make a garden, a good garden of herbs, lavender and roses, a garden for the nose. Although one can smell the river even from here.

I recommend always that the best-loved pieces—the sofa in which one curled while Mother read from a favoured book, the table on whose under-side one secretly carved one's initials—that these be the very first items to appear on the auction block, otherwise one is like a prisoner to heavy clouds of memory (nota bene) which hover just above the by-now greasy sofa, scarred table and worn carpets.

Fortunately we have been able to install our own ebony dining table. When the men finally had it in, I thought we had made a terrible mistake and was on the point of ordering them to remove it. The gold griffin legs and inlaid porphyry edging seemed to make hanging pictures or anything else impossible in our "snug" dining-room; the table is too high as well as too large. Frederick has been clever about this; he put small architectural prints on the walls, severe, hung *low*, quite perfect foils. Our supper was charming; the rear windows give on empty fields and stables, there are even rows of cabbages and asparagus still defiantly planted, which perhaps I should also plant, fields now filling in with squares for young families, who will spy in turn upon us and discover masked ladies and Spanish men dining off marble, on blue Sèvres plates, drinking from silver goblets of the age of the First George.

A suburban wasteland "for a change"—what a multitude of disappoint-ments, unhappinesses and yearning do people pour into those simple three words, the forsaken women, ruined men, the mortally ill, the frightened who travel aimlessly, who move house as though fleeing, who avoid their old friends, who sell the clothes which remind them of days of glory and beauty, all "for a change," whilst we—but here is Frederick with a glass of something bubbling.

We have had good news, at least I think so. Brunel has offered to "let Frederick in" on the Great Exhibition Hall. Frederick will work on the iron dome which crowns the middle. We had the usual struggle with ourselves, this time not perhaps as ferocious as before: "It is detail and decorative work, not originating design." This leading to "Stephenson and Brunel have offered this to me only as a gesture, only because they rejected me in the competition," ending in "It might be a more effective statement were I to stand entirely aside."

This time, I say, I needed barely a battalion in the field. I was able to use his own observations that Brunel had lost his touch. Had not Frederick remarked that the central iron dome was the only unusual feature of Bru-nel's giant brick box, and had not he heard that this immense sheet-iron top had grave problems in passing light in and gas from the lower jets out? It is a compliment that Brunel turns to Frederick in these difficulties. I told him this offer only proves what I always said about the competition, that it was a sham conducted so that the judges could award the contract to themselves. And as to standing aside, this time I did not let my tongue in vexation say again that no one would notice; I had only to remark that anyone in an official capacity associated with the great exhibition appeared therefore under the patronage of the Prince Consort, since this exhibition was his adored child: Frederick would be seen to have standing as an official architect.

It was a matter of twenty minutes; indeed, the outcome could have been predicted by the champagne he brought us and which we sipped in the boudoir smelling of paint and pitch. He will be paid a thousand pounds, a good omen for the house, more than all last year. And so to bed.

12 June 1850

Brunel came to supper tonight, the two of them at work since dawn. I was in no doubt: Raymond laid the table with snifters, and I instructed him to pour the cognac as he would pour wine. No roast, instead two courses of game birds, served with the most pungent sauces the timid potato can bring herself to concoct. I do not like a woman in the kitchen who sniffles. By eleven, the colour was in their faces again and they spoke in whole sentences.

Crumpled in his chair, Brunel began to describe the rail termini, warehouses, bridges which he and Frederick might create together; the visions so large all thought of funds, clients, all impediments were swept aside. Frederick nodded agreement with each idea, as though it were reasonable and the collaboration one to which he might just possibly assent. In an hour Brunel has conceived a lifetime of wonders, whilst Frederick as he dreams becomes ever more precisely fixed, his mind refining the details and the elegant implications of one impossible thing.

Suddenly Brunel sat upright in his chair, the decanter and glasses rattling as he put his fist down upon the marble and he demanded angrily, "Know why we turned your plan aside?"

Frederick was taken aback. Not I. Sweetly I smiled at our guest and supplied, "No dear, why ever did you?"

"Revolutionaries!"

This roused Frederick. "Sir! Dare you imply that Anne or I—"

" 'Course not." He gurgled and I poured him another generous glass of our best cognac to help him further. "Think: a building entirely of glass, never mind, the glass turrets and towers and such, a building entirely of glass is the easiest target in the world. Think: Queen and Consort walk through the central aisle on opening day; one revolutionary pokes a rifle through one glass pane, that's all he needs to do, break one glass pane, *anywhere*, to take aim. Or knocks out an upper pane with a pole; tosses in a bomb; glass everywhere, blood, panic, one minute for the Festival of Arts, Commerce and Industry to end in disaster. It was beautiful, what you did. Beautiful. However, brick was the only answer." Even if he did keep the commission for himself, this was a handsome excuse. They parted warmly.

I shall do Rosalind in Birmingham next month. £80 weekly. They are so astounded I can play a girl. I say to Hayman, "It is not a matter of the face, it is a matter of the wrists, how you move the wrists; a girl doesn't know how to use them, she is awkward, so you do that," but she doesn't understand, and seems embarrassed by her own compliment. Have I not demonstrated by now to these people our complete command? The advantages of our *professional training*? But they love the inspired amateur and so they hang their jaws amazed whenever they see what we are able to do.

19 June 1850

There are disturbing rumours about that man Stephenson and a politician named Ellis, who owns a railway; they are said to be in secret negotiation with—Paxton! Unlike the 245 who submitted in the ordinary way to the Commission, he is to be given a special chance of his own. But this rumour is absurd, Frederick says. The Exhibition opens in ten months and they shall be lucky, evidently, to execute Brunel's plan, which is now completely drawn. On the other side, the public, led by a Colonel Sibthorp, wish to prevent the event entirely, in order that Hyde Park remain in its pristine state. Frightened by garlic, demanding their vegetables boiled to pulp, unable to make wine, these English lovers of nature!

I have, in this regard, set myself resolutely against the fashion of Paulton's Square; we shall not keep dogs, as though members of the "county"; we shall continue cats. Frederick and I had a little fun with our neighbour, who maintains three nipping beasts, assuring the banker that in France cats are also promenaded on leads, and that we intend to walk Violet and Hermione daily. His bloated cheeks stiffened in suspicion, then rouged in indignation, finally dropped again with incomprehension as we spun out the picture of gentleman striding behind cat, in the Tuileries at dusk, only the occasional miaow of acknowledgement breaking the stillness of the King's preserves in the very heart of the City of Light. Though he may expect this from us. In the other drawing-rooms of Paulton's Square it is evidently thought that the scandalous couple, even if of advanced age, lower the tone of the Square; no one has left cards on us.

Today I dismissed Potato Biggs, another old Turkey carpet, and engaged the cook of La Vestris, who, it appears, is ruined once again. No agreement yet with the people of Macready, the American tour consuming them.

Frederick gave me a lovely pearl on a thin chain of silver, which he presented to me quite prettily this evening; it was hidden in the folds of a rose lying between my wine glasses. He took for himself from the jeweller —Janner it must be—three pearl shirt studs of exactly matching size. We shall be as elegant as La Vestris, and at this rate soon no richer. The supper was made more charming by our fare, for the first time since we moved; one could imagine oneself in Rheims. Nota bene: £500 comes from Brunel on the 22nd, when the Committee's plans are published; reserve £200 immediately for the house. The jewellery should be about £50, there are, say, £200 of current common debts, the rest for his office box.

27 June 1850

On the 22nd a messenger appeared as we breakfasted, bearing a cheque for £500 as promised from Brunel. The young man who called shortly thereafter to accompany Frederick to the atelier was furnished with a copy of *The Illustrated London News*. To be sure, I am no connoisseur; to me, however, the Committee plans did not look entirely bad, and one certainly noted the iron dome at the top as the principal feature of interest. Frederick and the young man stared at *The Illustrated London News* as if seeing the official Exhibition Hall for the first time.

"The false arches," the young man murmured.

"The false arches indeed," Frederick murmured.

"Remark the awkward excess of the verandah."

Frederick's eyes still rested in fascination on *The Illustrated London News*. "It is, after all, an international exposition. A verandah is characteristic, not only in India, but also in the American Southern states."

"Yes, sir."

Perhaps the newspaper had drawn the hall askew for political reasons? Perhaps the editor was Sibthorpian in sympathy?

"Oh, Madame," protested the earnest youth, "this is exactly in proportion: the brick arches are indeed sixty feet in height, the verandah as you see it, and the ceremonial dome should be as it is in scale here, one hundred and fifty feet more in height."

It did indeed appear as though an enormous bowler had been placed upon a shoe box. I refrained from further comment, however, as Frederick treats the staff with the utmost gravity, and these boys adore him for making it all matter, every last marking. This I have observed in architects: the mocking spirit does not provoke men to build, and they are seldom gay when engaged.

"Of course one had scrutinised the whole design, then tended to forget, working only upon the dome sections . . . Well," he rallied his draughtsman with a surprising smile, "we will at least make a dome which gives the eye pleasure when it rises to heaven, imploring relief. We must be off."

I was much taken up that day with the men from Covent Garden, so I thought no more of the matter until I met Frederick for a late supper at the Blue Fox. Crab in the English manner: braised out of the shell in mustard. By then his ears were full of what people are calling the "scandal." Colonel Sibthorp and his troops trumpet that the great elms in Hyde Park will be destroyed. More aesthetically minded sectors of the public collared Frederick in the afternoon at the Garrick to vent criticisms similar to those made over our breakfast. Frederick must appear in the halls of the Garrick like a Saint Bernard racing to the rescue with a restorative iron dome between its jaws (nota bene !!!!), which, as I did tell him after we sent back the crab, is all to the good.

"You treat of the matter as though Brunel and I were equals. He has employed me, and I accepted not only his commission but his fee. When accosted today, therefore, I sought to meet all objections. Honour obliges me to defend my master."

Sometimes I want to cry when he talks in this manner, sometimes I want to slap him. That night neither. His hand was bad. We touched on equally painful gossip; one hears everywhere that Paxton is furiously at work upon a competing plan. We were served an entrecôte, quite passable. Once more over the same ground: a fault ten years old. However, Frederick roused himself in explaining that no one could ensure the Exhibition's opening the following May other than by following the official plans. To accept Paxton would be to delay the Exhibition for at least a year, which would be fatal for various administrative and economic reasons, and so this rumour of sending for Paxton was merely an echo of the propensity of Englishmen, when in distress, to say "It's time to send for the Duke," the Duke in question being that of Wellington, the one who sought illumination from Le Normand in the old days. So matters lay on the 22nd.

On the 25th, the complexion of events changed. A special meeting of the Commissioners was held at which Paxton in fact presented a design, in detail, and which they have taken seriously enough to refer to their building committee, chaired by Brunel. Evidently the day *The Illustrated London News* published the official plan was the day upon which Paxton returned from a feverish retreat of nine days in the country, drawing; now he has had three for conspiracy. Brunel learnt that Paxton went first to Lord Brougham, another decayed politician, and "converted" him—merely the ancient's ploy to claim public notice. Yet his patronage caused the Prince Consort to convene a special meeting on these drawings, which we have since heard has to do with Brougham and the King of Hanover. One feels quite in Paris! Now Brunel worries that if Paxton produces a persuasive plan, this can serve as a pretext for further German intrigue, causing British pique, resulting in all building being postponed for further study, meaning no Hall will ever rise. This, "they say," will suit Brougham perfectly, he who is converted only to make use of Paxton in embarrassing the German Prince Consort, or so "they" told Brunel, who confided his fears to us last evening over supper. I shall order a cask of cognac if this continues.

Frederick of course asked him, in the off-handed way which deceived neither Brunel nor myself, what were the plans produced by Paxton. Brunel replied equally off-handedly that they had points of interest. From the lightness of his tone we also understood he would produce nothing further. And yet he is maladroit.

In rising from the table, he fumbled in his waistcoat, producing an envelope; he began to stammer. On such occasions Frederick's courtesy is impeccable. To relieve Brunel of whatever embarrassment the envelope contained, Frederick took it, threw it negligently upon the table, remarked that Anne had bought an interesting drawing said to be by a pupil of Inigo Jones about which Frederick would like his opinion, and so led Brunel out of the room. Once we had conveyed Brunel into a hansom, we returned to the dining room to retrieve the document. It contained the further £500 payment for Frederick's work upon the official design, the cheque marked "final disbursement." This has plunged Frederick today into the most profound gloom, from which I cannot shake him. "Here is my answer, Anne, this is what he thinks of Paxton's design."

They say of M. de Balzac that, when he appeared at the Bourse, impatiently tapping his cane, scanning the boards for the prices of the latest bonds on which he had squandered francs he had yet to call his own, they say that at these impatient moments the entire cast of the characters forged by him might commence darting to and fro; scenes, entire tales spilt unbidden into his mind whilst he watched the clerks chalking up the numbers. Sometimes Balzac, distracted by this invasion, nodded to the clerks, buying further and yet more disastrously, and all the while he conceived. Or, if he merely watched the elaborate ballet of already-made personages passing within his brain, he is said often to have smiled benignly at tallies which shewed his current holdings plummeting towards disaster. Today in the newspaper they published a picture of Mr Paxton which recalled these stories. What I knew of him was contrary: M. de Balzac, gentleman, promenading slowly in the Bois, his enormous head dropped forward on his breast, seemingly lost to the world. Probably at those moments not a single scene, not a sentence came to him, he could barely remember the names. I liked to imagine he resembled me when I am lost in thought, looking mentally through his wardrobes, drawing up plans for improvements to his house. Balzac's was magnificent, the new house; everyone knew he built and furnished it on credit, a mansion that much more splendid for depending upon his dealings on the Bourse. In the picture of Mr Paxton, who certainly dreams, the eyes are clear, looking directly at the viewer. You do not imagine Mr Paxton a man with debts.

I put the paper away, since Frederick would not enjoy being greeted at breakfast by the laudatory essay on the Committee's rival. A few hours later, however, it was still with me, a little. Chopin's last concert in Paris was the one for which he insisted tickets be printed on thick board, as if invitations to a private soirée. Chopin gave away half these elegant boards to his friends, as generous as M. de Balzac, who gave confidential information about certain bonds to people he held in affectionate regard. I know for a fact, however, that Chopin after this concert took a mound of gold coins from the Stirling woman who loved and bored him, he accepted La Stirling's help without a murmur. As though she owed him the gift. And this made me think, in all those years no one said they ever saw Chopin smile.

Today I had a great number of things to do, and I was glad of it, as one mustn't succumb too often to measuring then against now, at least, not here. Still, it came to me that I had never found Chopin an attractive man; his complexion was liverish. Mr Paxton seems decidedly handsome, if rotund, but I sometimes like a solid man. His smile is most engaging.

While reading Rosalind to Mrs Burton in the green room, I wandered off again, though now positively I would have given anything to close the door upon unbidden memory. It was the day that young, avid doctor gave me his newly concocted restorative, the sachet of minerals which caused me instead to miscarry. Frederick could have killed him and been acquitted by any jury, a secretive madman so in love with his phials and retorts he risked murder—for it is that—to observe the effect of his confection. Yet when Frederick pounded this alchemist against the wall, the head rapping against the plaster so hard, I remember his entreaty, "I only sought to try it," like a child bewildered by poisoning its dog, and how I was surprised into a momentary sympathy. No noble sentiment moved me to intercede for this pasty, unkempt experimenter, this exterminator of the greatest happiness we could have shared. I still hate him.

In the hansom to Paulton's Square these ramblings throughout the day began to explain themselves. Even the suddenly sobbing Dufort has his little corner in the same painting in which M. de Balzac appears so magnificent and M. Chopin accepts the francs from the adoring spinster without a word. Gazing upon this tableau, the viewer exclaims at a gesture or pose he recognises, something akin, some connexion between each of the figures and himself. For me that is how it has been; whether bemused or outraged, I discovered something of myself in the other, and so, now, I remember.

Admirable, handsome Paxton, your eyes never flickering for a moment, prompted by a guilty secret. Confident, responsible and kind. They say your daughters have charmed even the Queen. Earnest, handsome Paxton, I cannot find you in my painting.

7 July 1850

I came to breakfast yesterday morning to discover Frederick studying—he had that sort of intentness, a boy at his books—studying *The Illustrated London News*. I asked what absorbed him.

"Paxton has published an engraving of his plan, and an excellent description of its principles."

"Here, let me see."

Frederick kept the newspaper at his place. "Do you remember when we first met, the precise task Fontaine set me? Yes, it was the walls. I had hoped

I might be assigned to detailing on the roof. The genius of Fontaine's arcade lay in the roof." You are so often surprised by what it is they *do*. The old one would say, "Monsieur Courtland, to be elegant we must acquire a taste for the severe," his hair powder was strongly scented of verbena, a courtesy of the old régime, the nose of the lady caressed when the gentleman bent forward to kiss her hand. Frederick proceeded calmly in our suburban dining-room. "However, that too was a lost opportunity. The usual way of arcading, here and in France, is simply to span the space between two close-set ordinary buildings with a cover of glass; the walls are another matter, altogether. Once the weight of the roof can be accommodated by iron frames on the side, one has a structure which may be erected rapidly, produced by machine, and altered to suit the changes in the usage of the building."

I stared at *The Illustrated London News,* which Frederick continued to guard in front of him on the table.

"Fontaine cheated a little; the Galérie d'Orléans is buttressed by stone columns, behind its metal walls, though I argued it needn't be. The railway termini of Henderson, of Fox, these are simply wider, enlarged arcades, since their glass tops rest on brick and masonry bases."

Now we had come to it. "And Paxton, has he cheated?"

"Paxton has not cheated."

In so saying, he handed me *The Illustrated London News.* It shewed, indeed, a building entirely of glass bound in iron, one huge glass box at the base, a smaller box stepped back on two sides perched above it, crowned on top with yet a third, smaller box. In the middle, Paxton cut through his wedding cake with a similar stack of boxes running at right angles, just like a glass cathedral with a nave and transept. I said, "But my dear, they are exaggerating, you know how these papers are. They have drawn the building taller than the trees."

"It is taller; the nave roofs over Colonel Sibthorp's elms."

I began to understand the curious state of surrender in which I discovered my friend when I entered the room.

"Taller than your towers?"

"Taller."

I sent a note to Covent Garden that I would not come in; I was meant yesterday to do only two scenes. Then I asked him to help me choose stuff for curtains in the drawing-room, then to give me his judgement on the vermilion cape I shall wear next week in Manchester. We dined, retired to our rooms to read, as if we were on holiday. In the afternoon we took the carriage to Royal Avenue, then sat in the hospital gardens, or rather, I sat,

Frederick reclined, half propped up on an elbow, upon that wondrously thick, manicured grass they manage here. Usually when they recline on one side, men in their forties, the trunk sags, fat hangs from the upper arms, gravity revealing what can be masked if a man knows how to walk upright with an air. Frederick's torso remains unyielding whether he stands or lounges. The sun brought out the lighter tones of his mouse mop, the hand not supporting his head lightly holding a cigar. We must have made a fine couple, this elegant and I in my yellow silk shaded by the light lavender parasol with the bone handle. Several old soldiers distantly about the grounds stared at us.

"Fox helped him."

"Who is Fox?"

"A luminary of locomotion." Frederick puffed on his cigar and smiled slightly. "The phrase is my father's. When only a boy, Fox worked on the screw propeller. Later he advised Brunel on his ship."

The sky was fine. We were far from other people, and it seemed not too great a risk. These Turkish come from a cigarette maker in the Burlington Arcade and are quite sweet, also quick burning. I inserted one in the horn holder, bent forward, Frederick's arm reached up without his straining his body, like swimming, the smoke curling into the air, the smokes of the cigar and cigarette mingling; it was lovely.

"It is quite ingenious; lock-bolts, no rivets"—which evidently means the men would find it simple to construct. I assumed my air of intelligence. The cigarette spent, we rose, the soft wide-brim I found in Milan tilting superbly on his head, and promenaded through the hospital grounds. I asked how much harm the day's news had brought him.

"In fact? None. There isn't enough time for their plan this year. Paxton says they shall need eighteen acres of glass. Ours will be built, and I shall have something further, evidently, from that." This was news to me, Brunel's "final disbursement" not a farewell. "People will credit Paxton when eventually some edifice of this sort rises; there will be another exposition in twenty years. Credit him as they should. As they should." A soldier on crutches gaped at the beauty, the elegance which was us. "The perspective certainly is very fine; worthy of Ledoux." This said, we walked in silence to the gate. Not in dejection. Perhaps we were both relieved that Paxton had taken the burden of Frederick's great dream upon his own shoulders. So that Frederick might be free for something else. At least, at the gate, he rallied. "But, my dear, this is aerial. Perhaps I will have a word myself with Fox before the twenty years are out." A last jet of smoke floated up and over the brim of the Borsalino, and we entered our carriage for Paulton's Square.

While Delphine unlaced me tonight I thought, It will be best for us to return as soon as possible to Paris. The moment the sheets of metal for Frederick's dome are cut next month. We will be home in September. Frederick has Marsane's house and the fire brigade station in the rue de Grenelle to complete; I will speak to Horton about cancelling the October appearances. The atelier here can be run by someone else. Once the Exhibition Hall is built, then excellent, he will be Courtland of the Exhibition. Paulton's Square is perhaps a pity, but we shall rent another, nearer to town, where the neighbours do not fear to call.

28 July 1850

An announcement from the Royal Commissioners greeted Frederick when he arrived at the atelier yesterday morning. It conveyed the great appreciation of the Prince Consort and the Members of the Commission for the work of all those who, like Mr Courtland, had laboured with such dedication, etc., in the service of contriving an Exhibition Hall. This appreciation filled all of page one. "Circumstances" now however suggested the unusual step of a recourse to another plan, that advanced by Joseph Paxton. Frederick could not tell whether or not the next part of the announcement was inserted for his benefit. Happily, the Chairman of the Building Committee and Author of the prior plan, Mr Brunel, fully subscribed to this decision, and wished, as surely will you, Mr Courtland, those now charged with the erection of the Exhibition Hall God speed. End of page two.

A few days ago *Punch* had dubbed the Paxton box "The Crystal Palace." It was then I knew the tide had turned, for it is a brilliant stroke, by Paxton himself, surely.

Frederick says he called in his boys, announcing there would be no dome. He offered two months' wages to the three youngest, whom he had assigned to work with the ironmen. Those boys; struggling to disguise their disappointment, whilst he speaks quietly of their great futures, the boys nodding, trying not to look away.

Evidently one draughtsman asked Frederick the very question which puzzled me when I in turn read the thanks. Had Brunel voted against himself? I thought, surely not with any passion; equally, so, after the formality of endorsement, he must resign his place on the Commission, which will lead to a wide and negative reaction, it being so arrogant a way for the German Prince Consort to reward his friend the Duke of Devonshire's man. Then it will all collapse into politics, and, as in France, nothing will happen. Which at least leaves Frederick the title of one of the official architects before the débâcle of calling in Paxton.

But evidently not. Brunel spoke with great fervour in Paxton's behalf, and against his own plan, whilst the crazed Barrie opposed the new work, Barrie who previously voted against Brunel.

"Frederick, how strange!"

"Indeed. I know nothing of the duelling at the meeting which produced this result."

It was at this moment that I made my proposal. It had ripened somewhat in my mind. I suggested, with just the right note of hesitation, I hope, that he sell the partnership, conducting whatever English commissions he received from his quarters in Paris.

"Dissolve Courtland & Courtland?"

"It is not a shrine, my dear, it is a business. It were no tribute to him to maintain this family firm, when here there is so little to maintain. Your life is in France."

Frederick promised to give it serious thought.

So often it happens. We are in the first flush, in a restaurant, ordering food we cannot afford, but the bill comes later, or we are in the drawing-room of older persons who, miraculously, smile rather than frown as we laugh at our own stories. Someone says, "You have such a lovely voice," or "Your drawing shows real talent." The next day we are lyric coloraturas; we belong to that branch of modern painting associated with Delacroix, but seeking new forms. That is how I think the father decided for Frederick. Not in one evening, but like that. And happily, after it was decided Frederick was an architect he discovered he loved to draw. He could go back to the wondrous moment when he first said to himself, Yes, I can draw. Perhaps paint now, perhaps sculpt? The first discovery did not come to him in London. It came "abroad," where they sought to prepare him for his future, the abroad which is now his home. And now, if he re-traces his steps, he must admit he is not the son they had planned on, the son he too hoped to become.

I had a deep and satisfying rest this afternoon. Later I said to Frederick that soon we will be dining at Foyot's, and I shall give a few little parties in our garden on the roof. Perhaps a masked midnight supper there, dishes of shallots, snails, asparagus, celeriac, caviare, sorrel, leeks—"Ugh! All of them?" "Yes, and all mixed together"—dishes unknown in suburban squares for young families and yet too fine for exhibition in a Hall of Wares from Borneo, Marrakesh, Pongo Tongo Bongo and Manchester, places where there is manufacturing for lack of enough lurid gossip and champagne.

Tonight, we were in the midst of accounts of Macready's lucrative and prolonged progress in retiring from each and every stage of the world when we heard the bell. I was vexed, as this month we have decided no visitors on Sundays. It was Brunel. Saying farewell for a month, because he has decided to take his holidays now, so that he could return refreshed to "my duties" in September.

"Your duties?" Frederick raised an eyebrow.

"My position. Chairman of the Building Committee. Obliged to assist Paxton or Fox any way I can." Brunel, I think, leaves out many words, not for the sake of speed, but that the listener may colour the others with whatever meaning he wishes.

They say here a man learns respect of self through control of self. Imagine a calm Hugo; that is no man!

"It is most courageous of you, Biggy, to continue on the Commission."

Brunel brightened at the word "courageous."

"I mean, the rabble will be asking themselves, 'How much did they pay him to vote against his own building? My word, he's gone across to the other fellow's side. It must have been quite a present for him to swallow his pride.' So hard to make these vulgarians understand Service and our devotion to the Ideal."

These acid words flooded me with happiness. Brunel attempted to pass it off as a joke.

"Or they will say our plan was so good, we were obliged to make amends."

"Our?" At every word I could feel Frederick lighter. "I was in your service, on the only metal in the hall. You, however, conceived a building in brick, you who have never worked in brick before. You chose brick, when you could find no worthy entry, you who were then obliged to build something yourself."

"I told you, Frederick, it was a matter of the safety of the Royal Family." We had been in the drawing-room, disposed, as usual, on the divans. Now Frederick stood, rang for Raymond, and then took Brunel's arm, who had also risen, Frederick conducting him to the door as if escorting a favoured guest after a most enjoyable, if impromptu, visit. Raymond held the door, Frederick took our friend's hand and sped him on his way with words of comfort.

"My dear Biggy, in that case it is a matter for the politicians, not us. Formerly a glass structure was an invitation to revolutionary attack, now it happily is not. The duty of governments and ministers is to explain. Refer all questions to Lord Brougham. You need only say, You are content, at last working in the medium that has earned you the regard of people throughout the world minded to Progress." Brunel fled.

Tonight we decided to advance our own travel plans, and then we retired to separate bathrooms. I hear him soaping with the sponge. At home, no servant gives notice upon learning I perform this office for him. The windows of both our bathrooms are open to the breeze, which rustles the papers in the mud rectangle before our house. Frederick soaps. In the years before Frederick returned, Brunel used often to drink himself insensible in the company of Frederick's father; they say Barrie also drank steadily, it was the men's fashion to do so without women. Frederick thinks about the old draughtsman who retired when he returned, saying his time had come. Frederick calls out, "Anne, where are the towels, you have stolen all the towels!" His father, he says, never asked him to continue for them both; of course, by the last year there was no need of words. Cold and wet and cursing, Frederick does not think there is dishonour in breaking an un-spoken word to the dead. Instead, he rummages about in our room, until finally I hear the bed groan with weight; he has had a long day. I write for a while so that he can gather himself, I ring Raymond for coffee, Raymond brings it into my boudoir, silently, as this service too might cause others to give notice. While I write, Frederick lies in bed awake. The clever words to *Punch*. Our duty to the Crown. In bed he shivers, and I shall tell him if he complains it is from his own freedom, Frederick who cut into Brunel as delicately, as deeply, as any man would who no longer cares for the regard of his victim. You cannot carve well with a shaking hand. I drink my coffee. At last we are no longer in mourning; he has returned to thinking that, here, he is abroad.

24 February 1851

I believe this is the first time I have been alone in London since '27. If possible, Paulton's Square has become ruder, muddier in the last six months; it is filled with builders' planks for a hideous dispensary across the King's Road. The rear garden, however, is a miracle of grass edged by lavender, which will be quite tall in the spring. I suppose M. Snigs has advised us wisely about the lease. Tired. Everyone receives me with evident pleasure. I know there was a dinner at the Veronica a few evenings past to which Madame Mercure could not be invited; they have filled my ears since with stories of the intrigues and pretty histories of the evening. A winter bulb has cast up a stalk with a flower just opening, not crocus.

In a single day, four or five people have declared to me I must, I simply can't miss, I will thrill to a visit to Hyde Park to witness the construction of the Crystal Palace, but I would surely betray to Frederick some sign that I had gone.

M. Snigs has sent the most extraordinary note, agreeing to chaperone me to Macready's last ever performance before the public. "That a lady should think of a wizened old creature like myself fills me, Madame, with Alarm and Pleasure compounded in equal measure, these elements mixed in extravagant quantities that the invitation should be to one of the greatest events in the history of the theatre, and by a lady whose own place in that noblest and most unfairly derided art . . ." it goes on and on thus. Of course, I too was thrilled that Macready had thought to remember me. I have just written to my chaperone that we shall make the most of this adventure. This adventure. Sometimes the bell which rings steadily sends us raving.

Perhaps wise to have a last fitting now for the sable cape, then store it in the cellar at home; to leave furs in a shop here for six or seven months a risk. Nota bene: the fox pelts for the hood are to run horizontally round the head, not up and down, and they may even keep the heads, yes, the fox heads will appear at either side of my face when the hood is up. This is superb! a face garlanded by the large staring eyes of those animals. Send Raymond to Volkoff's tomorrow with a note.

In my house, all alone.

27 February 1851

I have always said that the established actor is no more secure than the young things struggling to make themselves known. The public arrive ready to shed rivers of tears or ache from laughing, too ready. This was Kean's undoing when he continued as an old man to play Hamlet, Macready's downfall in that rôle also, both gallant accounts of an unsuitable part; they were cruelly jeered. So I feared for Macready, little as I like his condescending airs, his egotism, when I saw the immense crowd in Brydges Street surrounding Drury Lane. The people waited for hours, they say, in the freezing air in hopes of a returned ticket, warming themselves with the thought of the greatest Macbeth of all time. By the time M. Snigs and I arrived at the stage door, Vinegar Yard and Little Russell Street were also filled with chilled believers.

We struggled through them, they who surged expectantly towards us, one boy accosting M. Snigs for an autograph—which, were I not there, I am sure he would have given! The stage doors closed on the mob. Clement received me as always: Bone swore, Mawdamn, go mint ally vooh? He was presented to M. Snigs, who thought to give him a coin, which Clement held up to the light for a moment, then returned to M. Snigs. "Looks right enough to me, Guv'nor." M. Snigs took the impertinence in good enough part. Clement conducted us to box 7. Across from us, in 32, was Dion Boucicault and his young man, Adèle's suitor. Dion had placed himself in the light so that his disappointment, his understanding and his respect for the failing actor would be visible to as many of the audience as possible. The puffy eyes betray the gay smile. Dion, La Vestris, Mathews, these dukes and duchesses of burletta, priests of the silvery laugh, the strangled sob: tonight when Macready began to fail these enemies of Natural Acting would say, "Ah well, you see? It isn't worth all that effort. Lemaître or Macready, any of that school; they act 'naturally' and the public today are only bored."

Never, never was there such an ovation, all of us instantly rising to our feet, men waving their hats, stamping, people by their own shouts rousing themselves to that pitch where they turn to one another and shrug as though What can one do? when Macready made his first appearance. He had thus far been heard to speak offstage the words, "Command they make a halt upon the heath."

From the moment Macbeth faces the three witches I realised Macready had chosen to make his farewell by showing us a Macbeth no one had ever seen before. One would love to see it again and again, to study it for years, if only the actor were not retiring to the provinces to live as an English county gentleman upon his earnings. A single shattering, revelatory evening—we would miss its creator more this way. I succumbed in the scene following, when the witches' prophecy is confirmed, Macbeth proclaimed Thane of Cawdor. The stage clears; Macready is about to begin Macbeth's soliloquy. For years Macready had played it as a man whose lust for power seems to him justified by the supernatural forces; Macready used to rub his hands together in pleasure at Macbeth's new title, he smiled the terrifyingly greedy smile which he produces from that wide mouth.

Tonight instead Macbeth is shaken, as if the supernatural powers have brought this power-lust to him, unbidden, a lust larger than the desire of the man Macbeth. Macready walked downstage to the apron for his soliloquy, just to the side of the prompt box, where he also liked to stand for his Hamlet, and indeed his bowed head and absolutely still body recalled some of the brooding abstraction he infused into that character. Then all at once Macready jerked the head up and turned to the wings stage right, to acknowledge once more those kind messengers who have brought Macbeth news of his elevation—for a last moment Macbeth is a man with ordinary courtesies. The messengers disappear into the wings; the lights dim on the figures in the background; Macready cried out, a man desperately seeking to convince himself, "This supernatural soliciting cannot be ill . . ." His body shook—not as the old Kean would have shaken, every limb wobbling like jelly, instead just once, an electrical, evil current passing through him as Macbeth alters the words, in a last attempt to hold on, ". . . cannot be good!" The lights come up on the crowd, towards whom Macbeth now walks blindly, oblivious. At this moment Macready revealed an aspect of his genius which I had never suspected. Banquo calls out to his friend to rouse him; Macbeth responds with a sickly sweet affection, the wide smile stretched to the limits of Macready's jaw, just trembling at the edges while the lips speak caressingly, Macbeth's hand comes up to pat the shoulder of his friend Banquo, the fingers and thumb of the patting hand wide apart, tensed, as if a stretched claw: at this moment we know the Devil has rendered this possessed soul capable of murder.

Such is the Macbeth Macready made ever more powerful from scene to scene, a man in the hands of a perverse god. The Macbeth last night with sure steps calculated so that we, who are also visited by these terrible urges beyond our ordinary desire, we felt as he felt, we half became murderers too.

Even the mild, gentle M. Snigs was by the penultimate scene overcome, a scene whose *idea*, at least, one could easily re-create, though it might fail for the lack of Macready's voice. The Birnam Wood moving towards Dunsinane is usually a farce of props, and Macready's former version was no better than Forrest's or Kean's, the horror predictable. Last night Macbeth, when he learns the Wood is moving, after a moment of disbelief gives way almost to relief. As Macready spoke the words "to doubt the equivocation of the fiend that lies like truth," he seemed bewildered, confused; we began to hope that magically he would cast off the spell which had caused Macbeth to murder, that it would pass like a bad dream. My companion was so rapt at this point that he began audibly to mutter at Macbeth, urging him to mend his ways. Macbeth knows the end is at hand, but will he give way? Will he yield?

The cunning smile of a possessed man faded, and in answer Macready contrived a new face. The square jaw framing the lips tightened, Macready pulled down tight the skin of the brow, the voice became metallic, the words pushed through the teeth, as never we heard Macbeth speak before in the evening. This man will not be afraid of any apparition, he will be resolute, at the end of the scene he rings out the words "Blow, wind! come, wrack! At least we'll die with harness on our back." Resolute Macbeth, who no longer believes in the fiend who lies like truth, who no longer believes himself, he will do battle with an army of moving, enchanted trees.

The flats drawn aside, we were suddenly shown the entire depth of the Drury Lane stage, the backcloth painted as hills, covered with trees. Dotted about the stage were the painted paste trees concealing men who hold the trees by shield grips. Malcolm appears on stage, trumpets sound, the soldiers set the trees aside, flaps set upon the backcloth fly up, revealing painted soldiers underneath those painted trees—as I say, the usual. Then, offstage, we heard the voice of Macready, laughing. The soldiers marched forward towards the apron, their little trees behind, as the offstage voice rises in pitch, almost braying at the whole business; these fools needn't have bothered, he would have welcomed them, disguised or not, welcomed his avengers. The army reached the apron, Macready panting for breath as a man will who has laughed himself silly. Curtain.

M. Snigs turned to me. There was a pandemonium of applause, so he had to shout.

"It was not at all the same!"

"Not at all! Infinitely better than before."

The scene had quite unstrung M. Snigs. "He thought it was a device of imagination, a play of props."

"Yes, but he doesn't any more."

Abruptly the applause died as the curtain rose on the duelling scene; M. Snigs continued to stare at me, and, in the hush of the audience, stated quite audibly, "Madame, you haven't the least idea what I am talking about."

Often it happens this way, the effect of theatre will so rouse people they become quite angry if others intrude upon them. Still, I was taken aback by his outburst. The final duelling scene was rather lost on me, though I have never taken much interest in battles fought with papier-mâché swords, consummated by spurts of pig's blood. The audience, however, was wild at the end; Boucicault had retired to a less exposed position within his box.

We were then subjected to a very long interval. After directing Clement to leave the champagne in its bucket, "Absolute cold, Madame, while dangerous to the lungs, is necessary to the fevered brain," removing the covers of the collation, sniffing suspiciously and replacing them, M. Snigs took my hand. He said he regretted his outburst. I thought to deflect further embarrassment by telling him the story of the gentleman who once jumped from a stage box into the boudoir where I was playing the part of a cruel mistress, the intruder ordering me to reform.

"No," M. Snigs insisted. "I regret this extraordinary player so stirred memories within me that I forgot that you had not journeyed, as it were, with me." His timing, too, is superb. He paused as though making another fleeting visit. "Frederick's father once enacted a burlesque of Macbeth; Macready recalled it to me." Another pause; as I have often observed with members of the legal profession, they are wont to deploy silence as preparation for an important utterance. Nothing came. It was my cue. I sipped. I observed that the elder Courtland, blessed with a lively wit, must have made an excellent player.

M. Snigs rose and poured us champagne—Verrières '46. Now he spoke indeed gravely. "Those who practise law are constantly berated for defending clients or cases in which the barrister hasn't an ounce of belief; when I was young, this indifference, as I called it, quite disturbed me. Then I learnt that here is the genius of our legal arrangements; the barrister who believes too earnestly in his own side loses the power for nimble play with his opponent; he sees only the justice of his own case. To attack or defend well, to serve your client to the best of your ability, you must not lose yourself. In the dramatic arts matters must be the same. I am sure, Madame, that at this very moment the great Macready is nearly as collected as ourselves; at least, he remained throughout the evening sufficiently in control of his own powers, so that he could watch and calculate and play upon us to contrive our surrender. The difficulty with Courtland was, he lacked this higher power. He revelled in his own dramaticality. Revelled, and loved and lost himself in it, which close love literally blinded him. I have long considered this matter," M. Snigs ended. "It is the failing of the entire family. They could, none of them, have lasted an hour in a court of law." He looked at me expectantly, but I was not in the mood last night. We passed the rest of the interval instead by reviewing the prayers of the ladies in waiting, the evenings of Mendelssohn songs (which contain neither words nor spirit), the dinners at which there is an abundance of iced water, the hundred signs by which their Court equates virtue and boredom.

About Macready's speech in front of the curtain, after the interval, I will say only this: I know Macready is contemptuous, even of his own worthy Queen and Prince Consort. He did not stay the night after the command performance at Windsor, which he boasted of to me, and he treats me well only because he curries the favour of Lemaître. Once when we played *Bérénice* in English he came off after the long peroration and remarked, "Say anything you like, the rabble are dull tonight," they who had made the effort of attending to *Bérénice* because of him. He made the life of his dresser a nightmare and, after some trivial misunderstanding, told Clement he was an amusing clown only when playing a stage-door guardian. This Macready appeared now dressed in a sombre gentleman's black suit, with a black hat in his hand, as though he were on the point of leaving his house.

After quelling the tumult, he spoke for a few minutes. The speech had but one idea: Macready thanked the public for permitting him to act. He thanked them, he left the stage, and though they stamped and screamed and begged, he did not come again from the wings. These cries rose to a pitch, three thousand people pleading; the gas lights were turned up, still they cheered and begged, to no avail. They believed in him; I suppose, in our profession, that is all that matters.

1 March 1851

Yesterday morning, as I made my toilette, I heard Frederick enter the house. At first I feared an accident had befallen the girls, one so terrible he had to come himself, like the fire in Caen. I rushed down to the drawing-room and saw instantly there was no disaster, for in the room of furniture covered with sheets and bare walls he had composed himself next to the fireplace, shifting from foot to foot, his arm draped in an effort at languor on the mantel.

"I hope my coming does not disconcert you?"

"Of course it does." Not quite what I meant. Still, it kept me at the door and him at the fireplace.

"Clients' business has obliged me." Now he moved to me. "I shall accompany you back to Paris."

As we embraced I whispered to him, "Frederick, in telling a lie the important thing is to keep still. The words may be entirely well spoken yet shifting back and forth like that on your feet gives you away." He released me. "Also, I have found that the best lies contain the most detail. You should not say 'clients' business,' you should tell me that there is a problem with the ironworks at Lille, the threat of a strike, say. Thus you come to London on your way to Birmingham but will be able to conclude your business in time for our departure together. As it happens, I have just been offered work myself in Birmingham next month, at £105 a week, which we must discuss, so it is as well you came. Now my dear, why?"

We resumed our original places. Languid, mantel-draping Frederick purred, "You must help me contrive a story you are willing to believe." *Le Moniteur*, it transpired, had published a picture of the glazing train Paxton uses for the Crystal Palace. Frederick's curiosity was thoroughly aroused.

"That I well believe."

And it might be useful in building factories in France, he might gain the export of it, he who has finally a life good enough which he has made for himself, I thought, on his own terms.

"I am satisfied with the indubitable fact that your curiosity is aroused."

We have hardly spoken the rest of the day. My fitting was scheduled for the afternoon at three, and I kept them at it until five. It was impossible to return to the suburb for tea.

2 March 1851

I was bitterly angry all yesterday.

5 March 1851

Behind the locked door, in the silent room, Vigny sang. Of course he spoke incessantly of his need for Solitude. Thus, instead of taking the early train back to London today with Charles, I remain here in my hotel room, under the covers; I shall return on the slow, overnight service. By then Frederick will have filled his eyes with the progress of his enemy's palace.

As to Birmingham. Not Rosalind but Jaques, a Jaques in Birmingham! The breeches of Madame! How Charles has aged. He was born the same year as the priest Newman and looks the much elder brother. The skin of his face and hands begins to be translucent, the eyes sag heavily in their sockets (if only men of these times would allow themselves the practises of their grandfathers; a little wheat powder mixed in cream is all that one needs to take off ten years), whereas Newman looks a very solemn boy, the complexion blooming, the modelled lips ruby, the hands seeming without veins. Rejuvenated by prayer.

This I believe is the first time I have spent an evening with Charles alone. I teased him about it, causing him to blush, even as he said, "The good Newman would hardly think attending one of his sermons improper." Perhaps had we occasion earlier. But this evening was amusing and pleasant enough for me.

His baby face, Newman's, I mean, was his principal attraction. When dear Lamennais preached, one felt oneself transported to the library, if not the drawing-room, of a most civilised gentleman who had travelled the world; as he spoke, he drew casually upon this store of experience, illuminating some arcane point of theology. He asked only that you do him the courtesy of following his thoughts, and as he was courtesy itself, you did more. Whereas this Newman is like the ordinary run of such persons, hectoring, loud; he has not learnt in public speaking to disguise that he is quite pleased with himself.

Charles took notes, as he is to write about the Newman–Achilli battle for his *Free-Thinker*. The delicious Achilli has put it about that these new English Catholics not only dream of imposing the faith again upon all England, they also have returned to the exuberances of the Church in the time of the Borgias; Newman is whispered to be secretly . . . married. In his Birmingham pulpit the English priest fights back. He maligns Achilli as crudely as he was maligned. Achilli is in the pay of the Freemasons, who pay him by the insult. Newman's reedy voice proceeded to detail Achilli's personal history. The parishioners sat bolt upright; no latin here! The whole attack was disguised as an example of the sufferings Catholics are likely to encounter in a secular society. Newman, I believe, was also encouraged to see Charles scribbling as he spoke, for he glanced at the pen frequently to espy which telling phrases caused the pen to move.

This was the first sight Charles has had of Newman since the conversion. Once Newman entered the Church his platform manner, evidently, became more combative. I remarked to Charles that it is only natural, the convert more ardent than those of us who take our religion for granted. "No, he has the gentlest voice of any living writer." Charles toyed with the spoons and glasses on our table, in the dining room of this hotel. I do not like men to fidget. "He has forged the gentlest voice of any living writer," Charles repeated. I thought to end the cutlery ballet by remarking, "The public like a man who treats them with a certain brutality." He paid no attention. I finally relieved him of his gloom, quite cleverly. I rounded immediately. "Indeed, this is the secret of carnal passion!" Now he blushed furiously again.

I wish I had gone back to London with Charles. This shabby hotel room is no relief.

18 March 1851

All they say is true; it is quite remarkable. When clouds pass overhead, shadows dapple the hall starting at one end, passing through the curving glass in the centre, then disappear like giant moths through the other wall. What most struck me today, which was mostly clear, almost summery, is that the sun seems to come from everywhere, the sides, even the floors, rather than beat down through the roof. Frederick says they have contrived the effect by stretching long bands of canvas over the top, suspended just above the glass. It is all so high up, you see nothing; the light seems to spread evenly and indirectly thanks to this ingenious invention. It was another idea of Paxton's.

I wanted to go without Frederick, rather only with M. Snigs, who has been several times and who offered to play *cavalier servant*. Frederick insisted. He tests himself, pointing to all the wonders of his adversary.

One imagined the Crystal Palace like a closed theatre, save for the workingmen. Not at all. Crowds of the most fashionably dressed ladies and gentlemen, conducted by trained guides, fill the vast hall, the course of fabrication itself dramatic. We watched, for instance, men ride upon a sort of miniature railroad whose tracks are the beams in the roof; in their carts steaming high, high above us, these sons of Vulcan replaced several defective panes of glass. Several persons attached themselves casually to our party from time to time, listening to Frederick explain these marvels.

My friend had the happy idea of pointing out to Snigs and myself the advances the Crystal Palace makes over the Galerie d'Orléans. "If only we had known then" introduces points of particular finesse. For instance, the old stone arches around the Palais-Royal—they offer both shade and the circulation of air, while in his arcade you have one or the other. In the Galerie d'Orléans they hang calico curtains inside to block the light; these curtains also block out air from the vents on top. (Here is the genius of strolling in nature. The tangling of parasols, hundreds of brilliantly coloured parasols raised aloft, a waving striped and dotted blue, red, yellow and white crêpe-de-chine sea, while under the stifling still heat of the sun-screen the parasol is useless.) "Paxton's genius is to put the shield outside; notice, Anne, that the invention which functions better also creates a more beautiful light." There is so much space in this palace, a thousand women could walk even with enormous Florentine umbrellas and never touch, such bliss for them, never obliged to touch. Then he found the iron posts and beams of the interior more graceful than those in the Galerie d'Orléans, because simpler than the Doric columns whose casting Frederick had overseen, the final responsibility given him by Fontaine.

After some minutes of this, I took Frederick aside. "Have you no pride?" I cared not who heard us, and indeed our words were lost in the hall.

"Would it be more manly to carp?" Frederick rounded. "This is the greatest work of the nineteenth century; men will continue to study it long after they have forgotten the dates of the revolutions or the clauses of the bills of reform. You must see things for what they are." This from the inventor of the iron San Gimignano! Even in England I would have taken him in my arms! If only he let me.

Both M. Snigs and I were relieved when our stroll led us to the central section of the Crystal Palace. Here statues, plants and domestic objects of British manufacture had begun to be laid out. Relieved because this actual exhibition, so contrary to the look of the Exhibition building, put an end to Frederick's praises. The statues! Stone Dianas and Nestors sagging under the weight of their fig leaves, the plinths swathed in swirling velvet draperies, set among pots of . . . ferns! How very very English, the same building which encompasses entire elm trees is swaddled in these "cosy," these wretched, dusty ferns with their ever-browning edges.

Laid within glass cases lined with brown velvet were: a cast-iron fire tongs shaped in the form of two hands grasping each other as for a handshake; an iron tea-cosy shaped in the form of a foot-high cathedral; a table lamp of iron and glass, the glass globes blown in the form of mannequin heads. Over these, a sort of iron tracery mask slips on, the iron cast in the features of leading politicians, royalties or, if the client prefers, at extra charge, the Mr and Mrs of the house. The effect is a sort of illuminated skull. As we gazed, stupefied, a boy placed on a stand the following placard, in elaborately sculpted letters of ivory:

The fruits of invention,
plucked when ripe.

BURSTON IRONMASTERS, LTD

We now positively gaped. The boy consulted an elaborate vest watch which he held prominently in his hand; when some determined moment of time elapsed, he nodded politely, then removed the placard from its stand. The little pantomime tells the visitor he or she must move on so that others may have a chance to look.

"Come, Sir," Snigs rounded on Frederick, when we sought repose at the great fountain. "Your labours may seem outmoded in comparison to the present establishment, yet the worthy Galerie d'Orléans houses objects of the most pleasing refinement. Does not this entire edifice, no matter how wondrous, strike you as consecrated for purposes little different from those of a Greenwich warehouse?" Those rolling sentences! "Is not it always thus? Invention for its own sake cannot ripen into art."

Frederick replied only that he had not before seen the structure furnished.

We exited past display chambers contrived of canvas or velvet flats.

Groups of similar objects were shown in these. One little stage was, however, discreetly curtained in front as well. Peeping within we saw a collection of the new water closets, which rather reminded me of Charles' collection of pottery jugs, some of these seats cast as elaborate Louis Quatorze thrones, others as benches such as one would find in an Italian Garden; some of the water closets were plain white, others glazed in green and yellow and even brown. Here a sign explained that the porcelain had been cast employing new principles derived from recent advances in the casting of iron.

By the time we achieved Park Lane, Frederick reminded me of a man who unwillingly has been shown an obscene drawing. The eminently sane comment of M. Snigs offered him no comfort, but it must in time, just as the disaster of this furnishing will bring the public back to those whose taste is refined.

I shall end with this contrast, which I did not think of in the afternoon. I remember the day I came to fetch Frederick from the Palais-Royal during the plague of '32. It stank appallingly, as much from the carbolic as from the discharges of the dying, the sight of those blotched writhing bodies a nightmare to me ever since. Frederick moved among that horror as a man absorbed in his work, without permitting himself to evince to the still living the slightest sign of distaste, or, even, of recognition.

1 April 1851

I will say about scenes that I admit—how could I not?—all my life to have succumbed to their unfolding, even when I had felt myself sucked down once they start. This was how we mis-stepped in the beginning. I can still picture every moment of our posturing, our false words then; we believed we could conquer each other, just as our words and our fine poses had conquered thousands! Now our daughters are grown women. He says Cécile's little boys run him ragged when he visits, "the little scamps treat me like a grandpapa," and he spoils them, just as he should. Our daughters; our son-in-law, who was willing to be told the truth. Some days *even now* I rehearse those terrible scenes so that they end differently, the door does not slam or I do not tease, I do not reach for another glass, or Lemaître does not play with his cane, which always gives him away. He does not roll his cane between his fingers whilst saluting me, "You seem to have yourself well in hand with this youth." Instead, we forbid Marie Dorval ever to come to the house. M. and Mme Lemaître visit their grandsons every

Sunday. Probably I would have as well yielded place to him and retired young.

Lemaître is the one I first thought about when we learnt today that Frederick has been included in the list of the Official Architects, all of which rejected or re-aligned persons are eligible for tickets to the inauguration of the Crystal Palace. Moreover, the invitation is to Mr and Mrs Frederick Courtland. The courtesy must entirely be Brunel's doing—I was perhaps mistaken in him. I thought of the legitimately married M. and Mme Lemaître, who would hardly be included in the opening of a trade exposition in France, indeed never invited as guests to the Tuileries, who would easily, very easily brush aside their failure to be invited to an exposition of trade. We are not in France, we are not married and we are invited on behalf of the Queen. I said we must at least write Brunel some letter of thanks, using as our excuse the fact that I shall be in Denmark then.

When Lamartine offered Lemaître the title rôle in *Toussaint L'Ouverture,* the poet asked him to go to the Château de Monceau to re-work the manuscript. "Lemaître, what an honour!" I said. "It was better than Meilhac," he replied with that little smile turning down. "I was able to give myself several grand scenes; superb indeed." I wanted to know if he had struggled with the poet for them. "Not at all! He has very little faith in his work." This is Lemaître. He knew if the dull play succeeded, all the credit would be for him. It was; Vacquerie, Houssaye, the mob, they all loved him. Yet he still has those terrible days as of old, staring out into my garden, refusing to eat, hating the sound of the human voice, disgusted with his own cunning.

Unlike powerful men, Frederick does not abandon himself to rage or grief, or loathing of self, nor could he utter the word "superb" with such satisfaction. Slowly, slowly, what Frederick loves makes him heartsick. He looked at me, then at the invitation. The words his eyes spoke were, "I'll bear it."

"The invitation is impossible for me. Most of the men of your circle know our relation; it would make for scandal."

So instead of discussing whether *he* should, we fell into this other matter of whether *we* should. About this he is quite firm; still, never to retreat, never to hide, he didn't give Lady Edwardes an inch last year, and why should we now, among thousands; our music.

Which made me think of the line Lemaître added one night to the last act of *Robert Macaire:* "I surrendered before the battle began; in my grief, I have become indifferent to others." This was the greatest of all the lies Lemaître told.

Thus I ended by asking Frederick if he knew the correct forms of address we should use in accepting a royal invitation, which, for no good reason, he did.

2 April 1851

I would like to write down the story of Guaradino. Guaradino was a Sicilian child whose purity of voice and grace of movement attracted the notice of a Venetian nobleman; Guaradino was taken to Venice and enrolled in the little school behind La Fenice, to prepare him to enter the Count's service as a player. The boy grew into quite a beauty; even when I met him, and he was well past seventy, the bones of the face and the hands were perfect, the skin unblemished. This prize was jealously guarded by his protector for no venal reason, simply that the house gained lustre from having in service the handsomest, most talented actor in Venice.

Guaradino's reward was an excellent life. His rooms in the Count's palazzo were decorated with furnishings of his choosing, and quite splendid frescos. When I met him, in '21, he was ordering the personal servants the Count provided him to dispose about his *salone* some extravagant pieces which he had caused to be copied from Hope's *Household Furniture*. I asked Guaradino how he passed his days as a private actor. I think even then he was one of the last.

"Most purposefully, most energetically. I rise early, take a large collation, in the German manner. When the light is sufficient in His Lordship's theatre, I gather the players of his troupe on stage. We discuss together, as equal colleagues, which pieces we think we might suggest to His Lordship; after all these years, we understand his tastes and the tastes of his guests, so the discussions are amicable. Then I begin to rehearse the work chosen for that night's performance; as the leading player, I have the right to dispose the others about the stage and to correct them if necessary, but again, I am careful to do so in a friendly and open manner. To give a truly pleasing performance, especially in a small theatre with perhaps twenty, thirty in the audience, the player must be in good humour; pique, nerves or little games will soon be remarked by those watching so close.

"We work until the dinner hour. This meal is served to us in an old refectory which has been refurbished by me for our common use, at His Lordship's expense. We continue our discussions in this agreeable room.

After our dinner, I insist that my people walk, rather than repose, as does everyone else—I insist on this even during the hottest days, since sleep after eating is the surest means of growing fat, and I can't be changing the costumes constantly. Also, the boys and girls of the troupe exercise in the city when the fewest temptations are about; temptors, fortunately, are persons much in need of sleep.

"We return to our labours, and then, while the Count's guests are arriving and assembling, we at last have an hour's repose. Your great Napoleon brought to Venice the custom of presenting ourselves first as men and women before the curtain; in a house like the Count's, this practise we have somewhat altered. We appear, in costume, singly, before the play is to begin, bowing or curtseying to the Count and his guests, briefly explaining what character we are to be and what we are likely or not likely to do. This presentation gives the assembled company great pleasure, and we strive to make our little introductions as graceful as possible.

"Then there is the play itself. We have performed everything; the Count has taste so refined and so catholic we have played rôles you cannot begin to dream of." Here Guaradino excused himself to me and his other auditors, who were performing *Alceste* once again at the Fenice. "This has been my greatest pleasure in His Lordship's service. He has given me the opportunity to explore all dramatic literature, wherever my imagination roams, with adequate if not lavish funds for performance, and with complete freedom in execution. My patron is a man of advanced ideas. If the result displeases him, well, he does not entirely blame us, for it was he who chose what we merely proposed. As I say, I have acquired the most profound knowledge of theatre, without experiencing the slightest vulgarity.

"The performance done, we bid farewell to his guests, retiring to change our costumes as the audience goes in to supper. At this point in the day, or, I should say, night, for it is now perhaps eleven in the evening, I withdraw to my own chambers, where I am served a repast in private, after which I read. I usually wait for the Count, who kindly visits me on the evening of a performance once he has bid his guests farewell. We discuss as friends, you understand, the evening's labours, during which I do try to ascertain what has pleased him, and what will be likely to amuse or surprise him agreeably in future works. He departs, and I retire to a well-earned slumber."

Though none of us was invited by the Count to see him play, Guaradino was reputed to be ever finer the longer he had performed for his master.

4 April 1851

M. Snigs came in. He also had news; finally they have decided to make another small gesture to the Liberals; he is to be knighted.

"I shall be obliged to call you Sir Snigs?"

"My dear Madame Mercure, you have netted me. Were I to forbid you, upon your lips would ever hover that absurd sobriquet, one you might threaten to produce during the most august occasions, as, for example, in presenting me to the artistes of the Comédie-Française, or during the round of jubilations, celebrations and kindred ceremonies during this season of Great Exhibitions—"

"Then you are going to the inauguration of the Crystal Palace?" Frederick cut in.

"I am, to witness Authority confer Legitimacy upon Industry. I shall attend in my exalted state."

We decided to drive to the ceremony together.

2 May 1851

I returned from Denmark only two days before the opening. One could tell from the trains; they were crowded with country people in their best clothes, and also with foreigners who complained of the stuffiness and the cold in the carriages. Frederick met me at the terminus mid-morning. We went directly to Miss Floss, who had the feathers on the hat at last, to Bates' for Frederick's smart new stove-pipe; with our tops thus provisioned, we journeyed home to await help with the lower regions.

But neither dressmaker nor tailor arrived that afternoon. I sent Raymond with urgent messages, which brought distraught replies from both; the crush of commerce proved overwhelming. Our invitations now proved invaluable, as Raymond returned to both in the early evening with a command from me that our costumers devote themselves to us, as we in turn were commanded attendance by Her Majesty, etc. The next morning both appeared early, full of their trials, but ready to work.

It is many years since I have made the slightest mistake in costume. Dressed as an English lady, the ambiguity, not to say falseness, of my position might be brought to the fore. The quilted dress Hortense had confected from Nemours cloth was excellent of its kind; the matching shawl was an uninspired complement only a proper English lady would wear.

"Fur!"

"Madame, it is May, and you will be amongst ten thousand people under glass."

"Fur! Take the fox heads off the sable cape; replace the satin lining with cut silk. Here, Hortense," I took the offending shawl, "use the silk you employed for this garment; it is more subtle, to match underneath." By this means, I contrived the appearance of a lady unacquainted with the English climate, prepared by rumour for endless, freezing rain, a Russian lady probably. This change required nearly the entire day of the disgruntled Hortense, for which I paid her handsomely.

Frederick was surprisingly more difficult. The order of the day is what we would think of as a Military Drawing-Room: decorations worn, excluding swords. (Logical, amidst the crush of ten thousand spectators; only those in the procession allowed them.) Frederick has no foreign or domestic orders, so all seemed quite simple with the tailor, until this personage let drop, "I am glad, Sir, you shall appear in such a sober state of black and white. Two other members of your committee positively tinkle and twinkle."

Fortunately I happened to be in the room. I motioned Frederick to come outside.

"You must wear something. I will send Raymond to that shop in the Burlington Arcade; let us hope they have something left—even a Belgian Star of Merit."

"Anne, I will do nothing of the sort! We are going as mere spectators and—"

There was no time for metaphysics; the tailor was pawing the ground. I returned to Herzfeld.

"Herr Herzfeld, confess"—he always succumbs if you treat him confidentially—"confess that we must do something more, no matter if the hour is late. We must impart some touch of individuality to the black and white sobriety of this costume."

Herzfeld has dressed the old Kean as a Moor, Phillips as a Martian, and also contrived several animal costumes. I knew he was capable, indeed his eyes lit up.

"A double silver chain for the waistcoat watch?"

"No," I said.

"A shawl collar in gold braid with matching braid at the cuffs?"

"No!" said Frederick, but we were progressing. Finally we agreed on the effect: a thin white satin stripe down the outside of each trouser leg, suggesting something military, quite smart, and, although I didn't say this, suggesting also that many decorations could adorn this young general; he had refrained for reasons best known to himself. To achieve this touch, it was necessary to add a silver bar on the chest pocket, where the medals would go, an addition I explained to Frederick as a simple horizontal of white necessary to balance the long verticals on the legs. Herzfeld spent the entire day re-fitting, and earned a minor fortune.

I arranged for Sir Snigs to spend that night with us, as we would be obliged to depart from Paulton's Square early in the morning in order to be in place by ten, two hours before the Royal Procession was due to enter the building. He arrived for the night as if prepared for an extended journey abroad, his cases jingling with bottles and boxes of pills. Frederick arranged with Snigs' man to help in dressing him.

They descended to the dining-room the next morning in amazing state, the young general handing in a most distinguished figure. A long crescent row of pins and crosses hung upon Snigs' sash, the sash framed by a court gown so old its cloth had turned from black-blue to green-black, this gown draped over a suit which gathered in bags around the emaciated frame. The court wig was also yellowed with age, yet perfectly hardened. The true distinction was the elderly man's gait; he moved *under* these garments, not in them, as though the vestments were solid enough to stand on their own and he was free enough within not to be weighted down—again, as ever, it is shoulder control, always the shoulders which manage the carriage of the body, even at eighty. However. Youth now had a reason to efface itself in the presence of age.

Although I had thus prepared us, if not for feigning, at least as though we two belonged with the old man, I was not reassured, not in my fur, not by Frederick's cunning simplicity. I was not reassured. I did not belong there. A moment of panic seized me, I would be discovered, and I felt ever so tired. I was on the verge of telling them I was ill, of withdrawing from this great scene where I would be exposed, I was sure of it, and I was tired of their caring, all of them caring save these two—as I say, I was on the verge of withdrawing when M. Snigs addressed me with a smile,

"Do you remember, Madame Mercure, we once before had occasion to depart in state? "It was the grand soirée of the Comtesse d'Agoult."

For a moment this caused me to keep silent, during which Raymond opened the door and motioned to us urgently; the King's Road was impassable from Royal Avenue, in minutes we would be unable to leave Paulton's Square. It was thus all my fault, I had ceased to think for one moment, one moment only! Marie's evening, so many memories for which I had no time either, we now hurrying down the steps to our carriage, a blue brougham with four dappled greys; the coachman showed himself impatient and worried, snapping his reins, our dreadful respectable neighbours amazed at the little flag upon the brougham indicating that we, the brazen Jezebel and her ageing lover, were part of the Official Party.

I shall not describe the manoeuvrings of this excellent person, save to remark that I thought he was leading us towards Richmond, then to Oxford, before, by a series of turnings, he established us on the north side of the Serpentine, down which we descended to the West Door of the Crystal Palace. Even along this rear route there were crowds waving and shouting at nothing, the women waving with their white kerchiefs, the men with their caps. In France, this holiday would be a festival for drunkards, pickpurses, a test for revolutionaries; police lining the streets would face the people. Yesterday men raised both hands without fear, soldiers turned their backs upon the crowd, that their ceremonial emblems would be displayed to the dignitaries.

The moment we entered the Serpentine drive in our carriage, the guerdons of officialdom draped by blue cords over our doors, people began cheering us. Frederick stared out dazed. Only the size of the crowd and the fervour of the shouting was new to me. Sir Snigs was put in bad humour by our reception; "These are the enemies of Deliberation, Madame, these loyal subjects." When at last we achieved the West Door, as he descended step by slow step, Sir Snigs received a wild ovation from the people, they who had no idea who he was.

Inside, the mass of notables seemed even more dense, and more exuberant, than the sea outside. An organ blared at the east end, and we could barely hear it. Frederick stumbled forward to an usher, our invitation held in both hands. I might have paid more attention to this. However, I thought him under the same delirious spell as was I, the sheer noise of it, the exuberance of light and colour. Looking up one saw the giant flags of all nations through the glass, the flags flapped and dappled the light like clouds. The Crystal Palace had been painted, every piece of metal coloured; the floor was carpeted, hectares of red and blue.

In this cauldron of light and colour, our friend soon arrested our attention. Rain began to fall. The ushers urged M. Snigs to walk as quickly as possible to our position, in order that those waiting outside could be more rapidly received within. The draughts proved Colonel Sibthorp quite wrong; the thousands inside had not heated the building, rather their ebb and flow swirled fresh, cold, damp air. I was glad of my fur. M. Snigs began coughing.

Coughing and coughing, slowly bending over with the racking pains, the ushers looking ever more concerned but still hoping he would move forward even in his fit, so that the others could come in. The stars of a Companion of St Stephen, of a Knight Templar, hung forward from his breast. Slower and slower, more bent; and the crush behind him threatened to topple him forward. Frederick supported him with one arm, I with the other, thinking how to exit, since all was stopped behind us, when suddenly M. Snigs jerked free of my arm, reached within his cape, and produced a vapour bottle. This he raised feebly to his lips, squeezed the bulb, straightened a bit, squeezed again, straightened more, squeezed a third time and was erect.

"Well, Madame," he managed as he hid the vaporiser again in his breast pocket, "you see I, too, make obeisance to the value of mechanical devices in the conduct of civilised life." In these circumstances we guided him to ours, the left side of the main aisle, rather than to the right, where by rank he belonged.

Our place was thirty yards east of the Royal Party; the more eminent sub-delegates of the Commissioners of the Exhibition were a mere ten yards from the throne, which was placed in the very centre of the hall, before the great fountain. Frederick busied himself with his godfather until we were seated, on chairs rather than stools, a further relief to the old man. Surrounding us were those who had advised Brunel or laboured for Paxton's seconds; there were also several colleagues of Frederick's father, who had secured official invitations on the strength of their worldly standing. All these persons could be said to have mixed sentiments about the event, even the Paxton delegates, who had not yet been paid. None betrayed themselves; benevolent smiles, warm fellowship the order of the day. Sir Snigs was also welcomed with benevolent smiles and warm fellowship by the architects and engineers, who assumed him to be an elder, distinguished colleague also excluded or unpaid.

Once disposed on our chairs, I remarked softly to M. Snigs, "It is an awkward group," and explained.

"Indeed. Companions in neglect."

And now I needed Frederick, more I think at that moment than ever before. Sir Severus Rood might make his little joke to show he had recovered, but these persons seemed all so many accusations to me, even though they were no more acceptable by their own lights than I. Still, none of them needed disguise. I did not want to be among the wives of these dimmed English luminaries, I wanted to go home, but we were surrounded by thousands of persons, and the next best would be for Frederick to hold my hand—although even this, amongst the wives of the dimmed luminaries, would have caused comment. The shameless woman!

Frederick has a peculiar smile for persons whose names he can't quite remember. It is frank, polite, sometimes accompanied by a little shrug, suggesting he would love to stop and chat if only he weren't so pressed for time, or in the midst of performing a social duty elsewhere. He gave this smile to several of his colleagues who called to him as we sat. I held myself in; I would have screamed if he had also thus favoured me. It was now noon.

Suddenly we heard a choir of trumpets add to the blurring noise of the organ. Her Majesty the Queen had arrived with the Prince Consort; there was a booming of guns. A tasteless Fate against which not even Guaradino could protect himself decreed that at this moment the rain should stop and sunlight pour through the roof and sides of the canvas-shrouded Crystal Palace.

When this spectacle commenced, the Lord Chancellor was still amusing himself by turning the fountain on and off with the flip of a lever; we saw a horrified chamberlain rush up to interrupt his fun. Then, parading down the centre aisle, the Great Officers of the Household walked backwards(!) facing the Royal Party, which had yet to begin its progress through the hall. These Great Officers of the Household did not know how to use their shoulders to lift their cloaks, and were in constant danger of tripping. Only two did; the Great Officers passed backwards to the centre where nave and transept met, and where the relieved Great Officers disposed themselves in a circle. Two gentlemen of M. Snigs' age paraded facing forward down the red centre carpet; they supported each other arm-in-arm, one walking on a wooden leg which he exposed almost in its entirety. A hush fell upon those whom they passed.

"Who are they?" I demanded.

"The disabled man is the Marquess of Anglesey, Master of the Ordnance; the rheumatic personage is the Duke of Wellington, Commander-in-Chief."

Like fabulous birds, these legends hopped and hobbled forward, speaking easily, as if indeed alone in a drawing-room.

"They are perhaps too feeble to account the circumstances."

"My dear Anne," Sir Snigs reproved me, "you still have something to learn of the English. This insouciant, comfortable gabbling establishes them to be the first among our noblemen."

As they arrived at the centre, a Chinaman wearing intense blue and vermilion robes moved forward, the mandarin bowing to them and the two of them nodding in return to another old friend; though exotic, evidently known and equal. (Later in the day it was discovered this foreign dignitary was entirely spurious, a naïf, an inquisitive sailor who had donned the ordinary ceremonial robes possessed by the men of his race.)

Finally the Queen. She too was in fur. Ermine. This irrationally made me ever more acutely uncomfortable. She too was in fur, though hers was ermine.

She is quite a sweet-appearing young woman, with the loose features of those who have engaged in much bearing of children. Her posture is stooped, and the forward, rigid carriage of the head gives the impression she is worried her crown will fall off. On the other hand, when she arrived at the centre of the Crystal Palace, she indicated with a single gesture that she would neither mount the dais, nor sit upon its throne; instead she would stand among her subjects. This wave of the hand was the merest half arc, the palm down, the arm moving out from the body to the side—but it was final, absolute, this rejection of the place others had appointed for her, an entire picture discomposed by a few inches of movement. I have been the wife of an Egyptian Pharaoh, a ruler of Amazons, a Roman Empress, Queen Theodoric, both Mary, Queen of Scots and her enemy Elizabeth, not to count all the queens and dignitaries of the classic French repertoire. In each of these rôles every step I took, every accent in my voice contributed to the impression. This young mother was under no such obligation. A building conceived with the sovereign sitting in state, just here; a ceremony calculated around her assumption of a Crystal Palace throne: at the last moment, she chose not. The little wave of the pudgy hand, refusing to mount this throne, was enough to establish her as their ruler, Queen Victoria. I looked at Frederick, but he had not noticed; the ceremony meant little to him and he gazed round and measured in his head. I do not think I have ever felt so lonely.

Because she stood, we stood, through the immensely long report which her husband, in his capacity as head of the Royal Commission, addressed to her as Queen. Much escaped me, since the German stumbled through an English text filled with numbers and technical phrases. But I was not alone in my boredom; all around us people shuffled from one leg to the other. The wives of the companions-in-neglect inspected the perfection of my dress. While everywhere the fatal commentary of coughing and sniffling began to be heard, heads not in the Royal line of vision turned round idly. Only at one point did the crowd spring to life: this was when the Prince announced there were nearly 25,000 people in the Crystal Palace at that moment, which statistic was passed back from those close enough to hear to those unfortunates too far away.

Everyone, I say, hearing or not hearing, was bored—save Frederick. To this German Prince whose committee had blasted his last chances, who mumbled, who had never handed him a glass of champagne nor would ever soothe him with light gossip, to him Frederick attended carefully, leaning forward in the chair next to mine. The Prince is filled with numbers; at several points Frederick commented "Not quite correct" or "hardly." Prince Albert spoke of the Crystal Palace as a Pope in mediaeval times might in consecrating a cathedral; indeed, at one moment, he declared this painted metal building to be as durable, as lasting, as churches of stone— to which Frederick nodded. As Germans do, he spoke more slowly to underline his words: the Exhibition will inaugurate an era of international peace, achieved through the free exchange of the goods we see disposed about the hall. The Crystal Palace expresses mankind's faith in the orderly march of progress. He seemed sincere. I hated him the few times I looked next to me, but I know he will pay for that speech; he too had not noticed, not attended to his wife. He does not understand even a single wave of her hand.

At the termination of this endless mumbling, we braced ourselves for an equally long reply of thanks from the Queen, but she was mercifully brief. Then there was a prayer, led by the Archbishop of Canterbury, spoken by seemingly all the 25,000 faithful in the hall, then singing; the Queen had requested the "Hallelujah" chorus from Handel. The echo was so great, the hall so vast, that one end was two measures behind the other, the "Hallelujah" chorus rolling back and forth across the hall like a turbulent sea.

"Will the glass shatter?" I shouted at Frederick.

"No," he said firmly. Had it, would he be curious just where the waves of sound would send showers of glass down upon the 25,000? The only unexpected event, however, was that the Chinese mandarin chose this moment to come forward to the Queen, prostrating himself upon the rug beneath her feet, his lips kissing the ground.

At the end of the music, the Lord Breadalbane announced in a loud voice which sounded pathetically weak after the tumult we had all just made, "Her Majesty commands me to declare this Exhibition open!" After the Royal Recession, there was one more ceremony to be completed before people were free to wander, a step we never knew we should be obliged to take. The Commissioners, Joseph Paxton and subordinates would now officially receive the thanks of other official delegations.

"Did you know anything of this?" I demanded as the ushers began to organise our progress of twenty yards.

"Nothing," Frederick returned, "nothing, nothing." For ten years, he had successfully avoided meeting Paxton. But there was nowhere to hide now.

We moved forward. It was agony to me. I confess I was not thinking of Frederick in that moment, I was thinking only of myself, the words "This is not where I want to be" screaming within me as a beadle bawled out "Mr and Mrs Henry Venable!," we then taking three steps forward, "Mr and Mrs Wilfred Smith," moving forward, while somewhere else in this vast glass church another beadle bawled at the same time to other thousands the words of the proclamation of thanks which floated to us in between our names . . . "genius . . . ingenuity of conception . . . Mr and Mrs Frederick Courtland . . . brilliance of execution . . ."

Frederick walked forward to Paxton slowly and erect; I was at his side, Sir Snigs enrolled behind us. Frederick held his head up, fixed a smile upon his face and marched.

". . . a grateful Nation . . ."

Now we began to mount the rostrum towards Paxton. I turned to see if M. Snigs was in any difficulty over the steps, but Frederick did not. He kept himself face forward, erect, the head smiling towards Paxton.

The party climbed half-way up the rostrum steps before halting temporarily. The proclamation of thanks was almost ended.

". . . a new era in architecture in Great Britain . . . Lord and Lady Monroe," the beadle frowning at the solitary Sir Snigs.

No matter what anyone thought, I sought for Frederick's hand. Which pressure he returned as absently as he had the greetings of his colleagues or considering if the Crystal Palace might shatter from noise. Still he smiled, the lips not tight, not forced, now the smile of the benevolent unpaid contractors and other rejected architects. For the first time, I saw Joseph Paxton close. He was only two yards away now.

I thought, "This is a man I would like to know," in the midst of this hideous ceremony that is what I thought, I would like to know him. Close up, watching him speak, one remarked the open gestures with his hands, the mobility of his features; he reminded me of a certain kind of Italian, recognisably from the country and comfortably of the people, vivid, lively, and no fool. The man before us complimented Joseph Paxton; the compliment he acknowledged with a shrug.

Then we stepped forward. Frederick, taller, shapelier and more beautiful than Paxton, stretched out his hand in greeting, the smile of twenty yards ago still upon his face. Frederick's hand was steady. Paxton smiled back. He now gave no sign of recognising Frederick's name. Frederick spoke mine, as his wife. Paxton bowed, I inclined my head, and then he looked behind us, saying to the man next to M. Snigs, "Robert! The great day is at last at hand."

Now we moved forward, still in line, towards the stairs on the other side of the rostrum; there were so many people about that the descent was no more swift than the mount. As a treat, the planners had moved to the base of this rostrum the most flamboyant of all the exhibits in the Crystal Palace.

It is called "Count Dunin's Man of Steel" after its creator. The Count has caused to be forged over seven thousand pieces of steel into plates and springs and wheels. These compose a metal man in the shape of the Apollo Belvedere, whose one arm, however, stretches out before him as for a handshake. At the turn of a single crank this metal figure begins to expand, the springs and wheels within him pushing out concealed plates, so that he retains the perfection of the Apollo of Belvedere's form, but becomes the size of a welcoming Goliath. It takes but thirty seconds to inflate Count Dunin's Man of Steel to double life-size, or to shrink him back to our own.

This elaborate device was given a place of honour at the base of the rostrum because of its ingenuity; also, Paxton begins to interest himself in steel. I suppose it is laughable; as people descended the rostrum, however, they turned the crank of the man of steel with more interest than amusement. Now our turn arrived.

Frederick still wore his smile. He turned the crank. Slowly, as if he were testing how much effort was required. It seemed to give quite smoothly. He made one turn, a second, a third. The toy now loomed over us, as high as the men upon the platform. Frederick cranked it back down, again searching its weight. When it had arrived at human size, ever smiling, Frederick reached out to shake the Man of Steel's hand with a firm, confident grasp.

It is now late evening. Paulton's Square smells sweet. I have been to visit Frederick, who, although awake, is still resting in bed. I have re-read my account of yesterday. The men laughing at Frederick will soon forget him, especially as he will have gone abroad. I caressed Frederick's hair tonight while he spoke of our plans; there is a little grey in it but it is still thick— heavy, brown and thick. I urged him to drink more tea, the rose-hip tea from Brand which is soothing. Tonight, he began to return to himself, as I told M. Snigs he would; he does not break.

The gay remark reverberated over and over in my mind. "Do you remember, Madame, we once before had occasion to depart in state?" Running my fingers through Frederick's hair, I thought how far we have travelled indeed, how far since we three last departed in state.

III

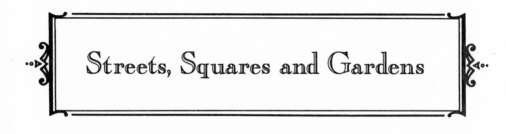

Streets, Squares and Gardens

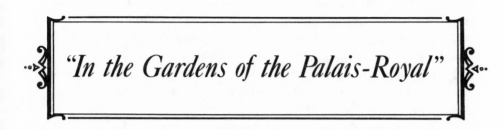

"In the Gardens of the Palais-Royal"

Undated Manuscript by
Charles Courtland, first part

Having during the past year retired from the editorial chair of this demanding if rewarding review, I determined to pass the first official months of old age in the city of my youth. In truth, I could give no reason why I, afflicted with gout and aching joints, wished to make so arduous a journey; my editorial retirement meant only that I was free to write that history of agnostic thought upon which I long meditated. Ideas for this *magnum opus* had previously visited me whilst I corrected errors of spelling in reams of galley proof, cajoled unpaid printers, threatened languid authors, soothed eccentric subscribers. At last in retreat, I could gather my thoughts in peace. Yet there also come times in one's life when the urge to travel seems however blindly the promise of discovery, times not confined to youth, discoveries which may break the bonds of mere adventure.

I was warned by more fortunate travelling spirits to prepare myself for a shock: the Paris I had last seen in 1860 would be unrecognisable in 1868. The very heart of the old Paris, they warned, had been ripped from the body of the city, the twisted streets annihilated, replaced by long, straight boulevards down which carriages careen at race-course speed, down which also troops and cannon can be deployed. In 1860, said my advisors, you saw only the beginnings, the merest preparation; the Emperor and the Baron Haussmann knew that publication then of their true intentions might indeed stir the entire metropolis, save the army and the architects, to resistance. It is not merely the streets that have succumbed to laws of geometry: I was also warned that the buildings lining them have been disciplined to a uniformity of six storeys, that hectare upon hectare of respectable housing had been added to the west as the poor were confined behind the *grands boulevards* of the north and the east.

I discounted these complaints because I had heard them from the moment I arrived in Paris in 1829. Victor Hugo proclaimed in his *Notre Dame de Paris* that the city would soon have the "opulence," the "diversity of aspect," the "hint of the grandiose" of a chequerboard; as for Balzac, who can forget the extraordinary evocation in *Les Illusions Perdues* of the destruction in the Palais-Royal of the old Galerie de Bois and its replacement by the chaste, cold iron Galerie d'Orléans?

(Do I too abruptly push him forward in this manner? And I seem to remember that I, too, in my own little sphere, was prepared to regret the passing of Old Paris before I had set foot in it that year.)

Thus I hastened to the scenes of my youth thinking not much would have changed, certainly not the love of the inconveniently picturesque amongst the poets of Paris, as well as amongst its leisured elegants, its concierges, and even its cabmen. In general, we find the hatred of modernity a comfort. However, as I directed my servants in the removal of my files of correspondence, my framed miniatures, the best of my Staffordshire jugs from my desk into dun tea-chests for storage, the siren voices of Paris were not of old friends. I have found one of the great surprises of ageing to be the curiosity to know, roughly as one must, what might happen after one is gone, to look forward into that absence.

(This is a more accurate beginning. For in honesty, I would otherwise be obliged to admit that even as I planned my boat and my trains to Paris, I feared hearing again in memory the confident ring of Frederick's voice in company with celebrated artists and writers, feared hearing his light banter tinged with insolence when amongst his colleagues. Paris, the bright ante-chamber of youth. Now I could also look behind him as he spoke, into the suite of the ever darker rooms through which later he would pass. But my fear should not be the point of the memoir, since it did not deter me from my journey. Nor should I account how Frederick, after the débâcle of the Crystal Palace, also shunned Paris, afraid to be reminded. Perhaps the best beginning is to remark simply that every man holds in sentimental regard the place where he first could say to himself exuberantly, "I am alive!" Save this problem for a later draught.)

I arrived one fine May morning at the Gare St-Lazare, having ambled slowly by little trains across the northwest of France, and passed the night previous in the far suburban home of a Protestant family. The countryside shewed few marks of change from the days of my youth, or, I suspect, the youth of my grandfathers. The family with whom I lodged, although persons of means, permitted themselves no display of fashion, under which rubric they would have included all modern convenience; this too was very much of the tradition of Huguenot France. When, however, our little train pulled into the St-Lazare station, I began to understand that my London advisors warned me not from idle fancy. This, the oldest of the rail termini in Paris, had just been roofed over with a vast iron-and-glass canopy, as large as those in London. It loomed and lorded over its surroundings as ours do not; the streets giving upon St-Lazare were in the midst of being cut and trimmed, much as one trims a hedge, the shaved sides of buildings now nakedly exposing the cut-away rooms within, rooms where only a few months ago there had been life; I could see, indeed, bits of furniture and clothing which had been left behind in the hasty removal of the tenants. These I watched an army of masons brick over, so that the rue de Rome on the side of the station will soon present a bald, blank face to the arriving and departing passengers.

I had come without advising any of my acquaintances in Paris; my voyage, whatever its course, would at least start free of the loving plans of friends. A cab was easily procured. The cabman asked me my address. I replied gaily, "Anywhere," which caused him to frown at the elderly madman, and so I relieved him by giving the name of my hotel, though I had no desire to be shut up.

Has Paris entirely imposed upon itself the modernity of an ugly utility? Not at all. My carriage sped me down the ramrod rue de Miromesnil and thence past the Palais de l'Exposition, certainly one of the largest iron-and-glass buildings in the world, and, to my untutored, tradition-minded eye, perhaps the most beautiful. Inspired by our Crystal Palace, this structure had already established itself as a part of the Parisian fabric by the time of my last visit, though it has far less surrounding turf than our own monument to Progress.

It has been four years now since the Crystal Palace disappeared from the London scene, unbolted and exiled to Sydenham, the palace obliterated as a painter might scrape away an obsessive patch of his canvas, the very part he had in the making thought, "This is superb!"; later he looked upon it more coolly, was surprised that the superb, important gesture rather bored him. However, there would be no great difficulty fixing it; the oil was still wet.

(How shall I ever forget my brother's face as he witnessed this scene! At first he watched in triumph, his face wreathed in smiles; these were the days in which they removed the glass panes, and he talked easily about what should replace Paxton's palace. But, perhaps after a fortnight, I detected an unease in Frederick, from a cause I could not then fathom. He asked me, with a casual air, "Should you like to come see the end of the Crystal

Palace?" but his hands were restless, as always the tell-tale sign. We arrived at the day when the iron skeleton began to be unbolted; there was but an immense frame around an empty volume. Men lowered triangles of roof from a sort of aerial rail coach fitted out with pulleys and counterweights; it was a spectacular sight, long beams and spars hanging over empty space, connected to nothing. Yet there were few people to witness this marvel, one Frederick said equalled the construction in technique. In truth, when the Exhibition ended, London did not take to congregating about the Crystal Palace. Frederick, however, viewed the destruction of this skeleton with ever-mounting unrest. The iron, as I say, methodically disappeared from the sky; would the assured young man have cared, would he have watched in awe, I mean the young man I remember dressed in a dashing ruby cape and oxblood riding boots? So far had Frederick come through trial, to the nobility of disinterested love. To quiet my brother's shaking I took his hand, which soon lay still in mine, but he would not come away. Anne says he insisted upon returning to Hyde Park until the site was once more level ground.)

Note and memoir are becoming so mingled I must go forward with more freedom in this Parisian account, if less polish. I shall insert nothing further in parentheses in this draught.

Owing to a momentary halt in traffic, I gazed at the enormous half-rounded Exhibition Hall, its flags flapping imperially high up in the breeze, so elevated that the patches of colour seem part of the sky. These are visible all along the Seine, even, they say, from the heights of Montmartre on a fine day. Though our avenue was broad, there were many carriages coming and going to the Exhibition, few of them smart but all respectable; there was an exhibition of tobacco at the moment, my coachman informed me as we rocked gently in the fine weather, indeed, a continual series of such displays which attracted families. We could see hordes of children disgorged from these serviceable vehicles; they shrieked at a troop of Negroes lining the staircase, puffing on lit cigars, this guard of the honour of tobacco blowing rings of smoke at the heads of the children. It is still a foreign country.

The evening before, in Courbevoie, my host, a most worthy pastor, described his pleasure in the English exhibits sent to the great International Exhibition. These were: a kiosk containing works of the Bible Society; an entire Protestant Church dismantled on our shores, exported, retrieved and re-built precisely within a year; a phalanx of agricultural machines; a model farm in miniature and a model school for the poor, also in miniature. Visitors were puzzled by our offering, for the character of the other displays tended to the lavish or to frank announcements of might like Krupp's fifty-tonne gun. The modest, earnest face of England is her true visage, if cast temporarily in shadow by the Crystal Palace.

The admiring pastor's description of our display caused me a tinge of regret that I had not come a year earlier; this again caused me to think of Frederick. How could I imagine I made such a pilgrimage merely to ascertain the speed of carriages in a modern street? Or that "Paris" roused in my mind the lilting refrain of "When We Were Young"? For when offered the opportunity to travel to the International Exhibition, on behalf of a large London daily, I felt, for Frederick's sake, I should not. In 1855 he attempted to build part of the Palais de l'Exposition; this was his last effort to wrest from the world some tangible recognition of his genius. And it was the last time he sought to confide in me, when he failed. "I mustn't be a burden to you." Smiling, making the little French shrug he had guarded unthinkingly as a souvenir. "I mustn't be a burden to you." If only, Frederick, if only you had allowed me to shelter you in my arms! At our age, could a brother's embrace be a burden?

The radical surgery now being conducted upon the capital of France will make Paris the very capital of the nineteenth century. I, like every visitor, could sense it, a revolution in space which will produce an equal dislocation in the moral vision of the man of the city. This is easier. I shall, as it were, declaim from my coach.

When in the middle 1850s they effaced the façade of the old Church of St-Benoît to clear a path for the rue des Ecoles, I thought it a pity that this scene of a great conflict between the Church and the People would never be visible to a child born after 1848. Indeed, upon my prior visit in 1860, the entire Latin Quarter resembled one of those ravaged corpses in the dissection theatres of medical schools. Gone were the pothouses, the revolutionary cafés, the places of ill repute in the Latin Quarter; these disorderly sites smudged the clean-drawn lines of the boulevard St-Michel and the rue des Ecoles.

Near the ruins of the Cluny the modernisers created a particularly irrational scene. Here the shops of many booksellers, specialising in tomes of poetry, clustered round a fresh hole in the ground; in this hole, in my youth, stood the café frequented by the competing poets and their coteries when the poets were unknown and unformed. You could not buy so much as a piece of paper on credit from the watchful ladies in those bookshops, and they did a particularly good business, by their standard of penny profit, in distress purchases from customers to whom they had sold the very goods they now took back for a pittance. Only the wineshop gave credit, and too many learnt to eat wine. Imagine had I taken here a boy born after 1848, pointed to the ever so picturesque booksellers and said, "We hated them";

he could only think, looking at the colourful fragments of Old Paris, "The old man's wits wander."

By 1868 the authorities had removed these irrational jolts between past and present. The relentless regularity of the façades of these new streets, or of streets re-fashioned like the boulevard des Italiens, suggest nothing of what had stood before. Geometry is beautiful to the extent it is unblemished. At most we can say the practise of the geometric aesthetic in a city devastates another art form, the art of memory, an infinitely more feeble art, remembering subject to mental powers inexorably fading, in need of a corpse, to complete my metaphor, to aid in conception of what was the living body.

With my brother I used to debate such questions by the hour. His architecture revealed a most elegantly severe cast of mind, indeed he devoted his entire career to championing the virtues of honest geometric mass over those of richly ornamented detail. I thought more about him that first day under the impress of Haussmann's revolutionary city than I had for some time. This linear, regular Paris is the city he always wanted to build.

My carriage crossed the Seine to the Left Bank. I passed places on the map where Frederick and I had quarrelled, where we had fed particularly friendly squirrels, where I had explained Plato's theory of Forms at such length that he had fallen asleep upon the bench where we sat. But now the bench was gone, as was the squirrel corner, and the house in front of which we disputed until protest came from within, all these signs to nourish my memory of him, effaced by the very geometry he had hoped to build, *his* city taking him within its own abstract present.

As we hurtled towards my hotel, situated to the side of the hospital of the Invalides, I thus found the very speed of these efficient streets depressing my spirits; there was not enough time to look, to see if possibly some trace of him had been left. We gained the door of the hotel. Even in my mounting distress I realised the coachman would abandon me were I suddenly to tell him again to drive on, anywhere, and in the quiet *quartier* I had chosen there were few conveyances for easy hire. So I announced to him that after depositing my valise I should need him immediately for an appointment. The memory of my brother dictated the address.

We approached the Palais-Royal coming down the rue de Rivoli. The April sunshine promised to warm the noon-time, already men and women had taken their places in the cafés, some reading newspapers, some drowsing, above them the city, as I had earlier remarked, draped in flags and streamers. The looming hulk of the Palais-Royal, a squat pile of grimy stone, proclaimed itself a winter palace out of season, yet I made my coachman approach the West Gate of the Palais-Royal as slowly as possible, that I might savour our destination. At last I was home.

To speak at convocations on "Theology and the Modern World," to care for cats, to dine in the company of persons who have set themselves against superstition, ignorance and illusion—could any life be more reassuring in its purpose? Though I abhor the ferocity of zealots like Father Newman, the convictions of sound and serious persons arouse in me resolution, the free-thinker's version of inspiration. And yet I have waited a score of years for someone, though I am frightened of no honourable person in particular, I have waited a score of years for one worthy to ask me, "Charles, of what are you thinking?" I will reply, "I am dreaming of the arrows of Apollo and of Athena in her glade." No criticism will be voiced—the fancies of the vine-clad Greeks also, in their proper place, have Moral Value. But I shall be found out.

Safe in the precincts of the Comédie-Française, the theatre in which I spent nearly a decade understanding barely half of what I heard. The theatre was the scene of great battles, like that at the first night of *Hernani*, as of daily intrigues. Often the Comédie-Française was closed for frivolous causes, like the night the actresses declared they could not perform because of an unfortunate astrological confluence, or the theatre was judged dangerously arousing, as during the week of the tax scandals, during which the government forbade performances of *William Tell*.

I am too old to believe that excitements of these sorts have more claim to Truth than the calm labour of years. However, a man cries at imaginary woes in a darkened hall without embarrassment, and those anonymous tears may warm him more than any hearth fire. Sad, is it not?

I walked around the theatre. It, too, had altered with the years. Others in Paris also, evidently, had discovered the Comédie-Française to be a home; the theatre used to be as grimy as the rest of the palace; whereas now, a porter informed me, the gilding is freshened monthly. The exterior stone has been washed, a rose cream at one corner of the Palais-Royal rectangle in brown-grey. The discipline of cleanliness was even more remarkable to me when I wandered within, though the reasons for it are evident only when one spends time in the living theatre.

At the Comédie-Française today, passage through the halls and mingling in the foyer have become more important than the life of the boxes. The entertaining of friends within the boxes cedes to mere casual greeting on the stairs, again a matter of the momentary, the quick, the passing in the new allegro tempo of Paris. Intervals, indeed, have been shortened. Proper ladies now aimlessly freely wander the halls, demand the dustless, gleaming propriety which no doubt reigns within their own homes.

"Spiritual Unease," "The Homeless Spirit"—how freely these phrases flow from the pen! Indeed, we think a man lacking if he does not suffer from "spiritual unease." In England, the old priestly remedy for this complaint was marriage and children, the hearth a natural home for the spirit. But for those of us who lack the consolations of fecundity, or those who, in the midst of squalling infants, still endure heartsick pangs, had the French authorities *for us* arranged this other refuge, this theatre scrubbed as clean as home?

In the old days the theatre could provoke the city; no more. In those days the spectators were often as loud as the players, silence reigning in a theatre only when decreed by the police for the sake of public order. Now, the silence is voluntary, in the theatres for the people as well as in the more august precincts of the Comédie-Française. To pay attention to others, people still themselves; even when broad Thérésa sings at a café-concert, the workingmen shush you if you speak while she sings. In the old days at the Variétés they used to shout out the lines of the farce and the melodrama along with the actors, just as we, we more fastidious ones, learnt the lines of *Hernani* well enough after a few months to shout them in aid of our actors when the reactionaries hissed and hooted. Geometry and silence; the straight street and the silent crowd.

All this bears on Frederick, all of it. Imagine: at seventy a man can say, "I have only a little more to add to my life; the years have accumulated." Or he can suddenly realise that in truth the time of human life does not accumulate. There is not a little more to add, but *everything,* everything if he is honestly to say that he has lived the life he should have. Even at seventy. On the one hand a man can exclaim, "At last!" That was my first impression of the Palais-Royal. Or he may suddenly realise, "There is no home!" in which case he must waste not a moment more.

I do not claim the condition of the modern theatre taught me this difference, nor would I dare write it in an article on "The Geographical and Moral Climate of Modern Paris," if such an essay is ever to be written by me. It was a matter of stone and glass. The stones of the Comédie-Française contained a domestic life that was becoming ever more refined and polite. The theatre was settling into old age. But the edifice I had come for bore another mark of time, a scar which had not healed. After touring the halls of the Comédie-Française I passed within the Palais-Royal, turned right and gained the gardens.

It was in the precincts of this palace and its enclosed gardens, the very place in which that early monument to modernity, the Galerie d'Orléans, was erected. At the ripe age of twenty-three my brother had been instrumental in the making of the iron-and-glass arcade. He came to Paris in 1828 to work with Fontaine, an architect not previously noted for use of modern materials, but a canny surveyor of life. Fontaine had managed the first Emperor Napoleon, they said at the time, as his wives could not, resisting Napoleon's desire for iron-and-glass structures in Paris in the early 1800s. By the time my brother came to Fontaine, the old man was converted— that is, he wanted to keep working and the work to be had was in iron and glass. The manners which managed Napoleon seduced my younger brother. Frederick, like our father, delighted in charm, of which Fontaine possessed an abundance. Fontaine made the young Englishman his lieuten- ant; when they came to a misunderstanding, in 1832, again because of this arcade in the Palais-Royal, Fontaine turned on Frederick, blackening his name whenever and wherever he could. Old age had struck Fontaine the way it often seems to strike men who have conducted their lives as diplo- matic campaigns; he could not bear the thought others would soon do without him. Fontaine taught Frederick iron and, in the short time remain- ing to the old man after this quarrel in '32, he determined Frederick would not put that knowledge to further use.

I disclose this perfidy only to suggest that in our youth matters were reversed amongst us from the usual pattern: the older, serious brother idled his time away in Paris, hoping to find a new vocation for himself after abandoning, or having been abandoned by, his priestly calling. The younger, amusing son meanwhile worked hard, first for his teacher, then against him. Our reversed destiny showed itself in these gardens; I often sat at a table in the open air, reading Lamennais or Sénancour, or (still it seems so shameful to admit) day-dreaming, occasionally glancing towards the Galerie d'Orléans where I could see my little brother pointing to a pane of glass, explaining some change or refinement he wished to attentive labourers. It was a great comfort to watch him working.

I feared as I entered the gardens that Haussmann's minions might have subjected the Palais-Royal also to the tyranny of straight lines, perhaps bricking in the stone arcades so that the inner face of the Palais-Royal resembled the blank wall along the rue de Rome. But the palace was still safe. Round the fountain in the centre children cavorted as always, and even within its basin, though many of the great jets which used to splash water from the edge of the stone circle towards the centre are broken. As always, boys cannot resist the water's invitation, an adventure to which their nurses are also sensible, for the garden rings with women's shouts and children's laughter. The old sundial chronometer is still in place, or rather, it has been restored to its place after the desecration of the statuary within and without the Palais during the February Days of 1848. I used to set my watch by this fine instrument, and did so again with an air of satisfaction, as an old ditty about this sundial went through my mind:

En ce jardin tout se rencontre,
Hormis de l'ombrage et des fleurs;
Si l'on y dérègle ses moeurs,
Au moins on y regle sa montre.

These gardens, in the youth of Balzac the scene of lewdness, made by my brother in his youth a scene of elegance, now speak however of solitude, even with the boys and girls round the fountain. The gravel paths are unlike a lawn upon which generations of children have danced. And great ladies of the new Empire now prefer to be glimpsed at a distance in the Bois de Boulogne, rather than in this familial scene. My brother's garden has gained from their absence, even though in his youth he dreamt of beautiful human forms promenading here as the final touch of the floral elegance he contrived in converting the garden to the Italian style. When we were young, we had in London a little patch of earth behind a shed we called our secret garden, out of range of shouts from nurses or tutors, or at least so we maintained. In Paris, I sat upon a bench, equally unmolested; my adult companions on the other benches all had found those miraculous points in the middle distance where they could stare into their very souls. Still, I wished my brother were here; he would, I think, accommodate the change, he would take pleasure in this, again our secret garden.

In looking up, in the very heart of "home," I saw my rest was over. I was no longer to be "retired." This is what I saw:

The greatest of the cafés was under the arches of the Galerie de Montpensier, the Café de Foy, the greatest at least to me as a young man, because a curate in the English provinces may dream of a glittering wicked room in Paris which would conquer his fear of sensate life *for him.* He may, like most of his clerical brothers, harbour this dream, even for an entire night, and then take himself back, throw himself down upon the altar, he all unworthiness, and through the very agency of prayer the memory of that terrible night or nights dims and dims and perhaps after a few years entirely disappears and he is cleansed. It is given to few of us to discover we have dreamt something real. It was given to me the moment I stepped through the doors of the Café de Foy with my brother in 1829.

The Café de Foy was lined with mirrors which made the vast rooms glitter; upon the ceiling was a magnificently dashing fresco by Vernet. Crammed at overburdened little tables was a veritable horde of painters, persons of the theatre, some from the Comédie-Française still in costume, having come to the Café de Foy for quick refreshment between scenes; there were real legislators mixed amongst these Roman senators and Spanish kings, the real men of power dressed in the most sombre, discreet black. Elegant youths of the time moved amongst them. It was an age of informality, though not of languor; the young wished no shield from the flush of pique, or friendship, or sheer curiosity; manners were, one might say, implicit, and this expressed itself in a natural gait, the easy movement of one's arms, the willingness to expose upon the face the record of what passed within the soul, even here, in the very temple of mutual and self-regard. I remember I stood at the entrance struck by the sheer improbability that it was real, and that my brother turned to me with concern.

"Have I conducted you to a profane temple?" he demanded with a smile. No, all the requisites of my dream Paris were furnished here in fact.

I haunted this café during those early years in Paris. My brother being frequently engaged nearby, I had the excuse I needed—excuse because one could not quite come here casually. Never besmirched by the lewdness of the old gardens, the Café de Foy attracted, if I may so put it, those persons of note who had earned the right to be in the presence of one another, even if they were privately unacquainted. For instance, there was a famous game of backgammon here in the winter of '31, continuing day after day, player succeeding player in a sort of relay, even women joining in. This racy entertainment would be spoilt if the wrong sort of person watched; the waiters managed to make that clear. The wrong sort of person could wait an hour for a coffee. A young man in the black gown and round hat of an English cleric with worn black boots was the wrong sort of person, but after I was seen a few times in the company of my dashing, elegant brother, I no longer waited. I came, watched the backgammon games, listened to the gossip about persons I had never met, offered my opinions on the history of English letters when asked, which was seldom, learnt to smoke a long pipe, developed a confidential relation with one of the waiters who did me the favour of watering the punch he served to me, as I hadn't the head for spirits of my brother's friends. It was here I first began to enjoy writing, on a small board I brought with me for the purpose. I propped the board against the table, put my paper upon it and composed, occasionally reaching over to sip from my coffee. In the Café de Foy, I was regarded simply as someone who had thus learnt to dress himself suitably.

The visual scene has ever been for me spiritual evidence. In the course of a decade I wrote of many Parisian places, including cafés: the Café Bothier, the Café Turc, the Coin Vendôme; the Turc was the first and the most important, for it was on its terrace that I discovered a new and compelling vocation: combat against my vanity of worthiness. But I was never tempted to write *about* the Café de Foy: were I to write it down, perhaps the dream-room would then vanish for ever.

Even after I left Paris, this café continued to be a vessel of life for me, albeit a changed one. In the Forties the same people frequented it, but they were ageing and so the Café de Foy became more sedate. By 1852 it resembled a drawing-room. Its distinguished members spoke quietly; they had no news to give, and by now they had ceased to dispute one another. Now also a certain formality marked their movements; this came from the stiffness of their joints. A fortunate ageing: in 1852 the liberal Catholic reformer Lamennais came to live at number 33 of the Galerie de Montpensier, a few steps away, and the café now understood his need. The old waiters took care of him the last two years of his life, losing bills of the dinners he could not pay for, at the end taking food to his chambers when the priest abandoned alike by the Church and by his fashionable followers was too ill to quit his bed.

Now, in 1868, I stared at the Café de Foy. The door was locked, the windows tightly shuttered. A notice nailed across the door announced the establishment was for sale. I later learnt it had been for sale since 1863.

I suppose every young man looks to some older person in whom he hopes to see the reflection of himself. As a youth in Paris, temporarily retired from the duties of parish life in rural England, Lamennais seemed to be the epitome of my own best future. It was not so much what, as how, he believed. Romans 14:22 perhaps best depicts his character: "Happy is he that condemneth not himself in that thing which he alloweth."

In 1852, the year he sought refuge in the Palais-Royal, I sought out my youthful ideal once again. I spoke to him of the ever-mounting loneliness afflicting my bachelorhood, my despair of transmuting the genuine love I felt and feel for the world into love for woman; I described the impossible conditions of Catholic life in my own country, the converts made blind zealots by their very need to affirm a new faith; I asked him did he think I should try to find a place for my loneliness in the precincts of the French Church, among whose back corridors and nether rooms a more liberal home for a convert priest might be found. I had asked for an hour of his time in the afternoon; the hour passed into two, then the afternoon into dusk, we two smoking and drinking coffee, for he would take nothing else for fear of the expense, the waiters of the Café de Foy attending us—him —as if matters of state must be under discussion. I poured out my loneliness to M. de Lamennais, who listened, repeating again and again, "I have no answer for you, but continue."

The Café de Foy has closed.

Even when Lamennais allowed in himself confusion which would have caused others to wring their hands, he looked about steadily; he sought to account all circumstance, no matter how distasteful. He spoke to me of his own trials of solitude, trials which had come to him when young, rather than in the high season of middle age. He had examined his conscience for the sources of his own aching, asking what defect of character caused him to feel so abandoned while alone in his cell. He spoke of the mask of amiability behind which he dwelt, he described to me the almost physical pain of his drawing-room triumphs, as when an exhausted, dissolute countess one day said to him, thinking to make him a present, "Father, in your company I feel the most lively desire for God." Surely, I said, he was angered at such moments. "Not quite. You see, I hoped the light and chatter of the world would warm me; it did not: never was I lonelier than when in a crowd, yet I continued to frequent society." He would allow me no compliment upon his person. He said to me only, "In time I understood I should never understand myself; I have left the matter at that."

Once it seemed scarcely possible this devout priest could survive his own confusions. This was during his struggle with the Pope, who defeated him with the merest flick of the lash. Yet Lamennais taught us all to regret our lesser need for resolution. He continued ever alert, ever broad in his allowance, and ever convinced that in this fulness he would come ultimately closer to God. By birth an aristocrat, he evinced an inner nobility by his manner of faith, he who in his last years depended upon the waiters of the Café de Foy to lose his bills, which these minions of fashion knew it was a duty, perhaps the only spiritual duty possible in their labour, to perform.

The Café de Foy was shut; delay was no longer possible. I rose to explore my brother's arcade.

Its glass walls and roof form one end of the quadrangle enclosed on the other three sides by stone. Curiously, iron which has not been painted for some time appears to take on a furred patina harmonious with the stone. Nothing, however, could redeem to my eyes the awkward peculiarity of so much glass, however beautifully framed. Even for him I cannot gainsay the evidence of my senses, nor would he wish it, Frederick who watched in pain as Paxton's Crystal Palace was dismounted.

Within the Galerie d'Orléans several of the shops are closed, some even used as store-rooms. At one end the arcade still has a few bustling culinary enterprises whose clientèle wanders in from the displays of *foie gras*, truffles and galantines in the windows of Chevet's. After ten, when the major-domos have left with their provisions, one's steps echo clearly, singly against the glass. The Galerie d'Orléans is tenanted from mid-morning to early evening by occasional elderly couples; at six or seven it closes, in winter to save upon fuel, in summer because even these clients prefer the pleasures of the open air. Within, during the shortened daily life of the arcade, the pensioners and their wives walk slowly up and down its wings, glancing at chocolates in porcelain, at cases containing old medals from the *ancien régime,* at relics from Egypt and Greece. One shop still supplies headpieces of the American savages, rude mementoes much in fashion one spring—it must be thirty-five years ago, the spring of 1833 when "everyone" disposed of one of these costumes of the noble savage somewhere about the drawing-room, the fashion lasting fully a month. The elderly proprietor hopes, I suppose, another similar month will come; he will exhaust his stocks, close his books and shut up shop, his investment vindicated and his life-work done. The couples promenade but seldom purchase; they have no need of ownership for memory. And so, the purveyor of the mouldering headpieces is also held a prisoner of the past, his doors open, as he waits for release.

Unlike the Crystal Palace, the Galerie d'Orléans remains in place. Unlike the Café de Foy, it remains open.

I walked up the central aisle, then around to the flanking aisle which gives upon the Cour d'Honneur, the court now a storage yard for the Comédie-Française at the corner. Men were stacking mounds of chairs, then covering the mounds with canvas. I crossed to the other flanking aisle, which gives upon the garden. This was a prettier aspect, looking out. Only two shops of twenty were open on this side, both sellers of semi-precious and costume gems.

My volume on agnostic thought will open with the biblical scene in which man first began to pray. This honour falls to Cain, who first brought God an offering; of course the offering was spurned from divine distaste, leading the jealous Cain to murder. Only when Eve begat Seth, to take the place of the slain brother, and Seth begat Enos, only "then began men to call upon the name of the Lord" (Genesis 4:26). I have sought to imagine Adam and Eve watching their grandson Enos pray. I am almost certain that the words of supplication and fealty to God upon the lips of Enos rendered them heartsick. They see upon his face a joy at the discovery of prayer, Enos using words like "holy," "blessed" or "reverend" which they had never used or indeed heard before, his purity seeming to the exhausted Adam and Eve not so much a reproach to themselves as a pushing to the side of their history, the history of their pain so much less to the boy than his discovery of faith through clasping his hands together, kneeling and rising, repeating the new words over and over again, the magic never fading, since he is certain God hears. In his innocent, pure voice, Enos calls Grandfather and Grandmother to prayer as well, incantation they should sing instead of rehearsing once more their story. The invention of prayer was the means by which mankind avoided the problem of consolation. It was especially apt in shunting aside those whom history confused, victims of not knowing—how could anyone?—the gravity, the fatality of one act in time.

Now, when contemplating the Indian head-dress, all became evident to me. I had not known in London, at meetings on "Theology and Modern Life," what to make of this discovery about the invention of prayer. This was the real reason for my voyage to Paris. I came to find out if my brother was in need of consolation; he was, even though his building stands. But how was I to find solace for his history?

I had imagined Enos, when the grandparents sought his hand and began the history of their tribulations, I had imagined the uncomprehending youth making one effort. He would say, "But Grandfather, after all, here you are." The exiled couple turn dully to each other—"Yes we survived." Now you hold an old man's hand but you know nothing of what passes in his heart. Perhaps M. de Lamennais felt similarly isolated during our interview. Certainly it was not enough to observe that the iron-and-glass building still stood. On the contrary, as I observed the faded couples promenading in their worn, carefully tended clothes, the dust on the panes of glass obscuring the beautiful trinkets resting within on pillows of blue satin or shelves of rosewood, these very signs of survival roused in me the conviction that something must be done for Frederick.

Here are words I employed long, long ago to comfort those in my parish: "No man hath seen God at any time . . . for he that loveth not his brother whom he hath seen, how can he love God whom he hath not seen?" I think I told my flock the evidence of the eye will not aid us in faith, nor in love, but that was a very long while ago. Now I would try to see more for my brother; he needed me. We who were done with prayers. And I knew, even if obscurely at that moment, I should have to sacrifice something of my own desire for rest, for home, in order to comfort him.

"One Amongst Many"

Undated Manuscript by
Charles Courtland, second part

A spy that morning might have remarked an elderly gentleman arrive at the Gare St-Lazare, leave his luggage at a respectable, unfashionable hotel, thence proceed to gardens of the same character. Now this foreigner, whose condition was easily deduced from his heavy shoes and stiff hat, exited from the Palais-Royal, his eye deployed speculatively up the avenue de l'Opéra. Evidently he was in search of lunch.

As indeed I was. The restaurants along that straight line did not appeal to me and so I turned back towards the Comédie-Française. Here I remarked a woman of early middle age in the square before the theatre, a woman sombrely dressed with, however, relieving touches of colour, a small Greek medallion pinned upon, and a red striped scarf over, her dark shawl. She stood ten yards away, turned in profile, her attention expectant upon the square which drowsed in the May luncheon sun. I could not be sure; there was a greater generosity under the chin than I remembered, the nose perhaps more prominent than that of the young lady I knew twenty years ago. The carriage of this matron seemed however an indelible signature: she held herself straight without stiffness, the rod of pride still unbent.

Now her patience was rewarded. Into the square a handsome phaeton appeared. The gentleman holding the reins directed his steed towards her, and jumped down smartly when the carriage rocked to a halt in place. He was, I judged, of her own age, not remarkable of feature in any way, a man with full hair, his lips and jowls also fleshy; I thought the gesture of jumping down ill became him. This lady, however, appeared quite pleased. She extended her hand, over which he bent. Although my eyesight is not what it was, I am sure I saw no rings on her strangely ungloved fingers, yet nothing in their mutual comportment betrayed the slightest intimacy after his heavy, showy thud upon the paving stones of the Comédie-Française.

She made a comment to him I could not catch, to which he nodded—perhaps a suggestion about their luncheon. He assisted her into the phaeton, as well-brought-up Frenchmen do, one foot under the carriage step, one arm a few inches behind the lady's back. There was simply no way to be but half sure. When she mounted the two steps she exposed his show of protection as absurd, she was so securely balanced and perfectly upright, as became a girl bred amidst persons whose comportment was their profession. Then she gathered her dowdy shawl about her. The companion folded the steps, mounted more slowly and with more dignity than he had descended, took up the reins, and the pair came straight towards me.

I looked up at her, she down at me. Not a sign of recognition passed between us! Or rather, she looked at the man staring at her from the pavement, without placing him, yet equally wishing to give the elderly stranger no offence, and so she smiled uncertainly before turning to her companion to continue the conversation they had already begun on the way to their restaurant.

How can I account the reasons which impelled me now wildly to search for a cab of my own? If only I had not from parsimony dismissed my chariot of the morning! Now I wished only to catch them for a moment, to come abreast, to . . . what? To ask her, "Are you Mademoiselle X, whom I knew twenty years ago?" It was madness, besides which, during this sweet sleepy hour, there were no carriages of any sort, let alone those for hire, to be had.

A cleric acquires the habit of puffing out little nostrums of cheer when his thoughts are otherwise engaged, just as a man learns to smoke a pipe without choking. When I had left my brother's arcade, in passing through the Cour de Nemours, I produced the following banality: "One must go forward, one must accept that life goes on." One glance disproved it. She radiated matronly comfort, even complacency. Perhaps because of this very competency she did not remember me, perhaps I was effaced from her memory as so much of the rest of my life had been effaced from the very stones of Paris. If it was indeed her. And so I wanted to catch her, to tell her, if it was Adèle, that the end of our correspondence was only a step forward in knowing her; as I poured out my confession to M. de Lamennais it was her face I saw in the spectral reflections of the garden windows in the Café de Foy, though my lips never betrayed her name. At the very least I wanted to impress her features upon my memory a last time, and, perhaps, our eyes would make us the gift of communion.

How strange it seems that the resolve to console my brother had so quickly plunged me again into the conundrum. I had told myself, in the years after my final interview with M. de Lamennais, that this egotistical wound would heal if I did not rub it; I took his own confession that "I should not understand myself, and leave the matter at that" to be good advice. It is good advice, but now in the Palais-Royal, the sheerest accident had joined my desire to reach out with my need to look within.

In the years after our last painful exchange of letters, my brother and her mother alluded to Adèle in a carefully casual and spare manner. I knew she returned to Greece in '48, that during the revolutionary disturbance there had been talk of her returning in an English frigate. When I asked Frederick the manner of her labours, he replied only that Anne found museums dusty and glum, and that Adèle was unlikely to explain to *him*. A year later, I had succeeded in producing the thought, in my essay on "The Wish for Immortality," that a man must hope for the courage to die alone. During this uplifting year, I asked again for news of Adèle in a carefully casual tone matching that of my informants, but they were not deceived. By '52, when at night I held my cats in my arms, the purring bodies throbbing against my chest, I wondered if even the pets would stay with me, could they learn to talk. Absurdly, it was this abysmal moment of self-pity which prompted me to seek out the noble Lamennais; when I discovered his pockets were empty and that he walked painfully even with the aid of a cane, I then could no more throw myself upon him than Frederick wished to become a burden to me. In these tides of solitude, gradually the need to know of Adèle's movements receded in my mind. Indeed, I accepted that her mother would recount only that she had ventured to Alexandria, to Rome, back to Greece, without any further explanation. Usually this was prevented by Frederick or Anne remembering an amusing story about someone I knew in London, or sweeping me off to a splendid occasion they had almost forgotten, at which we three were instantly due. However, the fact vouchsafed me—was it '62 or '63?—that Adèle had returned at last to Paris permanently, this fact I carefully preserved in my memory.

My antic search for a conveyance obliged me to rest against the portico of the theatre. The one certainty was that I would not return within to the garden benches. The wall, however, was cold, an east face, and made my rheumatic shoulder ache; I supported myself as long as I could bear the cold, turned round to stare up the avenue de l'Opéra; the phaeton had disappeared.

After a light repast in the *quartier,* I returned to the hotel to rest. During the collation my shoulder became worse. Held still, a joint seems under great pressure which could be eased if only the joint moved, but one knows that the slightest change of position will send a shooting pain from its original seat throughout the body. So one is prisoner of the desire and the fear to move. Often the tension sends up one's fever, the pain becoming so intense.

That evening I descended for the first time in several months into this release, and the kindly servants of the hotel were afraid for me. The phantoms haunting Lethe's shores come forward at these moments. Strange ones visited me in the large, soft bed looking out upon the first Emperor's monument to himself, to military glory, to Roman France, this self-tribute drawing few pilgrims inside the Invalides, his old soldiers forlorn in the immense triumphal gardens set aside in their honour and for their pleasure, a view of time mocking power sufficiently arousing in itself. I—but to recount them I must recount the terrible, simple fact which I have assumed so far, like a child crying "it hurts," thinking Nurse will understand exactly to which part of the anatomy this declaration refers. An assumption which makes for bad literature, for very bad literature indeed. Why was not my first morning in the Palais-Royal the prelude to a family reunion? Because my brother died in London on 21 September 1866. When I wrote of bringing comfort to Frederick Courtland I meant to the man who will live within me so long as I draw breath.

Even on his deathbed my brother made no appeal for the pastoral care which I determined to bestow upon him after, according to common reasoning, it was too late. At the burial service I spoke the conventional words of consolation to the many persons present, not as a priest but as a brother; I lightly acknowledged his reverses but then declared that he, like most of us, had accepted civilised disappointment of his early dreams as inevitable. Decorum only spoke through me. His tears at the destruction of the Crystal Palace—what place have these on a mask of civilised disappointment? Or again, because of Frederick's passion, he was far different from our father, whose irony accommodated alike triumph and disaster. When the acolytes of Fontaine blocked Frederick's work at the Palais de l'Exposition, he sought consolation by recounting the awkwardness of these enemies in the salons of Paris during the 1830s, a history which neither consoled him nor gave him the means to challenge their intrigue in the press, a weapon which I urged him to use. So my first instinct of consolation was, I must admit this, to reduce his life to a flattering lie. In truth he had no choice but to accept, though he did not bear his defeat gracefully.

How vividly those two days stand out before me! First Frederick rushed into hospital, then the doctor shaking and slapping him to rouse him from the apoplectic fit; finally, still panting, the young doctor seeking suitably mournful words with which to regret that nothing more was possible. I thought I should miss the memorial event myself, so immediately did the horde of Frederick's creditors close about me and so tangled an affair was it for him even to die in hospital. I shall confess however that as I hastened forward through the crowd of mourners to mount the pulpit, my thoughts were far from my brother's blue, bulging face or the equally hideous faces of the men who pressed for payment of old bills; I scanned the pews of the bereaved looking for her. Perhaps this was but one of those mental tricks by which we seek to cheat grief for a moment, yet also, surely, decorum demanded she pay her last respects. The very spirit of decorum that led me to speak of Frederick's civilised equanimity in the face of life's trials.

Only her sister and mother, however, came over from Paris. Anne explained that Adèle was "abroad," wherever that meant. Again without further explanation. Yet by now she had no need or cause to avoid me.

As a cleric, I early learned a truth about last illnesses and funerals. These terrible moments of parting seldom stain the minds of the bereaved indelibly. Widows instead speak with pain of the moments their husbands suddenly plunged into gloom for no good reason, or the contradictory stories the men told of a friend, or inexplicable failures of nerve. I later learnt in parting from Adèle it is the same when you abandon someone, when, as it were, you die on them. You leave, yet your lasting impression is not of the departure but of odd moments before the voyage.

Everyone was puzzled by Frederick's later life. He taught in a peculiar way spatial principles which he could not practise. I remember him once, in the premises he had first shared with our father, an atelier become more an extension of the schoolroom than working quarters—I remember Frederick commending a young man who had designed a church in a pyramidal shape, my brother's voice warm with approval, "It will never be built!" I heard a certain warmth in his voice when he spoke of architecture as an exercise of intellect, its forms matters of serious choice, these choices to be maintained in the face of shifting fashion. Yet he invariably blew the candle out by then looking the young man in the eye and declaring, "My ideas have been the unmaking of me; they may well be of you."

Did he care about his students? I am certain that for Frederick the principles of spatial imagination were true, whether he was capable of propounding them to one young man, to a thousand, or to none. Yet at his funeral, facing his charges, who sat as a phalanx of young fallen faces who could feel grief only as loss, I said his late-blooming capacity to inspire them was his reward for a life of perseverance. They had helped to comfort him. I want to believe this is true; on the other hand, in the last decade of his life I could not bear his laugh. And, may I say, I would tell them this lie again and yet again if it would encourage them and dignify their own struggle.

Now my first night-work will seem less delirious raving, more the attempt to solve a mystery. At last I could discuss with Adèle matters we might have considered at the funeral, though, because of what I had just seen in Paris, I had to go one step further. I tried to imagine what had effaced the traces of bitterness from her smile. Never favoured in youth, she seemed so unlikely a candidate to escape forward, much less than either of us. Now in fever I imagined the furnishing of her life. She had found a circle of friends who perhaps shared a common interest in antiquities, who met regularly in each other's homes to discuss matters of common interest about the history of the Orient, Hammurabi's tomb featuring, say, as the subject for an after-dinner speech in an apartment on the Ile de la Cité, the guests having dined upon eels and a roasted hare in the most comfortable manner of the old days before food became so highly sauced, an after-dinner speech about Hammurabi's tomb by this very gentleman who jumped down from the phaeton. Of course: he is a professor used to clambering about ruined temples, his bulk that of a man who has not hesitated to take up the excavating shovel when required. At least, in my fever, I saw her holding up a cracked pot, encased in mud, and asking him a question, which he answered to her satisfaction, she then placing the pot back upon a table. Indeed, this was the entirety of my first night—an image absolutely without provocation, or, indeed, explicitness, but I found it haunting, the matron with her ample chin and engaging smile holding the pot out for an explanation which she at last received, though there was none I heard.

For whatever reason, this—I hardly dare call it so, but such is the prosaic cast of my mind that it suffices to be so for me—this vision stayed with me from time to time during my waking hours the next day. The hotel servants put hot compresses upon my shoulder, which helped a little; I was offered laudanum, but this remedy I shall ever eschew. Father resorted to it in increasing dosages after his accident; I prefer more natural responses to the attacks Nature makes upon my own body. However, the compresses, applied rhythmically over the course of a day, are slower in result than the drug. In the late afternoon, my shoulder was again intolerable and I descended to Lethe's banks, now for another glimpse of her, longer and more consequent.

My cabman of the morning had been waiting in my dream for me all the while I was inside. Without a word of instruction, he hurtled me down the avenue de l'Opéra, and we overtook them just as they were about to turn at the twisted crossing before the opera house, where we would have lost them for ever. Now I did ask her if she was the woman I once knew, but before she could draw breath for her reply she and I and the professor were seated at the re-opened Café de Foy. "You must have many matters to discuss, more freely, I am sure, without an intruder present." She acknowledged his courtesy with another smile, and watched his back until he had disappeared through the bolted door, a lengthy exit due to the crowding of tables and the scurrying of servants, I all the while waiting impatiently for her attention.

At last. I poured out once again my side of the misunderstanding which had parted us, I spoke forcefully to her, the years having sharpened the reasons why I could not marry her. Instantly she held out her hand, just as she had in the square to the professor for his kiss. I continued with my explanation even as I bent forward, across the table, examining her fingers for signs of a wedding band. Her hands were delicate, the skin pale, the veins visible beneath, but I couldn't see the rings, if there were rings. So long as she held out her hand steadily for inspection, a pained, submissive smile on her lips, she was my partner in recrimination. Our union, however, lasted a mere moment. Then her hands were in her lap, she was drawn slightly away from our table, on her face the same tentative glance with which she favoured me in the square. How could it be otherwise? They had given us the very best place, in the middle of the Café de Foy, the one we used to have after our brilliant evenings, when we came here for oysters and last glasses of champagne; this very best table made conversation difficult at less than a shout, and now I was not quite shouting. The agreeable matron sat silently, smiled uncertainly and perhaps heard nothing. Perhaps she thought of her next engagement, during which archaeological puns would be exchanged among sun-burnt, knowing persons. One of those sudden silences swept the Café de Foy, as it will by chance in crowded places when a number of conversations finish or pause at once; in this vacuum my final words rang out, the only of my own which were distinct, ". . . not particular to you, Adèle. I could not with any woman." She smiled a little from the awkwardness of it, but the proprieties had somehow managed to be preserved. The torrent of orders, chatter and rattling china burst forth again, an insuring noise of decorum; her hands remained modestly in her lap. I had been quite mistaken; they were rough and browned, evidently from her investigations abroad. The servant called me gently that it was time for the next application of heated towel, and I awoke with a feeling of great self-loathing.

Is not this the meaning of Job 9:27? "If I say, I will forget my complaint, I will leave off my heaviness, and comfort myself."

My brother was often accused of creating his own dissatisfaction. The last two or three years he seemed to go out of his way to present clients who had come to him with requests for a cottage, for an addition to their country estates, with impossible and expensive plans in response. Why could he not limit himself and leave off with his struggle?—that is what people asked him. Here is a bond in suffering between us. "Resignation" is priest-craft for "I forget," Frederick; resignation dismisses life-long struggles as if, in the end, they don't really signify; the others find our complaint and heaviness, moreover, so unattractive.

After a day of rest, I determined to go out. I let my presence be known to those few persons who might, I thought, still remember me. Once more was I astonished by the manner in which people regain old friends. When I entered drawing-rooms, it was as though I had been away for only a few months at most, my hosts plunging me into the deepest consideration of perplexing affairs or of personalities I knew not at all, relaying me from guest to guest with "Here is our dear friend M. Charles Courtland, just come back from London, where he did not know that . . ." This surprising capacity of the human being to consider his fellow creatures as ever imminent, ever thirsty for doings, was evinced by retired ecclesiastics, the editors of philosophical reviews and ladies devoted to good works amongst the heathen.

Soon I became quite fatigued, though pleasurably, by the social round. Among the kind invitations I received was one from the authoress "Daniel Stern," whom I had known thirty years before as the Comtesse d'Agoult. Her next "at home" occurred the Monday five days after I rose from my hotel bed; I thought to send her a second note, one of regrets, to conserve my strength, a note which would scarcely signify to her, since I never knew her well. Moreover, the Countess has become a most distinguished figure in Parisian society, even a great figure; by now we would have no one in common. The only subject between us could be the past, and I had discovered during this week that I did not wish to speak of him, did not wish to share him, with others of his former circle.

Indeed, the week amongst my buzzing friends brought me comfort, the wistful sighing of "I remember when . . ." heard so seldom compared to the outraged "I have just learnt of the most disgraceful . . ." Imminence: a remedy for what cannot be undone. By contrast, my friends warned me that, among the upper orders, in the circles Marie d'Agoult has again come to frequent, there is almost no talk of general events, of politics, of ideas, at least in mixed company. Spies are thought to be everywhere; the notables are by now divided bitterly amongst themselves. All conspired to make me fear an evening spent in the company of the Comtesse d'Agoult would be, for lack of open, common ground, a suffocating exercise in "I remember."

I could not have been more mistaken.

Entering the rue de Varenne mansion, I saw at first what I expected to see: a distinguished residence attended by footmen in splendid livery, the upper servants comporting themselves, as they do in France, with that air of discretion which always reminds me of diplomats at work. The drawing-room in which the Countess received was similarly splendid, panelled in a light wood, the ceiling painted in the manner of Tiepolo, the figures floating above engaged in their own aerial evening party. The soirée, to be sure, could not be described as a romp. Even with the many persons present, crowded into the drawing-room of the borrowed mansion, voices seldom needed to be raised. Thus I was taken aback to hear two gentlemen near the door disputing the possibility of establishing a confederacy of miners of coal. Surely they compromised their hostess.

She now came forward to greet me. Dressed in grey, leaning on a cane, her hair framed by a widow's fichu, a footman hovering behind her, the Comtesse d'Agoult took my hand with only the barest hint of uncertainty betraying she had forgotten who was the English visitor, the name "Court-land" whispered to her again by someone else after I had spoken it as slowly as I could. To smooth our conversation she immediately presented me to the two conspiring men, remarking, "M. Courtland, these gentlemen have never ceased to dream of National Workshops!" They smiled rather sheep-ishly. "Nor have I!" She smiled at them, a little wickedly, I thought.

I insisted that the noblewoman seat herself, which the Comtesse d'Agoult agreed to do only if I also would seat myself. Again her lips parted slightly.

"Tell me," she asked, "what calls you to Paris."

I mentioned the names of a few persons near to my brother, without invoking his. She listened as if these persons were unknown to her, and impatiently. Not boredom with me prompted her, but rather the desire to ask me, did I remember the cause of the National Workshops in '48? I did. What was my opinion of them? I replied frankly that they had mistaken fraternal sentiment for effective labour. "Daniel Stern" looked pleased: she had invited an acceptable Englishman, whoever he was.

"You are entirely mistaken, Monsieur." Her eyes fastened upon me and glistened. "Entirely mistaken; you no doubt think they were political in-struments whereas they were meant as self-sufficient communities. We might establish them today."

At my request, she recounted her "metamorphosis," as she called it, an account which I sensed she has perfected through practise. Her career as "Daniel Stern" was launched with a novel of a personal character, *Nélida*, appearing in 1846. Of course! I instantly remembered that this flaming tome had given Adèle much amusement during the days of our correspondence, I wondered indeed how I could have failed to connect Marie d'Agoult to Adèle, though my own visits to the Hôtel de France were infrequent, . . . but "Daniel Stern" swept on, her eyes demanding my complete and submissive attention. Two years later, the revolutions spreading across the face of Europe entirely claimed the attention of the noblewoman; she confessed to me, without the slightest trace of remorse, that until 1848 she had followed the "easy way" of holding politics in contempt because politicians are beneath it. This we all tended to do in those years. The Romantics, ever in search of faith, had decreed that only Utopia was a worthy kingdom; the nearer July Monarchy seemed an uninhabitable swamp. 1848 had, however, shaken her; the sheer display of suffering in Paris, the extent of the poverty, was beyond her imagining, and she felt that the revolution this time would either change everything, or fail so completely that there would never be revolution in Europe again. So she began to keep a journal, and from that journal had come the three volumes of her *History of the Revolution of 1848.*

The lady of the Palais-Royal and the Comtesse d'Agoult. There had once been a plan to attach the younger woman to the elder, in the days when Marie d'Agoult was a figure of Romantic fashion and fashionable pity. Evidently the noblewoman had decided pathos was out of date, but, when I asked her how far it was possible in modern France to discuss politics openly, having been told the contrary, she replied in full voice, "I have been outrageous for so long, I have earned the right to say anything."

Then she laughed at me, noticing me for the first time. "Monsieur, to retain the power to blush at our age!" More to establish myself again as a man of spirit than to pry, I ventured, "There were thousands in Paris who saw what you saw, among them hundreds of writers, and yet there is only one 'Daniel Stern.' "

But "Daniel Stern" was not interested in sharing her private life with me. She shrugged, and said merely, "I am pleased you read my work." She rose, painfully, as did I, the two of us acknowledging with a moment's look our mutual frailties, she shrugged slightly, she who could, and I was presented to one of the dignitaries of the French Church, who remembered my name and my work, as the next hour proved, all too well.

That evening I returned to my hotel, as fevered as the week before. The ecclesiastic unwisely sought to defend to me *Quanta cura,* with its infamous *Syllabus* of errors, which encyclical I had rebutted in *The Free-Thinker,* and which I rebutted again, decisively, I may say, to this papal agent; the effort, however, cost me my strength, and once to make a point I foolishly gestured with my arm, provoking my shoulder. In my dream now I could not entirely banish the pain of that gesture; the sufferer from rheumatism usually sleeps carefully, so as not to roll over onto his shoulder or cramp his arm, but that night I was too upset to practise this caution in sleep. In my delirium I confessed what in civility I had kept held back. I admitted to knowing the title rather than the contents of her three volumes of the *History of the Revolution of 1848*.

The moment I declared my ignorance, she called out to a gentleman passing by us, "Adolphe!" He was swathed in bandages and hobbled on a cane. As he turned to her I recognised my dearest friend in Paris, another whose art was scorned by the public. Scorned though he never sounded more glorious to me than in the year before his suicide. Adolphe Nourrit had guarded the raiments of his agony, although by now he had become enormous, too large to fit through a window. He made as if to bend down to assist her to rise, and groaned. I called out to him, but he too gave no sign of recognising me. The Countess waved away his offer of a bandaged arm with scorn, rising upon her own stick. "It has been a great pleasure to meet you, M. Carton."

Once I had commemorated this dear friend, honoured his memory with truth. I waited for "My dear!," his way of greeting friends, even those he had visited the night before, as though he were astonished to see them. I waited for "My dear!" although I perfectly understood he might find it too painful to raise his arms to embrace me. Marie d'Agoult droned on and on about the *Syllabus* of errors, though this may be no more than the effect of rolling over onto my shoulder, which I know I did, since I cried out in pain and woke up. Now I sank back into a half-dream, wary of what I might do in my sleep to my shoulder, still waiting for him to acknowledge me, perhaps even, shall I say, to thank me for my commemoration. Words of comfort are guineas which change hands in the business of loving. I waited, but all I could hear was ". . . National Workshops falling under no such ecclesiastical interdiction, my dear monsieur" in her high, impersonal voice; then she moved on to that day's clash of members of the same party on the floor of the Chamber, ever advancing, ever forward in her invincible armour of opinions. I woke up rudely in the middle of the explanation of party conflict in the imperial age, Adolphe and I having yet to speak.

I was to suffer only one night more, but intensely. I do not blame the *Syllabus* of errors, even in conjunction with the proposed revival of National Workshops, for this ultimate attack. It is unsound and unscientific, at least in my London circle, to ascribe to the "soul" (written thus) any influence over the body. However, the soirée of the Countess most certainly called up in fever the last of my visitations.

This brief vision was as repugnant to me as would my friend singing have been a joy, were the gods of sleep merciful. It was not even a face before me, but a passage from a book, graven in my memory. Newman's so-called history of his own life appeared in 1864, and not incidentally; the autobiography is a masquerade designed to illustrate, to exemplify, that document of Papal intolerance. In my review of it, I remarked that Newman's *Apologia* should have been more aptly titled *The Teleology of Submission.* He claims his entire life as having moved ineluctably towards Catholic conversion. His contemporaries at Oxford thought him to be as confused a soul as ourselves, a man who claimed no answer. His very conversion more impressed us because there was something shocking in this solution. In the twenty years since that event, he has, like the Countess, polished his life into a *meaningful* and coherent form, and, having told this lie, the juices of other evils within him have flowed ever more freely.

I said I saw no face when the worst words of that book came back to me, words which embody all that is evil in man's hunger to believe—no, not evil in the hunger itself, but in the gluttony with which religion satisfies that hunger. There was a face. Newman smiles, an elderly cherub as he prefers to be depicted now in official portraits, recalling the Cardinal de Rohan. He smiles at Lacordaire, to whom he extends a hand in friendship. Holding his hand sweetly, to disarm Lacordaire, who ever responded to kindness, Newman says in his rich, reassuring baritone, so surprising from such a boyish man, just as he addressed himself to Lacordaire in print, "Liberty of thought is in itself a good; but it gives an opening to false liberty. Now by Liberalism I mean false liberty of thought. . . . Liberalism is the mistake of subjecting to human judgement those revealed doctrines which are in their nature beyond and independent of it. . . ." Thus speaks a man willing to re-arrange even the history of his own life—I mean not the facts but the sense—so that it conforms to revealed doctrine, words which bespeak to me by contrast the dignity and *honesty* of a more liberal confusion.

Even during the nightmare I waited for Adolphe to return; the assured, implacable voice of the priest gave him no more chance to speak than did the woman performing her legend. And yet even emphatic persons do seek from shy listeners murmurs of assent, smiles or only a mobile play of the lips, the resolute arias of "I think!" so many researches into what will arouse those whose eyes are habitually downcast. Adolphe was essentially a shy man, despite performing before a large public. Priest and Countess waited for him to give some sign, to nod or even to look them in the eyes, but he did not, he would not, and so both of these emphatic persons disappeared; we had nothing for them.

Once Adolphe and I walked along the Seine in mid-afternoon during a hot summer day. The sun was intense, the river stank, but the very vivacity of heat, light and smell compounded themselves into an hour of beauty. At moments during our amble Adolphe was recognised by strangers, whom he greeted with dignified courtesy. At other moments he saw coming towards us persons he knew, important persons whom he saw before they saw him. He would then mop his brow furiously, straighten his coat, pat his hair, afraid that he would appear wilted, last season's hero of the boards. He greeted these persons with chirps, with exaggerated exclamations of "My dear!" or "How ravishing your hat!," he fluttered and danced; then, the moment they passed, he deflated like a balloon and we continued to speak in our ordinary calm way. After this puffing and deflating had occurred three or four times, I turned to Adolphe, taking both his hands in mine. "You are afraid." Adolphe made as if to turn away, but I would not let go his hands. "It is unworthy of you."

His hands struggled for a moment more in mine, then went limp, like two small animals of the field nestled for shelter in a cup. Adolphe looked at me, his eyes forced down neither by priest nor Countess, he looked at me steadily, all the while in my embrace. I remember the foul air of the Seine mingled with his eau de cologne. His palms were beautifully soft. After a moment he said only, "Thank you." Now, once more, in the troubled sleep of an old man, Adolphe gazed at me as he had that hot summer day. This time there were no words of thanks spoken, no words at all; perhaps the bandages made it too difficult for him.

I was awakened by the routine of the hotel compresses. These fragments required, perhaps, a minute or two to dream. But I needed to hold the hands of my friend, even though they were bruised from his terrible fall, even though I held these crushed animals but for a moment; now I could speak to my brother.

The Evangelical Revival in England, both its Low Church and its Dissenting forms, has sometimes been compared to the Romantic movement in the arts. Evangelical fervour poured often into works of reform and improvement, but its locus was the individual soul, the soul invited to contemplate sin only to surmount it through acts of prayer almost abandoned in character. An observer of Venn's services might indeed have imagined pastor and congregation transported from a play of Victor Hugo.

Yet this passionate faith did not look back, it regretted nothing, and still speaks in triumphant tones of contest with the world. Whereas the Romantics of my youth had no faith their passion would prevail over a soiled world. Indeed, they anticipated defeat, sensible young men of twenty already regretting, already enshrining the old. In architecture this was especially pronounced. The great Pugin resorted to the stained glass of the Gothic Age, to its spires and buttresses, because these represented in his mind the visible signs of a life in which men lived for greater ends than advancement and money. Thus, while an Evangelical was made bold for struggle against the wickedness of the world by his faith, the Romantic architect had already foreseen the outcome in his own mind, and longed for the days before the contest began.

The group in Oriel College, the "Oriel Noetics," Blanco White, Copleston, Thomas Arnold, were sirens calling the youth Newman to the exercise of his reason, to the toleration of reasoning which had led to different results than his own, to an abhorrence of dogma. When he gave way to bouts of rigidity, his friends could only respond with the unhappiness of their liberal humanity. It was the same in France. Lacordaire and Lamennais had no weapons to combat *L'Univers* save their courtesy, their irony, their generosity in listening to opposing views, their humanity, none of these bludgeons.

When my master Lamennais first read an attack on himself by the Vatican, he imagined that the longer he talked to his adversaries, the more responsive they would become. *Dialogue* would render them reasonable. This was in truth the Liberal error in religion. The adversaries of toleration are capable of endless, perfectly polite discussion, in the course of which they simply wait for the opportunity to make the points they have always made.

I advert to these tendencies because in my night-work I realised they form the spiritual bond between my brother and myself. Our father had been entirely mistaken in our characters. Lamennais, Lacordaire, my companions at university so confused as boys, myself—we sought to practise religion as though we were Romantic architects; we sought to build a large, commodious and sentimental home. We accepted the invitation in the first Book of Kings, "Come home with me, and refresh thyself," instead of heeding the warning in Ecclesiastes 12:5,7 that "Man goeth to his long home, and the mourners go about the streets," and "Then shall the dust return to the earth as it was: and the spirit shall return unto God who gave it." The world at last empty, void, the spirit free at last for the full exercise of its powers. A cold man understands this, for he does not believe in order to seek comfort.

My brother was the enemy of Romantic architecture, though his early years passed so easily in Romantic Paris. His severities, his belief in the classical forms and volumes, derived from the union of expressive art and the discipline of mathematics. His views might be compared to Newman in the days when he advocated celibacy for clergymen, and other persons of strong faith, with sheer spiritual discipline as the end in view, rather than Catholicism. My brother also practised a kind of chastity. He refused ornament on the grounds that it was inherently frivolous; he challenged Pugin to justify his Gothicking as visually pure, whatever symbolical purity the bits of stained glass and ornate iron castings had in Pugin's mind.

The arbitrary form I found so ugly in the Galérie d'Orleans, the contempt and indifference with which my brother treated those who in turn were cold to him—Father was quite wrong, Frederick shewed a true vocation, in caring for the play of lines rather than the contriving of plans for pleasing rooms, or amusing follies. These proved our father's taste and his undoing. While we clerics who sought to be "humane" proved incapable of building at all.

There is so much to be written about these matters. But not, perhaps, here. I shall say only that my ultimate delirium convinced me I was no more required to speak soothingly to Frederick than Adolphe was to me. Frederick believed in his principles, whether he taught them to a thousand or to none. Here was his solace. Frederick required no comfort from me to redeem his life. He was a man of faith. Just as now, at last, I will live and die alone without needing to hear my beloved friend say again, quietly, "Thank you."

After two days my shoulder moved freely, my spirits rose. I was rather pleased with myself that I had surmounted this crisis in what had become, after all, a foreign city, without recourse to laudanum. I had determined to give myself one pleasure before I left, sick or well, and now I was able to enjoy this reward without physical worry, and an easier mind. I went to the theatre, to watch Madame Mercure perform.

That spectacle ended my journey, and so it shall this draught. There is so much I might write freely of her and publish with the greatest pleasure.

Madame Mercure is my friend of longest standing in France. Her career began in the days when the stage was less respectable than it is now. Serious artists like herself confined themselves to a small number of rôles from the classical repertoire to vindicate, as it were, their characters off-stage. Though never acclaimed by the public at large, Madame Mercure was from her earliest days treated by her colleagues with consideration. She was spared the terrible intrigues of the French stage in the 1830s, a woman mutually relied upon by those at war with one another. Hers was a specialised art: she rendered supporting characters so vividly that they became individual presences. Yet neither the woman nor the artist pushed herself unnaturally forward. Private repute in an essentially public profession meant that even as a young woman she was received easily throughout Paris.

I owe the pleasure of my acquaintance with her to my brother, who met her soon after his own arrival in the city. As it sometimes happens, the relations of greatest regard in our lives require the longest to mature; not until we were both already of an age to have full memories did our friendship ripen. By this time, a year or so before the Revolution of 1848, I had returned to establish myself in London, and she came to visit our city far less frequently than I should have wished—as the standards of theatrical art rose in her country they declined in mine. Madame Mercure found the English public ever more restive at the performances of translated works in which she excelled, *Phèdre, Bérénice, Le Cid,* works in which the declaiming voice is the action, and the subtleties of declamation the drama. So, in 1856 I believe it was, she ceased to favour us with her art. It was the year after my brother failed to secure for himself a position amongst those building iron-and-glass structures in Paris. In the last decade I thus saw her only during her infrequent, brief visits of pleasure to London, whilst my knowledge of her in Paris dwindled as my brother found ever fewer occasions to journey to the city of his last defeat.

From the press, however, I deduced that in France she found little to her taste the serious "bourgeois drama" of the Forties and Fifties, the plays of daily life and ordinary affairs. A new love came to her in these years, the love of comedy. When a girl she had avoided comic rôles because they smacked of the boulevard, of burletta, of the crude. A woman of delicate sensibility, she sought to avoid the least taint. During the Second Empire, as actors and actresses of France are ever more accorded their due, she has evidently felt free to explore a new repertoire. Perhaps she does not range far; only as far as the classic Italian comedies, once a French translation of Wycherley; mostly she has added to her rôles in Molière, a safe author for anyone else, but freedom for her. This departure has brought her no more acclaim, and no less regard. It was Molière in which now I would see her again, at the end of my voyage. She would act Madame Jourdain in *Le Bourgeois Gentilhomme.*

As a young woman Madame Mercure made use of a fragile figure to tragic effect: when she played queens, her will was made to seem triumphant over her weak constitution. Once she said to me, "I am one of the very few before the public for whom death scenes are as easy as lying down." Moreover, her hands were the longest I have ever seen, an elongation she played with on stage, stretching them out at crucial moments as though to display a deformity. Her aura of fragility, that of a person emaciated by suffering rather than the porcelain delicacy of a Dresden china shepherdess, is the reason I wish at all to evoke the acting of my dear friend in this memoir.

Madame Mercure's fragility made it seem unlikely she could succeed in the character of the solid, earthy wife of the absurd Monsieur Jourdain. Indeed, there were certain scenes throughout the evening in which what we the audience saw made it difficult to believe what we heard. When Monsieur Jourdain declares he will marry their daughter to a marquis, for instance, Madame Jourdain rounds on his pretension, hands on hips, a woman who knows her place and intends to enjoy herself just as she is. We heard Monsieur Jourdain castigated by a wraith whose hands, hung indignant-wife fashion, seemed encased within evening gloves which had been half drawn off. Again, when Madame Mercure declared she was but a plain and unadorned woman, we saw a creature who had eschewed the usual exaggerated creams and paints applied to stage personages for a toilette more chaste, and I might say more vernal than the arts which would be logically possessed by Madame Jourdain. What most struck me, however, was that her diction was still so beautiful, her voice as clear as ever, as miraculous in its penetration throughout the hall of the Comédie-Française. Yet, as ever, the sound was of an oboe, not a trumpet, floating Madame Jourdain's words. She loved Molière, but in her restraint and physical vulnerability we could not follow her in this new love.

I intend no criticism of my friend in noting this discrepancy. It was rather that Madame Mercure seemed to display a severity, may I say a linearity, which reminded me of my brother. She guarded this character even when it was, again, perhaps ill-suited. The public remarked the inapposite match of actress to rôle by its inability to laugh much at her beautifully produced sallies, though it tried. At the conclusion of *Le Bourgeois Gentilhomme*, she was briefly if respectfully applauded.

She alone of the persons I knew in Paris I sought out for a common remembrance of my brother. In the reception salon, after the performance, the impression of their similarity was still strong upon me. I said nothing, of course, yet I may have betrayed myself. She was occupied for several minutes in receiving compliments when I entered, and I effaced myself in a corner, near M. Frédéric Lemaître, the great actor of more popular entertainments, who also, evidently, awaited her. When she finished she came to me, we hardly knowing what to say in our emotion. We had not seen one another since the funeral. We embraced, then silence fell upon us; M. Lemaître, the only person left, looked out the window into the courtyard where the chairs and scenery of the theatre were stored. This silence could not endure or we would collapse in tears. She at last found words she had used to the others: "If you were pleased, I am pleased."

Did I start, or frown?

"My dear Charles." Madame Mercure was suddenly alert indeed. "Of course she is *not quite me*, but Madame Jourdain and I are well enough acquainted to be friends. I thought the applause particularly warm this evening. What did you think, Lemaître?" She turned to the great man, who continued to stare out the window for a moment before responding, "Yes, yes, quite good, excellent."

"You don't believe a word of it, and you're still worrying about money." Madame Mercure laughed and pressed my hand. "We will take you to a café in Siberia that has been absolutely the rage for the last nine days!"

Thus I was not to have an evening of reminiscence. Shameful as it is to admit, the prospect of meeting the great Lemaître rather pushed aside the disappointment I should have felt. Of course I had heard Madame Mercure speak of him for years, but they seemed to have a professional friendship, and many times at her home, hoping to meet him, I found that his work had kept him away. Nor was he particularly the friend of my brother, though their social circle was the same in the old days and my brother spoke of him cordially enough. As we quitted the Palais-Royal, I told M. Lemaître that I had read all the notices of his triumph in *Le Crime de Faverne.*

"You are an English amateur of theatre?" he politely asked.

"Entirely amateur. I am the retired editor of the quarterly *The Free-Thinker.*"

"A journal of Masonry?"

"Not at all, though we take an interest in relations between Masonry and the established churches of all countries." The carriage waiting for us in the Place de la Comédie moved forward without instruction the moment the footman had closed us in. I sounded so dismally boring, but he persisted.

"Extraordinary. A man of religion who admits to liking the stage." He smiled. "In the old days, the priests made my life a misery, fretting me to change this or that rough word, fretting the police I mean, dreadful old ladies, all of them. No offence, that is just their French way, all of them busybody old ladies. But what, dear English sir," he clasped his hands devoutly to his bosom, "what can interest you, who consider eternal truth and fervent faith, in the doings of us poor creatures, masters of illusion for a franc, we who inspire faith in phantoms, only so long as the prompter remembers our lines for us and we are not so drunk we slur our words."

"Frédéric!" Madame Mercure rebuked him, though gently; she seemed indeed pleased with our evening. Nor was I at all offended. Theatre suspends our usual rules of decorum to provide us another order of belief and, besides, all the actors in the Romantic days had a provoking manner. The carriage struck a hole in the paving, Lemaître swore, Madame Mercure clutched his arm, my shoulder protested. I began to reply that I was an ex-priest of the Anglican persuasion, as a prologue to showing him that *The Free-Thinker*'s policies took his view, when the actor interrupted me, shouting over the clatter of our wheels upon planks laid in a new street, the darkness of half-built Paris without.

"An ex-priest! Damn this carriage, Anne! You wanted some fun! That explains it!"

For a night, this would do.

In reading over the whole of this memoir, I see it is unsuitable for publication, even the end. I have told too much and too little. I will consign it to our mountain of family and friendly papers which since Frederick Courtland's death I've not had the heart to scale. Perhaps, some day, someone else will. May this memoir be read as a testament to the radiant gift of life he made me in youth, and to my sympathy for him when the radiance faded.

A Note On The Type

This book was set in a digitized version of Janson. The hot-metal version of Janson was a recutting made direct from type cast from matrices long thought to have been made by the Dutchman Anton Janson, who was a practicing type founder in Leipzig during the years 1668–1687. However, it has been conclusively demonstrated that these types are actually the work of Nicholas Kis (1650–1702), a Hungarian, who most probably learned his trade from the master Dutch type founder Dirk Voskens. The type is an excellent example of the influential and sturdy Dutch types that prevailed in England up to the time William Caslon (1692–1766) developed his own incomparable designs from them.

Composed, Printed and Bound by The Haddon Craftsmen, Inc.
Scranton, Pennsylvania